T
LOST BOY

An unputdownable psychological thriller
full of breathtaking twists

Please note this book was first published as

Past Reason

MARGARET MURPHY

JOFFE
BOOKS

Revised edition 2020
Joffe Books, London
www.joffebooks.com

First published in Great Britain in 1999
as *Past Reason*

ISBN: 978-1-78931-622-3

In affectionate memory of my father, Harry Wright.

ACKNOWLEDGEMENTS

I would like to thank Joe and Gill Murphy for their advice on social services and foster care; Rinty Rogers, Trish Bates and Mike Mannion for background information on children's nursing; and Derek Bradshaw for insights into police procedure.

My research into false memory was greatly facilitated by Nicholas P. Spanos's text *Multiple Identities and False Memories*; his work was — and is — inspirational. I would also like to pay tribute to Hollida Wakefield and Ralph Underwager's exhaustive and informative text, *Return of the Furies: An Investigation into Recovered Memory Therapy*.

When I first read about 'recovered memory', I was convinced that people could not have invented such terrible scenarios of abuse and suffering, but careful scientific study has shown that in our eagerness to explain our unhappiness we can become victims of our own imagination.

PART I

PROLOGUE

The boy stood uncertainly next to the car. He sucked in his lower lip — a habit only recently acquired — and chewed on it.

Never get into a strange car. How many times had he been told? At home, at school, at Beavers and more recently at Cubs.

'Come *on*, for heaven's sake!'

But it wasn't like he was getting into a stranger's car. He wasn't daft.

'I can't wait all day.'

The boy darted a look over his shoulder, unconsciously twisting one foot behind the other.

'I'm getting cross now . . .'

He didn't like to be naughty, but if he *didn't* get in the car, he was being disobedient, and if he *did*—

'Stop pratting about and get in!'

The boy jumped, nearly fell over, just disentangling one leg from the other in time to save himself. 'Mummy said—' he ventured.

'Mummy said. Mummy said. Where's Mummy now?'

The boy frowned. He loved his mummy, and he wanted his mummy to love him, but she shouted at him all the time and made fun of him when he cried. He looked back towards the house again, hoping she would magically appear and take the decision out of his hands, but she didn't come. She never did.

'Come *on*! . . . Look, if you're so worried, we'll telephone your mother from—We'll telephone your mother later, so she doesn't worry. All right?'

The boy edged forward, scraping the toes of his shoes on the gravel.

* * *

The kitchen was pristine — its surfaces wiped and disinfected and its stainless steel buffed to a dull gleam. A tap dripped with measured solemnity into a solitary cup, steadily filling with water. A bumble bee passed through the open door, explored with absent-minded disinterest, butting into the glass fronts of the display cupboards, moving on to the brightly coloured picture tiles dotted about the walls, and bumbling out the way it came, ignoring the still form of a woman lying on the floor.

For a while — perhaps an hour — after she had first fallen, bleeding, to the floor, she had heard the tick-tick-tick of the tap and had mistaken it for her own blood pulsing in her throat, pooling on the floor beneath her. As the dripping of the tap slowed, she had felt her pulse diminish and falter, fluttering as if her heart had forgotten the rhythm, but she could not find the strength to save herself: she had used it all in saving him.

A sudden rapid, shallow clamour of systolic contractions, quickening as if to finish the job, to end her suffering. It ceased. Death came easily, after the pain, the initial shock of violence, her futile struggle against his fury. She had not known herself to be near death, had felt only a depletion, a weariness. She was not aware of the slow darkening from the edges of her vision, did not even have to summon the courage to face her fear. It was a quiet surrender, a gentle going. No celestial choir, no blinding light, no warmth of welcome, no one to greet her and guide the way. Only darkness, a void.

The pool around her head and neck stopped growing and began to congeal, and the tick-tick of dripping of water gradually changed tone, becoming a deeper, viscous splosh.

CHAPTER 1

They ran, laughing like lunatics, screaming through the night, their shoes echoing in the empty streets like the clamouring footsteps of killers in a forties film. A few muffled barks went up — half-hearted yelps mostly — the dogs' fury tempered by the physical barriers of locked doors and the high garden walls of the wealthy.

Lobo saw a light go on and yelled up at the window, 'What're you lookin' at, nosy 'ole?'

Lee-Anne grabbed his arm, still laughing, gasping for air. 'You'll get us done, you mad-arsed bastard!' She bent, both hands on her knees, trying to catch her breath. Which gave Lobo an idea. He pulled at his trouser belt and dropped his pants, mooning at the alarmed house-owner. They ran all the way down to Aigburth Road and flagged a taxi. Fell into it, still giggling.

'I couldn't believe it when you dropped your kecks! I thought the old biddy'd have a heart attack!'

'Give her somethin' to look at, didn't I? Nosy bitch!'

Lee-Anne hiccupped. 'God, Lobo, I think I'm gonna spew.'

''Ey! 'Ey!' The taxi driver had been watching them in his lower mirror but hadn't spoken till now. 'Don't go pukin' in my cab.'

'Why?' Lobo said. 'Isn't her puke good enough for yer?' He'd seen that on Harry Enfield — *The Scousers*. He was boss, him.

Lee-Anne made retching sounds and the driver went ''Ey, 'ey,' again. They imitated him, then cracked up. It was ace how they had the same sense of humour.

Lee-Anne looked up, tears running down her face with laughing. 'Don't worry, mate,' she said. 'I'm not gonna spew any more. I think I'm gonna piss meself instead!'

Pure comic genius, that. She should be on the telly, Lobo thought. Suddenly, he wanted her. ''Ey, come on, mate,' he said. 'Stop arsing about. We want to get home tonight, you know.'

'It might help if you told me where you wanna go,' the driver said.

Lobo gave an address a quarter of a mile from their flat and fumbled at the door of someone else's house until the cab driver disappeared — they didn't want the pigs tracing them to the right place, did they? And Lobo was easily remembered: dark, almost black hair that spiked aggressively, uncontrollably in all directions from his scalp, a wide, red mouth and a mad-eyed stare that he had been working on since his school days. Lee-Anne was small, red haired — hard looking but still easy on the eye. Put the two of them together and people were bound to recall the mad, bad lad and the skinny girl.

As the taxi clattered around the corner, Lobo stuck his hands in his pockets and started the trudge home, then stopped when he realized Lee-Anne wasn't following. She was leaning on the wall of the house the taxi had dropped them at.

'I really am gonna spew,' she said, miserably.

She did look green. Lobo tugged at her shirt and glanced over his shoulder. 'Come on,' he said. 'It's done now.'

'The state of her, Lobo. You should've never took me there. I wish we never — I never wanna see nothin' like that again. Never.' Instead of throwing up, she surprised him by bursting into tears.

'Come 'ead,' he said. 'We'll go the cash till. See if any of them numbers work. That'll cheer you up.'

She kept on bawling and he started getting rattled: anyone who saw her like that would make connections when they saw it on the news. He could see that talking would do no good, so he grabbed her by the scruff of the neck and dragged her down the street, crying. The barking in this part of town had a sharper edge, like the dogs really could get out of their back yards, given a plank of rotten timber and a bit of luck, and this gave Lobo an acid tingle of excitement in the pit of his stomach.

CHAPTER 2

'He's probably just wandered off,' DC Lisa Calcot said. It was meant to reassure, but Mrs Harvey was in no mood for reassurances.

'He's been gone bloody hours! He would never stay out this late.' Mrs Harvey paced the sitting room, rearranging ornaments, then stopped abruptly to light a cigarette. 'He's bussed twenty-odd miles to school every day. Most of his school friends live in Chester. Where the *hell* d'you think he *could* go?'

DC Lisa Calcot saw her point. There was half a street's length between each of the picturesque thatched houses of Hale village and nothing but busy roadway to the unassuming semis on the estate up the road. DC Calcot couldn't see Mrs Harvey allowing her son to associate with the occupants of such inferior dwellings.

She glanced at DC Olly Weston but could see she'd get no help there.

'Maybe he went to see a friend?'

Vi Harvey looked at her as if the concept of her son having friends was entirely alien. '*He's* taken him. That man. The one outside his school. He must have come back. He must have followed the school bus — found out where we live—'

'Mrs Harvey,' Weston interrupted, 'you're going to have to explain.'

Vi looked from one officer to the other. 'Don't you people communicate with each other? He's tried it before!'

'*Who's* tried *what*?' Calcot demanded.

'The kidnapper! Oh, God, he'll kill me when he finds out! You've got to find him!'

Calcot took Mrs Harvey by the elbows and eased her into a chair. 'You have to take it from the beginning or we won't be able to help you,' she said.

Vi looked up at the detective, opened and closed her mouth a couple of times and then burst into tears. Calcot fetched a tissue from a polished brass holder on the coffee table, taking her cigarette and stubbing it out for her. They waited for her to calm down.

Mrs Harvey had dialled emergency services on Friday afternoon and told the operator that someone had snatched her little boy. When they had arrived, twenty minutes later, she had modified the story, telling them that he had 'disappeared'. A search of the area had turned up nothing.

Vi Harvey dabbed at her eyes, trying to salvage her hopelessly smudged mascara. The bangles on her wrist jingled in tune with her agitation. She positively glistened with metal — gold mostly. Her belt buckle gleamed with it, her black mules were piped with it, and the cuffs of her jacket were embroidered with it. It dangled in expensive twists from her ears and lay in a matching rope against the tanned skin of her neck. Even her hair seemed to glow with gold highlights — it covered her in a faint sheen, as if she secreted precious metal from her pores.

She finished her make-up repairs and stared dolefully at the two officers. 'The nanny called in sick. I had to cancel a lunch appointment.' This was said in a tone of exclamation. 'He was playing upstairs.'

'Your son?'

She frowned irritated. 'Who else? He was in his room—'

'His name is?'

'Who?'

'Your son,' Weston said, swapping a tired glance with Calcot. 'What's his name?'

'I've been through all this,' she said, frowning with irritation. 'Connor.' Then again, as if dictating to a slow and rather dim secretary. 'His name . . . is Connor. I turn my back for five minutes — *five minutes!*'

'Turned your back?' Weston said.

Calcot saw guilty colour creeping into Vi's face. *Turned her back! Topping up her tan, more like. Snoozing in the garden.*

'He was gone before I knew it,' Vi went on. 'Bill will never forgive me. He said he might try again.' Sensing that she had pushed the officers' patience to the limit she made an effort to give some form of coherent explanation. 'Someone tried to abduct Connor last week. From his school. Connor got away, but . . . Oh, *God*!' She covered her face with her hands. 'What am I going to tell Bill?'

'Bill is your husband?' Weston asked. Vi nodded. 'Where is he now?'

'How the hell would *I* know?' she snarled, swinging from distraught to aggressive in an instant. 'In some dreary meeting, no doubt, discussing the wonders of shrink-wrap or something equally scintillating.'

Calcot made an automatic appraisal of the bitterness as the accumulated gall of years. 'Where can we reach him?' she asked.

'He travels about a lot.'

'Do you have his mobile number?'

'Here.' Vi scrawled the number on a piece of paper retrieved from a box (gold again) of notelets next to the phone. The bangles on her wrist clashed excitedly. 'You won't get him. His phone's switched off.' She seemed suddenly to realize that she didn't have a cigarette in her hands and went to the coffee table to fetch one. As she lit up, she said, 'Now will you *please* stop pissing about and find my son!'

Calcot stared at the woman and wondered if Connor hadn't simply put some distance between himself and that high-pitched, scratchy voice. 'A photograph would be useful,' she said. 'Of your son . . . Connor.'

For a moment she looked ready to fly at him, then she placed her cigarette with exaggerated care in an ashtray and walked to the bookcase on the far side of the room. She took a picture from a matching set of albums, elaborately disguised as leather-bound books, and handed it to Calcot.

'Now get out of my house.'

* * *

'What d'you reckon?' Weston asked. Calcot punched in the number for Mr Harvey's mobile for the fourth time.

'She's right about one thing — he has got it switched off.'

They had already tried his factory, but the management of Creative Plastics hadn't seen their boss since earlier that day.

'She seemed more worried about him finding out she was caught napping than the kid being in danger.'

Weston slid her a sideways glance. 'Think it's a domestic?'

Calcot smiled. She had a way of turning up one corner of her mouth, making a dimple that said, *Nothing would surprise me.*

'Doesn't square with the previous attempt, does it, though?' Weston said. Castle Esplanade had dealt with the initial incident — Connor's school being near Chester city centre — headquarters had confirmed that he hadn't recognized his assailant, and neither had anyone else who had seen the attempted abduction.

Calcot shrugged. 'I hate women like her. Big money, big hair, big ego.'

Weston laughed. 'Thank you, Professor Cantor.'

'Who?'

'You don't know who Cantor is?'

'Should I?'

'You want to read up on your profiling, Lisa.'

They were on their way to the nanny's flat. Calcot was out of the car ahead of him, and Weston watched appreciatively. Her face might be a bit square — her shoulders were certainly chunky from overenthusiastic training at the weights bench — but Lisa Calcot had a lovely pair of legs, and she didn't hide them in trousers.

'You coming?' Calcot demanded.

Weston dragged his eyes from her legs, up past the curve of her hips and finally focused on her face. She was smiling — not much — just enough to show him she knew his game, just enough to let him know the double meaning was deliberate. He coloured a little, and she turned and walked up the steps to the front door.

The nanny didn't answer. Eventually they got a reply from the occupant of the front flat, a bleary-eyed man of forty or so, who grumbled that he'd bloody well disconnect the sodding bell if any other bugger woke him up, that a man couldn't get a decent kip on nights, and he didn't care *who* they were, he still had a right to a bit of peace and quiet.

They tramped up the stairs to Miss Halliwell's flat and hammered on the door. A weak voice asked who was there.

'Police, Miss Halliwell, open up.'

She did, as far as the chain would allow. 'She's taking employers' rights a bit far, isn't she, sending the police to check on me?' she said.

Calcot introduced them both and Miss Halliwell demanded to see their ID. Calcot handed over hers, and it was withdrawn through the narrow gap between the door and jamb. She closed the door while she read it. Weston was unable to contain his irritation.

'We're losing time, Miss Halliwell. Connor Harvey's gone missing and we need your help.'

'Connor—?' They heard the click of the chain, and then she opened the door wide. 'Connor's missing? Is it the same man? The one outside his school?'

Neither of them replied. They were staring at her face. Even in the dim light of the hallway, they could see it was disfigured by irregularly shaped, raised weals of angry dark red. Suddenly aware of their scrutiny, she shook her hair over her face and pulled her dressing gown tighter around her neck.

'It's not contagious,' she reassured them. 'Some kind of allergy, the doctor said.' She walked through to the tiny sitting room, talking over her shoulder. The sofa was made up as a temporary bed, and the floor around it was littered with magazines. She seemed about to apologize for the mess, then changed her mind and invited them to sit.

Weston looked around. Apart from the sofa, there was only a rocking chair and a few dining chairs clustered around a drop-leaf table. He took one of the dining chairs while Calcot sat on the rocker.

'You called in sick,' Calcot said.

The nanny brushed a wisp of mousy hair from her face and Calcot noticed the dark red blotches had affected her hands as well.

'I hardly slept a wink,' she said. 'I couldn't go in looking like this. And anyway, I feel awful . . .'

'No one's blaming you,' Weston said, seeing that she was ready to burst into feverish tears. 'We're just trying to get the facts straight.'

Miss Halliwell nodded, trying to be brave. 'I'm usually there by eight thirty in the holidays, so she doesn't have to deal with him. She gets so cross, and he's really such a dear little boy. I phoned at half seven. I just couldn't—' She broke off. 'Do you think he's all right?'

Nice to know someone cares, Weston thought. 'You don't live in?' he asked.

'I used to, when he was little, but he boards odd days and weekends now his dad's busier, so they don't need me as much.'

'What about his mum?'

'What about her?'

'Couldn't she look after him?'

Miss Halliwell laughed. 'She's *far* too busy.'

'Have you worked for them long?' Weston asked.

'Eight and a half years. Since Connor was a baby. He was my first job after college.' Then, anticipating their disbelief that she could tolerate Mrs Harvey's autocratic regime for so long, she added, 'She's not about all that much. And when she is, we stay out of her way.'

'Do you get on with Mrs Harvey?' Weston asked.

She fixed Weston with a look she might use on a giddy five-year-old. 'Did you?'

'But you stayed.'

'Connor's a love. I couldn't leave him. And Mr Harvey made sure she didn't get rid of me.' Her face crumpled suddenly, and she said, 'It's all my fault, isn't it? If I'd been there—'

'His mother was there,' Calcot said.

Miss Halliwell folded her arms across her chest, wincing a little in apparent discomfort. 'You don't know what she's like.'

'So tell us,' Weston said.

'She acts like a spoilt brat. Barely notices Connor most of the time. Oh, he's trotted out for half an hour at parties and such, so she can show him off — impress her friends with the doting mother routine — then he's shoved up to his room and woe betide him if he interrupts her entertainment.'

'What about Mr Harvey?'

Her face softened. 'He does what he can, but his business . . . He works such long hours.'

'Do you know where he is now?'

Miss Halliwell turned pink, making the marks on her skin flare dully. She blinked at them. 'Of course not. I mean — I know he'd be away till late tonight — I was going to sleep over, but . . .'

'So, you don't know how we can reach him?'

'No! Good heavens, what *are* you suggesting?'

* * *

'What were you suggesting?' Calcot asked when they got back to the car.

'I'm not sure. D'you think she's carrying a torch for Mr H? Of course, she's only a bit of a kid—'

Calcot smiled. 'Twenty-seven. Maybe a bit older. Isn't that what middle-aged men are supposed to go for?'

'Why ask me?'

Calcot gave a short throaty laugh, and Weston pulled away from the kerb with a screech, scowling furiously.

CHAPTER 3

Jenny Campbell stopped in her tracks. Max Greenberg was seated opposite the stairway, across the polished Marley tiles of what was rather grandly termed the lobby of the third-floor administration section. He looked cool, if somewhat incongruous, in his pale green summer-weight suit. He sat on the dingy plastic chair — relaxed but poised, ready to strike. A small boy was seated next to him, dark haired, bright eyed. Even at this distance, Jenny could sense his fear: his eyes glittered, rather than shone. He was wearing the pyjamas and maroon dressing gown he had arrived in, and from time to time he plucked at the piping on the lapels and pockets.

Jenny smiled at the boy — a reflex response to his anxiety and an instinctive desire to put him at ease. Although his gaze was unfocused, his manner remote, he seemed to tense at this tentative contact and looked down, away, his eyes flitting about the lobby, avoiding her.

Jenny wondered if she should simply turn and walk away, but hospital policy was that nursing staff should change out of uniform before leaving the building, and anyway her car keys were in her locker. The only route to the changing room was past Dr Greenberg. The twinkle of mischief in his eye decided Jenny. She took a breath and stepped forward, quelling the expanding bubble of anger in her chest.

Max rose to meet her. On one lapel he wore his hospital pass, which announced his status as consultant paediatric psychiatrist, and on the other, one of his collection of badges — this time it was a clown. Jenny had seen it before: you pressed his nose and a semicircle of LEDs lit up in sequence, juggling light, while the clown gurgled with laughter.

Jenny was fond of Max. They had first met when he had sought her out to compliment her on an article she had written for *Counselling News* on foster carers as counsellors, and he had encouraged her to write a text on fostering, suggesting reading material and using his influence to set up meetings with eminent writers and practitioners in the field.

His sharp style of dress and quick wit seemed ill-suited to working with sick and emotionally disturbed children, but he emanated a warmth and a solemn respect for the children in his care, to which they responded with instinctive trust.

Max intercepted Jenny at the halfway point. Despite her rising indignation, she could not prevent herself observing that the boy showed no alarm that his chaperone had abandoned him. He sat passively in the chair, his arms loose at his sides, hands hidden by the sleeves of his dressing gown, his shoulders rounded, and his eyes now fixed on the ground.

Max offered Jenny a rueful smile.

'What a rotten bloody trick,' Jenny muttered under her breath.

'Ah-ah. *Pas devant l'enfant*,' Max returned, his smile broadening.

The boy stirred as if waking from a daydream, blinked and looked up. Jenny, who was facing him, took the full force of his luminous brown eyes. She closed her own momentarily.

'Why are you doing this to me, Max?' she pleaded.

They had discussed it earlier, on the ward, while Jenny tried to write up her case notes and obs for the night. She was too busy. Not just with the nursing — her lecture tour for the National Association of Foster Carers was due to start in two weeks, and she hadn't completed her notes and preparation. 'I told you I was busy. Sylvia from the emergency duty team has had a go as well. I told her the same thing: I won't have time to be with him as much as he needs.'

She realized she'd said *won't*, rather than *wouldn't*, and silently cursed her unguardedness.

Max glanced over his shoulder to check that the boy wasn't likely to wander off, then he took Jenny by the elbow and steered her to the far side of the lobby. Instinctively, they both turned their bodies so that they could keep an eye on the child. A steady stream of nurses came and went — the admin section was closed, but the nurses' changing rooms were housed on the same floor. It was mainly the night shift finishing — the early shift had started an hour earlier, to allow for exchange of information, reading notes, briefings. Most exclaimed at the boy who sat apparently so passively and yet, Jenny suspected, unnaturally alert to movement and sound around him.

The boy himself stole occasional looks in their direction while still avoiding their gaze, responded to the friendly greetings of the nurses by hunching into an even smaller huddle, and refused to look up until, shrugging with frustration, they carried on past him into the changing room.

'I can't let him go to just anyone, Jen,' Max said. 'You've seen the results of his medical exam.'

Jenny fought the emotional pull of the evidence, meticulously observed and carefully noted by her colleague: withdrawn, silent and fearful, the boy had submitted to the examination, but he bore scars that suggested that he had at some time been subjected to physical abuse. The behavioural evidence supported this view. More immediate and compelling proof was the fact that X-ray examination showed that all the fingers of both hands had been broken in one traumatic incident in the past.

Jenny frowned. 'I couldn't do him justice, Max.'

She said *couldn't* rather than *can't*, knowing that Max would interpret it as taking a step back from the possibility of accepting the placement.

'Fraser finishes for the holidays soon, doesn't he?' Max said.

'He'd love you for that,' Jenny said. 'Three weeks looking after a severely disturbed boy on his own, while I swan off on my lecture tour.'

'Not that long, I promise—'

'Look, Max, we agreed to some breathing space after Luke moved on to his adoptive parents . . .'

Max Greenberg wondered if he should tell Jenny that Luke was unsettled with his adoptive parents. Unsettled *and* disruptive. He decided against it. Jenny and Fraser would have him back quicker than a blink, but Luke had developed a strong bond with the two of them, and that was the reason for his present refusal to accept his new parents. It would only make the situation worse if he went back to Fraser and Jenny, only to be sent off to someone else in a few months.

Luke had been with them for nearly two years, and they had become more attached to him than to any of their previous children. He knew they had felt bereaved by the loss.

Max looked into his friend's face. 'I know if anyone can draw this boy out, you can. The wards are too busy, even if there was a bed available — and there isn't,' he said firmly, pre-empting Jenny's objections. 'There's no physical reason for him to be in hospital. His injuries are historic. He needs one-to-one, Jen.' There was no response to this, so he went on. 'Social Services are desperate to find somewhere for him. They'd do their best to accommodate you on backup support, emergency cover when you need it . . . Come on, Jenny, you know what it's like trying to get an emergency placement over a weekend. It'd just be for a week or two, till his parents turn up. Don't worry,' he added, noticing that Jenny's expression had changed from truculence to concern for the boy, 'we'll make sure he's safe to go back.'

Jenny was watching another failed interchange between a staff nurse and the tiny figure seated at some yards' distance. She sighed. 'How old is he?'

Max knew her better than to presume that he had got his way — Jenny had not yet agreed to take the child — and despite her soft-heartedness she could be stubborn if she felt she was being manoeuvred into a situation she didn't like. 'I'd estimate his age at between seven and eight.' He frowned, measuring the boy against a mental catalogue of the heights and physical features and behaviours of the thousands of children he had cared for in his fifteen years as consultant paediatric psychiatrist at the hospital. 'My guess would be a small eight-year-old.'

She shuddered. 'What would frighten a child so much he can't even be induced to speak?'

Max shrugged. 'It doesn't pay to anticipate what happened. He could be a gypsy child. He's the right skin colour for it. They teach their kids not to talk to the authorities. If he's been told to keep his mouth shut . . .' He raised his eyebrows. 'Children at this age can take things very literally.'

'Save the Piagetian theory for your students.'

Max grinned. 'It'd only be for a week — two at the most. He probably wandered off and wasn't missed till it was too late. They'll come back for him.'

Jenny fixed him with a distrustful stare. 'If you really believed he was a gypsy child you wouldn't be so keen on my taking him.' The clothes the boy was dressed in suggested money, and his fearfulness hinted at something far more sinister than merely having got lost.

Max hesitated. It didn't do to prevaricate with Jenny: she saw too readily through any attempt to fudge the truth and was too incensed by it to make it worth the aggravation. 'All right, I'll give you my gut reaction. His responses were worrying. I want him somewhere where he'll feel safe.'

'Isn't there *anyone* else?'

'The only other vacancy is a busy household with older foster children. It wouldn't be appropriate for him.'

'Where was he found?'

'South end, Garston, but he might've wandered some distance from home.'

Jenny shook her head. 'An eight-year-old wandering around the city in the early hours in his nightclothes and slippers. Anything might have happened to him.'

Max went on. 'The police are knocking on doors to ask if they've seen anything. In a day or so they may want to take a few pictures, see if they can get a response from the *Liverpool Echo* or local TV. The contact's Mike Delaney,' he added, knowing that Jenny had worked with Sergeant Delaney before and liked him.

Jenny repeated the sigh, more deeply this time, and Max thought he detected a promising note of resignation in it. 'What are you calling him?' Jenny asked.

'I thought perhaps Paul,' Max suggested, too cautious even now to believe that Jenny had finally capitulated.

At that moment all hell broke loose. Jarmon Willis, a charge nurse and old nursing college friend of Jenny's, had approached the boy, much as the female staff had done, but instead of recoiling and refusing to speak, the boy suddenly leapt to his feet and ran for the stairs screaming. Jenny intercepted him and picked him up. He was kicking and shouting: wordless, unearthly, terrified sounds that clattered off the bare walls and proliferated down the echoing staircase.

'It's all right,' she said, 'you're safe.' She repeated it over and over, catching his hands to prevent him gouging at her face, gently restraining him, turning from Jarmon. She waved the shocked charge nurse away and he disappeared through the door to the right of the female changing room. 'Look, he's gone.' The child stared wildly over her shoulder, then abruptly slumped in her arms, passive once more.

Max held back, as he had done when the boy had reacted so violently, hoping that once Jenny had established contact, she would find it impossible to walk away from him. Sometimes he was appalled by his willingness to manipulate adults for the benefit of the children in his care, but the child needed to be placed with someone he could trust. Max had a powerful feeling about this child: something that made him uneasy in himself and fearful for the boy. Jenny was the best person to look after him, and he could see that she was coming to a decision.

Jenny set the child gently on his feet, seemingly afraid that he would fall down, but he did not. He stood beside her, looking at the floor, panting slightly, tears rolling unchecked down his face, his nose running. She fished a paper handkerchief from her pocket and wiped his nose, then crouched down beside him. He responded by becoming unnaturally still, so that even the air around him seemed hushed, and Max was reminded of the freeze reflex of fawns.

Jenny turned at a slight angle to the boy and lowered her head so that he could look into her face if he chose to favour her with one of those fleeting, sidelong glances.

'My name is Jenny Campbell,' she said. 'I don't know your name.' The boy's stillness seemed to intensify. Max stood quietly apart, admiring her skill in knowing precisely how long she should wait for the boy to come up with a name if he chose to, without making the silence burdensome for the child. After a few seconds, she nodded, accepting his decision.

'I thought, if you don't mind, I'd call you Paul for now. Would that be all right?' The boy seemed to relax infinitesimally, and Jenny glanced up at Max. This was an acceptance.

'Max thinks it would be best if you came home with me for a little while, just until we find your mummy and daddy.' A movement at the periphery of her vision told her that the boy had stolen a glance at her.

She got up slowly. 'Will you come with me, Paul?' She held out her hand. The boy took half a minute to respond, then he put his tiny hand in hers.

* * *

The boy's hand was cold, but it was warmed by the lady's. Her hair was shiny and a bit ruffled. She had a freckle the colour and shape of a tea leaf on her right cheek. Her voice sounded like wind chimes: gentle and musical. When she wiped his nose, her hanky had smelled of mints. His experience, for the moment, was limited to the sensual. Colour and noise had been his first impression, after the numbing cold of the previous night. He had already forgotten the other lady's house, the small red house with its smells of toast and cabbage and damp, and the sound of a slowly ticking clock, but he remembered the blue light, the wailing siren. The inside of the ambulance smelled of the doctors — metal and special soap and the cold stuff they rub on you before they give you a needle.

Then pictures, toys, silvery fish, hanging by threads from the ceiling. Voices, voices. There may have been words, but he could make no sense of them. Colour-noise and sound-noise. Smells of something like cough sweets and camphor, but less comforting than home.

He whimpered a little at the picture in his head. He didn't like to think of home, so he concentrated on the sounds around him until all memory of home, even all thought, went away. The sounds here were thin metal against sharp edges: rasping, hard, clattering, unfriendly. It was cold noise, which made him think of pain, made him want to hide his hands, hide himself somewhere small and far away, where no one would find him. He felt all of this without words, for words — he knew this without anybody telling him — were dangerous.

CHAPTER 4

Jenny double-locked the front door. There was no sense in taking chances that the child might wander off again. He had sat slumped in the passenger seat beside her on the journey home, showing no interest in his surroundings, no recognition.

It was nearly nine o'clock by the time she had filled in the necessary forms and then changed out of her uniform. The morning traffic had already belched a brownish haze of nitrous oxide over the city. It was going to be hot. Jenny glanced over at the boy from time to time. He stared ahead, his eyes level with the dashboard, eyelids slightly lowered, not so much ignoring her as oblivious to her.

Jenny and Fraser lived in a large Victorian house on the edge of Sefton Park, which they had converted back from flats when they bought it ten years previously. The house was warm and welcoming, and judging by the light snore that was audible even from the hallway, Fraser was still in bed.

The boy stood by her side, unmoving, seeming to lack any personal volition, but he complied with Jenny's requests, following her to the kitchen, sitting up at the table and eating a little cereal. She gave him a glass of warm milk and a biscuit to follow and explained, despite the fact that he gave no indication of having understood, that her husband was upstairs, that he was asleep, that it was just the three of them in the house. She paused, watching him closely for a reaction, but the boy maintained the same bland, beautiful expression. She might almost think him deaf, except that Max had told her the boy's hearing appeared to be normal. Indeed, he seemed to be unusually sensitive to noise.

His breakfast finished, she showed him the bathroom, the playroom, the spare bedroom, and the master bedroom, which reverberated more emphatically with Fraser's snores at this close range. The boy edged past the closed door with his back to the banister and they went on to his bedroom, which until recently had been Luke's room. They had decorated it in pastel colours because the children who came to them often seemed to find the brighter, primary colours more typical of children's bedrooms too stimulating.

Jenny open and closed cupboard doors, ostensibly to show him what was in them — the toys and games they would play with when he had settled in — but her real purpose was to reassure the boy that there was nothing — no *one* — hidden in them, nothing to fear from them.

'Before you go to bed, d'you think you could brush your teeth?' Jenny asked.

He went to the door and waited by it, staring up at her with those great, wounded eyes. He followed her to the bathroom. A Mickey Mouse beaker — Luke's — the fad of the moment, with his toothbrush still propped up in it, stood on the shelf above the sink as he had left it four weeks previously. Neither of them had been able to bring themselves to throw it away.

Luke's adoptive parents had agreed to let him stay with Jenny and Fraser until he had celebrated his fifth birthday. They were kind, gentle people, keen to make the transition from foster care to a stable family life as easy and painless as they could. The birthday party had been a disaster: Luke had refused to blow out the candles on his birthday cake and had fled upstairs in tears as his friends sang happy birthday to him.

Jenny swallowed hard and reached for the beaker. The boy flinched at the sudden movement and she said a few light, reassuring words, telling him what she was doing as she took a new toothbrush from the cabinet and unwrapped it.

He brushed his teeth without help and then placed the toothbrush in the beaker himself. He offered his hand to Jenny and she took it, smiling. 'You can sleep as late as you like, Paul.' She felt uncomfortable with the name Max had given him for convenience and for the sake of paperwork. She felt it must confuse him, and she resolved not to use it unless she had to. Then perhaps he might offer his own name more readily.

They stepped from the bathroom onto the landing.

Fraser stood in the doorway of their bedroom, looking like he had just woken. 'Who—?' he said. The night-growth of stubble showed black against the terrible pallor of his skin.

Oh, God, Jenny thought. *Poor Fraser!* Half asleep, he had seen the boy and imagined Luke had come back. She felt the boy's grip tighten and he took a startled breath.

'Paul,' she said, calmly, aware that she had already broken her resolution. 'This is my husband, Fraser. He's going to help me look after you.'

Fraser held the banister as if he needed it for support. 'This is Paul,' she went on. 'It's not his real name, but we don't know that yet. He's going to stay with us for a little while.' She remembered the quick, nervous look when she had mentioned the boy's mother and father previously and decided not to mention his parents again until he was communicating properly.

'Paul is going to bed because he didn't get any sleep last night.' She carried on past her husband, and the boy cringed behind her. He didn't take his eyes off Fraser all the way down the landing, but twisted round, still grasping Jenny's hand tightly, and stared at Fraser until they reached his bedroom and Fraser was no longer in sight.

Jenny removed his dressing gown and pulled back the duvet. The boy climbed into bed, which made two things he had done unbidden: replacing his toothbrush and getting into bed. It gave Jenny an irrational surge of optimism on the boy's behalf.

He was staring at the ceiling, unblinking, wide awake. Occasionally his eyes would flicker to the door.

'Would you like me to close it?' Jenny asked, smoothing the curls from his eyes. He answered her with another darting look at the door.

'Tell you what,' she said, getting up. 'I'll put this sign on the handle outside, then nobody can come in unless you tell them to.' It had worked for Luke when he had nightmares about a monster that lived on the landing. She unhooked the 'Do Not Disturb' sign she had made for Luke and hung it outside, then she shut the door firmly. She thought she saw a glimmer of relief on the boy's face.

This room caught the morning sun and it was warming fast in the July sunshine. Jenny crossed the room to open the window and the boy uttered a guttural cry of dismay. She turned to him.

'You want me to keep this closed, too?'

The boy stared wildly. Jenny pulled the latch closed. His eyes were wide, filled with terror.

Jenny sat beside him, holding his hand, crooning a lullaby in her sweet soprano, and within minutes the boy's grip slackened and his head slipped to one side. She carried on a little longer and then crept to the door and looked back at him.

His face was slightly flushed, and his fringe, which was a little too long, had fallen in an inverted question mark onto the bridge of his nose. He moaned and turned towards the window, and warm patches of colour spilt from the curtains onto his sleeping form.

* * *

Flowers. The house smelled of flowers. It was silent. Even the colours were quiet. He had seen everything: the coral-coloured carpet of the hall, the bowl of roses on the kitchen table, the sparkling jars of biscuits and pasta and lentils and rice on the warm tops of the cupboards. And he had seen the pale lemon-coloured spider, its body matching the velvety petals, hiding in the folds of a yellow rose. *He would not tell.* The spider watched him from its hiding place. The slight movements of its long front legs trembled with tension — he had seen it once in a cat. It was on the lawn, and it sat, fat, like this spider, trembling in a half-crouch until he felt sorry for it, because it seemed so afraid to move. And then it pounced, rushing to the border and catching a bird, carrying it carelessly in its mouth, staring blankly at the window, and he realized with sickening certainty that the tremor was not caused by fear but excitement. He had seen all of this, until it hurt his eyes to look, and he wanted to shut it out.

The boy drowsed, alert to every sound, waking frequently, always afraid, disoriented by his strange surroundings. The lady with the shiny hair smelled of hand cream. He didn't like the man. The pillow slips were cool against the back of his head and he turned, to let them take the heat from his face. They smelled of ironing and linen chests. He saw in his mind the man's face, strange, sick-looking, and it made him afraid. *I don't like him!* This thought had no clarity, nor distinct form, rather he felt it as a visceral fear. He closed his eyes tightly, conjuring up a picture in his head of the lady making the man go away.

* * *

Fraser was in bed, sitting up, waiting for her. She undressed and slipped on a baggy T-shirt. He stared at her, unblinking.

'All right?' she asked, sliding under the duvet and moving one hand to his chest. He felt clammy and she propped herself onto one elbow to look at him. 'I know,' she said. 'We agreed. No more children until the autumn.' She shrugged apologetically. 'Max ambushed me — virtually twisted my arm up my back. I'm sorry, Fraser.'

Later, while they shared toast and tea at the kitchen table, he broached the subject. 'A week's preparation, then off on your lecture tour, you said. I was supposed to use the time to sort myself out for next term, then get a bit of decorating done.'

'Leaving two weeks for a trip away together, I know.' Sun streamed in through the open window, and with it, truncated bursts of bird song.

'You're not playing by the rules, hen,' he reproached.

When she had first met him, before seventeen years of living in England had softened it to no more than a burr, Fraser's Glaswegian accent had been virtually incomprehensible to her. She had been in the second year of a nursing degree and had returned to university after six weeks working in America over the summer with the kind of swagger that owed more to relief than self-confidence. She had never before been so far from home, even choosing her local university so that she could be near friends and family, and although she had enjoyed her time away, it was good to be back on familiar territory.

The term had started with a fog that had brought public transport to a standstill, but Jenny and a group of friends had decided to walk, rather than miss their first day back. It wasn't far from their rented terrace in Wavertree to the university, and they had laughed and chatted all the way, feeling cocooned and mysterious in the all-enveloping gloom.

Jenny had split up from the main group after the lecture, having decided to look up a few references at the Harold Cohen library before going to lunch. The route to the library was a short walk from the biological sciences building, past the quad and through an archway — easy on a clear day, if you were familiar with the layout of the buildings, their alleyways and dead ends. But this section of the university was a jumble of Victorian, 1940s Art Deco, and 1960s functional glass-and-concrete buildings — constructed, it seems, with no unifying theme in mind, and the resulting collection of railed and un-railed sections, basements, blind alleys and cul-de-sacs had been particularly confusing in the murk rolling in from the Mersey.

On her right, Jenny could hear the traffic on Brownlow Hill as a long, steady drone, rather than the usual high-note, low-note Doppler effect of speeding midday motorists.

From the brownish fug to her left Jenny heard a distinct and passionately articulated 'Fuck!' Then a dark and decidedly handsome figure stumbled from an alley on her left.

'You all right?' she asked, eyeing him up with unabashed interest. The stranger muttered something that sounded like:

'Am looken ferra bluedy staesh'n.'

She raised her eyebrows and smiled. 'Sorry?'

'Ah'm sicka this rrathole awrreddy an' it's owny ma firrst dae!'

Her ear was beginning to attune to the accent, and she was able to decipher this without asking him to repeat himself.

'I know what you mean,' she said. 'I'm a native of the rathole.'

'Ach, sorry, luv, it's just—' He looked about him at the dirty mist.

She laughed. 'It's not always like this. And my name's Jenny.'

Fraser, it seemed, had arrived late for his first lecture of his first term at Liverpool University, after getting hopelessly lost trying to walk it from the halls of residence in Mossley Hill with only an *A to Z* as a guide.

'Why didn't you wait for the bus?'

'Radio said the' werren't runnin''

'That's just the Mersey buses. The halls of residence have their own special fleet to carry the delicate darlings from A to B without their having to rub shoulders with the Great Unwashed.'

'How d'ye know sae much about it?' he demanded, when they were seated comfortably in the Augustus John pub with a pint and a packet of crisps each.

Jenny tugged at her scarf. 'Don't you recognize the university colours?' she asked.

'Like ah sae—'

'You only arrived last night, and you haven't got your bearings yet.' He grinned and Jenny had to grit her teeth to keep from sighing. He really was *gorgeous*. 'You weren't really going to get on the first train home, were you?'

He looked a bit sheepish.

'Look, they may seem like a load of snobs and public-school haw-haws at first, but that's because you missed freshers' week, so you haven't had the chance to sort out the worthies from the wankers. They aren't all bad.' He looked at her doubtfully and she added, 'Most of it's just a front. They're as terrified as you or me.'

He sipped his lager, still doubtful. 'D'ye reckon?'

She crossed her heart, kissed her two fingers and gave the scout salute. 'What are you studying?' she asked.

He blushed and took a long pull on his pint.

'I'm doing a combined honours in psychology and nursing,' she told him. 'Second year,' she added, grimacing at the unworthy smugness she felt at the status conferred by a whole year's extra experience. 'So?'

He shifted uncomfortably. 'A'hm dae'n combined honours, as well,' he said.

'In what?' His evasiveness was beginning to irritate.

'Sociology and' — he shrugged, colouring a little more deeply — 'geography.'

Jenny grinned, then raised her hands at his answering scowl. 'I promise I won't tell a soul,' she said.

She had persuaded him to stay and they had remained, somewhat disappointingly for Jenny, friends throughout university, but they had kept in touch after graduation, occasionally meeting with some of their university friends, but more and more frequently on their own and, without the distractions of the usual crowd they hung round with, they began to realize that their delight in each other's company was more than platonic. Fraser proposed to her the day he was appointed to his first teaching job, and Jenny had accepted without hesitation.

* * *

'We'll get a week away, I promise.' She took his hand. 'At *least* a week — two, if I can wangle the time off,' she went on, when she saw that he wasn't thawing. 'Max thinks it'll only take a couple of weeks to find the boy's parents. He thinks they might be Romanies — moved on and left him behind by accident.'

A fleeting shadow of the horror she had read in Fraser's face earlier returned and Jenny was reminded of something Max had once told her: 'It's easy to dispel the monsters of childhood — all it takes is a little magic and a lot of faith. But the devils of adulthood are much more tenacious.'

'Fraser,' she said, 'is everything okay? Before, on the landing — you looked terrible.'

'It was shock, that's all. I thought—' He bit his lower lip.

'You thought Luke had come home.' She shook her head. 'I'm so sorry.' She stood and, leaning across the table, kissed him. He responded, brushing her cheek with the back of his hand, then stroking the nape of her neck and pulling her to him.

Jenny broke away gently. 'Bed?' she said. He nodded, and she saw that he had forgiven her.

'You look like you could do with a few hours' sleep.'

Jenny smiled. 'Who said anything about sleep?'

She did get some sleep — about two hours, resting comfortably against the warmth of Fraser's shoulder and dreaming of the boy who was, for reasons that seemed perfectly obvious in the dream, a concert pianist. She woke as somebody rushed on stage and slammed the piano lid down on his fingers.

* * *

His heart pounding, he stared at the door.

I promised to be a good boy. I promised. But the shape at the door — behind the door — pulled him. *No . . . please, don't make me.*

* * *

Fraser woke with a start. The boy was standing in the bedroom doorway. His eyes were wide open, and he was mumbling something she couldn't hear properly.

'Lie still,' Jenny whispered, 'he's sleepwalking.' Outside she could hear the grind and groan of the bin lorry. They hadn't made their quota by five on Friday night, and privatization meant that it wasn't unusual for the bin collection for their area to be completed on Saturday.

'Bloody bin men disturbed him.' She reached for her dressing gown, draped over the chair next to the bed and got into it with as much dignity and with the least exposure of flesh she could manage.

Suddenly the boy's breathing grew shallow and quick. He made small yelping sounds which escalated to full-blown screams of terror. Jenny edged up to him, fearful of frightening him further, calming him, talking quietly, gently steering him back to bed.

Fraser stared at the photograph on the chest of drawers and back to the boy. A picture of himself aged nine or ten, a fish in one hand, fishing rod in the other, squinting into the light, both proud and shy. His first catch. A sprat, no more, but his father crowing about it to his friends as if Fraser had reeled in a pike big enough to swallow him whole.

When she returned half an hour later, Fraser was again sitting up in bed. She crawled next to him and kissed the tangle of dark hair on his chest.

'You see why I couldn't refuse to take him?' she said.

He sighed. 'What can I do?'

'I'll introduce you when he's properly awake. Play with him — that's if he'll have anything to do with you — he doesn't seem to take to men. Talk to him, try and gain his trust. But don't try and persuade him to talk about what happened. We have to be careful not to plant ideas in his head. He'll tell us what went on when he's ready.'

'Okay.' He was silent for some time, then he asked, 'What if I don't gain his trust?'

'You could always move out.' She could tell by Fraser's tension that she had gone too far. 'Joke, Fraser. Bad joke, I know — I'm sorry, but I'm tired.'

He kissed the top of her head. Her hair gleamed in the sunlight slipping through the hastily drawn curtains. 'Did he make any sense?'

She shook her head, then snuggled closer and kissed him under the chin. 'Think he looks like you?' This had been their stock question since their first foster child, Daniel O'Hare, had come to them on a short-term placement eight years before. It was a running gag, meant to make them laugh and, more importantly, to distract them from wondering with each successive placement why it couldn't be their own child.

Mostly they did laugh, but not this time.

Jenny frowned. There had been children who had her eye colour, Fraser's hair colour, children who had been with them long enough to pick up his or her mannerisms. Once, they'd even taken a boy whose mother had fallen ill and been rushed to hospital days after moving to Liverpool from Glasgow. Jamie had got on like a house on fire with Fraser and they had talked for hours in an incomprehensible dialect until she had felt quite excluded.

This child, more than any other, this dark-eyed, dark-haired little fawn really did look like Fraser. He even had the slightly sallow skin colouring that Fraser claimed he owed to his European ancestry.

Fraser kissed the crown of Jenny's head again and stared at the space on the dresser where the photograph had been. The bedroom door stood ajar, casting a wedge of pale, greenish light from the hallway onto the dresser — spotlight on deception.

* * *

Honeysuckle. The air was thick with it. As a child I would break the long thin teat of the flower at the base and suck the tiny bead of nectar from it. Sweet, scented — a forbidden pleasure. Who knew what dirt and germs were harboured in the folds of its petals?

Light shone from a window at the rear of the house. The kitchen. She finished her coffee, placed it in the sink. And then he was there. He ran into the room. Ran to her. Hugged her. Laughed with her.

A bat swooped and circled overhead, its very silence demanding attention. I stopped and watched, listened to the silence. It calmed me. The front of the house would be best — less suspicious.

I knocked and he came into the entrance hall. I could see his shadow, faint, blurred behind the glass. I focused silently on him, demanding his attention.

CHAPTER 5

'Jen, are you with me?'

Jenny shook herself and took a swig of her orange juice. 'I'm sorry, Max, it's . . .' She had been thinking that something was not quite right at home. Not just in Fraser's reaction to the boy, but an atmosphere, something she couldn't quite pin down. And when she had dusted that afternoon, there was something odd about their bedroom. It felt like a fixture, something she took for granted, barely noticing it, had been shifted, or perhaps it simply wasn't there . . .

'You're worried about Paul?'

'Yes.' But if she was honest it wasn't concern for Paul that was preoccupying her thoughts at that moment. Working the night shift had proved a convenient arrangement. They had almost forgotten the importance of such things in their year and a half with Luke, who had adored them both equally and unequivocally, and who was placid and easy-going in a way that none of their other children had been. As it worked out, Paul had slept through most of her absence on Saturday night, and then again on Sunday. In fact, he slept rather more than was healthy for his age, but Max had assured her that this was only to be expected in a child who had been through some kind of trauma, as seemed increasingly likely in Paul's case.

'I shouldn't be bothering you with this.' They had been discussing the problems of false memory syndrome, a subject of one of Jenny's lectures and a sideline — even a hobby horse — of Max's. Occasionally, they gave lectures at the same conventions. Once, they had even given a joint presentation to a group of undergraduate nurses.

She made an effort to concentrate. 'If a person claiming recovered memory of abuse is unlikely to recant while still under the influence of the therapist they made the original disclosure to, doesn't that mean that by the time you get to them they're almost past help?'

'It certainly doesn't make the job any easier. You see, they have entered into a kind of compact with their therapist in which they play the good abuse victim and the therapist gives them the positive reinforcement of attention. It's not a conscious decision — they're not trying to fool anyone — they are absolutely convinced they *have* been abused. The people I see only begin to question the truth of the appalling stories they tell *after* they've broken away from the therapist — or the group which is feeding their fantasies. Some even go through a period of psychosis before they eventually start to mend.'

Jenny nodded, assimilating this, trying to find a way to work the information into her lecture.

'It's difficult to get the balance right,' she said. 'I don't want to trivialize the devastating effect of abuse, but I want to warn people that carelessly framed questions can lead children to remember abuse that never took place.'

'Memory's a tricky thing,' Max agreed. 'Once an idea is planted it takes root and grows. I've known people invent complex and intricate histories which are pure fabrication — and yet they believe them as absolute truth.'

'And when you challenge those beliefs?'

'Immediate reaction?' he said. '"You're calling me a liar. I went through this and you're disbelieving me. You're traumatizing me all over again, making me feel I have to prove what I know to be true."'

Jenny sighed.

'Now,' Max's eyes crinkled as he leaned forward and peered into her face. 'Let's get back to what you are worried about.'

Jenny smiled. 'You'd be charging your Rodney Street patients at least eighty quid an hour for this.'

Max Greenberg drew his eyebrows together and gave his head a little shake. 'Minimum. And they would not all be allowed their consultation in such a conducive setting.' They had agreed to meet in the Knotty Ash pub an hour before Jenny's shift was due to begin. He waited, sipping his half-pint of Guinness and watching her over the rim of his glass.

She gazed into his eyes but could not withstand his cool appraisal, so, to avoid the steady, unhurried and perceptive scrutiny of the psychiatrist, she let her examination of his features travel on to his broad, intelligent forehead and the receding line of fine brown hair.

It wasn't that she didn't trust Max — she trusted him almost as much as she trusted Fraser — but she didn't like to waste his time, and it all seemed so trivial when put into perspective. She could read from his expression that Max would not let this go, however, so she sighed again, and began:

'I had a phone call yesterday.'

Max's whole body signalled interest and attention.

'At first, I thought it was a heavy breather, but I think he was hesitating, wondering whether to hang up.'

'He?'

'Definitely a he.'

She fell silent and Max prompted, 'He did speak eventually?'

'Eventually, yes.' She took a breath, remembering the effect the caller's question had had on her: slow, cold pain, followed by an emptiness in the pit of her stomach. 'Max, he asked if I had any children.' She swallowed. 'Wanted to know if I'd had a child adopted.'

Max would know the effect such a question would have on Jenny. He placed one hand over hers for a moment, then asked, 'What did you tell him?'

'I asked who he was. He called himself Mr Hunter. Said he was a private detective — I know, not a very original alias, was it? He said he was working for a client who'd been adopted and was trying to trace his parents.' She laughed a little shakily and pushed her fingers through her hair. 'At first I thought it was a joke — someone at the hospital — I don't know. I told him I don't have any children. Of course, I *should* have asked him which agency he worked for, tried to get some proof of identification from him, but it was all so unreal. He'd hung up before I could gather my wits and think what to say to him. I tried last number trace, but he'd withheld it.'

'It worries you?'

'You're dead right it does. How did he get my telephone number?'

'From the phone book? You know, you have been in the papers rather a lot recently — "NURSE-WRITER DOCTORS THE PAST" — and then there was that radio interview. People are intrigued by such things. Perhaps he saw a publicity photo and thought there was some physical resemblance.'

'That's what Fraser said.' Jenny was surprised and flattered that Dr Greenberg had paid such close attention to her press coverage — she had almost forgotten the launch of *Poisoned Chalice* three weeks previously. There had been unexpected, if fleeting, media interest generated by the controversial subject matter of her book, centred around a single chapter on the false/recovered memories debate. The text was meant for academic readers in the fields of nursing and Social Services, but the Brandon report had stirred up a lot of interest, even in the tabloid press, and she found herself, briefly, a celebrity. It was a momentary distraction from the pain of Luke's disappearance from their lives, too transient to provide more than a temporary respite.

'You may be right,' she added. Nevertheless, the phone call had been disturbing. Fraser's reaction had upset her, too. He had been out shopping when the call came, and his immediate response was: 'He asked *you* if you'd had any children adopted?'

'It's not written in big letters on my forehead, Fraser,' she had said. 'I haven't always been like this, you know.'

Of course, Fraser knew. He knew because he had been with her when the dreadful pains started. He had held her hand as she screamed and writhed in agony on a trolley in the casualty department of the Royal Hospital. He had signed the consent form for the operation to save her life because, by the time they discovered that she had an ectopic pregnancy and was bleeding internally, she was delirious and unable to make any rational decisions for herself. Not that Fraser's decision was entirely rational. Until that moment they hadn't known that she was pregnant.

Fraser had recoiled, hurt, and Jenny had silently cursed herself. She swilled the remnants of her orange juice around the glass. 'I'm afraid I was a bit short with Fraser and he's done one of his tactical withdrawals.' She smiled. 'The only person talking in our house at the moment is me. It's a bit eerie, having all these one-sided conversations.'

'I take it the boy still isn't communicating.'

Jenny noticed that he hadn't used their agreed pseudonym for the boy, and wondered if Max shared her reservations about giving the child a name other than his own.

'No,' she said. 'Well, yes, I suppose he *is* communicating, in his own way — he just won't talk.'

'The level of communication?'

'Gestures, facial expressions, body language.'

'Has he used the paints and crayons?'

Max had recommended encouraging Paul to draw or paint.

'He draws the same thing over and over. A house with a brick wall at the front of it. Then he paints black bars on all the windows and a lock on the front door.'

'To keep him in, or someone else out, I wonder?'

'I really don't know, Max.' She remembered the 'Do Not Disturb' sign and told Max that the boy now placed it outside his door whenever he went into his room. 'He seems to find it reassuring.'

'How does he get on with Fraser?'

Jenny thought about this for a time, torn between loyalty to Fraser and the welfare of the boy. 'He tolerates him. I don't know if he's aware I'm not there at night — I put him to bed before I leave and I'm usually back before he wakes up — but he does sleepwalk, and he's more agitated if Fraser tries to settle him than when I'm there.' She looked up at Max, perplexed and worried. 'I don't *want* to rush him — I know it'd be best to let him dictate the pace. I know you think there's no urgency, Max, but . . .'

'You're not so sure?'

She nodded. 'You think I'm wrong?'

Max grunted. 'Asking questions can give the appearance of moving things along, but what if it's in the wrong direction? We bring our own prejudices, our own hang-ups, our own night terrors and demons to these situations. Even if you could persuade him to nod or shake his head in answer, your questions would be closed — a narrow yes or no is often not the answer we would like to give — life is too complex for such simplicity. In his mind, he may see his answers as being right or wrong.'

'You're telling me to take my own advice.' She smiled and he reciprocated.

'I suspect he's trying to be a good boy, to do the right thing, and in forcing him to answer questions set from your own agenda, you could find he'll give the answers he thinks fit in with your expectations.'

'Okay,' she said, 'point taken. We don't want any false memory scenarios, right?'

'In a nutshell. Now, have you sorted out what you intend to say about false memory in your lectures?'

Jenny held up her notebook. 'I'll type these up when I get home tomorrow. Then I'll jot down a few suggestions and arrive in Nottingham armed and dangerous.' She had a one-off lecture at a conference of social workers and health visitors, which she intended to use as a dress rehearsal for the tour. 'I'll need to do some reading at the university library when I get back. I need the corroboration of recent research.' The Brandon report had sparked off a whole raft of papers on recovered memory. 'I'll incorporate what I can into the Nottingham lecture and use the rest for the tour.'

Max nodded, approving. 'Will those two be all right together for a whole day while you're away?'

'Max,' Jenny laughed, 'you think of everything. Social Services have arranged for a female social work assistant to stay with them for the twenty-four hours I'll be away.' She checked her watch, drained the last of her orange juice and stood to leave. 'Thanks again.' She bent to kiss his cheek and he caught her hand as she took it from his shoulder.

'Jenny . . .' She looked at him, startled, eyes wide. He squeezed her hand, embarrassed, then released it. 'Be careful.'

Max watched her leave, a trim thirty-five-year-old who could pass for ten years younger. Black jeans, white T-shirt, golden hair cascading shaggily over her shoulders, and he felt a surge of almost fatherly pride, followed by a stab of concern for her safety. 'Ridiculous,' he muttered, taking a cool swallow of Guinness and pinching the creamy moustache from his upper lip between his forefinger and thumb. It was unlikely, he reasoned, that her telephone call and his crank calls were linked. His calls had been distorted by a voice scrambler, so he couldn't be sure if the caller was male or female. Jenny's caller was definitely male — she'd seemed quite certain of that — and he had made no specific threats. No — there was no point worrying her unnecessarily.

* * *

'How're you getting on with the little lad?'

'Jeez!' Jenny jumped like a startled cat. She hadn't heard anyone come into the changing room. She had twenty minutes before her shift started and was first to arrive.

'Shona,' she said, taking a few breaths and attempting to get the pounding of her heart under control.

'Is he all right, like?' Shona seemed unaware of the fright she had given Jenny.

'He's fine.' Shona had taken a personal interest in the boy ever since the story had broken on local radio.

'They're gonna put his picture in the *Echo*. And on the telly.'

'How did you know that?' Mike Delaney at the *Liverpool Echo* had arranged for a photographer to come to the house at seven on Tuesday morning, so that the pictures would make Wednesday's *Echo* and *Granada News*.

Shona tapped the side of her thin, pretty nose. 'There's not many advantages to working on the switchboard, but . . .' She smiled, revealing slightly crooked teeth. 'Anyway, it was on Radio Merseyside at teatime.'

Shona, it would appear, divided her time between listening to local radio and TV news, watching soaps and reading the *Liverpool Echo*.

'What are you doing here so late?' Jenny asked. It was twenty to eight, and the offices closed at five, leaving only a skeleton staff on the switchboard.

'Oh, you know,' Shona said, shrugging her bony shoulders. 'No rest for the wicked.'

Jenny continued dressing, while Shona hovered uncertainly, sitting, then standing, then pacing the room uneasily. She had the slightly gawky movements of a teenager, though she must have been in her mid-twenties. She was dressed in a short denim skirt and a tight-fitting cotton top with bootlace straps. Her hair, dark brown and unruly, was brushed back from her face, a small hank of it caught in a slide which she had trouble keeping in place, so that it slipped sideways and she was constantly having to pull it back into position, until a snarl of knotted hair gathered behind it.

'Has he said anything yet?'

'Paul? No. Why do you ask?'

'Well, they're not gonna find his mum and dad if he doesn't talk, are they?'

'I think the police are hoping someone will come forward when they show his picture on the TV and in the *Echo*.'

Shona clasped her hands anxiously in front of her. 'But they'll have to make sure they're his real parents and, like, that he's gonna be okay.'

Jenny smiled. 'I'm sure they will. In fact, I can't understand why his parents haven't come forward already.'

'You know what I think?' She paused, and Jenny saw that she was deeply troubled.

Jenny tilted her head to show that she was listening.

Shona shrugged. 'Well, never mind what I think. You've only got to look at his little face to see that poor lad's suffered.'

'I don't think we should jump to conclusions,' Jenny said, folding her jeans and T-shirt and stowing them on the shelf in her locker. Privately, she agreed with Shona, but the telephonist was susceptible to even the mildest suggestion, and she had a vivid imagination.

'It's not jumping to conclusions when a kiddy comes in and he's so traumatized he can't even talk!'

'*Traumatized*?' Jenny repeated.

Shona stared back at her. 'I'm seeing this therapist,' she said by way of explanation. 'She says we've got to unlock the anger bottled up inside us or it'll eat us up from the inside.'

'Shona,' Jenny said, 'releasing anger in that way can be dangerous. It feeds on itself. *Being* angry *makes* us angry.'

'You've got to get him to talk, Jen.'

'He'll talk when he's ready.'

'He's blocking it out — what happened to him.'

'I know that.'

'He's got to get his memory back or it'll arrest his development.'

Jenny sighed. 'I think the whole problem is he *can't* forget. He wants to, but he can't.'

Shona's smile was pitying. 'I know what I'm talking about, Jen.'

'Well, thanks,' Jenny said briskly, 'but I'll stick with the experts' advice.'

Shona recoiled as if she had slapped her, and Jenny saw that she had spoken too sharply. 'We have to go very carefully, Shona. We have to be sure that anything he does say — when he decides to talk to us — is real. It's a hazard when you're trying to draw children out: you can inadvertently plant ideas — things that never happened.'

'And what about his hands, eh? He didn't get them injuries playing "knuckles", did he?'

Jenny winced. 'How do you know about his hands?' They were old injuries and, until a satisfactory explanation could be found as to how he got them, Max had decided to keep quiet about them. Shona shrugged, offering her a coy smile. Jenny stared for a moment. 'His case notes are confidential, Shona,' she rebuked gently.

'Oh yeah, blame me for showing an interest,' Shona said, huffily. 'I'm only trying to help, aren't I?'

Jenny stared at her until she blushed.

'Ar 'ey, Jen. You're not gonna grass me up, are you? I only had a little squint over Trish's shoulder while she typed them up.' Trish was Max's secretary.

'Let the police do their job,' Jenny said, hoping that an ambiguous answer might make Shona more circumspect about looking at confidential medical records without authorization — cross-eyed or otherwise.

* * *

Still, Jenny thought, as she trotted down three flights to Ward A2, Shona has a point. In the three days since he'd come to them, the boy *had* shown signs of trauma. Jenny had kept notes, as Max had asked.

On Saturday, she had made burgers and chips for him — a safe fall-back option with all the other children they had ever fostered.

Paul sat staring at his plate for a full five minutes with that look of unfathomable sadness on his face, and when she had asked, quietly, 'Don't you like chips?' he had started violently and hastily eaten a few mouthfuls, then promptly burst into tears, hitching and choking and balking like she had made him eat raw chopped liver.

* * *

He tried to eat it. But the man kept watching him. He tried not to think about the other time—

'Throw up, and I'll make you eat THAT! I'll get you a fucking straw and you can suck it up!'

—even closed his eyes to make the remembering go away. But you can't shut your eyes to a memory. It only makes it come more.

* * *

Shona sat down in the pub, a glass of cider and a packet of crisps for her dinner and poked about in her shoulder bag until she found the photocopy she had made of Jenny's behavioural diary on Paul. They had sat on Trish's desk, waiting to be passed on to Max Greenberg all day, and nobody missed them in the five minutes it took to make a duplicate set. 'He glances up at me frequently,' Shona read from the photocopied notes, 'but he quickly averts his eyes.'

He started at the top of the house, in the playroom, then worked down to the main landing, checking the window in his room was shut, even though it was hot and sunny. Then he opened the cupboards and touched each item — toy or clothing — closed them after him, then moved on to the bed, the cabinet, the chair, the radiator.

I suspected that he was asking for information with his quick, shy sideways glances, and so I began a commentary: what each room was for, who had owned the clothes in the wardrobes and drawers. Once or twice he seemed to nod, as if to say, 'Explanation accepted,' but mostly he simply moved on to the next thing, touching it, picking it up, sometimes smelling it. He cuddled some of the toys, but always replaced them where he'd found them.

In the study, he went through the ritual of checking the window locks, and then he stood with his back to it and surveyed the room. I told him that we use it as an office, and he showed an interest in the computer, the desk, my papers. The only thing he wouldn't touch was the filing cabinet. He kept turning away from it, so that it was out of his field of vision. In the end, I touched it and named it and he blanched and hid his hands behind his back.

Shona flinched. Her own hands felt a sympathetic rap of sharp pain and, looking down at them, she saw that her fingers were hooked so severely that her nails had pierced the paper.

He gave the spare bedroom a cursory check-over, and secured the window, but at our bedroom he paused, touched the door and tilted his head, as if in question.

'That's mine and Fraser's bedroom. You can go in, if you like.'

Instead, he returned to his own room, unhooked the sign from the inside of the door handle, and placed it on our door after pulling it shut.

I said, 'You've put your "Do Not Disturb" sign on our bedroom door.' He patted the door, then moved on.

Fraser was in the sitting room when we went in. He put down his paper and pretended to be absorbed in the TV. The boy switched his attention to Fraser — checking his reaction when he touched things. He touched the remote control like it was a live snake, then again, when there was no reaction. Then he picked it up, watching Fraser closely. I asked him if he'd like to watch something else, but he put the control down where he'd found it and then went back to his tactile catalogue.

In the kitchen, he climbed onto a stool and lifted the lids off every jar, taking a great sniff of each. He rearranged them — the only items he did not return to their original places. Coffee, then tea, sugar, mint tea, then the pastas: tagliatelle, penne, vermicelli, spaghetti. The herbs and spices he arranged in alphabetical order in the spice rack.

I sat and watched him, offering the same commentary, neither approving nor disapproving his actions. It must have taken him an hour in all. He replaced the stool at the breakfast bar and clambered up onto my lap and rested his head on my chest. At first, I thought he was listening to my heartbeat, but he was crying silently, great rivers of silent tears, until I thought his little heart would break.

'All right, Queen?' The barmaid was standing over her, concern and curiosity both showing on her face.

Shona found a tissue and wiped her eyes. 'Don't you sometimes wish you could take someone's pain away from them?' she asked.

'I've got enough of me own to be goin' on with, thanks very much.' The barmaid gathered the first empties of the night and retired, clinking, behind the bar.

Shona smoothed out the crumpled sheet of paper before replacing it in her bag. The pain in her hands abated to a dull throb as she sipped her drink, but a deeper, yearning ache pulled at her heart.

CHAPTER 6

Lee-Anne picked up the handbag. 'Credit cards,' she said. 'Purse.' She handed both over to Lobo. 'Fuck!'

'What?'

'She moved.'

'No, she never. It was the—'

—Blood. It crept like a tidal flow, threatening to break over the tips of her shoes, heaving and sighing. She stepped back, appalled. Lobo clicked the purse clasp and his eyes opened wide. Blood bubbled and churned, rising and falling like the agonized breathing of the dying woman. Then it flowed over the clasp of the purse, over the green leather and down Lobo's arms, dripping from his elbows. He threw back his head and laughed.

She sensed another movement and looked down. The woman had rolled onto her back. Her neck was slashed and from the gash, more blood flowed, frothing, bright red from her lungs. Her mouth formed the words, but the sound came, hideously, a watery whisper, from the gaping wound in her throat.

'Help me . . .'

Lee-Anne screamed and sat bolt upright. She panted, terrified, watching blood course down the walls from the ceiling, congealing in lumps, slowing and stopping. Lobo slept on beside her.

She whimpered, her heart hammering in her chest. 'It's a dream,' she told herself. 'Just a dream.'

But the blood flowed on, forming rivulets like rain on glass. Its smell filled the room with its butcher's-slab reek, metallic, rich, repugnant. She stepped out of bed and crept to the wall, stretched out a hand and, overcoming her revulsion, she touched it.

It was dry.

She woke a second time with the lumpy, uneven feel of woodchip wallpaper under her fingertips. No rivers of blood, no coppery smell. A dream, after all.

* * *

'Is this it, then? Have you had enough?'

Lee-Anne looked at the clutter of bags around their table and giggled. She'd hardly even started, but Lobo was hungry, and she knew better than to push him when he was hungry.

'Isn't it great?' she said.

'What?'

'Gettin' what you want instead of what you can afford.'

Lobo pouched a mouthful of steak pie into the side of his cheek. 'What we want and what we can afford is one and the same thing now, Lee.'

She felt a warm glow just below her rib cage. He only called her Lee when he was feeling mellow. 'When I get home, I'm gonna throw out all my old togs. Every last stitch.'

He laughed and stuffed another forkful of pie and chips into his mouth.

'I never in my *life* thought I'd be out buying Hugo Boss and CK jeans.'

'Well, you've got half a dozen to choose from now, eh, girl?'

'I can't wait till you try that suit on again. You look gorgeous in that suit,' Lee-Anne said.

Lobo shrugged. He'd only bought it to shut her up. If it was down to him, he'd've got more sports gear, but like she said, they'd bring out a new Liverpool strip next season and he'd be out of date. Anyway, if wearing a suit made Lee-Anne look at him like he was Leonardo DiCaprio, it was worth it.

'Makes you sorry you've got to go back to all that manky furniture in the flat,' Lee-Anne added, with a little grimace of disgust. 'Dusty old tat.'

She nibbled her tuna sandwich while she waited for Lobo to get the idea she wanted him to get. He'd nearly finished his meal and the extra calories and strong tea had restored his good mood.

'What's to stop us binning the lot?' he said, waving the waitress over.

'The landlord, for one,' Lee-Anne said, feigning shock, knowing that thinking he was flouting all the rules was just the thing to egg Lobo on. 'What would we sit on?'

He laughed. 'What would we sit on . . .' The waitress arrived and he gave her his full attention. 'Have you got any apple pie and custard, love?'

'The waitress smiled. 'How much d'you want?'

'Just the two.' The waitress made a note and left. 'How much have we spent since Saturday?' he asked. 'A couple of thou'? More? No one's batted an eyelid. She must be minted!'

Have been, Lee-Anne thought. Past tense. She wished Lobo wouldn't keep bringing her up. It took the shine off things, thinking about her.

'What's up with you?' Lobo was getting sick of her moods. One minute she was up, spending like a pop star, acting like a Spice Girl, the next she was crying her eyes out and saying she couldn't sleep — all over some bint she didn't even know.

'The stupid mare had her PIN numbers with her cards — she was *begging* to be ripped off!'

'Don't say that, Lobo.' It didn't seem right, taking her money and then calling her names.

'Just 'cos she's got money doesn't make her better than you and me.'

'She hasn't got it no more, though, has she?' Lee-Ann said.

'No. We have. It was hers, now it's ours. So, are we gonna spend it or mope over it?'

Lee-Anne bit her lip. She *did* feel bad about it, but on the bright side, Lobo had taken the bait. She looked at the bags of shopping. 'What else did you have in mind?' she asked.

'Something decent to sit on,' he said. 'A bed that doesn't put holes in me when I lie on it. New lino for the kitchen, carpet for the bedroom.'

Lee-Anne frowned. 'That'd mean decorating.'

'I'll get our Kyle and the lads to lend a hand. It'll only take a couple of days.'

Blue, she thought. I want the bedroom blue, to wipe out every trace of the red and black Lobo had painted the room when they had first moved in. Blue and yellow. Sun and sky. She'd had that dream every night for three days, sometimes more than once in a night. A bit of blue and yellow wallpaper might not stop the bad dreams, but at least when she woke up she wouldn't think she was still living them.

'It would be nice . . .' Lee-Anne said, putting just the right balance of doubt and timid appreciation into it.

'Eat up,' Lobo said. 'We've got stuff to buy.'

* * *

Mr Wood sat in an armchair next to his daughter's empty bed. He had paced up and down the corridor with frantic energy for half an hour after Jarmon, the charge nurse, had asked him to leave the ward because his exclamations and groans had begun to unsettle the children.

Jarmon glanced up from his notes when Jenny came into the office. 'How is he?'

'He's not wearing out the lino anymore, but he's not coping well.'

Jarmon shook his head. 'When I suggested he should go for a walk, I meant *out*side the building.'

‘When’s Carla due back?’

‘She’s still in the operating room. Could be an hour, could be more.’

‘I’ll make him a cuppa when I’ve a quiet moment,’ Jenny said.

She went on her rounds, stopping to check Georgie’s temperature and pulse rate: it had surged alarmingly in the first half of the night, because of an adverse reaction to the anaesthetic. Her mother had gone home after seeing her come up from theatre — she had four others to look after and her husband was working nights. The staff had debated whether to bring her back in, but Georgie had rallied in the last hour and it looked as though she would be all right.

She was a tiny, skinny little four-year-old, and the padded patch over her left eye increased the appearance of vulnerability. She moaned as Jenny pulled a sheet over her. Her unpatched eye half opened. ‘Mummy . . .’

Jenny stroked the little girl’s face. ‘All right, chicken.’ Georgie’s pet name. ‘Everything’s fine.’ Georgie mumbled something and drifted off again.

When Jenny looked up, Mr Wood was wiping his eyes. Carla’s Donald Duck sat on his knee and he stroked it compulsively. Jenny updated Georgie’s chart, then went and sat beside Mr Wood.

‘It may take a while yet,’ she said.

Mr Wood nodded, pressing his lips together and frowning as if in physical pain.

‘I’ll make you a cuppa, shall I?’

He nodded again, then looked up, puzzled. ‘What, love?’

Jenny began repeating what she had just said, but he interrupted, seizing her hand and telling her in a whisper, ‘She’s such a bonny lass. If she loses her eye, what’ll I do? What’ll I tell her?’

‘Tell who? Carla?’

He flung Jenny’s hand from him. ‘She’ll blame me! I told her if she was fretting so much, I’d tell Carla she wasn’t to play in the back till I got it cleared.’ His eyes, a pale, clear blue, were red and swollen at the rim. 'But it was such a nice day, and I can't let her play out the front with the traffic . . .' He paused and sighed. 'It was meant to be a surprise. She's been on at me for months about Carla's bedroom. I thought I'll decorate her room and then sort out the garden, have it looking nice for when Sue — that's my wife — for when she gets back.

'"Carla," I said, "Keep away from the rubbish!" I *told* her . . .' He squeezed the toy close to his chest, looking both angry and defensive. Then his face crumpled, and Jenny saw only his distress and anxiety for his child.

'She'll have a nice new bedroom to come home to, won't she?' Jenny said, gently.

He shook his head. 'I've ruined her life.'

'Mr Wood,' Jenny said, 'does your wife know what's happened to Carla?'

He nodded, miserably. 'She's on her way. She only went for a few days to her sister's.'

People always used a qualifier in these situations: 'She only . . . I was just . . . I'd only turned my back a minute . . .' As if the scant lapse of time should have kept their child safe. For some, the closeness of death changed their view of life, so that safety, order, reliability became ephemeral, transitory, and every moment was filled with the menace of potential disaster. What, Jenny wondered, would Paul's parents say, when they were found? And why hadn't they reported him missing? From Friday to Monday night and not a word. Did they fear police prosecution — or had they been prevented from coming forward for some other reason?

CHAPTER 7

The surprise had been how easily it had been accomplished. Messy, yes, but astonishingly brief. A sliver of steel had destroyed what had seemed, until the moment it ceased to be, invincible. It was remarkable, awesome. Hatred had been the driving force: she had prevented the achievement of an objective. She had got in the way, had become an obstacle to be overcome. Afterwards, there had even been a kind of sorrow, a kind of regret. But death was ugly, it banished real pity, and so both sorrow and regret were muted, and all that was left was a throb of anger.

The boy's memory played like a colour video with surround sound. He tried to make it stop, but the pictures wouldn't go away.

'EAT the fucking burger. You wanted it, now eat it. Don't you—Don't you DARE throw up, you little pig. Throw up, and I'll make you eat THAT! I'll get you a straw and you can suck it up!'

Jenny's face stared down at him. Her eyes were the same shade of green as the cat's. Her jaws were empty, but a deadly cunning flickered behind the blank, dull lifelessness of her eyes. He tried to eat, but he couldn't make his stomach stay still, and he retched.

He was awakened by the sound of his own thin cries. The dream had confused him: everything had got mixed up — the now and the before. People, even. Jenny was nice, wasn't she? Jenny, with the glow of light around her face, and the voice like wind chimes. She never shouted. She would never hurt him. Would she? He wasn't sure of anything anymore. Trust, safety, love, all seem so fleeting, so easily taken away. Like the big, solid, cheery, snowman he built after an April snowfall — by midday he was gone, leaving an untidy jumble of scarf and carrot nose and umbrella in a dirty melt of snow. He never found the button eyes. They had vanished for good.

He gathered together the soft toys — teddy bears, donkeys, lions, polar bears, owls, monkeys, penguins (not the pigs — *not the pigs!*) — and placed some by the door, facing out. Two more guarded the window. He kept a polar bear and a lion for himself, tucking them in either side of him and waited, unsleeping, for the morning to come.

* * *

Paul looked too tired for the photo session on the Tuesday morning, but the photographer promised it would take no more than twenty minutes. Sergeant Mike Delaney arrived just in time for the session. He had been called out when the boy was found and it was he who had requested a Police Protection Order, so he felt a responsibility for the child, and he wanted to be there when Diane Seward took her photographs.

Mike was first-generation Irish — part of the constant stream of Irish émigrés that had quit the Old Country, first during the Potato Famine of the 1840s, and later, when the depression of the 1930s wiped whole families from the face of Ireland. His parents had come over in 1935, in the hope of finding work and decent housing. What they had found was the squalid, sooty, back-to-back terraced slums of Scotland Road and Everton Brow.

His parents had raised a family of five girls and a boy in a two up, two down with an outside privy and no bathroom.

Mike remembered the gas mantles, and although his sisters told him they were long defunct when he was born, he could swear he could recall the yellow-blue light, the throaty exhalation of gas down the pipes, and a faint smell of coal tar. Bath night was once a week: buckets of water heated on the stove and poured into a zinc bath in front of the fire in the back room. Mike was the youngest. He had been born when Eileen was forty, and they had all but given up on a boy to complete their family. He had also been their favourite — doted on by his mother, viewed with distant pride by his father and fussed over by the girls, adored for his curly hair that had darkened from ash blond to tawny in his late teens. His mother, now in her eighties, still regarded him as her boy, even though he was now the age she had been when she gave birth to him. He had dealt with Saturday-night drunks, the riots of the 1980s and more recently the drug addicts and their gun-carrying pushers, but his mother's chief worry was that he might catch cold if he didn't wrap up well, and she constantly fussed that he couldn't be eating enough, sneaking him extra cheese sandwiches for his carrying out if he chanced to call in on his rounds. Eileen believed that the rosary would protect from any evil, and to please her, Mike carried one with him on duty, despite having given up the faith some fifteen years earlier.

* * *

The warmth, the strange mixture of stillness and vibrancy which he associated with the Campbells' house was marred by something between Jenny and Fraser. He sensed a restraint — even strain — beneath Fraser and Jenny's polite conversation, and so it came as no surprise, when the photographer took Paul into the garden for the better light, that Fraser said, 'Look, I'm as much in the dark as you are.'

Jenny glanced over at Mike.

'Don't mind me,' he said, knowing full well it was difficult *not* to mind six foot four of solid flesh.

'Can't this wait?' Jenny asked.

'I don't think it can,' Fraser said.

'All right,' Jenny said, as if making up her mind not to be embarrassed. 'All right. You get a call from the same weirdo who called me, and you say nothing. What am I supposed to think? Why didn't you tell me?'

'I didn't want to worry you.'

It sounded lame. They all heard it, and Mike felt embarrassed on Fraser's behalf.

'Very considerate,' Jenny said, then seemed to regret the heavy sarcasm of her reply. 'What did he say?' she asked.

'More or less what he said to you.'

'More — or less?'

'The same, okay?'

Mike felt it was time to step in. 'An anonymous phone call or what?'

Jenny took a breath and ran her fingers through her hair. 'I'm sorry, Mike. I had a call from someone claiming to be a private detective. He asked if I'd had any children adopted and rang off when I said I hadn't.'

Fraser nodded, indicating that his call had followed the same pattern.

'And you think it could have something to do with young Paul?'

She hesitated, balking at the use of that name, then shrugged. 'I really don't know, but it spooked me.'

Mike thought for a moment. 'If he calls again—'

'He did,' Jenny said. 'Just before you arrived. I answered. He asked to speak to Fraser.'

Mike turned his steady gaze on Fraser. No wonder Jenny was upset. She must be wondering what else he was hiding from her.

'I tried the number trace,' Fraser said, and Mike noted the defensive hunch of his shoulders. 'He'd dialled 141. The number was withheld.'

'Maybe. When was the first call?'

'Sunday. As far as I know,' Jenny said, glaring at her husband.

Fraser looked uncomfortable.

'Fraser?'

'I don't know, Mike. Earlier in the week. Wednesday — no, Tuesday.'

Jenny's gasped in outrage and Fraser carried on, not speaking loudly but in a firm, clear voice. 'A couple of calls — that's all. I thought it was a crank, Jen — if we ignored him, he'd stop.'

'Look,' Mike said, 'it could be just a crank, like you said. Someone local, making connections from the news coverage and the appearance of a little boy at your house.'

'You think they could be watching us?' Jenny said, simultaneously glancing out into the garden to see that the boy was safe. Mike followed her gaze and saw the photographer positioning him gently, checking the light, talking to him, trying to get a response, failing.

* * *

He had learned early to be still and very quiet.

Hide away. Hide away from the sharp eyes and the angry voices, be small, go far away, and they won't see you. They won't hurt you.

The boy looked to the left of the photographer. They wouldn't let him hide. They had found him and brought him here. He knew instinctively there are other ways of hiding, of finding refuge. He retreated, locking the doors and barring the windows of himself, fleeing down a pathway, losing himself in a maze until even he can't find where he is. And still he did not feel safe.

* * *

'There's no point in jumping to conclusions,' Mike said. 'We'll see what the media come up with. If we get no joy and you get another call, we'll set up a phone trace, okay?'

Diane had finished and was occupying the boy by pushing him on the swing at the end of the garden. They watched him for some moments through the open door, his passivity an expression in itself of his extreme unhappiness, and then Mike said, 'Case conference Friday, yeah?'

'Yes,' Jenny answered. 'Hopefully we'll know who his parents are by then.' She was back in professional mode, her spat with Fraser set aside in the interests of the child. 'I'll be away in Nottingham until late tomorrow,' she added, 'but Fraser will deal with anything that comes out of the media coverage.'

Mike drove the photographer back to Merseyside Constabulary Headquarters, through the potholed and grimy streets that edged the leafy, middle-class park community like the outer crust of a geode.

'Nice-looking kid,' Mike commented.

'Beats taking snapshots of corpses.'

Mike grimaced. Diane Seward was a scene-of-crime officer, her main strength being forensic photography.

'Sorry,' she said. 'The gallows humour doesn't appeal to everyone. He's gorgeous.' She patted her camera bag. 'If these don't bring 'em out in droves looking to claim him, I'll give up photography and become a garage mechanic.'

Mike winced. 'We're not *Pet Rescue,* you know, Di. If his mum and dad come forward, I'll be happy.'

Diane shot him a sideways look. 'I wouldn't build my hopes up of happy ever after, if I were you,' she said. 'I did a voluntary stint in Bosnia a couple of years back. It was with a charity trying to get families back together who'd been split up by the war. That boy has the look of the kids I photographed. A look of horror like you couldn't imagine, let alone fathom. I don't think he feels he can ever be safe again.'

* * *

Most of the children placed in Jenny and Fraser's care were school-aged and, barring holidays, that gave Jenny long stretches of writing time. She had never needed much sleep. Her mother had called her 'Jumping Jenny', and since the loss of her child and all hopes of motherhood as a result of her ectopic pregnancy, Jenny's writing maintained her link with sanity during the long hours of the night.

She had worked Friday to Monday night and would have the next four days off, giving her the opportunity to present her pre-tour lecture — or lectures, to be precise. She was timetabled to present the same talk twice, to allow nurses on shifts to have the choice of a morning or afternoon session. She saw the Nottingham trip as a kind of dress rehearsal for the full tour and would adjust the content in line with audience reaction, adding or subtracting material depending on the make-up of each group she was scheduled to speak to.

She hated leaving Fraser to cope with the boy, especially since *Granada News* would be making an appeal on their Wednesday bulletins to anyone who thought they might know him to contact the police, but her lecture had been set up months ago and would be difficult to reschedule before the autumn because of the full lecture tour, and her promise to Fraser that they would go on holiday together.

She had missed her customary four hours of sleep because of the photographer's session, but the train journey provided a pleasant prospect of three hours' snoozing, followed by a good meal and a drop of wine before getting an early night.

The social work assistant arrived. Amy was a big, friendly woman, extrovert and lively. 'Hiya, Paul,' she said, ruffling his hair. Paul shied away, but she seemed not to notice. 'We're going to have a great time tonight, aren't we? Has he eaten?'

'No,' Jenny said.

'Well, I'll rustle us up something in a jiffy, eh, love?'

They had been lucky to be allocated Amy: it was rare for social work assistants to be asked to supervise children in the home, they were often simply too busy anyway, but Jenny had contacted Roz, their link worker, and explained her worries about Paul: he was evidently wary of men, and she was concerned that he wouldn't cope without a female presence for a full twenty-four hours. Normally she would have taken advantage of a reciprocal arrangement she had with another foster carer for babysitting, but Phyllis could hardly stay a night away from her own foster children, and Jenny didn't want to put Paul through spending a night in strange surroundings.

Paul flung his arms around Jenny and refused to let go. 'Amy's here to take care of you,' Jenny said, adding, 'Fraser will be here, too.' Paul's grip tightened, and she realized this had been the wrong thing to say.

Jenny carried him to a chair and sat with him clamped to her, talking over his whimpers of protest, giving details of where she was going and what she was going to do. Fraser looked on with a hurt, puzzled expression on his face.

She's going, and I'll be all alone again. What if—?

A flash of light, a glint of steel—

Paul raised his hands, striking out, defending himself.

Jenny held him, gently restraining him, and he twisted round to look at her. She saw stark terror in his eyes. He clung to her once more, and she explained that she would be away for only a day. 'I'm going to check the house over, to make sure everything's all right before I leave. Will you help me?'

Fatigue had slackened the boy's grip, but for a moment he held her tighter, then he got down from her lap and took her hand, leading her to the kitchen. He went to the little cupboard that housed the boiler and, opening the door, reached inside and took out the back-door key. He had been with them only four days, but he knew all the door keys, window keys, hooks, locks and latches in the house.

He took Jenny on a tour, securing every lock, but hesitated outside Jenny and Fraser's bedroom. She knew that he wouldn't feel safe unless he had been through all of the house, so she said, 'I think *all* the locks need checking, don't you?' Jenny led the way, but Paul secured the locks himself. She made it Paul's responsibility to lock the front door after her, and her last image of him was his face staring solemnly out at her, before he put his weight behind the door and slammed it shut.

There had been something stoical in his expression as she waved to him, and he stared back, unresponsive, his hands by his sides. As if he did not expect her to return.

The rhythm of the train lulled her, and she slipped into a doze, waking with a start when the tannoy clacked and the driver warned them of an approaching station stop. Something had been bothering her since the first day she had brought Paul into their home. So intangible she could not say, 'This isn't right' or 'That makes me uneasy.' Rather, it was a vacancy, an empty place. She thought hard. Something different about Fraser? God knows he's been acting strangely. Something *about* Fraser . . . The ghost of an image taunted her for some minutes, and she took to replaying the day she brought Paul home. Fraser shocked, pale. Paul's night terrors. She had gone to him, and when she returned, something had changed. Something tangible, real . . .

The picture! The one on the chest of drawers. It was missing. Had Fraser hidden it? Why would he do that? The way he watched the boy unsettled her. He had a muddled, distracted look — the look of someone trying to find something he had lost . . .

* * *

Amy was to stay with them overnight and through the following day, until Jenny's return. They were in the kitchen, the portable TV on as background noise. Fraser rose half out of his chair, then collapsed back into it. The boy on screen was dark haired and sallow skinned. He had been snatched from outside his own front door. The police were looking for him. Amy heard the name — Connor something. Fraser looked from the boy, sitting at the kitchen table, painting himself safe with the carefully constructed bars of his house, to the television. Amy sensed his tension and glancing up from the pancakes she was making, saw him lining up the two images in his sights, making a comparison.

'Fraser?' she said, following his gaze, but the boy's image had gone, and the presenter had moved on to another news item.

The telephone rang and Fraser jumped up. 'I'll take it in the sitting room,' he said. 'I'm expecting a call from school.'

He picked up the receiver on the fourth ring. At first, he thought the caller had hung up. When he spoke, Fraser recognized 'Mr Hunter's' voice immediately.

'Would you know him?'

No time for interruptions, just one question and then the line was dead. No point in trying to trace the call. He tried anyway — carefully, precisely punching in the numbers: one . . . four . . . seven . . . one . . . and heard the message: 'The caller withheld their number.'

He replaced the receiver, his hand shaking. As he stood looking stupidly at the phone, it rang again. Fraser snatched it up. 'Meet me,' he begged, not waiting for the caller to speak. 'Please — at least talk to me.'

When he returned to the kitchen, Amy was watching with satisfaction as the boy wolfed down the pancakes, which she had filled with jam and cream.

'My God! What's happened?' she gasped.

'I . . . have to go out,' he said. 'I don't know how long it'll take . . .'

'You look ghastly — sit down and get your colour back.'

Fraser shook his head. He stared at the boy for a second or two, then reached out to touch him, but Paul flinched away, staring with furious concentration at his plate until Fraser turned and staggered from the room.

* * *

It was raining up on the moors. Reflections of grey-white light from the car park security lamps shivered on pools of water and sump oil puddling the scabrous asphalt. Fraser waited.

He had followed Hunter's instructions, driving almost sick with terror to the cold, sodden crest of the Pennines, and waited, sitting hunched in the car beside the slumped single-storey café. Its window frames were pulpy from the incessant seepage of condensation within and the persistent drift of moorland mist without. The window glass hung with greasy lace, so that he could see little of the interior. He had watched the customers come and go, as the gloom gathered and deepened.

Strip lights inside the café, filtered through the accumulated layers of nicotine and grease, cast a jaundiced circle of smudged light a few yards' distance from the windows, and Fraser watched as each customer stepped out, zipping up jackets, fastening coats, glancing left and right before moving to their cars. Once or twice, men leaving the dingy comfort of the café chanced to look in his direction, and he tensed, bracing himself for contact, but none of them approached him.

Within half an hour the car's windscreen was fogged and Fraser had opened a window to clear it. In the trees to the edge of the car park starlings had gathered, their constant bubbling warble like a prolonged murmur of discontent. The insistent drone of traffic on the A road only yards away overlaid the sound. The air smelled of chip fat and fried bacon, and the sweeter, lonely smell of damp moorland. Was Hunter there, hidden in the gathering darkness? Watching him?

Hunter had called the night before Jenny brought Paul home. When Paul had appeared on the landing, he had thought — for a moment had been certain — and he'd felt the clash of opposite emotions: hope and dread.

* * *

The back door is ajar. Has he returned? Is it possible? I don't know why I am here, except perhaps to try and find some clue to his whereabouts. I can't find him. I must *find him.*

A faint sound, like a low sob. Dear God — she can't have survived? Her blood is on my clothing. Could it be the boy? No — of course they wouldn't bring him back here. But the police would have secured the place. If they had been here. If they had seen her . . .

She is there, still. I can smell her, but I can't look at her again. I won't.

CHAPTER 8

'Shona.' The therapist's voice was warm, compassionate, but Shona heard the note of disappointment. 'Haven't you anything to tell us?'

Shona glanced quickly at the others. They stared back at her, all four of them, their faces unreadable. It was only when she looked away that she felt their hostility. It fell on her like rain pattering on an overcoat — large gobs, like spittle, falling on her. They demanded her full allegiance, the lowering of barriers. Commitment and integration could not be achieved without honesty, without pain.

She had tried, for weeks she had tried to let go of her anger. At first, she had said she couldn't let go of something she didn't feel. Now she admitted that she had suppressed her rage, and although she tried, she couldn't get in touch with it.

Pam told her she was making progress, that she was progressing towards release. And then nothing. The others had gradually recalled terrible events — not all at once, more like a story building in a TV series, sometimes going back to the triggering event. Mostly, they started with vague feelings of unhappiness, but with Pam's help those feelings took shape and became real, and they began to experience the awful things they had hidden from themselves for so long.

Pam gave them permission to express their rage, their hurt, the devastating sense of loss, and she was ready to take the group forward. But Shona held them back. Shona had let them down. She hadn't remembered anything, and she began to feel again the desperation that had driven her two years earlier to try to take her own life.

'Perhaps,' Pam suggested in her gentle, forgiving voice, 'you feel you can't identify with the rest of the group.'

Pit, pat, pat — Shona felt the spatter of hateful looks.

'It's not like that,' she said. 'I've tried, honest I have, but—'

'Perhaps it would be best if you and I continued on an individual basis.'

'But I want to . . .' What did she want? To stay, certainly. To be accepted, trusted. She wanted to be wanted.

'You could join another group when you feel more able to share.'

A murmur of agreement went around the group and Shona began to cry. 'Please, give me one more chance!' She could not bear to be banished.

'We don't want to hurt you, Shona, but you can't be healed until you have confronted what is making you unhappy.'

'I know, I know,' Shona sobbed. They were so kind, and she was cutting herself off from them, inhibiting the others with her aloofness, her reserve. She didn't deserve to belong. In her mind she saw herself in a vast black featureless landscape: alone, unwanted.

Pam put her hand on Shona's head. Shona felt the kind of gratitude, the soaring sense of love she had experienced when the priest had blessed her at her confirmation. The same authority rested in Pam's hands: she had the power of forgiveness and of healing.

Pam left her hand there as she spoke. 'I believe that Shona has suffered something so terrible that she has buried it deep. We have to help her unearth it. But it's up to the group . . .'

Shona felt a burning heat radiate outwards, from her scalp to the skin of her face. She knew what would happen next. Knew that they would reject her — push her away as her mother had done so many times, disgusted by her displays of affection. Then, something magical happened, a small miracle, and Shona encountered her first truly spiritual experience. No one spoke, but all four gathered around her and Pam, and collectively they joined arms, holding her close, sharing her tears.

* * *

Vi Harvey stood in the middle of the sitting room, a cigarette in one hand and the cordless phone in the other. 'Where is he?' she demanded. 'I should call the police. They know he's missing.'

There was a silence. She heard his breathing at the other end of the line.

'You really shouldn't have told them,' he said.

Vi shivered and took a nervy puff of her cigarette. 'What was I supposed to—'

'Be quiet,' he said sharply. 'Be quiet and listen. I'm going to tell you what to do. If you're reasonable, we'll both get what we want out of this.'

The doorbell rang moments later. It was the two detectives who had called on Friday.

'Oh, God,' she said. 'I was about to phone you. Come in. There's been a terrible mistake.'

Weston and Calcot exchanged a suspicious look. This was not the angry, offensive Mrs Harvey who had told them to stop pissing about and find her son. Weston shrugged and they followed her through to the sitting room. She stubbed out her cigarette, immediately taking a fresh one from a pack on the mantelpiece. She picked up the lighter and flicked the trigger in agitated embarrassment.

Calcot fastened her gaze on the lighter, interested to note that it was the cheap, throwaway kind and not another chunky, gold-plated ornament.

'You said there'd been a mistake,' she said.

Vi looked up at them, her head bent over the flame, then drew deeply, inhaling gratefully. 'Some stupid bloody shit didn't pass on a message and of course, after what happened last week, it was hardly surprising I jumped to the conclusion.'

'Let's start with the mistake, shall we?' Weston said.

'I'm trying to, if you'd just . . .' Vi seemed to notice that her mask of effusive repentance had slipped and gave it an almost visible hitch, beginning again, with a smile that could crack ice. 'Do sit down. I'm afraid my nerves are a little on edge with all this . . .' She waved an arm encompassing all of her present difficulties in its majestic sweep, then plumped herself into a chair, armed with cigarettes and ashtray.

She took a deep breath and started again. 'Connor is quite safe.'

'Oh?' Calcot said.

'I was *supposed* to get a message,' she went on. 'But the incompetent menial who was given the task of contacting me forgot to telephone. I mean *completely* forgot.'

'The content of the message?' Calcot asked.

Vi gave a rueful smile. Neither Calcot nor Weston responded.

Connor's mother took a fresh cigarette from the packet on the arm of the chair and lit it using the one she had only half finished. 'He's with his father. The bloody idiot secretary was supposed to ring me and tell me. They've gone fishing in the Lakes.'

Mrs Harvey coloured beneath her tan. 'I'm sorry! All right? I know I've wasted your time. I really can't apologize enough.'

'You've got that right,' Calcot muttered.

'I beg your pardon?'

'When did you find out he was safe?'

'Oh, just this minute — just before you arrived. Really!'

Calcot paused, thinking. 'Your son's playing in his room. Next minute, he's vanished, and you want us to believe his dad took him?'

Vi looked bewildered. 'It's true . . .'

'And he didn't think to put his head round the door and let you know?'

'I *told* you! He thought I *did* know.'

Weston took up the story. 'So he just picks Connor up from the driveway and zooms off.'

'That was the arrangement. "Have Connor waiting outside at twelve thirty." It was pure chance that Connor was actually there at that time, and of course Bill — Mr Harvey — assumed I'd got him ready.'

'He didn't think it strange you didn't come to wave them goodbye?'

She stiffened slightly. 'I was otherwise occupied. I can't keep track of the child twenty-four hours a day.'

Calcot sucked her teeth. 'What about a suitcase?'

'What?'

'Wouldn't Mr Harvey expect to have some clothes packed?'

Vi seemed momentarily confused. She tapped her cigarette ash into the ashtray, frowning, then came up with that dazzling smile again. 'Part of the message. "Don't bother to pack, we'll get you some new gear when we arrive."'

'You expect us to believe that?' Weston said.

'Why not?' she snapped. 'He can afford it.' She shrugged, stubbing out her cigarette and trying to regain her composure. 'Connor has grown so much over these past months. It's almost as if the lengthening days have made him shoot up like a sapling.'

She sounded like someone trying to imitate a proud mother, and Calcot was reminded of Miss Halliwell's contemptuous remark: *Oh, he's trotted out for half an hour at parties to impress her friends with the doting mother routine.*

Vi became increasingly nervous under their continued scrutiny. 'Do you have children, Constable Calcot?' she asked, her voice unsteady.

'I don't believe that's what happened, Mrs Harvey,' Calcot said, ignoring the question. 'I think you were angry with your husband because he suggested you should cancel your lunch appointment. You told him you wouldn't mess up your arrangements to suit him. You had a row. Maybe he threatened to leave you. He stormed off, taking Connor with him.'

Vi Harvey paled visibly. Evidently Calcot had hit the mark with at least some of the story.

'So,' Calcot went on, 'you called us and make up some cock-and-bull story about your son being abducted, hoping to get the media involved and maximize your husband's embarrassment.' She paused and watched as Vi fiddled with a fresh cigarette. 'How am I doing so far?'

'You're entering the realms of pure fantasy, if you must know.'

Vi took a moment to light her cigarette. She flicked the trigger of her lighter several times to no effect, then flung it away in frustration, strode to a bookcase and rummaged in one of its drawers, retrieving a new one.

'None of this would have happened if that stupid girl had passed on his message.'

Pert to petulant, and all because of a faulty lighter, Calcot thought. 'It's odd, isn't it, that a businessman would switch off his mobile phone on a busy working day?'

'His work had been trying to contact him all afternoon,' Weston explained.

Her frown deepened. 'That damned mobile. He's so sickeningly correct about these things. Switches it off in restaurants — and he wouldn't *dream* of having it switched on if he's driving on the motorway.'

'But he's in the Lakes, isn't he? No one to disturb for miles.'

Vi laughed. The sound made Calcot think of broken glass. 'Bill wouldn't despoil a beauty spot with the trill of a phone. The fact that I'm half out of my mind with worry is neither here nor there.'

'Save the histrionics for the magistrate's court,' Weston said, unable to stand any more.

'Magistrates . . .' she whispered, bringing a hand to her collar bone.

'Wasting police time, Mrs Harvey,' Calcot said, 'is a very serious matter.'

They left while she was still trying to splutter a reply.

* * *

I should be happy, Lee-Anne thought. Lobo and Kyle up a ladder, wallpapering the living room, and his mates Beefy and Mazzer working on the bedroom. She shut out an image of blood dripping down the walls and told herself that they would be finished by Wednesday, and by Thursday the new carpets would be laid.

It did no good, the restless nervous energy caused by excitement and lack of sleep was uncontrollable. She threw down the *Daily Post*, which she had been scanning for news of the woman, and got up to make a brew.

As she passed the radio, the newsreader's voice took on a sombre tone.

'A woman's body was found today.'

Lee-Anne shrieked and turned up the volume.

Lobo and Kyle shouted ''Ey!' and 'Bloody hell!' simultaneously.

Lee-Anne bent her head to the speaker, despite the deafening volume.

'Police are asking for anyone who may have been in the Dock Road area between two and four o'clock this morning to come forward, as they may have vital information . . .'

Lee-Anne looked up, shame-faced, as Lobo descended the ladder and turned the radio volume down. Kyle watched them both as he continued smoothing the piece of paper he was hanging.

'What's up with her?' he asked.

Lobo kept his back to his brother. 'What *is* she like, 'eh?' he asked. His voice sounded relaxed, but his eyes bulged, and his face was red with rage. 'No one's gonna hurt you,' he soothed. 'Not while I'm around.' He bent to kiss her cheek. 'Not unless it's me,' he hissed in her ear. Then, returning to normal conversational level, 'Come on, I'll help you make us some coffee and sarnies.' He took her by the elbow and led her to the kitchen, closing the door after him.

'What the *fuck* d'you think you're playing at?' he whispered.

Lee-Anne backed away from him. 'I can't help it, Lobo. I keep getting them dreams. I keep getting them, and every time I close my eyes, I can see her face.'

'It's a dream, right?' He poked her hard in the chest. 'A fucking *dream*.'

'Why hasn't it been in the news? They must've found her by now. I keep thinking they know, and they're just gonna come and knock on the door one day, and—'

Lobo covered her mouth with his hand. 'You keep talking like that, you'll bring the bizzies down on us, and if you do . . .' When he took his hand away there were four pale lines on her cheeks, which quickly filled with blood, becoming raised, red weals.

'Sorry, Lobo.' Lee-Anne knew when to play humble, but it was no good Lobo threatening. She still couldn't get that girl's face out of her mind. What good was it, having all this stuff, getting the flat nice and everything, if she kept seeing that girl's horrified face staring up at her, like some ghost at a feast?

CHAPTER 9

'The claims made by false memory syndrome sufferers are preposterous.' Not bad for an opening line, Max thought, and it certainly got their attention. 'I will attempt, in my presentation, to underline the significance of the therapist's role in planting ideas of abuse.'

There was a rustle of movement, a metaphorical ruffling of feathers among the abuse therapy proponents. Max nodded. His eyes swept the auditorium, assessing the composition of his audience. The venue — the arts lecture theatre — was a short walk from the psychology building, and he had expected a large proportion of students, despite the fact that this was a mid-week slot and, being an evening lecture, meant their sacrificing valuable drinking time. There was a number, clustered mainly at the back, within easy reach of the doors and hence unobtrusive escape, but there was also a large contingent of older people. The preponderance of women was not a promising sign: Max's position on recovered memory was well known, and several of his lectures had been disrupted by recovered memory therapists, the majority of whom were women. He resigned himself to the fact that he had a hostile audience this evening.

'For many genuine abuse victims, the memory of abuse — and they *do* remember it, make no mistake — the memory is unpleasant, uncomfortable, distasteful, often deeply upsetting. But it is nothing like as traumatic as the experiences some of these so-called recovered memory victims have been put through by the very people who claim to be trying to help them.'

For a few minutes there was uproar. Max could not make himself heard. He was not sure if he would be able to continue, but just as he was about to give up, those who were there genuinely to hear his viewpoint imposed their will on the gathering and there was a restless quiet.

'I'm not trying to shock you — this is too serious a subject for sensationalism,' he went on. 'But it is a fact that many people are being made ill by therapy.'

In the audience, Shona looked at Pam. Pam reassured her with a smile, but she was angry, Shona could see that. Angry and upset. She felt an answering sting of hurt at the injustice of it — Pam was a healer, she helped people, gave far more of her time than was ever expected of her, gave emotionally — gave of herself. Pam had let down the barriers that for Shona had acted as an obstacle to the establishment of a trusting relationship with her therapists in the past. Dr Greenberg was the type who viewed his patients from the lofty heights of professional reserve. And he was saying that Pam made people *ill*?

Max patted the air, trying to quiet the protestations of the audience. 'People go for counselling, therapy, whatever, because they are unhappy. Why should they be unhappy? The majority of recovered memory sufferers are middle-class, successful career people. They have every reason to be happy. What right have they to be *un*happy?' He paused. 'But success does not necessarily make us happy. Material comfort — even security — aren't enough. Good food and wine, holidays abroad, delightful children, a comfortable house in a good area — a car and a mobile phone do not bring contentment.' He spread his fingers.

'Well, then, if we are unhappy, there must be a cause. It's a rather bleak prospect to look to oneself for such a cause, but who else can we blame? Why, our parents — our upbringing. So these unhappy people go to a therapist to find permission for their misery and the therapist coaxes from them dreadful things their parents did to them. "No wonder you're screwed up!" they tell their clients. "It's amazing you've coped so well with all this inside of you."'

There was a murmur of dissent from the audience, but a few remained still, and he could see them thinking about what he was saying.

'And *then* what do the recovered memory therapists do?' he said. 'They encourage the expression of rage, the acting out of violent feelings.' He shook his head. 'This is not healing, my friends.

'Therapists invite their patients to channel their hatred, their vitriol, to let it flow out of them, in a variety of cathartic acts.' He shrugged. 'What is the point of this? There's no *reservoir* of anger within us, any more than there is a finite quota of love which we are capable of bestowing, no conduit of expression — we need not empty out the reservoir of bitter gall for fear the dam will break. Rage . . .' He balled his hand into a fist, and raised his arm, glaring out at the assembly and finishing at a roar. 'Rage is generated by the manifestation of it!'

He saw one or two heads nod here and took a few seconds to catch his breath before going on. 'I ask you to consider statistical fact: first, in a survey of American clinicians, who, let's face it, lead the field in recovered memory therapy,' — there was an ironic cheer from the sceptics in the auditorium — 'the modal number of professional publications read by clinical psychologists specializing in recovered memory was' — he paused — 'nought.'

A few in the audience exchanged uneasy glances.

'That's right,' he said, 'recovered memory specialists read . . . nothing. A big . . . fat . . . zero. Which leads me to my next statistical fact: the bulk of treatment decisions are made on the basis of their intuitive appeal. Now, we all know the problems that a clinician's personal bias can cause. We're all victims of our own past, aren't we?' He smiled and felt a ripple of positive response — hardly a tidal wave, but he was making some headway.

'But what if that past has been reinvented through the subtle coercion of a recovered memory therapist?' He shook his head. 'Recovered memory! Let's call it by its real name — make no mistake, it's false memory.'

At that moment, Shona began to hate him. She hated his smugness, his sureness, the arrogance with which he dismissed the sincere hard work of hundreds — thousands — of people. And in dismissing them, he dismissed the suffering of those they tried to help as just so much hysterical ranting.

* * *

Max arrived home at ten thirty, having stopped to take questions from the audience at the end of the lecture. No one had threatened him, which was a refreshing change, although one woman, after telling him that she fervently hoped he would go through what she had suffered one day, tore up the reading list he had distributed and threw it in his face.

The police were at his house when Max arrived. He suppressed mild irritation at being stopped on his own doorstep by a police constable and explained that he owned the place. There was a broken pane of glass in the back door, but otherwise no damage. Thanks to Miss Bembridge's swift action, the intruder had got no further than the kitchen when the police had arrived. Max called in an emergency glazier, resigning himself to paying the extra for a night-time call-out, and resolved to have flowers delivered to his neighbour the following morning.

It wasn't until later, when he'd had a chance to sit and think, that he started wondering if it *had* been a normal burglary or if the boy in Jenny and Fraser's care might have something to do with it. There had been a number of calls to the hospital switchboard, asking where the boy could be found. Shona had taken one of the calls and had sought him out to warn him.

Shona. She had been at the lecture that evening, sitting in the middle section with a group of others, her face shining with something approaching reverence for the woman at the centre of the little huddle. Shona had been his patient when she had suffered a breakdown in her late teens. She had recovered and was discharged from his care, but there had remained a fragility in her which made her particularly vulnerable to the influence of others. She would come into his sessions bubbling with happiness about some new organization she had joined, only to return in a week or two, disillusioned and despondent. If she'd hooked up with a recovered memory counsellor . . .

Max froze. He thought he had heard something. He listened. There it was again — a small, metallic squeak — a door hinge, perhaps the back gate. He set his whisky tumbler down on the table next to his chair and crept to the door of his sitting room. His heart was thudding, and he wondered for a moment if he should do the sensible thing and run like hell. He picked up the telephone receiver and heard the steady buzz of the dialling tone. There was definitely someone outside, moving cautiously around the back of the house. Perhaps the burglar had returned, thinking that the back door would be left insecure overnight.

Max jumped as the three-tone warning sounded and a recorded voice suggested to *hang up and try again*.

'This is ridiculous!' he muttered. Hearing his own voice gave him courage. He replaced the handset, crossed to the doorway and, pausing only to return and pick up the whisky bottle as a weapon, went into the hall. The kitchen door stood open, and as he approached, he saw the back-door handle turn, slowly, carefully. The key was in the lock. He had meant to remove it, as the police constable had advised, but he'd been side-tracked. The window above it had been boarded, so he couldn't see out. He tiptoed into the kitchen, his heart thudding faster. Licking his lips nervously, he adjusted his grip on the bottle, which was now slick with sweat. Quickly, he turned the key in the latch and flung the door open, the bottle raised, ready.

A bright light shone in his eyes and he stepped back, the bottle still raised above his head. He heard a muffled cry of alarm, followed by a scuffle of footsteps. He blinked into the darkness, yelling, 'Stay away from here! I'm onto you and so are the police!' Neither of which were true, but he hoped he sounded convincing.

* * *

How much does she know? Fraser wondered. *Does she suspect?*

He watched Jenny in the darkness, her face peaceful, serene, vulnerable. She had arrived home late, exhausted by her lectures and travel. Her arm rested on his chest, the pulse of her wrist a barely discernible throb against the cantle of his collarbone.

Why does she love me? This had always been a puzzle to him, ever since that first day, when she swept down on him, smiling, coat flapping, like a bird from the fog. *How can she trust me?* She had always found trust so easy, had given it so readily, only rarely being disillusioned, and he, who had been so careful, so circumspect in giving his trust, had been so catastrophically wrong. He thought how frail trust is, how easily lost. And to regain it? He feared that would prove impossible.

Why did any of this have to happen? He raged against their childlessness, against the single, devastating event that had led them to this existence, to the constant shift of affections from one child to the next — substitutes for the children they could never have. The remorseless drift of children in and out of their lives, each loss a new bereavement. Although it hadn't seemed this way until now. He had imagined — had persuaded himself — that they were happy. But life, it seemed, had a way of jolting him from a smooth, untroubled, anaesthetized course in quite another direction. As when he had proposed to Jenny, convinced that he would otherwise have lost her entirely to Simon. She was young, lovely — not a beauty perhaps, but Jenny had a rare glow about her. Was it goodness? Happiness? Whatever it was, it made her blindingly, compulsively attractive, then as now. She hadn't yet noticed Simon, but Fraser had known — had recognized the signs from his own infatuation — that Simon was in love with Jenny.

So they had married, and would have drifted gently for a few years, planning for parenthood, in no immediate hurry, but then Jenny had lost the baby they hadn't even known she was carrying, had nearly died, and suddenly having children seemed a matter of supreme importance.

Should he have told Jenny his wishes, his desire to adopt? Perhaps if he had told her, she might have come around to his way of thinking. It seemed she had blanked off that part of her mind, so that adoption had never entered into the discussion. Fostering was to fill the void in their lives. Fostering meant constant change, never making a permanent commitment, never having to admit that this was the closest she would get to having her own child.

With time, they had accepted their childlessness, and had thought themselves content to help other people's children. Now Paul had happened. He didn't *arrive*, he hadn't *come into* their lives. This enigmatic stranger was an event, an incident, a *happening* — and he had changed everything. *Would you know him?* Hunter had first asked the question, and he had repeated it to himself a hundred times since.

Fraser sighed, and when he bent to kiss the nape of Jenny's neck, she stirred and moaned, and in his heightened emotional state his kiss felt like a betrayal.

They were late getting up on Thursday morning. Fraser and the boy were badly rested, hollow eyed. Jenny, exhausted by her lectures and late return home on Wednesday night, woke with a vague sense of resentment foolishly harboured after a dream in which Fraser had spoken unkindly to her.

There had, as yet, been nothing conclusive from the media exposure — a word that made Jenny uneasy, for she felt that the pictures of the boy, beautiful and strangely haunting, would somehow put him at risk. The police were following up leads, checking information. Mike had told them he would let them know as soon as he had anything useful.

Anything useful. The phrase filled Jenny with dread. She felt a gnawing apprehension that what was useful to the police might prove cataclysmic for the boy. She sensed a deep and entrenched terror in him. It was in the fearful sidelong glances he gave them, in the silence that had persisted now for the six days he had been in their care. She knew that his social worker was having no more success with Paul than she was, although Fraser said that he had heard Paul humming once or twice the previous day, behind the closed door of his room, safe behind the barrier of wood and protected by the talisman of a cardboard sign — snatches Fraser could not identify but which had the repetitive quality of nursery rhymes.

The phone rang. Jenny pushed Fraser gently back into his chair. 'Finish your breakfast,' she said. She took the call in the hallway, her hand wavering over the receiver, momentarily anxious that this might be another disturbing message from Mr Hunter. Judging by Fraser's troubled look as she left the kitchen, the same thought had crossed his mind.

When she returned, the boy had paused from painting to listen to a bird singing on the hawthorn at the bottom of the garden, and Fraser was watching him with rapt attention.

'That was Max,' Jenny said, breaking into Fraser's reverie.

Fraser looked into her face, but she saw that his mind was still on the boy.

'Fraser, are you listening?' she asked.

He shook himself. 'Yes,' he said. 'Max. Is he all right?'

Jenny frowned. 'He's been burgled. During his lecture last night, or shortly after.'

'Did they do much damage?' Fraser asked.

'No. A neighbour heard them and called the police.'

'Lucky escape,' he murmured, his mind already drifting elsewhere again.

'He should have that place alarmed.'

'Hmm . . .' Fraser said. 'I might be late tonight — staff meeting — and I need to call in at the library on the way home.'

'Fraser?' Jenny stared, appalled that he had so easily dismissed the burglary.

For a moment, it seemed that Fraser had forgotten the subject of their conversation. 'He should be more careful.'

'Careful — of what?'

'Security and that.'

'Have you had another call?' Jenny asked, immediately suspicious as to the cause of his distraction.

'No!' he exclaimed. Then, more softly, 'No . . .'

'Because if you have, we should tell Mike.'

'I'm just tired,' he said. 'End of term addles the brain. It's pretty fast and furious just now: exams, reports, getting up to date with coursework you've not managed to cover earlier in the term. And the kids don't make it any easier — they're getting bolshier by the day.'

'I expect they're tired, too.' She looked at him, wondering if she would regret bringing Paul to their home. She knew that Fraser was missing Luke. Maybe Paul was reminding him just how much he was missing: the very difference between the boys recalled how easy their relationship with Luke had been, how affectionate he was, how lively and open. Fraser could do without that kind of reminder, just now.

'If you want to go and see Max, I'll look after the boy,' Fraser said.

Paul looked over at Jenny. She had thought he wasn't listening, but the sheer terror in his face convinced her otherwise. 'I think it'll wait until tomorrow,' she said. 'Anyway, you're already late for work, and I'd like to see Paul's picture, when it's finished.'

The boy looked sharply away and for some minutes he simply sat, staring at the painting. Then he carefully folded it into four, climbed down from the chair and threw the paper into the bin.

Breathe softly. Look ahead, close your mind. Make it safe, make it safe. They're watching! But if you don't look, they won't see you. Won't harm you.

Jenny put out a hand to the boy, but he shrank from her, clasping both hands to his chest, avoiding eye contact. So much of his behaviour was contradictory in this way. He would use the 'Do Not Disturb' sign whenever he went to his room, but once or twice when Jenny had gone upstairs his door had been open, as if he was listening, or perhaps he wanted the reassurance that they were still there, even though he refused even basic contact with them.

* * *

'Max seemed worried, Fraser,' Jenny said. She had coaxed the boy to eat a little breakfast and had persuaded him into the garden, so their discussion had continued with less restraint.

'It's more likely one of his recovered memory folk, isn't it?'

'You don't approve of Max's methods, do you?' she said.

She could see Paul through the open door. He was staring at the swing and the other toys as if he had forgotten what they were for. Or had he never learned, Jenny wondered, distracted for a moment from their conversation.

'He asked if we'd had any more phone calls—'

'Now don't start that again, Jenny!'

'I'm not starting anything. He said the hospital switchboard has had a few funny calls. He thinks they could be linked to ours.'

'I don't think so.'

'Why not?'

Fraser started clearing away dishes and Jenny automatically picked up a tea towel.

'I just don't. Can we leave it now?' He looked at his watch. 'Hell! I'll be late for work.'

'Go,' Jenny said. 'You might as well.'

* * *

'I told you I'd be there, didn't I?' Vi Harvey chain-lit her fourth cigarette. This had been a long, difficult call. 'I said I'd agree to your terms. You can have whatever the bloody hell you want. But you go back on your word and I swear I'll fucking kill you. Do you hear me? I'll find you and I'll kill you.'

She meant it. The heat of her rage and frustration, even with the fire-break of distance and telephone cable between them, was fierce.

'I'll keep my word,' he said. 'If you keep yours.'

CHAPTER 10

Jenny saw an outline: a blurred, fuzzy hulking shape beyond the frosted glass of the front door. She felt a momentary stab of alarm and turned to check that Paul hadn't followed her from the kitchen. He was painting one of his house pictures, but this one was all in red. The walls, door, windows, even the bars were painted in livid crimson.

The doorbell rang. Fraser had gone to work. She wondered if she should simply ignore the bell, but then dismissed the idea as a nervy response to her disturbed sleep. She opened the door and almost took a step back from the aggressive stare of the man on the step.

'Took your time, didn't you?' He was big. He carried the sort of muscle that makes a man look fat in a suit.

Her first impulse was to slam the front door and run for the boy. Then the man produced a warrant card. Jenny stared at it stupidly. DC Douglas. How could this shaven-headed thug be a policeman?

He turned sideways, jerking his head to indicate a smaller man behind him. 'Can we come in, then?' he asked.

'No.' There was no room for negotiation. Jenny began closing the door and the second man stepped forward.

'Hang on, love,' he said. 'You can't just refuse to talk to us, you know!'

Jenny looked past Douglas to the second man. He seemed astonished by her reaction. He dipped into his jacket pocket and produced his own warrant card.

'DC Sallis.'

Jenny glanced over her shoulder to the interior of the house. She was worried that the conversation would bring Paul out of the kitchen, and she knew that Douglas would frighten him.

'Look, you've seen our ID,' Sallis said.

'Mike promised me he'd come himself if there was any news,' Jenny said.

'Mike who?'

'I know things get busy, but he's usually reliable on these things. He'd at least send a female officer. The boy's scared enough as it is.'

Jenny caught the exchanged looks of bafflement between Sallis and Douglas. 'If you're not here about Paul . . . Oh, Jesus.' Her hand went to her mouth. 'Max. Is he—?'

Douglas rolled his eyes. 'Max,' he said, in his curiously monotonous voice. 'That'd be Max Bygraves, would it? Max Headroom?' He snapped his fingers. 'Got it! Mad Max, right?'

All Jenny's suspicion returned. 'Give me your warrant card,' she said to Douglas. 'I'll phone through to Canning Place and get confirmation you are who you say you are.'

Douglas tilted his head, leaned back a little. 'Tell you what, love. You can let us in, or we can have our little chin-wag down the station.'

'Try it,' she said, a slow, smouldering heat building in her chest. 'I dare you.'

Sallis — the smaller one — intervened. 'She's got a point, Dave,' he said. 'She's within her rights. Give her your card.'

Douglas glared at Jenny but made no move to comply.

'Give her the card, will you?' Sallis growled.

Douglas took out his warrant card with great reluctance and with very bad grace handed it over.

'You might want to see if you can get through to Mike Delaney,' Jenny said, addressing Sallis. 'He'll give you my background.' She closed the door.

Douglas blinked a couple of times. 'Think she's a Tom or what?'

Sallis grinned. 'Don't let Mike hear you say that. Thinking the only good-looking bint he'd be on speaking terms with'd have to be a Tom. Anyway, she doesn't look like a Tom.' He fished in the inside pocket of his jacket for his mobile.

Douglas was disdainful. 'They don't all wear fishnet tights and leather boots, you know.'

Everyone got their name shortened down the nick, or else a 'y' was tacked on the end: he was Dougy, Wright was Wrighty, MacBride was Macca. But Sallis didn't like it. Douglas had tried calling him Sally — only tried it the once, mind — and the experience had created a dark area in his subconscious, which would not admit to actually being wary of Sallis's temper but which nevertheless caused him to avoid using his name altogether.

'Oh, yeah?' Sallis said, keying in the number. 'What do Toms wear, then?'

'You know. *Normal* clothes. Like normal girls.'

Sallis finished punching the numbers on the keypad and frowned. 'So, what's normal?'

Douglas got halfway through a careful description of what normal girls wear before he realized Sallis was taking the piss, by which time the smart-arsed little runt had got through to Sergeant Delaney and he couldn't give him a dig to let him know he didn't appreciate the joke.

When Jenny Campbell opened the door, after speaking to DI Crank at police headquarters, the men had changed places. With Douglas looming behind him, Sallis, who was head and shoulders shorter, looked like a slightly shady businessman with his minder.

Sallis was quick to apologize. 'Didn't know you were looking after the little lad,' he said. 'No wonder you were a bit jumpy, like.'

'You weren't to know,' Jenny said, returning Douglas's warrant card.

He waited a moment and, no invitation forthcoming, said, 'Any chance of a chat inside, love?'

She opened the door wider, allowing them in. 'Ms Campbell. Or Jenny,' she said.

Douglas prodded Sallis in the back to let him know what he thought of tarts who called themselves *Miz*. They followed her through to the front sitting room, Sallis unconsciously taking in extraneous information on the way. The house was big, by his standards — high ceilings and big, square rooms. *Hell to heat in winter*, he thought. They'd looked after it well — recent decoration, stripped wood floors. Seemed like Ms Campbell had looked after herself pretty well, too. Shaggy blond hair that moved very nicely when she walked, likewise her hips, which had just the right amount of flare to stimulate interest. Her jeans fitted in all the right places. She wore a pale blue cotton shirt and was delicately tanned — golden, rather than brown.

Sallis shook his head. His wife had told him he had become a drooling old codger when he'd hit thirty. He was beginning to think she could be right. She did have nice skin, though, Ms Campbell — *Jenny* — and she was wearing some light, citrusy perfume that made him think of summer, gardens and fresh, clean air. The sitting room was sort of golden as well: yellows and shades of orange and parchment. Rugs on the floor, rather than a carpet, which Sallis disapproved of as impractical: dusty in the summer and cold in the winter. The settees were a bit plain as well, just white linen. Seemed to him she'd want a dark colour to hide the sticky paw prints of the kids she fostered.

'They're washable,' Jenny said, clearly amused by Sallis's open appraisal of her decor. 'Would you like to sit down?'

Sallis sat on the sofa, tapped the arm and said, 'Nice,' not very convincingly. Douglas wedged himself into one of the armchairs without a word. DS Delaney had asked to speak to him on the phone, and he'd been subdued ever since.

'Is he about, like? The lad?' Sallis asked. 'We've had loads of calls from the *Granada* thing.'

'I've taken Paul to his room. He's nervous of men.' Douglas shot her a look that said, *Not the only one, is he?* and Sallis gave him a hard stare that said, *Behave.*

'So,' Jenny said, 'if you could keep it down, I'd be grateful.'

'Doesn't he want to play out, like?' Sallis asked. He had a lad of his own, about the same age. He was probably tear-arsing around the school playground at this time of the morning. Seemed a shame for the kid to be indoors when he could be out in the fresh air.

'He doesn't want to do much of anything.'

Sallis nodded, digesting the full meaning of that remark.

'So,' she said, 'what was it you wanted to talk to me about?'

'Oh yeah, right,' Sallis said, pulling himself together. 'Failing to report an accident.' He watched her reaction. It was incredulous, faintly amused.

'Accident? As in car accident?'

'That's right.'

She shook her head. 'Not me.'

'Sorry, lu—Jenny. Your car. Has to be. We got it on video.'

'When?'

'Tuesday. At around six p.m.' He consulted his notebook. 'Seven minutes past, to be precise.'

Jenny raised her eyebrows. 'That *is* precise.'

'Security video. They log the time.'

Jenny shrugged, told Sallis the time her train had left Lime Street, and approximately where she would have been when she was supposed to have crashed her car.

'You say you were going to give a lecture?' Sallis said. 'I thought you were a nurse.'

'I am, part-time. Part-time lecturer and academic writer.'

'Oh yeah?' He turned down the corners of his mouth, jotted a few points in his notebook. 'What kind of books d'you write, then?' he asked, curiosity getting the better of cool insouciance.

She didn't answer straight away. Sallis looked up from his notes. Was she wondering whether to make an issue of the irrelevance of the question?

But after a moment, she said, 'Articles, mostly, rather than books. Child care, fostering, that sort of thing.'

Sallis nodded. 'Fits in, like, with what you do.'

'I hate to interrupt,' Douglas butted in and Sallis shot him a withering look. The man had no subtlety.

He dragged his eyes away from Douglas and addressed Jenny again: 'Where did you park the car?'

'At the multi-storey car park next to the station.' Jenny thought for a moment. 'I can't remember exactly where, but I wrote the level on the ticket. The car was where I'd left it.'

'Was the petrol down, when you got back?'

'Sorry,' Jenny said, 'I didn't notice.'

Sallis grunted, making more notes. 'What time did you get home?' Sallis asked, looking up from his writing into iridescent eyes, and feeling slightly disconcerted to find her scrutinizing him.

'I was in Nottingham all day Wednesday. I got the last train home. Arrived back in Liverpool at about eleven thirty, I think. Wouldn't your video tape tell you all this?'

He glanced over at Douglas, embarrassed to have been caught out. 'Thing is,' Sallis said, 'the bloke whose car was dented didn't get back from *his* business trip till this morning. He reported the damage to the car park's security, and they went through the tapes till they got your car backing out.'

Jenny sat forward, resting her forearms on her knees. 'Well, can't you see it isn't me driving out of the car park?' Jenny asked. 'I really *didn't* crash my car.'

He dipped his head apologetically. 'The video camera was filming another area of the car park when — whoever

— got into the car. All we got was the crash and the car driving away.'

Jenny nodded, thoughtfully. 'If you play your tape on, you might see *whoever* bringing it back. I found the car exactly where I'd parked it on Tuesday.'

'We'll do that,' Sallis said.

'Yeah, yeah,' Douglas said. 'But it doesn't change the evidence, does it? We've still got your car backing into the Laguna and then buggering off.'

'Is the car here?' Sallis asked.

Jenny led them out through the front door. The garage had been built into the basement of the house. 'I'm sure I'd've noticed if the car had been damaged,' Jenny said, opening the garage door. The garage took up the whole of the floor area of the house, with brick-built pillars to support the weight of the building above. The place smelled faintly of engine oil but more pungently of apples, and Sallis noticed there were boxes of fruit and vegetables stacked in one corner. The whole of the far wall was given over to shelving and a series of hooks for storing larger tools. They were in pristine condition and everything was neatly stowed. He wondered whether it was Jenny or her husband who was the DIYer.

He turned his attention to the car, walking around it and squinting along the edge of the paintwork, looking for scratches or dents. It did, indeed, seem to be untouched. He crouched down at the rear of the car and examined the tow bar. 'Here y'are,' he said, inviting Jenny to hunker down beside him. 'See that?' He pointed with a pen. There were a few scratches on the metal.

'We have a caravan. Those could be . . .'

'And this.' He took out a small plastic bag and scraped a few flakes of pale blue paint into it from the tow bar.

'I take it that's—'

'The same colour as the car that was damaged. Right.'

Jenny shook her head. 'I can't explain it. The car was there on Wednesday night when I got back. Exactly where I'd left it.'

'Who else uses it?' Sallis asked, sealing the bag before standing up.

'No one.'

'Husband? Children?'

'We have no children.' No matter how often she said that, it always sounded like an admission, the acknowledgement of a guilty secret. 'My husband hates cars,' she went on, quickly. 'He doesn't drive. Comes out in a cold sweat just sitting in the driver's seat.'

'Yeah?'

This was from Douglas.

'Yes,' Jenny answered, meeting his aggression with a cool stare.

* * *

Paul was at the window, watching them leave. He heard the clunk of their car doors and the engine starting up.

He had left the door open as a sign she could come in, but she knocked anyway, and asked for permission. He didn't answer, but waited until they had disappeared from sight, even pressing his cheek to the pane. Perplexed momentarily by the paradox of cold glass and hot sun, he watched his breath steam and then vanish on the windowpane.

She came and stood next to him.

'They were policemen,' Jenny said.

He slid past her, avoiding contact.

He sat on the edge of the bed and hummed a few bars of something but shut up when he realized she was listening. He sat looking at his watch, waiting for her to leave. The sun streamed into the room and bounced off the watch, making a green doughnut at the back of his eyes. He screwed them up tightly, then opened them again. A circle of gold danced on the ceiling above him and to the left. He watched the disk of light, entranced, and noticed that as he moved, it moved.

Guardian angel, he thought. When you were all alone, your guardian angel looked after you. They stood just behind your shoulder, just out of sight, but sometimes, if you turned really fast, you saw a faint glitter of light, or heard the rustle of feathers as they flew up to heaven. He sighed.

Guardian angels were unreliable, he had found.

Gradually, he became aware that the light was coming from his watch face. It used to make him laugh, the idea that a watch had a face: happy face was ten past ten or ten to two, sad face at twenty past eight or twenty to four. His watch had a happy face, just now.

He made it beam off the walls and ceiling onto the teddy bears and polar bears and donkeys and penguins (he had hidden the pigs in the wardrobe). Then something wonderful happened. A second disk of gold joined his, darting like a fairy, a sprite, following his, playing tag. Once, he laughed out loud, because he had foxed it, sent it entirely the wrong way.

She laughed as well. Her watch must have its happy face on, too. He looked up at her, into her eyes and, for the first time, consciously acknowledged her presence, her status as a person, as another human being.

* * *

He watched as Jenny and the boy walked toward the main entrance of the hospital, weaving between the parked cars, Jenny talking all the time, encouraging the child, no doubt trying to keep his mind off the therapy session. They passed right in front of his car, but neither looked into it.

'Do you know this boy?' What a question! The TV presenter couldn't know how crass he was in asking it.

I know every scratch and scar on his eight-year-old body. He has a purple birth mark, small, hidden by his hair, just above his left ear, and a chickenpox scar on his back, between his shoulder blades. I know him, all right. I know every thought, every hope, every wish, dream and desire of his lying, selfish little heart.

'Despite daily therapy, the boy has not been able to tell the police what happened to him . . .'

Well, that's something, I suppose. And the reference to therapy was enough to bring me here. Now that I've found him, we'll soon have him back to his old self.

As she stepped through the door, Jenny glanced over her shoulder, and her face changed from calm and smiling to an expression of sudden shock. Had she felt his presence? The boy looked up at her, his eyes widening with fear.

Yes, I'm here — you feel it, too, don't you? I'm coming for you, child, and you will know my displeasure.

CHAPTER 11

'You have to work on your feelings,' Pam had told them. 'You have been out of touch with yourself for such a long time, you've forgotten what it is to allow your feelings free rein.'

Shona knew she was right. It reminded her of that time she had put off phoning her mother. 'Time . . .' she told herself. 'I've never got the time.' So, time went by and her guilty feelings turned to resentment. 'There's two ends to a phone,' she would mutter, eyeing the handset as if her mother's face was staring reproachfully up at her from the telephone table. But she could never quite convince herself. Her mother had loaded her with the burden of responsibility since childhood. It was Shona's job to do the phoning, to visit and cheer up and shop and make sure that her mother was happy. Except she never was. Never happy — never satisfied.

The truth was, she didn't *want* to phone her mother. She was depressed even by the sound of her mother's voice. Her loneliness, her obsession with TV soaps and *Oprah* and *Esther* and all the other chat shows that proved to her that her own life was dull, boring and empty reproved Shona for failing as a daughter. Shona despised her mother, a woman who couldn't tell drama from real life, while hiding from life herself in the drama of those same soaps.

When, finally, the burden of guilt became too heavy and she did make the call, her mother would spend half of it moaning how Shona never phoned, never came to see her — adding to her guilt and depressing her further. She often demanded to know, as if Shona had planned it, why she hadn't found herself a nice young man, why she hadn't given her any grandchildren, making Shona hate herself to the point of angry tears and her mother to point of murderous fantasy. Then, suddenly, the fury would abandon her and she would feel bereft, aching for acknowledgement, and she would find herself weeping.

'What're you crying for?' Like it was a surprise. Not to be outdone, her mother would start snuffling and blubbing down the line like some maudlin drunk. 'You know I love you, girl . . .'

Shona wanted to say, *How? How do I know? You* tell *me, but you never show it. You criticize and you whine and complain, and then, once in a while you say you love me, and that's supposed to make everything all right.* But she didn't say it. She never confronted her mother with her hypocrisy, because she knew that her mother wouldn't have anything to say that really meant anything. Shona just became more careful, telephoning once a week, remembering her mother's birthday, sending flowers on Mother's Day, visiting at Christmas, maintaining a polite, formal distance. Conversations were kept to safe topics and tears were forbidden. It was easier this way, less demanding on the emotions.

Yet now Pam was asking her to give herself up to those same emotions she had kept in check for so long and with such stern vigilance. Shona knew the dangers that compliance posed, but she did want to get better. She had never found it easy, fitting in, being one of the gang, but Pam had been kind to her, understanding, and she yearned for her therapist's approval. The others in the group said they wanted to share in her healing. When they had gathered around her the other night, she had felt protected, shielded, included. She did not want to go back to the awful colourless days — the days when she hated herself and envied the world its companionship.

Pam had shown her what it was like to be welcome, to be needed and loved. The others had accepted her because they respected Pam, and now they were beginning to see her as part of the group. Perhaps they would even come to like her. Max Greenberg's lecture had belittled Pam, had rubbished her work and ridiculed the people she helped. People like Shona. She felt a sudden rush of feeling, an overwhelming urge to prove her love for Pam in some courageous act.

* * *

Shona moved cautiously, quietly, down the side of the building. She knew the house was empty: she had watched Max Greenberg leave, just as she had watched him arrive the previous night, swaggering and smug from his evening lecture.

Now she crept like a cat from light into darkness. The shadow of the neighbouring building sliced through the evening sunshine, throwing the side of Dr Greenberg's house into shade so deep that she hesitated in the darkness, momentarily blinded.

Quivering, alert to sounds and smells, even her skin was sensitive to the subtlest vibration of movement. The faintest of breezes, warm and unrefreshing, stirred the air. The wall felt smooth and cold to her fingertips and she extended her arm until its length was in contact with its surface, its coolness calming the fever of terror within her. Mingled smells of lawn clippings and garbage drifted to her as she edged deeper into the shadows, close to the brickwork, using her fingers to guide her, lacking the gift of feline night vision. The bricks soothed the hot ache in her joints.

The stink of waste became overpowering just as her fingertips brushed metal and her knee made contact with something hard and abrasive. She yelped in pain and surprise, jumping back, flailing, fending off an imagined attacker before the familiar outline of a bin began to emerge from the gloom, and she sobbed, half-laughing.

Somehow it did seem grotesque and funny that a man like Greenberg would perform such mundane tasks as putting the bins out for collection.

She waited a minute, two minutes, panting, pressed against the wall, listening for noises from the neighbouring house, signs that they had heard her yell, the scrape of the bin, moved by her knee. Abruptly, music screamed from an ice-cream van near the house. It played 'Greensleeves' at a manic pace, waited less than a minute, then roared off down the street. She calmed herself, willing the thudding of her heart to slow. Radio music floated tinnily from somewhere within, but there were no windows on this blind, blank wall, and when she was sure no one would come to investigate, she continued to the gate.

A brick wall divided the two gardens, and the gates into the respective properties were angled at forty-five degrees to the centre. She lifted the latch and drifted, silent as a wraith, into his domain. The garden was in shade, save for one small wedge of sunlight at the south eastern corner.

She listened: traffic noise, and that radio, playing jazz. An aeroplane, somewhere high and distant, its engine noise a single, faint note, stirred an intense longing in her.

She had suffered, but she was a survivor and she would put a stake through the heart of Max Greenberg. Put a stop to his venomous attacks.

The broken pane of glass had been repaired. She looked round for something to heave at it and almost screamed when the door opened a crack, creaking in the slight current of air. It was open. Every fibre, every muscle and sinew tensed to run, she stepped forward and pushed the door with her fingernail. It gave.

She almost walked past the envelope pinned to the kitchen door, but something made her stop and take it down.

I don't know your name yet, but I soon will, it read.

I think we should talk, don't you?

Her hand began to shake so violently that she dropped the paper. My God. My God! He must have seen her! Her head felt suddenly helium-light, expanded, explosive. She brought her hands to her head to convince herself that it was still its normal shape and size, to pull herself back to earth. Then she turned and ran from the house to her car. She had parked it only a few yards from his front door. She threw up in the gutter, then dry-heaved wretchedly, near collapse for several minutes longer. When she came to herself again, a cold, wet sheen glistened on her skin. Her hands were hurting. She examined them: they looked swollen, and when she touched them the skin was sensitive and hot. A brief flutter of excitement — this was the sort of sign she had been waiting for — then she had a fleeting impression of fear. She faced it, doing as Pam had instructed, thinking into the pain, into the fear, into the darkness that obscured her memory.

You cannot be *what you are, until you* know *what you are.* Pam's wisdom confronted her, as she must confront her deepest terror. It eluded her until she had a brief flash of something, an image and a feeling. The horror was too awful, she shook her head, forcing it away, pushing it back into the shadows.

CHAPTER 12

Paul had finally gone off to sleep, and Jenny was watching TV in the sitting room. Fraser folded the paper he was reading and dumped it by the side of his chair. 'I think I'll go up,' he said.

Jenny looked at him. She wanted to ask if everything was all right, but she knew it would irritate him, and anyway, she wouldn't get an honest answer. 'I'll be up in a few minutes,' she said.

The phone rang just as Fraser got into the hallway. Jenny reached for the extension near her chair, but Fraser got to the hall phone before her. Why was he so jumpy? She felt sure it had something to do with the calls from Mr Hunter, but whenever she suggested that they could be linked to the telephone calls to the hospital switchboard, he rubbished the idea.

Fraser put his head round the door. 'For you,' he said. 'Max.'

'I've had another visit,' Max said, without preamble.

'Oh, Max — did they do any damage?'

'No, I—' He checked and said instead, 'Have you heard anything more from your Mr Hunter?'

'*I* haven't.' Jenny hadn't meant to put the emphasis on the 'I', but it was there, nevertheless, and of course Max heard it. 'Why are you so sure there's a connection?' Jenny went on, to deflect him from probing further.

'I don't know, Jenny. It may be coincidence that your phone calls started at the same time as . . . all this. But the burglaries . . . What if they're after reports on Paul?'

'But you don't keep your hospital files at home,' she said, surprised.

'Not the full files, but I do take notes home to complete them, and to prepare for case meetings and consultations. Anyway, it's a hell of a lot easier breaking into my place than the hospital records office.'

'It could be recovered memory protesters,' she suggested. 'You know how paranoid they be.'

'What could they hope to gain?'

'Making you as fearful as they are?'

Jenny could hear Max's smile in his reply. 'Who's supposed to be the psychiatrist around here?'

She laughed, but when he spoke again, all trace of humour was gone from his voice. 'Jenny, promise me you will be very, very careful.'

* * *

'He wants *you* to be careful!' Fraser put his book face down on top of the bedcovers and looked at her in frank amazement. 'He leaves his house empty eighteen hours a day with no security system, a back door that could be blown open with one good sneeze — leaves the damn key in the lock, just to make it easier for any would-be burglar — and he says *you* should be careful!'

'His security arrangements may be a bit haphazard, Fraser, but he's not reckless.'

Fraser snorted derisively. 'Have you seen the car he drives? If it was a building it'd be condemned. *And* his driving's pure radge.'

'Be fair,' Jenny said, laughing. 'You think anyone who drives a car is a certifiable loon.'

He didn't reply to that, only shrugged.

Which reminded Jenny that someone — whether certifiable or just plain criminal she could not say — had taken their car, crashed it, driven it away and then replaced it exactly where they had found it. The phenomenon was not exactly common, Mike had told her, but neither was it unheard of, for criminals to test drive cars they intended to use on a robbery — a kind of dry run — replacing it where they found it and returning a day or so later to use it in the real thing. But wouldn't that apply to cars parked in the same contract parking bay every day — office hours, reliable? Her occasional trips hardly fit into that category.

So who had taken the car, and why had they taken pains to make her think it had never been moved? When she had told Fraser that the police had called and why, he had sat down heavily and said, 'Fuck.'

Fraser, who had got out of the habit of swearing entirely after they had started fostering, anxious to set a good example to the children in their care, no matter how brief their stay might be.

Then, looking up at her, he had asked, 'What did you tell them?'

'What *could* I tell them? I didn't even know the damned car had been moved. They were convinced it was me — got the whole thing on video.'

'Then how could they think it was you?'

'That's exactly what I said,' Jenny replied, touched by Fraser's unquestioning trust in both her driving ability and her honesty.

'And?'

'And. The important bit, with the thief getting into the car, wasn't on tape. I don't know if that was good luck or good management on his part.'

'His?'

'I assume it's a man. You don't get that many women stealing cars.'

'Oh.'

‘Fraser,’ she said, ‘are you all right?’

He had stood impulsively and paced the room. ‘Funny phone calls, Max’s house burgled, now the car taken and mysteriously replaced. No, Jenny, I’m not all right.’

There did seem to be too many coincidences, and in a sense she was comforted to think that she wasn’t alone in feeling disturbed by the accumulation of circumstances, but she could not push from her mind his shrug, his failure to respond to her joke that he classed all drivers as lunatics. That *was* surprising, because he always did. Respond, that is. He always made some remark that if it weren’t for other drivers, he wouldn’t be afraid to drive at all, or cars didn’t scare him, people did. But this time he had shrugged and said nothing.

* * *

Damp. Cold. Without warning. The boy was wrapped in something. Twisted tight. Suffocating. His face, shoulders imprisoned, his arms pinned. A cold, soapy smell. A towel.

Then he was picked up bodily.

There was a silence lasting a few seconds — long enough to hear the water drip, once, from the tap. Then shock. Sharp. Hard.

Icy water. He opened his mouth to scream, but he couldn’t breathe, and for what seemed like an age, he gasped, open mouthed, unable to draw breath.

* * *

Fraser was out of bed and halfway into his dressing gown before he realized what was happening.

‘I’ll go,’ Jenny said. ‘You may panic him.’

The screams continued — prolonged, high pitched, interspersed with a few gabbled words.

Jenny reached the boy’s bedroom within seconds. He was sitting up in bed, his eyes wide open. He was drenched in sweat, the window closed and locked despite the heat. She spoke to him, approaching him slowly, calming him, telling him where he was, who she was, that he was safe.

Oh, dear God, she thought, *Safe from what?*

'Darling,' she soothed, knowing that it would only make things worse if she were to address him by a name not his own, 'you've had a dream. A bad dream, that's all. Just a dream.' She repeated these words over and over, cautiously lowering herself onto the bed next to him, slipping her arm around his shoulders, talking above his screams. After a few moments, he subsided into babbled apologies.

'Please I'llbegood. Sorrysorrysorry. I didn't mean it. Please — didn't mean it. I'll wash myself. I'll wash myself clean. *Pleasepleaseplease!*'

This went on for several minutes, Jenny talking calmly all the time, wanting to weep for the boy. He replying with his pathetic apologies, until they moderated to a whisper and he wept, sobbed, hugged her tightly, and she kissed his hot forehead, murmuring reassurances until he was calm, exhausted.

She changed his pyjamas. He had wet the bed, too, and he watched Jenny change the bedding from the safety of a little nest of beanbags in a corner of the room. He had gathered to him a polar bear and a lion and had them sitting on either side of him, like sentinels, while he sucked on an ice lolly Jenny had given him to serve the dual purpose of cooling him down and soothing his throat, which must surely be sore after all that screaming.

He had insisted on coming with her, mutely refusing to be alone, clinging to her and whimpering, so they had fetched the fresh bedding together, and his pyjamas, and the ice lolly, and she had not had the chance to talk, even for the briefest moment, to Fraser. She spoke on in a conversational tone as she worked, telling the boy about the following day. Jenny had arranged for Paul to be looked after by Phyllis, another foster carer, while they attended his case conference. Gina Vance, the senior social worker in charge, had cleared it. It was standard practice, in these circumstances, to use the network of foster care contacts — social services preferred to leave the child in the care of another foster carer, rather than someone who hadn't been thoroughly vetted.

Phyllis planned to take Paul, along with her own foster children, to Chester Zoo. Jenny tried to interest Paul in the trip, but he responded to none of her questions about his favourite animals, returning to his mute state as if he had never spoken. She could not discover if he had pets at home, nor if he had visited the zoo before. He had merely sat, licking his ice lolly and staring at her with his huge, dark eyes, but when she put him into bed he had caught her hand and held it tightly, tightly, as if he were afraid of her leaving him.

'D'you want me to stay?' she asked, expecting no reply, but going through the motions, for surely, some day he would talk to her. His grip tightened and his eyes widened, and she considered herself answered.

'Of course I'll stay,' she said, adding, 'You *are* safe now, Paul.' He understood, she was certain of it. 'I won't let anything hurt you.' She thought she saw a fleeting dread in his face, then he looked away. She tucked his favourite toys either side of him, telling him that polar bear and lion would guard over him while he slept. This seemed to console him, and he relaxed a little.

The therapy sessions didn't seem to be having any impact on him at all. He isolated himself from the other children, crawling under tables to avoid physical contact, staring at the toys as if their purpose were unknown to him. The only activity he would participate in was art, during which he repeated the obsessive routine of painting a house and then barring the windows with thick, black lines, adding a huge padlock for the front door. Once, another child had become overexcited and had splashed paint from his brush onto Paul's painting. Paul had looked at the fine spray of carmine red, watched it blur and merge with the primrose yellow curtains behind the barred windows of his house. The child beside him laughed in delight and flicked his paint brush again. A few drops fell on Paul's hand, one or two on his face, and he began screaming—

A sudden spurt, as fine as mist, but he felt it — felt the heat of it on his face. 'Come here, you little bastard! Come and take your punishment.'

—short staccato bursts of sound, which no one could stop, until Paul had been washed clean of paint. After that, he had sat slumped in a chair, totally withdrawn, unable to look at the psychologist who spoke to him, perhaps unaware of his presence.

Jenny had wanted to keep him at home after that, but Max told her it would be unwise to increase his isolation — they would just have to be more careful during group activity sessions. So she had taken him each morning, even though his condition seemed unaltered. She did not notice the car parked outside the hospital every day, for it was hidden among scores of others, always in different areas of the car park, but always with a clear view of the main entrance.

She sat beside Paul, in the chair that had served for so many night vigils, and watched over him for an hour after he slept. No dreams seemed to trouble him now, but she lingered, unwilling to leave him.

She knew that Fraser would be lying awake, wanting to help, but knowing that his presence would only alarm the boy. She felt for him: he hated to be isolated in this way, unable to support and solace, barred from all but the most superficial contact. It was imperative to Fraser that they function as a family — he had worked hard to achieve that with all their foster children — and for some reason it seemed even more important to him in Paul's case. And yet, with Paul, more than any other child, he was locked out, emotionally and physically, since Paul avoided physical contact except at times of extreme distress, even with her.

She had hoped that the police would have discovered something about him by now — even DC Sallis had said they'd had a good response from the *Granada News* appeal. Fraser had decided to come with her to the boy's case conference and had even arranged for time off school so that he could be there. Often, she would go alone to these reviews and Fraser would occupy the child, but occasionally, as with Jamie, the boy from Glasgow, the roles would be reversed. It didn't matter — whichever of them was closer to the child attended. In truth, neither of them knew much about Paul. All they knew was what they had been able to observe. He told them nothing and communicated little in other ways, and yet Fraser had wanted to be there. He had explained that since he couldn't make himself useful looking after the boy he may as well go with her. There was an ache of longing hidden beneath his feigned indifference, and Jenny wished she could do something to soothe his pain, but that was not within her power — perhaps not even within the boy's power, for it did seem that it was the boy's arrival that had triggered this disquiet in Fraser. Perhaps, also, the crank caller, who may or may not be linked with the boy, or with Max.

Now, in the small hours of the morning, the silence and solitude were somehow more substantial, more tangible than ever they were in the daytime. Her vigil over a small boy whose secrets were locked within him, unknown and unknowable, made her see just how alone this little scrap of humanity was. In the broader picture, his isolation reflected her own, for since his arrival, Jenny had come to see how little she knew of anyone — even Fraser. What little she did know was what he chose to tell her, and how much of that could she — *should she* — believe?

A thought came to her that made her catch her breath. She had insisted to the police that only she drove the car, that Fraser didn't drive — hated even the idea. But did she know that for certain? All through their marriage, he had resisted the idea of learning to drive. The one time she had coaxed him to sit behind the wheel and try the controls in the broad expanse of an empty supermarket car park, he had panicked as soon as the car started to creep forward.

That was ten years ago. How could she be sure that Fraser didn't drive? That he hadn't learned? She believed it because Fraser her told her. But did that make it true? The car hadn't been broken into — there was no damage to the lock or the steering column — and she kept a set of spare keys in her dressing table drawer.

She tutted, impatient with herself. 'For God's sake, Jenny,' she whispered. 'This is paranoid.' Paranoid, unreasonable, morbid and disloyal. Fraser had been a rock. A steady, constant, dependable landmark during an almost impossible transitional period in which she had had to reassess her concept of womanhood, marriage and family. He had never given up on her, had never once doubted her.

She looked at the boy once more. He was in a deep sleep. She tiptoed from the room and returned to bed. Fraser was reading. She slipped in beside him and nuzzled his neck.

'What's this for?' he asked.

'For being you.'

She felt him tense and withdraw slightly. 'How's the wee lad?'

'He's asleep,' she said, puzzled, but prepared to try again. She slid her arm under his and stroked his abdomen.

'So should you be,' he said, briskly, tapping her hand and flicking out the side light. She heard his novel thump to the floor beside the bed. 'Case conference in the morning.' He turned away from her, moving so that a cool strip of cotton sheeting separated them, and their bodies did not touch, except for her arm draped over him.

His dismissal of her felt like a body-blow. She was reminded of her dream, the dream in which Fraser rejected her. 'Fraser,' she said, 'is something wrong? Are you okay?'

'Fine.' He patted her hand again. 'Get some sleep, will you?'

He said he was fine, and she knew that it was a lie. He wasn't fine. Neither of them was, for reasons she could not begin to fathom. Nothing was fine. And she wouldn't get a wink of sleep.

* * *

Max pinched the bridge of his nose and sighed. He felt a migraine coming on. Was he doing the right thing, not telling Jenny why he wanted her to be careful? As well as the second break-in at his house, the hospital switchboard had received several more phone calls, asking for information about the boy. Some of the callers claimed to be his mother but refused to give a name or a contact number, others simply wanted to know where he was being housed. These, he felt, were the most menacing.

The police are monitoring the situation, he told himself. It would be unfair to Jenny to add to her worries by telling her to watch out for lunatics lurking in the undergrowth every time she brought Paul for a counselling session or took him for a walk in the park. It was probably nothing to worry about, simply people who wanted to give a sense of importance to their lives by pretending a relationship to a mystery child.

A voice, small but persistent screamed for him to listen to his instincts that Jenny and Paul were in danger. But when he examined the facts, the hidden menace was insubstantial, no more than a shadow at his back, and he convinced himself that his own situation had made him unduly apprehensive.

* * *

When the group therapy session started, Pam asked if anyone had anything they wanted to share with the group. Shona started to put up her hand, like a schoolgirl, then put it down, embarrassed, and stood instead.

'I've got something to say — well, to show, really.' She saw distrust in one or two of their faces, but she went on, describing what had happened.

'Will you show us your hands?' Pam asked.

They gasped at the swelling, the black and purple discoloration.

'Does it hurt?' That was Angela.

‘A bit,’ Shona replied, suddenly shy. ‘Not as much as before.’

‘Before.’

‘At home. In my flat.’ She couldn’t say that she had returned to Greenberg’s house. How could she tell them that she had found the door open and had turned and fled?

‘You *said* “before”,’ Pam repeated. ‘Think, Shona. When did this happen before?’

Shona shrugged helplessly. She had tried to remember, but it was gone.

‘This is a body memory,’ Pam explained. ‘Sometimes the body remembers abuse which the mind can’t bear to recall. Now, you said, “before, at home”. Think of home. A place in your home that frightened you. A sound or a smell. Something that speaks to your pain.’

Shona began to shake her head, but Pam asked them all to close their eyes and help Shona to travel back, back, back until she could see what had hurt her.

Shona listened to Pam’s voice. It went on and on, a gentle, persistent undertone, now whispering, now loud with urgency. ‘Who hurt you, Shona? Can you remember who gave you this pain?’

Someone groaned. Shona was drifting. She had the strangest sensation of floating, then—

She cried out and looked down at her hands. A ridge of new swelling ran from the half-moons of her nails to just below the first knuckle of her index fingers. An attic room. A rumbling sound. Ball bearings. A runner. She knew.

CHAPTER 13

Mike Delaney checked his watch. Eight thirty. They'd had a huge response to the television appeal for information about the lad, and perhaps a score or more of the respondents had pointed out the similarity between this boy and a lad who had disappeared from outside his home in Cheshire. It took a phone call to Granada TV and half a dozen transfers before he got hold of someone from Cheshire Constabulary who could tell him more. One further switchboard transfer put him in contact with DC Weston, one of the investigating officers. He arranged to meet in Widnes and was shown by a WPC to the canteen, where a few people were eating breakfast.

'That's Weston over there,' the WPC said, indicating a slightly paunchy man, tucking in to a full English, with toast to follow. He made his way to the table, but Weston didn't look up from tearing through his meal until Mike stood over him.

'Mike Delaney,' he said, offering his hand.

Weston licked his fingers and wiped them on a paper napkin before taking it. 'Hope you don't mind,' he said, 'but I can't go without my grub, and we've got a briefing at nine.'

'It was good of you to see me,' Mike said.

A woman approached the table with a tray holding several rounds of toast and two mugs. She had broad shoulders and a solid, tough look, but she moved gracefully. 'Hope you don't mind coffee,' she said, passing Mike one of the mugs.

'Coffee's great,' he said. Weston mumbled an introduction through half-chewed fried bread and egg.

'I'll do the honours, shall I?' she said to Weston. 'While you fill your face.' Since Weston's face was filled to bursting at the time, he couldn't reply, only managing a grimace. 'I'm DC Lisa Calcot.'

They shook hands and sat at the table.

'Connor's mum phoned us on Friday,' Calcot said. 'Said he'd gone missing from outside the house. She told us someone had tried to snatch him from outside his school in Chester earlier in the week — a parent waiting to pick up his own son saw a man trying to drag Connor into a car. He intervened and the bloke drove off.'

'Nobody recognized him?'

'No.'

'Got a picture?'

Weston wiped his hands again and reached inside his briefcase next to his chair. 'That's him,' he said.

Mike took out his photograph of Paul and placed it next to Connor's.

'Similar,' he said, 'but it's not the same lad.'

'No, but they could be twins,' Calcot breathed, dragging the two images to her for closer inspection.

'Maybe you could show this to Connor's mother,' Mike suggested, handing the photograph of Paul to Weston. 'If they're related, maybe there's a link.'

'Sure,' Weston said, sliding both photographs back into the folder. 'You know our lad's turned up?'

'That's putting it a bit strongly,' Calcot said. 'His mum says he's with his dad, but we haven't spoken to him or the boy yet.'

'But there was a previous abduction attempt,' Mike said. 'That was genuine.'

'Yeah,' Calcot said. 'D'you think the kidnapper got the wrong boy, is that it?' She had stopped munching on her toast and was giving him her full attention.

'I suppose it's possible, if you didn't know the boys well . . .'

'You might go for Connor, first try, outside the school, realize your mistake and then try and snatch Paul from his home. He botched his first attempt, there was no reason why he'd do any better on the second,' Weston suggested.

'Hard to say, until we know the order of events,' Mike said. 'We don't know what happened to Paul — we're not even sure when. Maybe the bloke who tried to snatch Connor actually took Paul first, and the kid got away somehow. Or maybe he didn't. Perhaps the abductor had got what he wanted from the lad — information? Something else? And just let him go.' Mike sighed. There were too many could-bes, what-ifs and maybes.

'Are you any nearer identifying your little boy?' Calcot asked.

'I'm seeing someone this morning.' Mike tilted his head. 'Hopefully . . .' He frowned. 'What did you make of Connor's mum?'

'A hard-faced bitch.' Calcot said it without missing a beat.

Weston laughed. 'Lisa didn't hit it off with Mrs Harvey.'

'So what's your opinion of her?' Mike asked.

Weston sucked food from between his teeth. 'She's a strong-willed woman,' he said, smiling as Calcot rolled her eyes.

'Strong-willed enough to try and bargain with kidnappers?' Mike asked.

CHAPTER 14

'Do you know this boy?' the presenter asked. Paul's photograph stared out from the television screen. *'He was found wandering the streets of the Garston area of Liverpool in his nightclothes early last Saturday morning. He was clearly distressed and refusing to speak. Despite daily therapy, the boy has not been able to tell the police what happened to him and they are still no nearer tracing his parents. If you have any information which might help reunite this boy with his family, Merseyside Police have set up a confidential telephone hotline. The number is—'*

Mike Delaney pushed the stop button on the remote control and switched off the TV.

'We had hundreds of calls after that appeal,' he said. 'It's been a painstaking process, following every one of them up, but we didn't want the lad upset by gawkers and publicity seekers, so we had to be sure callers were genuine. Which is why it's taken till today.'

'You've found his parents?' Jenny said, leaning forward eagerly.

The room reserved for the case conference was crammed full. Aside from the independent chairperson and the secretary taking the minutes of the meeting, there were representatives of all interested official bodies in Paul's case: the doctor who had examined Paul when he was first brought to hospital, the local authority solicitor, education department and health authority representatives, Paul's social worker, Mike Delaney, representing the police force, Max, Fraser and Jenny, and Gina Vance, the senior social worker with responsibility for Paul. Roz, who was Jenny and Fraser's link worker, had turned up at the last minute.

The tables had been arranged in a U-shape, with the TV and video recorder placed at the open end of it. The room was a uniform grey: the tables and chairs selected for the tonal neutrality that was the trend in institutions in the late seventies, in tune with the depression of the times, and the walls — originally icicle blue — had gradually faded and with accumulated grime had taken on the new shade of dove grey, in conformity with the rest of the decor.

The plastic seat covers were sticky in the heat of another swelteringly hot and humid morning, and the security latches on the windows allowed only a couple of centimetres' gap for air circulation. The blinds were stuck in the open position.

Mike felt a trickle of sweat slide between his shoulder blades and work its way down to the waistband of his trousers. *To hell with this*, he thought. He loosened his tie and popped the top button of his shirt. 'Any reason why I shouldn't open the door?' he asked.

'Dozens,' Max said, with characteristic dryness. 'But in the overriding interests of sanity, I think you must.' He had taken off his jacket and was wearing a short-sleeved shirt which seemed curiously at odds with the formality of his yellow bow tie. His fun badge, a push-button affair that played 'Raindrops Keep Falling on My Head' when triggered, had been transferred from his jacket lapel to his shirt pocket. While they waited for Mike Delaney to arrive, he had demonstrated to the rest of the assembly.

The distraction of the exchange between Mike and Max seemed to relax the group. Gina Vance grinned and reached for the iced water. 'Glad someone had the common sense to suggest it,' she said.

They had to prop the door open, but the cooling effect of the resulting draught was pure bliss.

'Okay, have we found his parents?' Mike said, rephrasing Jenny's question. 'To be honest, not yet. But we think we know his name.'

There was a collective movement, an almost visible poising of pens.

'Alain Fournier,' Mike said, carefully spelling both names for all concerned.

'Hmm,' Max said. 'Like the writer.'

'That's what his headmaster said. Can't say I've heard of him myself.'

'Died young,' Max said.

'Headmaster?' Fraser interrupted, irritably. He had been out of sorts ever since he had got up. 'He's been identified by his headmaster?' he demanded.

'He attends Harcourt Prep School in Mossley Hill. A private school. Not cheap.'

* * *

Mike had visited the headmaster, Mr Radleigh, and his wife immediately after his chat with Cheshire CID. The school was in a quiet drive which curved elegantly from an only slightly busier road, arching back to the main roadway a quarter of a mile further west of its ingress. He supposed it must be Victorian in origin: all red brick and false crenellations, splendid in its way, and certainly unexpected in this corner of suburbia. It was hidden behind a high sandstone wall and an immaculately clipped beech hedge. The driveway, in black tarmac speckled with pink stones, swept with courtly splendour, looping back on itself at a spectacular roundabout planted with begonias and a box hedge in the school's crest. There was room for two-way traffic, and speed ramps had been built in, presumably to discourage parents who were late delivering their darlings to school from speeding to the front door.

He had parked in front of a sandstone portico with slate roof, which sheltered a wide doorway complete with studded double oak doors hung from huge trefoil-shaped iron hinges. He scanned the layout while he locked his car. The main building seemed to be one street-long rectangle. Set back from it, and a little to its right, was a squat, solid-looking house. A little further down the driveway, at an angle to the school building, was another, modern-looking construction with a reflecting glass front, which Mike assumed was some kind of sports hall or perhaps a swimming pool. It reflected the powder-blue and cotton-wool sky and the best features of the main building to impressive effect. He could hear the buzz of a mower somewhere nearby and wondered if there were fields behind the main frontage.

He walked up a shallow set of steps to the imposing doorway and rang at the doorbell marked 'Headmaster's Secretary'. He was shown by a tall, mousy-haired woman across the tarmac and down a pretty, lavender-lined path to the house. The latticed windows gleamed in the early morning sun and the scent of lavender wafted up to him as his trousers brushed the tips of the flowers. This, he thought, was very different from the dilapidated 1960s flat-roofed, leaky secondary modern he had attended.

The headmaster answered the door. He was younger than Mike had expected, and tall. Dressed casually but immaculately in chinos and a polo shirt, he looked ready for a morning on the golf course.

'So good of you to come,' he said, as though Mike were a visiting friend. 'We're in the drawing room.' He showed Mike through a panelled hallway to a large and gleaming room which Mike's mother would have called a 'parlour'. Except that it was on a much grander scale than any best room they had ever had. It must have been twenty-five feet long, and the sheen of freshly waxed wood seemed to compete with the warm glow of the copper and brass plate ranged on rails around the room.

Mrs Radleigh sat on a pale silk-covered settee. She smiled over at Mike as her husband introduced him, then busied herself pouring tea.

Mike began by asking why it had taken them until Thursday evening to telephone the police.

Mr Radleigh rubbed the back of his neck. 'We were up in London for a few days, as it's the *exeat*. Didn't arrive back until Thursday morning.'

'Joanne — my secretary — had taken a few calls from parents who thought it might be Alain, but she had no way of telling,' the headmaster went on. 'And, bless her, she didn't want to trouble us with something that might be entirely irrelevant.'

Mike raised his eyebrows and Mr Radleigh dipped his head in apology. 'Joanne can be a bit of a dragon when it comes to protecting our time away.'

'The appeal made national news,' Mike said. 'Surely—'

'We don't watch much television — even when we're here,' Radleigh said with a disapproving frown. 'Rather like watching the world through one's letterbox, I always feel.'

'But you did see his picture, eventually,' Mike said, stifling his irritation at the man's dismissive tone. 'If not on TV, where? In the *Echo*?'

Radleigh shook his head. 'We'd cancelled the papers, as we were going away, but Joanne managed to track down a parent who'd actually had the presence of mind to tape the thing on TV. Apparently, the news programme showed Alain's photograph, and naturally, when Joanne realized that it was he, she contacted me immediately.' He stopped, perhaps aware that he was explaining himself more than was strictly necessary.

'Milk or lemon, Sergeant?' Mrs Radleigh asked.

'Milk, thanks.'

Mrs Radleigh bent to complete the task. She smiled as she handed over the cup.

Must take years of training, that, Mike thought. The tea-making ritual, the gracious smile, not spilling a drop.

Years of patient coaching. He tasted the tea and made an effort not to grimace. It was bitter, though it smelled faintly of flowers or some sweet herb — nothing like his normal brew — and he was almost grateful for the stronger scent of beeswax and cigars that pervaded the room, masking the strange flavour. The room was chilly, despite the heat of the day: it faced south-west, and the morning sun had not crept in through its windows. Mike was reminded of one of his mother's pronouncements on the English: 'Meanness or stubbornness, I don't know which, but May to September you'll not see a fire in an Englishman's grate.'

She had formed her opinions of the English gentry from her time in service in Ireland, and in all essential features, they had remained unmodified, unmoderated by the years.

'You're sure the boy is Alan Fournier?' Mike asked.

'Al*ain*,' Mr Radleigh corrected. 'Like the author. His mother is French. Alain speaks the language fluently.'

Mike sipped his tea and stole a look at Mrs Radleigh. She wore a plain linen dress with a matching short-sleeved jacket. An expensive-looking diamond brooch was pinned to one lapel. Gold earrings and a plain gold chain in matching twists gleamed against her pale skin.

'What about his father?' he asked. 'Is he around?'

The headmaster and his wife exchanged a look. 'They're divorced,' Mr Radleigh said. 'When Madame Fournier signed Alain up with us, she insisted on using her maiden name. We did ask for the father's name — it helps if we're having trouble chasing up fees to have more than one point of contact — but she left that section of the registration form blank, and we didn't insist.'

'I'd like a list of names and addresses of Alain's classmates,' Mike said.

Mrs Radleigh cleared her throat. 'We would, of course, have to ask for parental permission before divulging such details.'

'Mrs Radleigh,' Mike said, 'we don't know what happened to the lad, but it must have been pretty bad for him to run off in the middle of the night and end up miles away from home, unable or unwilling to speak.'

Mrs Radleigh frowned. Her hair, an astonishing construction of body perm and hair spray, positively quivered with indignation at the contradiction. Mr Radleigh took a step forward. 'I'm sure our parents would be eager to do all they can to help, Sergeant,' he said, smiling. 'I suppose you will already have one or two names from your hotline . . .'

Mike looked up sharply. The headmaster's pale blue eyes showed guileless interest. 'The full list would be nice,' Mike said.

'You shall have it.' The courteous little bow was implied, a fabrication of the mind only, but it created a powerful image of the headmaster charming parents — circulating with easy grace at a social gathering, exchanging a decorous word here, a moment or two of gentle banter there, before moving on, beguiling and entertaining as he despatched cocktails.

'D'you keep pictures of the kids for the records?'

'Of course!' Radleigh slapped his forehead. 'It never occurred to me. His is fairly recent, which should help — he's only been with us for about eight months. You can pick it up from my secretary when I take you across for the class list.'

'Has there been any unusual activity around the school in the past week or so — anyone hanging around, any break-ins?'

The headmaster looked at his wife, his eyebrows raised slightly. She gazed back, wide eyed. 'None at all. We do have a problem from time to time with youths from Aigburth and Garston hopping over the wall to see if there's anything worth stealing, but we have a permanent night watchman now — ex-police dog patrol — he has two very well-trained dogs.'

'Would he have said if he'd had any trouble?'

'We have a debriefing every morning before school begins.'

Mrs Radleigh glanced at her husband, and then looked demurely away as she murmured something Mike couldn't quite catch.

'Oh, yes,' Radleigh said. 'Thank you darling. A couple of lads tried to steal some chairs from the pavilion a few nights ago, but apart from that, there's been nothing in the past two weeks.'

'What about daytime? No one loitering by the gates, no unfamiliar faces?'

'We have staff at the main gate to make sure the boys arrive and leave in an orderly fashion. They would have reported anything suspicious to me at the staff briefing at break time.'

'Didn't you think it was strange when Alain didn't turn up for school on Monday?' Mike asked.

'I should have thought it strange if he *had*. You see, term ended a week ago last Thursday for Harcourt, Sergeant.'

Radleigh's wife made a fluttering gesture with her hands, and murmured something like, 'Do you think we ought . . . ?'

Mr Radleigh frowned. 'If you think it may be relevant . . .'

'Oh, but I *do*, darling.'

Mike broke in, impatient that the conversation was being carried on as though he had become temporarily blind and deaf. 'It's hard to say what's relevant until it's been said. Sometimes not even then.'

'Quite,' Radleigh said, bringing his hand to the back of his head again and smoothing a hair that he must have imagined had contrived to get itself out of place. His hand finished up on the back of his neck and stayed there. 'We must allow the sergeant to judge for himself. You see, Sergeant Delaney, even if it had been term time, we should not have been unduly alarmed by Alain's absence.'

He paused. Mike could see that the headmaster was uncomfortable breaking a confidence in this way. 'If you can give us something on Alain's background it could help us trace his mother and give the people working with him a better chance of getting through to him,' he said.

'Yes, I can see that it would.' The hand came down and Radleigh took a deep breath before continuing. 'Madame

Fournier is rather prone to taking Alain out of school without permission.'

'Oh, yeah? What did you do about that?'

'We complained, of course. It is disruptive to a boy's education, having him out of school for two or three days at a time, but when it comes right down to it, there's really very little we *can* do.'

'There are laws covering unauthorized school absence, Mr Radleigh.'

Radleigh smiled. 'We are not the state sector, Mr Delaney. We like to think we can be a little more flexible.'

'Pays her fees on time, does she?'

The remark was calculated to cause offence, but Radleigh took it with a smile and a nod. 'I won't deny that it's a factor. Prep schools are going to the wall all over the country. Even in the more affluent areas of Merseyside there have been closures in the last few years, but I think we can safely say that we get the best from our boys, Sergeant, even with a lenient approach to occasional absences.'

'I can believe that,' Mike conceded, without irony. 'So, why does she keep him off — Sickness? Holidays? Or what?'

'Madame Fournier does a lot of business in France and Italy. She's an interior designer, and she buys ceramics, pottery and fabrics on the continent. She will, from time to time, leave the boy in our care, but . . .' He shrugged.

'Leave him in your care?' Mike asked. 'Is this a boarding school, then?'

'We have day boys as well as boarders — forty full-time and fifteen . . .' He turned to his wife. 'Is it fifteen, darling?' He turned back to Mike, having received confirmation. 'Fifteen weekly boarders.'

Mike formed a frivolous picture of fifteen *weakly* boys, cold and shivering, coughing and sniffing through whatever served as assembly here. He placed his cup and saucer on a spindle-legged table and wrote a few notes, while Mr and Mrs Radleigh waited courteously for him to finish.

'We have a little extra room, a few spare beds in case of emergencies, but Madame Fournier prefers not to let Alain stay over, if she can avoid it.' He hesitated, and Mike looked up.

'Sir?'

Radleigh glanced at his wife, but she looked away, leaving the decision to speak or remain silent to her husband. 'Alain's mother is, at times, a little oversolicitous of the boy.'

'That's it?' There was a silence. 'The lad won't talk to us, Mr Radleigh. Won't you speak *for* him?' The appeal to the man's sense of decency worked.

He took a breath, hesitated, then said, 'This is only an impression, Sergeant Delaney . . .'

'Whatever you can tell me . . .'

Radleigh paused, composing his thoughts. 'Alain was — *is* — a pleasant, quiet, hard-working little chap. He doesn't exactly light up a room when he enters it, but he's well-liked and he has friends. He's never a problem in school — except when his mother is around.'

'Yeah?'

'The fact is, he seems tense, anxious — perhaps even fearful — when his mother is present.' He shrugged. 'Perhaps I'm being unfair . . .' Mrs Radleigh murmured a reassurance that he was not.

'One occasionally comes across a parent, usually a mother, who will explain at length that her little boy is delicate, sensitive, nervous — and yet our picture of the child is very different. Often, it's a sort of projection of her anxieties onto the child. We did try to persuade her to let him board on a termly basis, but she wouldn't have it.'

'Said she needed him near her.' Mrs Radleigh's expression said she neither gave the notion much credence, nor did she sympathize with Madame Fournier.

'Have you got anyone staying at the moment?' Mike asked.

'As I explained, Sergeant,' Radleigh said patiently, 'the summer *exeat* began just over a week ago.'

'And none of the lads go home a bit late?'

They both laughed. 'We are *very* fond of our boys, Sergeant,' the headmaster said, 'but we wouldn't allow *that*.'

'Not even a day or two late, like Saturday morning?'

'What *are* you suggesting?' Radleigh demanded, momentarily losing his good humour and impeccable manners. 'That Alain boarded with us on Friday evening and we let him wander off and did nothing to prevent it? Worse still, that we didn't report his disappearance to the police?'

Mike heard a little gasp from Mrs Radleigh and she exclaimed, 'What an extraordinary idea!'

'Who looks after the boarders?' Mike asked, determined to follow through his 'extraordinary idea'.

'Cannon Jones,' Radleigh said.

'A vicar, is he?'

Radleigh shook his head. 'Cannon with two Ns — it's is his nickname.'

'What's he called Cannon for?'

'I think it had something to do with a television detective in the 1970s — the name was bestowed upon him before our time. Look, is this really relevant?'

'Like I said—'

'Yes, yes,' Radleigh interrupted. 'It's difficult to know.'

'How long have you been here?' Mike asked.

'Twelve years.'

Long enough to know what he's on about, Mike thought. Long enough to be given the boot if he didn't fit in. 'Where is Madame Fournier now?' he asked.

'I really couldn't say.' Radleigh sounded genuinely apologetic. 'During the holidays, we simply don't know what family arrangements might be.'

Mike nodded. 'Okay. I'd like a word with "Cannon" Jones.'

* * *

They called in at his secretary's office to provide Mike with photocopies of school documentation on Alain. Mike looked over the secretary's shoulder as she riffled through the files. 'Can you photocopy any forms or letters for me, as well?'

She did not answer, but looked to the headmaster for approval, passing Mike a photograph of Alain — Paul, as Mike knew him — before getting up from her desk to go to the photocopier.

'It's a good likeness,' he said. 'I'll take the original, if that's okay. We'll take copies and let you have it back.' He stepped outside to phone through to the incident room and gave the boy's name and address to DI Crank.

Radleigh showed him to Jones's flat personally. Whether this was because he didn't trust his secretary to keep her mouth shut or another example of the old-world courtesy that Mike found both charming and infuriating in the man, he couldn't be sure, but he was glad of the escort. The school layout was confusing — a clutter of doorways and corridors and narrow staircases which seemed to serve single rooms and store cupboards. The headmaster fell silent. Mike sensed that he was struggling with something, wondering if he should say what was on his mind.

'Whatever it is, it's best said.' Mike glanced at the headmaster. 'If it helps us find out what happened to Alain . . .'

Radleigh nodded gravely. 'No doubt the Social Services people have already told you this, but . . . Alain—' He stopped. 'One notices when boys board, you see. We insist on them having a bath when they stay — even if it's only overnight.'

'You noticed the scars.'

'The duty staff did, and of course they reported it to me. Some of them looked like cigarette burns.' He shuddered. 'He also suffers from enuresis.'

'Enu—?'

'Bed-wetting. Of course, he's only eight, but it is relatively unusual in our boys. And a sign of psychological disturbance.'

'Yeah,' Mike said. 'So I'm told.'

Cannon Jones's rooms were in a far corner of the main building, and this, too, was a maze of corridors and cubby-holes, stairways and landings.

‘There is a corpus of staff who live in,’ Radleigh explained. ‘It’s essential to provide the level of cover we need to look after the boarders.’

They were walking down a long corridor, having taken several turns after entering through the central doorway — it seemed the school building was constructed in the shape of a letter E. The gleaming wood block floors looked newly polished, and the smell of wax was sharp. Mike remembered his own school corridors as steeped in the old smells of smoked haddock and steamed pudding, its classrooms reeking of stale sweat and fresh farts. At Harcourt, it seemed all unsavoury odours were eradicated by the vigorous attentions of the cleaning staff, who were present in impressive numbers but seen only at a distance.

As they passed, Mike glanced at the oil paintings which lined the walls of the corridor. Each bore a small explanatory plaque.

‘Former headmasters and old boys who have made a significant contribution to society,’ Radleigh said, adding after a moment’s thought, ‘Or to the school.’ He was going through the motions of his prospective parents’ tour speech. The pauses, and the sly, self-effacing jokes were obviously well-rehearsed, and Mike guessed he could generally rely upon getting a laugh from that one. Unless the ‘prospectives’ were foreign, or below the blurred boundary of middle and working class.

Mike jerked his chin. ‘If my old school carried pictures of past notables, they’d be mostly mug shots.’

Radleigh made a small sound of commiseration.

At the end of the corridor there were two broad staircases, both wooden, both freshly waxed. ‘The left staircase leads to the dorms, the right one to the staff bedrooms,’ the headmaster explained.

They mounted the right staircase and, glancing left, Mike saw that there was a connecting door through to the dormitories.

‘It’s left unlocked at night,’ Radleigh told him. ‘Should a boy need access to the duty master.’

Mr Jones's rooms were at the end of a dark, creaking corridor, one flight of stairs up from the main staff accommodation. Radleigh knocked, and within seconds the door was flung open and a barrel-shaped man with a straight, nailbrush-stiff moustache bounced out into the corridor and ushered them in. Mike suddenly made the connection: Frank Cannon, the seventies TV detective whose trademark was obesity. Introductions completed, he led them through to a large and comfortably furnished room. It was redolent of bachelorhood: the all-pervading smell of cigars that Mike had noticed in the Radleighs' sitting room, leather sofas and brass reading lamps and acres and acres of books. The room seemed a little fusty, in want of some fresh air, but it had the well-kept look of a place routinely swept out and polished by someone paid to do the job.

Mr Jones was already dressed, and had apparently breakfasted, if the tantalizing smell of bacon and toast was anything to go by. It appeared that Mr Jones rated a higher specification of accommodation than the bedroom and shared bathroom that most staff were granted: there were doors either end of the main sitting room, and the breakfast smells attested to the fact that he evidently had his own kitchen.

'Do sit down, Sergeant,' Jones said.

Mike walked to an armchair by the window. The sound of the mower was clearer here, and through the latticework of the lead lights he could see a tractor trundling up and down the sunny field at the back of the school.

'Now, what can I do for you?' Mr Jones asked.

'When did Alain Fournier last stay over?' Mike asked.

'Ah.' He looked momentarily troubled.

Mike narrowed his eyes. 'Mr Jones?'

'Alain . . . Alain? My memory! Well, it can't have been during the summer term because — well, because it's only just gone and I'm sure I should have remembered.' He laughed nervously, and Mike, immediately suspicious, asked if he kept a register of the boys.

'Yes,' Jones said, flustered. 'Yes, of course.' He shuffled his bulk to the edge of the sofa and boosted himself up. 'I, um . . .' He rooted around in a dark, roughly carved sideboard, shuffling papers and thumping books one on top of another until he found what he was looking for. 'Here we are!' The register was an A4 hard-bound book, labelled *Short-Stay Boarders*. Jones flipped through. 'There. He last stayed with us from March the tenth to the thirteenth.'

Mike put his hand out, and for a moment the old man seemed reluctant to give up the book, then he handed it over, with a quick glance at his headmaster.

The entries started in 1996 and continued through to the summer of 1999. Each new day was ruled off in black ink and the boys' names were entered by hand.

'Rising oblique for presence at evening roll call, falling oblique for morning,' Jones said, plucking at the edges of the book, but Mike wasn't ready to surrender it yet. 'We wouldn't want to lose any of the blighters during the night!'

'It's a lot of work, filling in the names like that every day.' Cannon Jones was jumpy, and Mike wanted to know why.

'We found it worked best for the Irregulars — our name for short-stay boarders. One doesn't know day to day who will be here and who not. To avoid confusion, we enter those present at evening roll call.'

'A list is provided by my secretary for the duty master, so he knows what to expect,' Radleigh interrupted. 'We can't have boys just turning up unexpectedly.'

'Right,' Mike said, then tapped the entry for the twelfth of March. 'There he is.' He continued thumbing through the pages. He could feel Mr Jones's increasing agitation, and this made him study them even more closely. 'So, there's a separate register for the regular boarders?' he asked.

'Hmm,' said Jones. 'The same as a day register.' Then, as if suddenly realizing that this might be his deliverance, with a little bound, he returned to the sideboard and withdrew a standard school register. 'Here it is! All the Regulars are listed, as you see . . .'

But Mike did not see. He was looking at the entry for the thirtieth of June. Alain Fournier's name had been added to the end of the list. A rising oblique in the first column noted the boy's presence at evening roll call, and a neat, oval nought in the second column recorded his absence in the morning. A red capital L had been entered over the nought.

Mr Jones had fallen silent.

'I thought you said Alain hadn't stayed over during the summer term, Mr Jones.'

'Oh dear, oh dear . . .' The man was positively quivering with nervous energy. 'What will you think of me, Sergeant?'

'And why is he in the regular boarders' register, if he's — what did you call them — an *Ir*regular?'

'Cannon,' said Radleigh carefully, 'please explain.'

'Yes,' Mike said, 'I'd be interested to hear this.'

Cannon Jones look deeply distressed. 'I assure you, it has absolutely no relevance.'

Mike almost laughed outright. 'You know,' he said, 'I'm getting really hacked off with people here telling me what's relevant and what isn't.'

Mr Jones looked near to tears. 'Alain did stay with us for one night on the thirtieth of June. His listing in the Regulars' register was a simple error — the duty master is a new member of staff, and he mistakenly entered Alain in the wrong book.'

'I'll want a word with him,' Mike said, and Mr Radleigh nodded. 'But I'm more interested in why Alain was initially marked absent for morning roll call on the first of July.'

Cannon Jones had turned brick red. 'I'm afraid . . .' he said, addressing his headmaster, rather than Mike, 'that Alain was missing at morning registration. We looked for him all over the building — you can imagine, we were frantic — but he wasn't to be found. Eventually one of the boys suggested we try the pavilion.' He smoothed his moustache, his hand atremble. 'We found him asleep on one of the benches. A sleepwalking incident — they happen from time to time, when boys are in strange surroundings. Simply that.

There was *nothing* sinister in it.' He turned away from Mike, appealing directly to Radleigh. 'It wasn't worth mentioning. A minor incident, no harm done.'

'When a boy goes missing, it is always worth mentioning,' Radleigh said, stiffly. Then, 'We'll discuss this further.'

Mr Jones mumbled a meek, 'Yes, Headmaster.'

Mike leafed through the remaining pages of the register. Alain had not stayed overnight at the school after the thirtieth of June.

'Right,' Mike said, embarrassed on Jones's behalf. 'I think I've got all I need.'

'Let me show you out, Sergeant,' Radleigh said, but he did not take his eyes from Jones. Mike began to demur, but he wasn't sure he could find the way back without a guide, so he didn't argue when the headmaster said, 'I insist. This will wait until later.'

At the bottom of the stairs, Radleigh turned to him. 'Mr Delaney, I can only apologize. I assure you—'

'Mr Radleigh, maybe it's significant that Alain's prone to sleepwalking, maybe it isn't — it could have some bearing on what happened to him, or how he came to be wandering the streets, but since he wasn't in your care at the time . . .'

The headmaster inclined his head, graciously. 'If you've time, I can ask my secretary to telephone the duty master who checked Alain in on the thirtieth.'

Mike checked his watch. 'I've got a meeting at ten thirty — I'll barely make it in time, through the rush hour traffic.'

'Of course — I'm sorry to keep you. I'll ask her to find his number and pass it on to you.' He frowned, all surface gloss and pretence gone. 'I can assure you this lapse of care *will* be dealt with.'

'I don't doubt it,' Mike said.

Radleigh nodded, coughed. 'Will you call at Alain's home address before you go to your meeting?'

'I wish I could.' Mike had come so far with this side of the investigation. He would like to have carried it through at least to questioning the mother — if she was fit for questioning. DI Crank would have called the hospital with the news and despatched a team to the Fournier residence as soon as he'd ended the call. 'I can't miss this meeting,' he said, in half-admonishment to himself.

CHAPTER 15

As it turned out, Mike Delaney made it to the case review meeting at the hospital with minutes to spare, after spending fifteen minutes snarled in traffic behind a minor shunt. But ten minutes into the meeting, DC Sallis had interrupted, and Mike knew before Sallis had said a word — knew from the look on his face — that a body had been found.

'She's been positively identified?'

Sallis nodded. 'By the cleaning lady — it's Mrs Fournier, all right. She got to the house at half past nine and found the body in the kitchen.'

The men were talking in a small office adjacent to the conference room and sweltering in the soaring heat — there were too many compelling reasons for keeping the door shut to ignore them.

'Looks like the motive was robbery,' Sallis said. 'Money scattered about, and her purse was missing from her handbag. Possibly credit cards an' all.'

'Cause of death?'

'We're waiting on the pathologist, but there was a hell of a lot of blood, Mike. Cuts to her arms, too. It looks like she's been there a while.'

'Maybe since last weekend?'

Sallis shrugged. 'This hot weather, it's hard to say. Scene-of-Crime team are picking over the house as we speak. The pathologist asked for them to leave the body *in situ*.'

Mike nodded. 'Well, we'll just have to wait for him to get there,' he said.

* * *

DC Sallis watched DS Delaney leave, keeping his back straight until the door closed. Then he slumped against a table and wiped his brow.

The place had been teaming with uniformed police when he'd arrived. A WPC stood guard at the door. The facade bowed outward at the centre of the building, drawing a smooth white curve to form the portico, which was supported by two pillars of gleaming white stone. She might almost have been a token bobby standing outside an embassy building. He showed his warrant card and stepped into the hallway. Only it wasn't a hallway, it was an entrance hall like he had only ever seen in films: black and white tiles in a geometric design and the concave sweep of the outer wall painted in an abstract fresco of yellow and black. A staircase curved left from the centre of the entrance, mirroring the line of the portico, but reddish-brown stains marred the pristine beauty of the marble balustrade. He could smell it already. Death permeated the entire house, declaring its presence, staking its claim.

The cleaning woman sat in a chair just inside the front door. She looked grey, in shock, and kept wiping her hand with a tissue and muttering over and over: 'I thought I saw her move. I touched her . . . Under the skin, there was—God help me!' She shuddered violently.

He got her details and a brief statement of how she'd found the body, then touched her lightly on the shoulder before heading inside.

A second constable stood at the door of a room to the right of the staircase.

‘In there?’ Sallis asked, unnecessarily. He really didn’t want to go into that room, although he knew he had to, because DI Crank would be expecting a detailed report and such things cannot be had second hand. All that stopped him from turning around and walking out were self-respect and self-interest. By speaking to the PC, even those two words, he had established contact, which would make it more difficult for him to do the cowardly thing and leave. Sallis did not have a strong stomach and did not find death any easier for having seen it before and in a number of guises.

He tried a trick that sometimes worked: he studied the PC. Looking for signs of distress in others was apt to make him forget his own. The officer was pale. He had removed his jacket, and damp patches of sweat showed under the arms of his short-sleeved shirt. He seemed to be having trouble with his breathing.

No bloody wonder, his inner voice intruded. *The corpse is ripe. Very ripe.*

As he drew closer, he, too, modified his breathing, taking shallower breaths, exhaling through his nose in snuffling little snorts. ‘Has anyone contacted the Home Office pathologist?’ Sallis asked, knowing the answer, but needing the distraction of words to prevent him thinking.

‘He’s out on a call. Be here as soon as he can. A police surgeon’s on his way to confirm death.’ The young officer was staring past him, towards the staircase. He sounded strained, strangulated almost, trying to swallow down as he spoke.

‘SOCOs?’ Sallis asked. This was not working.

‘Hmm.’

‘Look,’ Sallis said, taking pity on the lad, ‘why don’t you get a breath of air? I’ll keep an eye on things till you feel a bit brighter. It’s okay, I’m not gonna trample all over the evidence. I’ll just take a look from the doorway, all right?’ He waited for the constable to flee, then, taking a clean, pressed handkerchief from his pocket and holding it to his mouth and nose, he opened the door.

The woman lay face down in a dried and cracked oasis of blood. She had dark, curly hair, at about shoulder length, and she was wearing a sleeveless dress. She was barefoot. Sallis didn't need a pathologist to tell him that those marks on her arms were defence cuts, any more than he needed a police surgeon to confirm that she was dead.

Across an expanse of Italian floor tiles, a few brownish footprints led to the outer door. It stood ajar. He did a sweep of the kitchen, trying to concentrate but finding it difficult with the distracting buzz of flies busily zipping in and out through the open door. Sallis swallowed, thinking about the cleaner's horrified exclamation: *I touched her . . . Under the skin, there was—*

No. He didn't want to think about that — leave the grisly details for the SOCOs and the pathologists who get paid to look at that sort of thing.

The kitchen was the size of an average family restaurant. Streaks of green in the tiles echoed the carefully distressed effect of the rustic green units. The wall tiles were a patchwork of cream, darker green and terracotta. The oven and hob looked like it belonged in a restaurant, too: it dominated the centre of the room in a square island of steel technology, industrial quality. Serious housekeeping, this.

He tried to prevent his eye being drawn to the body, but it was constantly dragged back to that one focal point in the room. She lay to the right of the central island, her right arm curved over her head, her left leg slightly bent. He forced himself to try again. This time, he noticed something else, something partly hidden by the oven housing: the leather strap of a shoulder bag and a few coins scattered across the floor. He'd asked the SOCOs to check the bag, knowing the forensics team would have his guts if he messed with the scene. No purse. Robbery, then. And had the little boy seen it happen? He'd found it hard enough to look at this — how much harder for a child of seven or eight years old?

* * *

'D'you want to wait for Mike to get back or shall we carry on?' Jenny asked.

'Let's get on with it,' Fraser said. He had been ill-tempered and impatient all morning.

Max leaned back in his chair and peered through the open door into the corridor. 'No sign of him,' he said. 'I'm with Fraser on this.'

'But if he has some news of Alain's parents—'

'We'll backtrack,' Fraser insisted.

Jenny gave him a long, cool stare, then started distributing copies of her notes, and after a few minutes silence, in which the conference members read through them, she and Fraser began giving details of their observations over the past week.

'He — Alain—' She had to remind herself that he had a name now. 'Alain is vocalizing more now, but he won't speak directly to us.'

'I've heard nursery rhymes — something like that,' Fraser said. 'I couldn't make it out. Could've been French, now that I think of it.'

'The nightmares are getting worse,' Jenny went on. 'He's terrified, but it's difficult to make sense of what he says.'

'Now we have a name, perhaps Social Services can trawl the records for any history of abuse?'

'If he isn't registered "at risk" he could be difficult to trace, even with a name,' Gina said.

Max spread his hands. 'We may be able to find the hospital that treated the injuries to his hands. But it'll take time.'

'What about the interim care order?' Jenny asked.

'Granted. I was in court yesterday. But we need more on the kid.' Gina laughed. 'Correction — we need *something* on him!'

'We've a name, at least,' Max said.

'We've a lot more than that.'

They all looked toward the doorway, where Mike Delaney stood. He crossed the room and stood by the open window.

'Bad news?' Jenny asked.

Mike took a gulp of air, then sat down. 'The worst. A body's been found at the Fournier house. We've had a positive ID . . . It's his mother.'

There was a moment's silence. Fraser reached for Jenny's hand. 'Murder?' he asked.

'Looks like. We'll have to wait for the pathologist's report—' He shrugged. 'What the hell — yeah, it looks very much like murder.'

Jenny threw Max a look which said, *So much for the gypsy child theory.*

Max's eyebrows quirked in silent apology, then, turning again to Mike, he asked, 'What next?'

'We try and trace next of kin,' Mike said. 'His school gave me a contact number in France for Maurice and Dominique Fournier — her parents — we'll speak to them first, and we'll see if we can track down the father at the same time.' In the silence that followed, Mike looked at each person around the conference table. 'We can't rule out the father as a suspect, of course, but it looks more like a random attack. They're divorced and probably weren't even in contact. She may have disturbed a burglar, got into a fight with him, ended up dead.'

'And Alain may have witnessed it,' Max said.

PART II

CHAPTER 16

'Getting a good eyeful, Olly?'

DC Weston looked up, startled from his leisurely appreciation of Lisa Calcot's legs. 'What?' She had her bloody back to him. 'How the hell—?'

'Eyes in the back of my head.'

'Sorry.'

She smiled, turning to him. 'All is forgiven — if you make the coffee — I know it's not your turn,' she added before he could complain. 'That's the point.' She waited for him to brew up, while she doodled on the notebook next to the phone. They had been discussing Mike Delaney's suggestion that Connor Harvey may have been abducted, talking in circles for half an hour.

The phone rang and Calcot answered it. 'Mike, we were just talking about you.' There was a pause. Calcot stopped doodling and started writing with a purpose. 'When? . . . Rough guess, Mike — we've got a MisPer this end as well, don't forget.'

Weston heard the urgency on her tone and signalled her, wanting to know what was being said. She waved for him to be quiet.

'Oh, shit!' A pause, then, 'Yeah, I know, but if there *is* a connection and we've been sitting on our hands for a week—' Mike interrupted and she listened for a moment or two, then said, 'Thanks for the info. If your lad does say anything . . . You will? Cheers.' She hung up and stared at the phone.

'So?' Weston demanded.

'Mike Delaney.'

'I gathered that much. What did he want?'

'Liverpool's found a body. Their lad's mum.' She looked up at Weston. 'She's been there a while, Jim.'

'Oh, shit!'

'That's what I said.' For a while, neither of them said a word, then the kettle clicked off and Weston made their drinks, going through the motions without thinking.

'So,' Calcot said, taking the coffee mug Weston offered to her. 'What've we got? Two lads who look pretty much the same. One — Connor — is attacked outside his school. Attempted abduction. A few days later, he goes missing, and we've still not located him. The other — Alain — witnesses the murder of his mum and runs for it.'

'Speculation,' Weston said, blowing on his tea. He dragged a chair over and sat next to Calcot, took a digestive biscuit from the packet on her desk and began crunching thoughtfully.

'It may well be speculation, but it's the best guess we've got for now.' Calcot took a sip of coffee, grimaced and added a couple of sweeteners from the dispenser she always carried in her pocket. 'The same day Connor disappears Alain's mother is killed. He runs off — escapes?'

Weston shrugged. 'Maybe.'

'And is found miles from home.'

'Struck dumb,' Weston reminded her.

'Yes.'

Weston took a second biscuit and dipped it into his tea. 'There's nothing to connect the two boys, bar a passing resemblance to each other. Chances are young Connor's having a whale of a time getting spoilt rotten by his dad.'

'I bloody hope so,' Calcot said fervently. 'But if that *is* the case, why hasn't Mr Harvey got in touch?'

'His wife's told us they're safe and well. Why should he?'

'Because we've asked him to.'

Weston conceded the point.

'Anyway, Mrs H isn't exactly playing straight with us.'

Weston nodded — another point to Lisa Calcot. In fact, Weston reflected, Mrs Harvey was treading a very narrow line between guileless disorganization and culpable obstructiveness. He opened his mouth, but Lisa asked the question for him.

'So where *is* dad?'

Disconcerting, he thought, *the way she seems to know what I'm about to say*. Weston sucked the last piece of tea-soaked biscuit between his teeth with great satisfaction. 'Come on then, if you're coming,' he said, heading for the door.

'Where to?'

'That's a relief,' Weston said, enjoying Calcot's puzzlement. 'I was beginning to think you could read my bloody mind!'

* * *

The staff at Creative Plastics were very cooperative. The receptionist gave them coffee while she located Mr Preston, their senior manager. Mr Preston was charm itself. He was immaculately dressed, in the sharp, hard-edged manner of young businessmen, and his clear blue eyes betrayed no sign of caprice. He showed them to his office and instructed his secretary to hold all calls.

'We last heard from Mr Harvey last Friday,' he said. 'He went home for lunch. We got a brief call at about half one to say he'd decided to take some time off.'

'Does he do that?' Weston asked, 'I mean, is it usual?'

Preston debated a moment. 'It depends what you mean by usual.' He flicked a speck of lint from the sleeve of his suit jacket. Calcot thought she saw a hint of a blush on his face.

‘When was the last time he took time off at short notice?’ she asked.

‘I’m not sure . . .’ He couldn’t meet her eye.

‘Well,’ Calcot said, ‘was it recent? Say, in the last six months.’ Preston seemed to be having trouble thinking back. ‘Mr Preston, has he *ever* taken time off at short notice?’

Preston did not answer, and Weston reached over to the intercom on his desk. ‘Shall we call in your secretary and see if her memory’s any more reliable?’

Preston’s hand darted forward to prevent him pushing the button. Weston glared at him, and Preston withdrew, thrummed the desktop for a second or two, then with a slight shrug, he said, ‘Mr Harvey always plans his time off.’

‘How did he seem?’ Calcot asked. Preston stared blankly at her. ‘Did he sound like a man about to go off on a well-earned break or . . . ?’ Preston clamped his mouth shut as if afraid he would let something slip.

‘Your reluctance does you credit, Mr Preston,’ Calcot said, soothingly. ‘You don’t want to appear disloyal. But we’re here because we’re concerned about Mr Harvey.’

He dipped his head in a defensive gesture. ‘It’s really none of my business.’

‘You know his son’s missing?’ Calcot asked.

‘They found him — I mean, didn’t they? With Mr Harvey.’ He broke off, and Calcot gave him a moment to consider the illogicality of what he had said.

After a suitable pause, she spoke his thoughts for him. ‘Since we don’t know where Mr Harvey is, how could we have found his son?’

Preston grew decidedly red around the eyes. ‘It’s just — I mean Mrs Harvey—’

‘What about Mrs Harvey?’ Weston demanded.

‘She said there’d been a mistake — Connor was with his father — we weren’t to keep troubling him.’

‘Troubling him how?’

He shook his head, all trace of slick businessman gone.

'We just want to be sure they're both safe,' Calcot said, kindly.

She waited, and at last Preston said, 'We've been trying his mobile, but it's switched off. He's not answering his home phone, and he doesn't reply to his emails. I even went to his home address.'

'Is there anything that might have triggered his sudden disappearance?'

Preston picked up his pen and clicked it agitatedly.

'Mr Preston?' she said sharply.

He twitched, then with a sigh put down the pen. 'I think there may have been some trouble at home.'

CHAPTER 17

'Shona!'

She had virtually run into Max at the main entrance. She was looking over her shoulder as if in terror of some pursuing evil. She gave a yelp of surprise and dismay and glanced around the foyer, searching for an escape route.

'Shona?' He reached to touch her arm, but she shrank back, and he let his hand fall. She looked terrible. He hadn't seen her like this since he had treated her as an in-patient over two years previously. He looked into her face, trying to establish eye contact, but she looked at the floor, the murals decorating the walls, the reception desk, anywhere but at him.

He had seen her at the lecture, with the recovered memory lobbyists, gazing adoringly at the woman at the centre of her group. Shona was impressionable, emotionally vulnerable, and she would believe whatever was suggested to her, whatever they *wanted* her to believe.

'They can't help you,' he said.

She gave a little cry and covered her mouth.

'I saw you,' he said, gently. 'On Wednesday.'

She looked up at him, fleetingly, her eyes wide with alarm.

'Why don't you come and see me? We'll sort something out.' He was busy, and strictly speaking, at nineteen years of age, Shona was no longer within his remit: he was paediatric psychiatry. But since he had already blurred the boundaries by taking an interest in recovered memory, why not take it a step further? Anyway, Shona was an ex-patient. He couldn't very well abandon her simply because she had passed an arbitrary line.

'I'm late!' she said, still refusing to look at him.

'All right, but I won't take no for an answer.'

She darted past him into the building, and he sighed as he stepped out.

Max had an afternoon appointment in Manchester. He sauntered out to his car in his shirt sleeves, deep in thought. The next few days would be crucial for Alain. He was confident Jenny could cope, but the discovery that the child's mother had been murdered confirmed the feeling that had returned again and again since he had first been found. There was a horrible tragedy at the centre of this particular mystery. While the boy remained mute, it would be impossible to broach the subject of his mother's murder with him. While he had nobody to correct his feelings of guilt, Alain might be taking the responsibility for his mother's death upon himself, and until he identified the killer, Alain must still be at risk of further attack.

The brickwork and the tarmac of the hospital car park had already begun to absorb the heat of the day and the buildings seemed almost to glow peach and gold, reflecting the accumulated warmth. Max fumbled in his jacket pocket for his keys, wondering how to advise Jenny to proceed.

He had left the driver's window partly open — foolish, perhaps, with opportunistic thieves always on the prowl, but Max was inclined to think that anyone who took a fancy to his ageing Rover V8 would have to be eccentric, if not stupid. And they would be more than welcome to the repair bills that had become a monthly feature over the past half year. Someone had told him the car was a modern classic, but Max himself could not see the attraction of a faded, mud-brown rust bucket, with its cracked vinyl seats, broken clock and temperamental gearbox, an engine that could burn a couple of pints of oil in as many weeks, and did twenty-seven miles to the gallon on a good day, with a following wind. He would get around to buying a new car when he found time, but there never seemed to be enough time for the simplest organizational tasks of living.

He got the door open and slid gingerly behind the wheel, concentrating too hard on the extreme discomfort of hot black vinyl against thinly covered skin to notice, at first, that the dashboard was tidy. His Liverpool, Manchester and Southport copies of the *A to Z* were stacked neatly on the passenger seat, together with a tape of Bob Dylan's *Blood on the Tracks,* discarded when his tape recorder had finally died two months previously, the tape disgorging its contents like some animal grossly parasitized by worms.

It was only when Max reached automatically for his bag of mint imperials that he noticed their absence. In their place was a small bottle in the shape of the Virgin Mary. He picked it up and turned it in his hands, making her perform a stately pirouette. The bottle was hot and soft and, as he turned the figure, he noticed that the crown, which also formed the lid of the bottle, had been put on askew, giving her a jaunty, less than dignified look. He glanced up and round, but, apart from a mother who had just arrived with her little girl, the car park seemed deserted.

He tipped the bottle. The line of water came to about waist height of the garments, about level with her sky-blue sash, and he wondered, with a slightly queasy sense of unease, if his car had been exorcized. An image of a crazed woman flicking holy water around the interior of his car, trying to dispel the evil pervading it, filled his mind's eye and he felt a chill of realization: Jenny was right, whoever had broken into his house — whoever was watching him — had nothing to do with the boy. It was his interest in recovered memory that had made him a target.

He glanced uneasily around the car park. It was now empty of people — the brief hiatus between morning and afternoon clinics creating a lull that allowed the constant tuneless chirrup of a sparrow to break into his consciousness. He stared at the metallic reflections of light and colour from the cars, aware of an unseen menace, watching, waiting to strike.

CHAPTER 18

'Memory isn't static, Fraser,' Jenny said. 'It's affected by our present state of mind, our present beliefs, by what's happened to us since the event.' She drove out of the hospital car park and headed for Queens Drive.

'So, the longer young Alain refuses to talk, the more likely his memory of what happened will become confused?'

She nodded. 'D'you remember what you were doing when you heard the news of Princess Diana's death?'

'Yeah, I was coming home from Sefton Park with that wee lad that was afraid of ducks — remember him? — Billy, that was it. Gordon Paget stopped me and told me what'd happened.'

'You're sure about that, are you?'

'Well, of course I'm sure. It's not the kind of thing you're likely to forget, is it?'

'You'd think not.'

'Okay, smart arse, tell me why I'm wrong.'

'I don't know if you're wrong. I was at work that day, so how would I know?'

'But . . . ?'

Traffic was light, and Jenny eased the car into the outside lane and accelerated, heading towards Penny Lane. 'In

1986, an American academic team did a survey — about a hundred students. Asked them to fill in a questionnaire the day after the Challenger disaster. What they were doing when they heard the news that the space shuttle had blown up: details of their lives, how they found out — that kind of thing. Then eighteen months later they asked the same people to fill in exactly the same questionnaire.'

'And they couldn't remember?'

'Oh, they remembered all right,' Jenny said. 'A totally different set of facts. The interviewing researchers were then instructed to check the new questionnaire against the old and give them clues as to what they had originally written. That didn't jog their memories. Then they showed them the questionnaires, written in their own hand eighteen months previously, and guess what?'

'I wouldn't want to spoil your fun.'

She shot him an amused glance. 'They insisted the original answers were wrong. That their new responses were what *really* happened. They discounted responses written *in their own hand* at the time of the disaster.'

Fraser was silent for some time. At last, he said, 'You're saying that people forget what actually happened to them, and unless they've written contemporaneous notes, you can't rely on anything they say.'

'Not quite. People don't forget what's important. I mean, it doesn't really *matter* that you were walking Billy home from the park when you heard. What matters is that Diana died. That fact is immutable.'

He shifted in his seat. 'Are you telling me it's impossible to forget that you were abused?'

'No. It *is* possible to forget abuse. Something like forty percent of victims can't remember documented abuse later in life. But the majority of abuse is not violent. And controversial though it sounds, not all abuse is traumatic. If it isn't traumatic, it's more likely to be forgotten.'

'Aren't you more likely to *want* to forget the more traumatic kind?' Fraser asked, thinking about the boy.

'God, yes,' she sighed. 'But forgetting is a passive process. You can't *make* yourself forget, you just . . . do, because you haven't thought about it for some time. Traumatic events are much harder to forget. Memories of fires, car crashes, violent events — including violent sexual assault — remain, even when we try to suppress them. They can get fragmented or muddled — and different people will remember the event in a different way, depending on their personal perspective — but the memory is not obliterated entirely.'

She felt his gaze on her.

'What does that mean for Alain?' he said at last.

'That's what worries me. He's so withdrawn. I mean, what if he witnessed the murder?'

'Why can't you just ask him straight out?'

'Because without the words to express how he feels, we would be asking him to relive a terrible thing all on his own. And even if he *didn't* see his mother murdered, there's a risk he might tell us what he thinks we want to hear.'

'No — surely . . . ?'

'There are dozens of documented cases,' she said. 'They had to *rewrite the book* on interviewing suspected victims after the Orkney child sexual abuse scandal in the early nineties. Four families torn apart, nine children traumatized, an entire community riven by spurious accusations of satanic sexual abuse. Children coerced into giving accounts of abuse that *never* happened.'

'I remember it,' Fraser said, nodding. 'Aye, it was horrible . . .'

'And that's why we can't ask Alain if he saw his mother murdered. When he's able to communicate, we can ask him what happened — why he was wandering the street in his nightclothes — but we have to be very, very careful not to put ideas in his head.'

* * *

They stopped off at the supermarket. Jenny would need to be around as much as possible over the next few days, and since Fraser couldn't drive, it made sense to stock up while they had the chance.

'I'll need to get back to work this afternoon,' Fraser said, reaching into a refrigerator cabinet for a packet of cheddar cheese. He placed it carefully in the trolley, avoiding her gaze.

'You're not serious?'

'What?' He straightened up, hands slightly spread, a picture of affronted innocence.

'Alain's mother is dead. I can't tell him that in his present state, but I'm going to go home and call him by name. I don't know what his reaction will be, maybe he'll carry on locking me out, but he's got to deal with it some time, I don't know when, but it might be today. I need you with me, love, please!'

'I've got some stuff to do,' Fraser said, when they reached the car.

'You've got the entire holiday for work, Fraser.'

'This won't wait.'

'What — taking down your "Farming around the world" posters and tidying your stockroom won't wait?'

'Thanks.'

She took a breath. 'I'm sorry. But look at it from my perspective: you're telling me this in Tesco's, between the cheeses and the cooked meats, an hour after we've been told the boy's mother has been murdered.'

'For pity's sake!' he whispered. 'Keep your voice down.'

'QED.' Jenny slapped a packet of boiled ham into the trolley.

'What's that supposed to mean?'

'It means you're bloody transparent. You wait until we're in a public place, where you imagine I won't make a scene and then tell me you're leaving me to do the hard bit.'

'You seem to be doing fine without any help from me.'

Jenny stopped the trolley. 'Fraser, we're not in competition here. The boy's mother was *murdered*, for God's sake!'

A middle-aged woman paused mid-reach and shot Jenny an alarmed look.

'It's probable the killer was a man,' Jenny went on. 'So it isn't all that surprising that he's a bit wary of you. Don't take it so damned personally.' The woman was transfixed by the extraordinary conversation and when Jenny asked her testily, 'Is my trolley in your way?' she took a packet of cooked meat at random and hurried on.

'If I could postpone this, I would,' Fraser said, 'but it's too important.'

Jenny stared at him. 'What's changed between this morning and now?'

He shrugged. 'I didn't ask you to bring him home.'

Jenny looked at him a little longer, trying to fathom what it was that was making him so mean tempered, then she shook her head and they completed the rest of the shopping in a confused mood of resentfulness and regret, both fuming, both unwilling to break the silence.

'It's end of term,' Jenny said, making a final plea as they made their way to the car. 'You said yourself you've only two lessons to teach with all your year eleven and upper sixth kids gone. You said you'd take the day off.'

It was at times like this that Jenny was reminded just how much she had depended on her mother. When they had retired, her parents had sold up in Liverpool, bought a cottage on the coast, not far from Blackpool, but her father had died suddenly, two days after they had moved in, and it seemed to Jenny that the onset of her mother's dementia could be dated to the funeral. They had tried taking her with them on holiday the previous year, but she became so distressed by the unfamiliar surroundings that Jenny had had to drive her back to the nursing home only days after they had set out.

'You take the car,' Fraser said. 'I'll get the bus.'

'You take it,' Jenny said. It was a cheap jibe, childish and spiteful, but Fraser's reaction was unexpectedly emphatic.

'What d'you mean by that? I can't drive, you know I can't drive.'

She knew it. They both did. It had been the subject of frequent discussions in the early years of their marriage. So why did he need to say it? She wanted to ask him, but he was already out of hailing distance, and instead she watched him until he turned the corner and was gone.

* * *

Who to follow? Him or her? The boy has always been with her. Except for this morning. Of course, that could be because there's no therapy session on Friday, but she was there — together with the big fellow. Her husband? Must be — they seem to get on so well.

She'll have to go home soon. She isn't going to let a boot load of shopping spoil in the heat just because she had a row with her husband.

The grey Vauxhall followed Jenny out of the car park, leaving a hundred yards distance between them until they reached Penny Lane, then it closed the gap, sliding in with just one car between them.

It had followed her twice before. The first time, she had accelerated away as the lights at Queens Drive had changed, trapping the Vauxhall, losing it only five minutes from where it had started, at the hospital gates.

This time, I'm sticking to you like a leech to a bloody rag.

* * *

Jenny chatted with Phyllis as she unpacked the shopping and restocked the fridge and cupboards. 'Not a flicker from him,' Phyllis told her, while her own children played on the swing in the garden for a few minutes, fighting over whose turn it was, whining for arbitration. Alain stood several feet away from them, watching, wary of them. 'He's in his own little world. Wouldn't talk to my two — and you know what Damon's like, never shuts up.'

'Didn't he show any interest in anything?' Jenny asked.

Phyllis fixed her with one of her meaningful looks. 'Only if you count lingering over the railings and gates and locks of the enclosures. Fascinated by them, he was.'

She was so evidently relieved to relinquish her responsibility for Alain that Jenny hadn't the heart to ask her to stick around while she broached the difficult subject of calling him by his real name. So she saw Phyllis and her children out and returned to the kitchen.

She asked Alain if he was hungry, used his name. He immediately ran to the kitchen table and dragged a chair, scrambling under the table and pulling the chair in front of him.

'If you don't want me to use your real name, I won't,' Jenny said. 'You can come out. It's all right. Really.' Except it wasn't. How could anything be all right when his mother was dead — murdered — and he had in all likelihood seen it happen?

He appeared a few minutes later, after Jenny had made a sandwich for each of them. He sat at the table and ate the sandwich, sipping the glass of milk she'd poured for him, avoiding her eye. She tried the name of his school, the names of his best friends at school. She mentioned Cannon Jones's name, the headmaster's — all of which she had committed to memory since the case review, so that she wouldn't have to refer to notes in front of the boy. Finally — tentatively — she named the road where he lived. Nothing. Not the faintest glimmer. Alain had retreated from her. She had temporarily lost him.

The doorbell rang. Jenny hesitated, and it chimed out again, more insistently. The boy vanished, cowering under the table, and Jenny crouched down to him. 'I'll be back in two ticks,' she said.

It was DC Douglas. 'What the hell do you want?' Jenny demanded.

'I'd like a word with your husband,' he said, peering past her.

'He isn't at home,' she said, then, curious, 'What's it about?'

'Where is he?'

Funny, Jenny thought, that policemen always expect an answer to their questions, but rarely feel under an obligation to answer questions themselves. She heard the scrape of a chair in the kitchen and glanced over her shoulder. Alain was standing in the doorway at the end of the hall.

'This is a bad time,' Jenny told Douglas. 'Come back in a couple of hours. Or try him at work.' She started to close the door, but Douglas caught it.

'You're sure he's not here?'

Jenny looked over her shoulder again, as something crashed to the floor in the kitchen. The back door was open, and the boy was gone. 'Paul!' she yelled. Shit. 'Alain!' She ran to the kitchen and out into the garden, followed by Douglas. The boy was already at the back fence. He jumped, got one hand to the top and tried to scramble over. 'Alain, it's all right. It's only a policeman.'

He ignored her and Jenny had to grab him and pull him away, kicking and biting. Douglas stood over them, unsure of what to do. He looked menacing even to Jenny, this great, ungainly bear of a man, moving from foot to foot — to the boy he must seem like a monstrous giant.

'For God's sake!' she hissed. 'Can't you see you're terrifying him?'

'It's all right, mate,' Douglas said, reaching out. Alain started screaming. 'Look. Look mate—' He fished in his jacket pocket for his warrant card and the boy panicked, trying to climb over Jenny to get away from him.

'Hey!' Douglas said, ineffectually. 'Hey . . .'

'*Laissez-moi tranquille!*' the boy screamed. '*Laissez-moi tranquille!*'

'Douglas!' Jenny said through gritted teeth.

'All right,' he said, evidently shocked by the boy's reaction. 'I'm going.' He turned back at the door to the house. 'D'you want me to send anyone round, like?' he asked.

'Just get *out*!' Jenny said, still struggling with Alain, regretting her refusal of help when she heard Douglas's car start, and she realized she was alone with the hysterical boy.

* * *

Shona came into the room and sat down at the switchboard, muttering to herself. Yvonne was taking a call, and having made the connection she asked Shona why she was back from lunch so early. Shona looked at her, through her, distracted, seemingly distraught. She kept fiddling with the slide in her hair, until a frazzled knot gathered on one side of it.

They can't help you. Shona looked over her shoulder, a prickle of sharp terror spiking her spine, half expecting to see him there. *They can't help you.* Dr Greenberg's voice echoed in her head. Pam, Angela, the others in her group — none of them could help. *He* wouldn't let them.

Sometimes she saw Dr Greenberg as a vampire, a bloodsucker who needed a dark, musty room — his books and papers — where he could return to roost and rest. Sometimes he seemed more like a warlock who used his books of spells to mix his poisonous brew of science and statistics to make liars of people who had suffered.

Her hands jerked and twitched, the knuckles felt hot and they throbbed with a pain that shouted down everything but his voice. Pam had warned her about the flashbacks. She had seen the others, heard their accounts of what they saw . . . but nothing could have prepared her for this. She had covered the bruising with plasters, four on each hand. Of course, people had asked. She told them she'd trapped them in a door. They didn't believe her, but she didn't care. She could have had time off, got herself signed off sick, but it was worse at home. Bad dreams and, more horribly, sudden, vivid flashes. It was coming back to her with frightening intensity. She couldn't sleep, didn't dare to.

Work was a distraction, but it was hard to concentrate. Tiredness and sometimes a voice or the noise of a filing cabinet closing, and she would have to get out. Yvonne had found her one time, crying in the toilets. Yvonne knew — about the other time — how she'd tried to harm herself. But she hadn't known then the reason — Shona herself hadn't known — hadn't remembered. Until now.

I saw you on Wednesday. He had seen her! But he was at the *lecture* on Wednesday. She had left an hour before it finished. How could he have seen her break into his house?

Oh, God! she thought. *The note!*

I don't know your name yet, but I soon will.

The note — it was meant for me!

She pulled off her headset and scuttled out of the room.

'Shona!' Yvonne rolled her eyes at Raj, who was working the day shift with her.

'D'you think you should go after her?'

'What's the point?' Yvonne said. 'She doesn't listen. She never bloody listens.'

'Well, someone should do something.'

Yvonne felt a stab of guilt. She was, after all, the senior member of the team, had trained Shona herself. She wasn't a bad operator, either. Conscientious, willing to step up in an emergency — someone off sick or delayed. She would always do an extra stint to help out.

'I'm not her mother,' Yvonne said, resentment getting the better of her good nature. 'Shona's a big girl now. I can't go poking my nose in where it's not wanted.'

* * *

Carol Ewart's face lit up when she saw Shona. As she came closer, Carol exclaimed, 'What the hell's up with you?'

Shona's eyes darted about the waiting area of the records office. Too many people. She tried to control the panic welling up in her, but all those people, all those eyes . . .

'Can we talk?' she asked.

'Sure.' Talking was what they did, the two of them, in the canteen, sometimes over the phone. Something one or the other had heard or seen, a sneaked glimpse of some report. Shona had a knack for finding juicy gossip and was generous in passing it on. But Carol could see that Shona's agitation was due to more than recently acquired information about who was sleeping with the new SHO.

She rang the bell to summon one of her colleagues to the serving hatch and slipped out of the side door.

'Come on,' she said, guiding Shona to the staff toilets at one corner of the foyer.

'You look awful.' It wasn't very tactful, but it was true. Shona's face was pale, almost grey in the harsh glare of the strip lights. The skin around her eyes was red and puffy, and she looked like she hadn't slept for days.

'You've got to help me, Carol.'

'Okay.'

'Someone's after me.'

'*What*? Who?'

'Can you check my records? See if they're still on the shelves?'

'You were a patient here?' This was news to Carol, she thought Shona told her everything, and this was a secret she had to know more about.

'*Please*, Carol. Just check it!'

'All right.' Carol was flustered by her friend's emotional state. 'For God's sake, calm down, will you? Go into the staff room and have a fag or a cup of tea, calm your nerves.'

CHAPTER 19

'We've friggin' had it now.' Lee-Anne was channel hopping unhappily. BBC 1, Channel 4 and Granada were all showing pictures of Mrs Angeline Fournier, found murdered in her home in Mossley Hill. Immediately after, two photofit pictures. The one of Lobo was remarkably accurate.

'. . . Police believe Mrs Fournier may have disturbed burglars and was subjected to what they describe as "a frenzied attack".' The shot cut to a detective inspector, but Lee-Anne turned off the television before he could open his mouth.

'What're we gonna *do*?' she pleaded, her eyes filling with tears.

Lobo slumped lower in his chair and tried to slip his hands nonchalantly into the front pockets of his jeans, but they wouldn't quite fit, so he ended up with four fingers of each hand jammed in up to the first knuckle, which made him feel foolish, and that made him bad tempered.

He scowled at Lee-Anne. '*I* don't know, do I? Don't ask me.'

Lee-Anne glared back at him with hate in her eyes. 'Well it was your idea in the first place, so bleedin' *think* of something, mastermind.'

Lobo stood up, pulling his hands from his pockets, and switched on the sound system. He liked that — *sound system* — much better than *radio* or *music centre*. It had a professional quality to it, like it meant business. The news was on.

'. . . trying to trace a young couple, seen knocking on doors in the area last Friday evening. Police believe the dead woman is the mother of a boy found wandering the streets of the Garston area of Liverpool early last Saturday morning.'

'Turn it off, will you?'

'The boy is in a state of shock, and, as yet, has been unable to give police details of the attack, but a team of trained specialists is working with him, to try and coax—'

Lee-Anne put her hands over her ears and screamed.

'*What*?' Lobo yelled.

'It's doin' me head in! Turn it *off*!'

Lobo turned up the volume and she screamed again, then, seeing that this was having no effect, she took off a shoe and threw it at the stereo. It bounced off the wall and Lobo caught it before it did any damage.

''Ey!' he yelled. 'You mad cow!' He threw the shoe back at her. His aim was better and it struck her full in the mouth.

Momentarily, they both froze, then Lee-Anne was out of her chair and lunging at him, hands clawed and teeth bared. He caught one arm, but the other flailed at him and her nails scraped the side of his head, drawing blood. He grabbed her free hand, but she threw herself forward, head-butting him, missing his forehead but splitting his lower lip. Lobo hated the taste of blood.

He threw Lee-Anne onto the settee and gave her an open-handed slap. She put a hand to her face, shocked. 'You hit me, you bastard!' Tears welled up again.

Lobo pulled up his trousers and smoothed his hair. 'You started it,' he said. Then, realizing that he sounded like a sulky kid, he added, 'There's more where that come from.'

Abruptly, Lee-Anne stopped crying and stared back at him, round eyed and furious. 'You *what*?'

Derek Spencer — his real name — had been called thick all his life, but he wasn't stupid and he certainly wasn't suicidal. He hitched up his trousers again, turned away and started fiddling with the volume control of the sound system. He even turned it down a little.

Lee-Anne was staring at his back, he could feel it, and his shoulders twitched feeling the burning hatred of that look. He turned to face her and saw triumph in her eyes. Satisfied that she had won the round, she took a tissue from the sleeve of her blouse and dabbed her mouth, checking for blood. Then she held out her hand. 'Giz them.'

Lobo hunched his shoulders.

'I said, giz them,' Lee-Anne repeated.

He sucked his teeth.

'Giz the cards, Lobo.'

'Why?' he said. Then, 'I won't.'

'*I won't*,' she mimicked. '*I won't. Why don't you make me, hey?* You're just like a bleedin' kid — "I won't."'

He turned now, grinning.

'Like a kid, am I?'

Lee-Anne took a step back but recovered quickly. 'You can't use the friggin' things,' she began, taking a reasonable stance. 'They'll get you. They know the cards've been nicked now. They'll be looking for them. Giz them and we'll cut them up together. It was nice while it lasted. We got some boss stuff out of it, but it's over.'

Lobo lowered his head, still grinning.

'Over?' he said, disbelievingly. 'I haven't even started yet, girl.'

She took swipe at him as he made for the door, but he shook her off and she didn't try again. Just as well.

She tried wheedling. 'Lobo, you'll get yourself locked up!'

He shoved his face up close to hers, grinning.

'Ahhh,' he breathed, tilting his head, knowing it gave him the look of a crazed clown. 'Worried about me, are you?'

That look had served him well through school. No one messed with him when he had that look on him.

She tried faking, of course, like she didn't care. But they'd known each other since school. His nickname — short for lobotomy but pronounced *Lowbow*, as in the wolf — was given to him after a particularly bloody playground brawl with a year-eleven twice his size. Lobo was still only in year eight. Lee-Anne had seen blood on Lobo's teeth that day and knew it wasn't his.

'I'm worried about both of us, Lobo,' she said. 'We've got everything nice. We've even got some spare cash for once. But if they catch us, we've had it — the woman's dead!'

'They're not gonna catch us,' he said, still grinning, and slapped the settee either side of her.

'But they—' Her words were cut off by his hand over her mouth.

'I said: They're not — *gonna* — catch us.'

* * *

Then he was gone, and Lee-Anne knew they were as good as caught. *He looks like the devil when he smiles like that*, she thought. All teeth and eyebrows and eyes horrible and glittering. She flinched at the memory of his breath on her cheek and in her mouth — the reek of last night's beer and fags an assault on her. And his teeth, so gleaming and white. Close — so *close* — to her face. Lobo hurt other people, not her. Never her. But today he'd hit her — twice.

She went from room to room, drinking in the colours and the fresh clean smell of it all, wishing she had a camera, to capture the colours, to keep hold of the feeling. Her mates had been dead jealous when she showed them all her new gear. Jade and Rhiannon still lived at home with their mums, and Lee-Anne had enjoyed acting the sophisticate, offering them a choice of tea or coffee, biscuits or cake. It wasn't *fair*! He was going to spoil it all out of spite.

She turned on the radio and flumped down on the sofa, then picked up a magazine to read. She was just getting into an article entitled 'Does your man please you?' when the radio cut out.

'Frig,' she said, and went to fiddle with the switches and dials. It didn't help. Then she noticed that the stand-by light on the new TV was out. She went into the tiny, windowless kitchen and switched on the light. Nothing happened. The microwave clock was blank as well. 'Shit,' she said. Bloody leccy.

She returned to her place on the sofa and tried to settle into her magazine, but she kept thinking about Lobo, coming home late, probably tanked up. One of two things would happen: either he would be too out of his skull to fix the power or he would make a big thing about how helpless girls were and how it takes a man to sort out an electrical problem. The fact that she'd got a B grade in physics GCSE and he'd got sweet FA was neither here nor there — anyway, she hadn't told him — but she knew she wouldn't be able to stomach him droning on about how girls didn't have a technical cell in their brains.

She put down her magazine and rummaged in the cardboard box under the sink until she found a pair of pliers and some fuse wire. She left the door on the latch and went downstairs. The meters were in the basement, so probably the fuse boxes were, too. The door opened inwards, and it was stiff, but she knew better than to put her shoulder to it: there were only three steps down from ground level. The rest had rotted and finally collapsed when the meter man called last autumn. No one had been since, which suited most of them fine, because they got estimated bills but used more juice than they would normally dare.

The light, a naked sixty-watt bulb, worked. Lee-Anne edged down to the third step and sat down. She turned around and lowered herself the rest of the way. It wasn't much of a drop, when you were expecting it.

She went to the bank of meters and mains switches, looking for the one labelled Flat 6. The switch was off.

'What the f—?' Lee-Anne caught a movement from the corner of her eye and wheeled round, just as the light went out. She screamed.

CHAPTER 20

Sallis clicked his fingers at Mike Delaney. Mike paused in his conversation with the manager of the credit card company. The clerical staff seated near Sallis also fell quiet.

'Where?' Sallis said. 'Long stay, level C. Right. Got it. Cheers, mate.' He hung up. 'Mrs Fournier's car,' he explained. 'Manchester airport. Did they find her car keys at the house?'

Mike shook his head. 'They'll have to break in.'

Sallis nodded at the receiver in Mike's hand. 'Sarge . . . you haven't put the credit card company on hold?'

Mike grinned. 'Taste of their own medicine.' The civilian clerical staff and CID had spent the afternoon checking all the major credit card companies to find out if Mrs Fournier had an account with them. It had taken an hour of phone calls, faxes, call backs and security checks to make contact with someone who had the authority to answer his questions. 'Ask the boss if we can have a forensics team sent over there.' Mike punched a number on the keypad of his desk phone.

'Mr Whittle, sorry about that. We need to know if anything has been cashed on Mrs Fournier's card since last Friday — here or abroad. Can you do that?'

‘We should be able to give you that information immediately a transaction is made,’ Mr Whittle said. He scrolled through Angeline Fournier’s account details. ‘There are a lot of outgoings in Italy and France.’

‘After Friday?’

‘No . . . nothing since then, but she did book a flight with BA ten days ago. You’d be able to get the flight details from the airline, if I give you her card number.’

It took another two hours to find out that Mrs Fournier had not used her credit cards since booking her airline tickets. She had bought £2,000 worth of traveller’s cheques and £500 in euros at the same time. Her flight out was on Wednesday the seventh, from Manchester to Hendaye, near the Spanish border. Her return flight was scheduled two weeks later.

‘The only money in her purse was a few euro cents,’ Douglas said.

Mike, Sallis and Douglas had gathered in DI Crank’s office. ‘American Express are trying to find out if she cashed any of the traveller’s cheques,’ Mike said. ‘But if they were spent in shops, it depends how fast they process them — it could be days before we know.’

DI Crank eyed Mike Delaney as if he had imparted this information with the distinct intention of spoiling his day. ‘Was she definitely on the flight out last Wednesday?’

‘According to BA.’

Crank scratched his chin. ‘So why did she come back early? And why didn’t she use her credit card?’

‘She had plenty of cash with her.’

‘Maybe. But why leave her car at the airport?’

‘Maybe she didn’t come back by plane,’ Sallis offered. ‘She could’ve come back on the ferry.’

‘Or she could’ve got a flight back,’ Mike suggested, ‘driven home, and then whoever killed her took the car and drove it back.’

‘A bit of a coincidence, isn’t it?’ Douglas chipped in. ‘She drives home, he tops her and then takes her car all the way back to the same airport.’

Mike wasn't fazed by his scepticism. 'Manchester is the only international airport I know of in the North West,' he said. 'And if he found all that foreign dosh on her, it might've given him the idea of taking a nice foreign trip.'

Crank grunted noncommittally. 'You can't get away from the fact her cards haven't been used,' he said. 'Normally, you'd expect thieves to squeeze as much as possible out of stolen credit cards in the first few days — before the shops are alerted.'

Mike shrugged. 'If he didn't have the PIN numbers, he'd be stuck. Unless he had a female accomplice, and an extra form of ID.'

'Her driving licence and passport weren't found,' Sallis said.

'So, he's got the ID, but he still hasn't used the cards. Maybe he's working alone, after all,' DI Crank said. 'Anything from the car?'

'Sorry, boss.' Sallis had checked with the SOCOs at the airport car park, just before the meeting. 'Nothing obvious. No travel documents or maps — and no obvious signs of violence. It'll be down to forensics now.'

Crank nodded his approval of Sallis's thoroughness. 'Did her parents give us anything useful?'

'They don't speak any English,' Mike said. 'And they're quite elderly. The French authorities are supposed to be getting back to me when they've got some answers.'

* * *

Fraser returned after five o'clock. Jenny was in the sitting room, exhausted, bruised and scratched. He reached to touch her cheek, but she flinched from him.

'I'd never have left you alone with him if I'd known,' he said. 'I'm sorry, love.'

'Sorry doesn't cut it, Fraser,' she said. 'Sorry doesn't even begin to fray the edges.'

He watched her for a few moments, then shrugged. 'What can I say?' He went to the drinks cabinet and poured himself a whisky. ‘Can I get you a drink?’ he asked. Jenny didn’t reply. He poured one anyway, carried it over and placed it on the table next to her.

‘Where were you?’ she asked.

‘I told you — I went to school, did some sorting out.’

He glanced sideways, avoiding her gaze, and Jenny said, ‘Wondering if I tried to contact you at school?’

He avoided her eye. ‘Ach, you know it’s impossible during the teaching day. Messages’re never passed on.’

‘And what if someone goes to your school, to your classroom, and finds it all locked up and no sign of the diligent schoolmaster?’

Annoyance and guilt fought for control of his features. ‘You came to *school*?’

‘Not me,’ Jenny said. ‘The police.’

Fraser blanched and looked towards the door. ‘The boy. Is he—?’

‘He’s sleeping,’ Jenny said.

‘Then I don’t get it.’

‘Neither do I,’ Jenny said, taking a swallow of whisky while she decided how much to tell him. ‘The charming constable Douglas called. He wanted to speak to you — wouldn’t tell me why.’ She laughed, one hand went to her cheek. ‘He didn’t really get much opportunity, come to think of it.’

‘Look, I said—’

She waved away his apology. ‘I imagine it has something to do with the car accident. He telephoned later when he couldn’t find you at work — it was his visit that set off Alain in the first place, and he didn’t want to cause any further upset.’ She flashed Fraser a bitter smile. ‘Nice to know the man has some sensibilities. He wanted you to contact him as soon as you got home.’

Fraser had become very quiet. A sudden shudder ran through him, sploshing his drink and he stared balefully into his glass, watching the streaks of whisky drain from the sides of the tumbler.

'I thought they said it could have been stolen by someone planning a robbery,' he suggested.

'They did say that, didn't they? After all, they know that *I* didn't drive the car that night. But it doesn't make sense, bringing it back — I mean who does that?' She was giving him the chance to come clean, but he was refusing to take it. 'They also said,' Jenny pressed on, unwilling to reach the conclusion she felt was inevitable, but needing to know the truth, 'that they will go back and run through the rest of the video tapes to see if they could catch the thief returning the car.'

Fraser closed his eyes and took a gulp of whisky.

'Was it you, Fraser? Did you take the car?' He took a breath, and in that unbearable hiatus Jenny blurted out, 'Please, don't lie to me.'

He exhaled. 'I *borrowed* the car,' he said. 'I didn't "take" it, I *borrowed* it. And I put the damned thing back exactly as I'd found it.'

'Not exactly, surely?'

He shrugged.

'Why?' she asked. 'And why lie about it?'

Fraser passed a tired hand over his eyes, and Jenny saw that he seemed ill with exhaustion. Over the past week they had both lost sleep, had both been worried and anxious. She had thought it was for Alain — but perhaps she had misinterpreted the cause of Fraser's restlessness.

'I needed the car,' he said. 'And I didn't lie. You just assumed it couldn't have been me. It was you told the police I couldn't drive.'

Jenny laughed. 'This is unbelievable! Leaving aside what you said to me in the supermarket car park, are you really trying to put this on me?'

'Jenny, I needed the car,' he repeated. 'I knew you wouldn't miss it.'

'So why didn't you *say* something? I'd have left the car at home. Why'd you let me think you can't drive?'

'I've been taking lessons. It was supposed to be a surprise. I've not passed my test yet, but I thought if I learned it would be a help.'

'Great help,' Jenny said. 'You know you're likely to lose your licence before you're even qualified to drive? What the hell was so important?'

Fraser stood and poured himself another drink. 'I can't say. Not yet.'

'You mean you *won't* say.'

He swung round. 'Look,' he began, hotly, 'I pay my share. It's my car as much as it's yours.'

'This has got nothing to do with money, Fraser. At least not for me. You drove the car uninsured. What if you'd hurt someone?'

'But I didn't hurt anyone, did I?' He set down his drink and crouched in front of Jenny, placing both hands on her shoulders. She shook him off.

'How do I know *what* you did?' she demanded. 'How can I be sure of anything anymore? What is it you're not telling me?'

'You'll just have to trust me a little longer, Jen. I promise I'll explain everything when I can.'

She stared at him. He really hadn't understood. 'Don't you get it, Fraser? The fact is I can't trust you at all. I can't trust a single word you say.' She walked out and he didn't try to stop her.

* * *

She was right. She couldn't trust him.

It's all about trust, Fraser thought, and he was losing it — had lost it. He didn't know if he could trust himself anymore, and if she didn't yet hate him, she soon would. And he would deserve that, too.

The nightmare, for him, had begun a week before Jenny had even heard of Mr Hunter. The same man had telephoned and asked Fraser the question that had so upset

Jenny: *Have you had any children adopted?* Her mind had gone immediately to the child they had lost, the children they had fostered who had moved on to adoptive parents, and the longing, the yearning, the pain each separation had caused them, but Fraser had thought of one child only. He had suspected even then the true nature of the call, the true identity of the caller.

Jenny had lost the baby two years before his affair. It had been enough, at the time, that she had survived. They had been grateful to be together, not to be lost to one another, but gradually, over the months that followed, the horror of that night had begun to fade.

His terror on that night, like Jenny's pain, became harder to recall, and the memory ceased to be a succession of breathless snapshots: Jenny in agony. Jenny screaming, flailing about on a hospital trolley, fighting the oxygen mask. Fraser trying to comfort her, out of his mind with worry. But as the months passed a creeping regret gradually displaced all other emotions, until all he could remember of the rush to the hospital, the howl of the ambulance chorusing with Jenny's screams, the blood and the anguish and the terrible dread, was the debilitating sadness that they would never — could never — have children of their own. The realization had incapacitated them both for a time. For months they barely spoke to each other. The effort of communication was beyond them. Then Jenny had suggested fostering, making the tacit acceptance of their situation explicit, incontrovertible.

He couldn't accept that. Not at first. It had made him desperate to a degree of which he had not thought himself capable. He never thought of leaving Jenny, not in the real sense of moving out, but he could not be *with* her, collude with her in the acceptance of their sterility. For a short time, he had hated her even for bringing up the idea of fostering, and although he would never have admitted this to himself, had wanted almost to punish her for having failed them both.

His hand went to his shirt pocket and he took out a raggedly torn scrap of fax paper. He stared at the address printed on it, still undecided.

* * *

'Fancy having another crack at Lynn Halliwell?' Calcot and Weston walked back to the car, the gravel of Vi Harvey's driveway crunching underfoot. The house was locked up. There was no one home.

Weston eased himself into the passenger seat. 'What I really fancy is a heart-to-heart with Mrs Harvey,' he said.

'Well, don't look so glum! Phone her up, leave a message on her answerphone. She'll get back to us.'

While Weston made the call, Calcot turned the car in the direction of Liverpool, and Lynn Halliwell's flat. They were just in time — the nanny was packing.

'Going somewhere, Miss Halliwell?' Calcot asked. Clothes were stacked in neatly ironed and folded piles, and the larger items had already been placed in the bottom of a large and well-travelled suitcase.

Lynn smiled, a touch nervously. The dark red blotches had faded, apart from one or two on her neck, and a sore-looking patch on one hand, leaving her skin pale, clear, almost translucent. She had a pretty mouth, but her smile was forced. 'Holiday,' she said. 'Since Mr Harvey won't be needing me for the next week, I thought I'd visit a college friend.'

'Where's that?' Calcot asked.

Miss Halliwell coloured slightly. 'Why?'

Calcot and Weston stared coldly at her, Calcot counting the beats — five — before she went on the defensive.

'I don't see that it's any of your business where I go in my free time. I mean, why are you here? What are you after?'

'A straight answer,' Weston said, annoyance making him laconic.

'I told you, I'm staying with a college friend. I don't have to tell you where.'

'He's been in touch, has he?' Calcot asked. Miss Halliwell looked confused by the question, as though afraid it was some kind of trap. 'You said Mr Harvey won't be needing you next week — presumably he told you that.'

'Oh . . . yes.'

'Only he hasn't found time to contact us,' Weston told her.

Miss Halliwell lifted one shoulder. 'He's a very busy man.'

Calcot gave her a disingenuously puzzled smile. 'I thought he was supposed to be on holiday.'

'He *is*, but he still has to fit all the office work in. He's busier on holiday than when he's at home.'

'Touching,' Weston said.

'What?'

'Your . . . admiration for your boss.'

Miss Halliwell looked from Weston to Calcot.

'Where is he?' Calcot asked.

'In the Lakes somewhere.'

'And Connor's with him?' They were playing a verbal game of ping-pong — Weston and Calcot alternating, trying to put Lynn off, spoil her concentration enough to make her slip up.

'I've already answered that question.'

'Not to our satisfaction.' Weston stared, waiting for Calcot to take over.

'Obstruction is a serious charge, Miss Halliwell.'

Lynn kept her eyes on Weston. 'I'm not a criminal,' she said. 'And this isn't a police state.' Before she could finish her little speech, Calcot was cautioning her. The colour fled from Lynn's face.

'Obstruction'll do for now,' Calcot went on conversationally.

'But if Connor doesn't turn up soon,' Weston said, taking up the baton, 'you could be facing a charge of abduction—'

'And conspiracy,' Calcot finished for him.

'You're not serious!' Tears sprang to her eyes. 'But I haven't *done* anything! I would never harm Connor!'

‘Give us an address,’ Weston said. ‘A location for Connor or Mr Harvey — doesn’t matter which. We’ll take it from there.’

‘And you can go off on your holiday,’ Calcot soothed.

Lynn’s face was closed. She had an obdurate look that suggested she could go on as long as it took — she was not going to help them. Calcot began to understand how this inoffensive, mild-looking young woman had withstood Mrs Harvey’s despotic rule for eight years.

CHAPTER 21

Lobo *liked* buying stuff — not shopping — he wouldn't call it that. Lee-Anne went shopping — *tarts* went shopping. Lobo *bought* stuff. He had been buying stuff all day, and now he felt happier, filled up with it, 'shopped out', Lee-Anne would've said. He would have said *sated*, had he known the word.

He stood on the corner of Ranleigh Street and Bold Street, deciding whether to have a look in at Lewis's on his way back, but the shops would be shutting any minute and he'd got enough for one day anyhow. The savoury-sweet smells of Chinese cooking wafted up to him on a light breeze from the restaurants of Chinatown, setting his stomach gurgling. Not that he'd be tempted. All that rice and shit. Lee-Anne made proper food. Food he could stomach. She made chips better than the chippy. Lobo felt himself weakening. He glanced down at the bags in his right hand. She wasn't gonna like the fact he'd been and bought more stuff. He shifted his grip on the cue in his left hand, bracing himself, and headed for his car.

He'd parked in Hope Street, around the corner from the Liverpool Institute of Performing Arts — what everyone called the Fame School. Uphill all the way. Even with a following wind from the Mersey, he'd broken out into a sweat within minutes and he felt his wheeze coming on. At the corner of Mount Street, one of the regular prozzies had turned out early, hoping to catch a bit of white-collar custom on their way home from the office.

'Got the time, lad?' she asked.

'I might have the time, but I wouldn't bet on having the energy, girl,' Lobo said, trying to control the harshness of his breathing.

'I'll give you chance to catch your breath,' she said, following him a few steps from the corner. 'No extra charge.'

Lobo shook his head and hurried on. They embarrassed him, the street girls, even though this one had a nice pair of legs and he would have liked to try her out. But he was frightened of diseases — a weakness Lee-Anne played on every opportunity she could — quoting facts and figures from her magazines, telling him about the threat of AIDS and syphilis. Bloody bitch even took him to see *The Madness of King George*, and for weeks she kidded him that old George had gone off his head because of some venereal disease or other. Oh, she knew his weak spots, Lee-Anne did.

He barely noticed the rest of the hike, passing the old-fashioned houses, with their balconies and vines climbing up to them — open invitation — without a second glance. He was about to turn the corner to where he'd parked the car, fifty yards from the cop shop, when a sharp whistle from behind made him turn and, on the steps of the Fame School, he saw his friend and sometime partner in crime, Dileep Khan.

Lobo waited on the corner, grinning foolishly until he caught himself at it and matched his friend's serious expression. 'All right, Randy, lad,' he said.

Dileep had been called Randy ever since year nine — something to do with his Pakistani name, Lobo couldn't remember. He looked past Randy to the steps of the Fame School, where a little cluster of students were posing in front of the big blue doorway. Three or four girls and a couple of lads. They seemed to be waiting for Randy.

'What're you doin' in there, lad?' Lobo asked. 'Robbin' the place, or wha'?

'Nah, man.' Randy stuck his hands into his jeans pockets and glanced over his shoulder to the waiting group. 'I'm doin' a course, aren't I?'

'What, like actin'?'

'Actin', singin', dancin',' Randy said, forgetting for the moment his elocution teacher's careful instruction to 'make the "ing" sing!'

'*Wha*?' Lobo roared with laughter. 'You — dancin'?'

Randy drew his heavy eyebrows together, so that they met in a straight line across the narrow bridge of his nose. 'What're you doin' then, Lobo?' he asked. 'Still signin' on?'

Lobo switched off the laughter instantaneously. 'Yeah, mate. Why?'

Randy shrugged. 'Just askin'.' He lifted his chin, indicating the bags Lobo was carrying. 'Have they bunked up the social since I signed off, or wha'?'

'Didn't they tell you?' Lobo said. 'They're givin' loyalty cards now. Anyone who's been signin' on for more than three years. Got mine last week. Twenty-five-percent discount on leading brand names.'

Randy allowed a twinkle of amusement to escape from under his eyebrows. 'Just my luck, 'ey? A few more months, I would've qualified.'

Lobo grinned. 'Nah. I just got lucky, didn't I?'

Randy nodded. 'Win on the gee-gees, or . . .'

'Or, mate,' Lobo laughed. 'Definitely "or".'

Randy tilted his head. 'Well,' he said. 'If you're so flush, how's about buying a poor student a drink?'

'I don't know about that, mate,' Lobo said doubtfully. 'I don't like to encourage spongin' off the state, like.' Randy punched him in the arm, and he laughed again — God, he'd missed Randy. 'Aren't you on your holidays, then?'

Randy shrugged. 'We're doin' this thing for a—' He stopped himself just in time. 'A kind of like show,' he finished. 'So,' he said, 'are you coming for a bevvy, or wha'?'

Lobo didn't need any encouragement to delay his next meeting with Lee-Anne. 'Okay, I'll just put this stuff out of sight of robbin' bastards.' He had expected Randy to follow him to the car, but when he turned to say something to his old schoolfriend, Khan was still standing on the corner.

'Where are we goin'?' Randy asked. 'So's I can tell me mates.'

Lobo stiffened. Randy was one thing, they'd gone to school together — they'd even done the odd bit of house breaking together — but students was a different matter. Students put his back up. He couldn't help it, they just did.

'Mate . . .' he began.

'I'll tell them the Phil, all right?'

Before Lobo could answer, Randy had sprinted across the road to the steps, where his friends were waiting.

CHAPTER 22

Jenny knocked at Alain's bedroom door. She waited a moment, listening, wondering whether to risk going in, when, unexpectedly, the door opened.

'Alain?' she said.

The boy stared up at her, his huge eyes dulled with misery. He held the polar bear under one arm, and now, beneath her gaze, he shifted it to the front of his body, its head partly covering his face, forming a protective barrier between them, and in the fraction of a second it took her to notice, Jenny wondered if, at home, he had a comforter. Luke had carried around a baby duvet which he'd had since infancy. He would suck one corner and when he was feeling tired or insecure, he would wrap it around his shoulders, even covering his face with it if he was shy of visitors. She would sneak it from his sleeping arms every so often to wash it — making sure she replaced it, clean and dry, before he awoke. Luke would be grumpy for a few hours, fixing her with a mistrustful stare, dragging it through every dusty corner until it had accumulated a satisfying layer of grime, so that it felt it belonged to him once more. Eventually it had fallen to pieces and he had forgotten it.

Luke's adoption had been a terrible blow to them. Of course, they had expected it, but he had been with them for so long that she — perhaps Fraser, too — had begun to think of him as their own. She had spoken to Gina after the case conference, and she had hinted that Luke was unsettled in his new home. Jenny felt that it was unfair to the child, asking him to accept two new people as his mummy and daddy, when all he could remember was her and Fraser.

Jenny smiled down at Alain. 'Are you ready for dinner?'

He turned from her and Jenny had a sense of having failed him, that she had missed a momentous chance, said entirely the wrong thing, that if she had not taken the easy route and asked that trite, meaningless question, she might have known everything. Jenny had occasionally experienced this feeling before, with other children, but in each case, the contact that had begun the process of healing had eventually been made, perhaps by a different route, but it had happened, and therefore she was not too despondent. Alain sat cross-legged on the beanbag, his eyes fixed on her face.

Had he witnessed his mother's murder? Jenny felt out of her depth. She didn't know what to say to him, what to ask him, how to help him.

'Grandma and Grandpa Fournier are coming and see you soon,' she said.

The boy's gaze never flinched from her face. *Grandma and Grandpa?* he thought. *Will* she *not come?* He hugged the bear closer to him, squashing its velvet-soft fur to his chest. *Of course. She hates me now. They all do. I promised to look after everything. I promised!*

Jenny saw a tear fall onto Alain's cheek. She sat beside him and put her arm around him. 'What is it, love?' she asked. 'If you tell me, I'll try to help, I promise.'

It was that word that did it. *Promise.* He shuddered. 'Do I have to see them?' he asked. Jenny gasped at the sound of his voice. 'Can't you tell them not to come?'

* * *

Vi Harvey finally returned DC Weston's call at six p.m. They had just about given up on her for the day. Calcot gave Weston an agonized look. She waited until he had finished the call and immediately started in with a list of reasons why he should have put off meeting up with Mrs Harvey until the following morning.

'I thought you were keen to get this cleared up?' Weston said.

'I am! But I'm meeting someone later.'

'Anyone in particular? Maybe I could tag along.'

'No one you'd know. And you wouldn't be welcome.'

'This won't take long. She says she'll pop into the station on the way home.'

'That's very accommodating of her.'

'I thought so.'

They only had to wait twenty minutes. Vi jangled into the station wearing enough gold to warrant a Securicor escort. 'You wanted to show me a picture,' she said.

'Thank you for reminding me,' Weston replied. He sifted through the drift of papers and document wallets on his desk, while Vi made herself comfortable in the chair opposite and eyed him coolly.

'Any news?' Calcot asked.

'No. But then I don't expect Bill to telephone me every five minutes while he's on holiday.' She didn't take her eyes off Weston.

'You haven't managed to get in touch with him, then?'

She favoured Calcot with a brief, withering glance. 'I'd have said.'

'You'd have said what?'

'If I'd got in touch with him. You've got his mobile number. Haven't you tried?'

'We have, Mrs Harvey. We have.'

Weston coughed. 'Sorry to interrupt,' he said, handing Vi a copy of the photograph of Alain.

'What about him?'

'You don't recognize him?'

'Should I?'

'Take a good look.'

She gave it one more cursory appraisal and sighed. 'It's not Connor, if that's what you think.'

'No relation?'

'No.'

Weston and Calcot exchanged a look. They were no further than they had been that morning, except they had the Harveys' nanny in a cell, and it looked like Mrs Harvey belonged in one right with her. Vi must have sensed their frustration, for she abruptly turned on the charm.

'I know this is difficult for you,' she said. 'And believe me, I appreciate your concern, but there's really nothing to worry about. Everything's *fine*.'

Yeah? Weston thought. *Then why do I get the feeling you're trying to convince yourself as much as us?*

* * *

Randy could feel the tension building. Lobo had been winding the others up steadily now for an hour and a half. Two of the group had left already, unable to stomach Lobo's increasingly offensive remarks as he got rat-arsed drunk. They were seated in the Liszt room of the Philharmonic pub. The evening light twinkled in through the stained-glass window, buffing the walnut panels of the room to a mellow golden orange.

Peter Merembe had made the mistake of treating Lobo as a rational being, capable of being persuaded by argument. 'I don't know why the burden on the state should worry you,' Peter said, with the gentlest emphasis on the word *you*.

Randy winced inwardly.

'What's that supposed to mean?' Lobo said.

As a rule, Lobo was a bit of a bigot, only allowing Randy the status of honorary white because they had gone to school together. Also, Lobo was forced to sit next to him for English and had discovered that Randy had a natural facility for the subject and didn't mind sharing ideas — even homework — with his mates. His friend's cleverness and generosity had saved Lobo a lot of bother going through school.

Randy tried to keep his eyes off Lobo's new pool cue, which he had had insisted on bringing with him when he discovered it didn't fit in the boot of the car. 'Are you calling me a scrounger?' he demanded.

'No more than I am,' Peter said, smiling. 'But you claim state money, just as I do.'

Lobo drew back his lips, baring his teeth in a warning snarl. '*Just as I do*,' he said, mimicking Peter's public-school accent. 'You've never had to claim dole in your life, you fucking gaylord poncy black *bastard*!' The angel in the stained-glass window looked on with an expression of dismay, but Peter's smile broadened, became a grin, and suddenly, alarmingly, he was laughing — a rich, mirthful, unaffected laugh.

Lobo turned to Randy, furious. 'What's he laughin' at?' he demanded.

Randy shrugged helplessly.

'What're you laughin' at?' he said, turning again to Peter.

Randy had expected this to come to blows by now, but Peter seemed genuinely amused. The rest of the group had shrunk back in their seats and were watching the two men warily.

Peter sank the rest of his pint, barely controlling his laughter enough to avoid choking. He patted Randy on the shoulder as he made his way to the door. 'I really think you should use him for your character study,' he said. 'There are acres of material in him. He's absolutely perfect.'

A low, guttural growl from Lobo, and he leapt to his feet, snatching up his cue as a weapon. One of the girls squeaked, but Peter carried on, turning left towards the main door. Lobo made to follow him, but Randy grabbed his cue arm. He was taller than Lobo, and sinewy.

'I'll fucking *burst* him!' Lobo screamed, struggling with Randy. He considered a head butt, abandoning the idea because Randy had apparently anticipated the possibility and held him at arm's length. 'I'll kill the bastard!'

'Sit down and shut up,' Randy said, adding quietly, so as not to embarrass his mate, 'or I'll put you to fucking *bed* early.'

Lobo eyed him, gauging the level of threat. It was touch-and-go for a minute as he paraphrased the old saying in his head: *Fucked if you do, fucked if you don't.* When it came down to it, it was his degree of intoxication that decided him. He wasn't up to chasing after the black guy in the state he was in, so he sat down instead.

Randy stood over him for a minute or two longer, breathing heavily through his nose and trying to get his temper under control. Randy's strong sense of personal dignity abhorred scenes. He hated name-calling more than physical aggression: at least if things got physical you could get some redress, but with name-calling, the damage was inside, like a slow burn, it went through layer after layer, flaying the skin, sensitizing the nerves for the next time.

Lobo gradually relaxed and huffed himself into a sulk. Randy gave his friends a significant look. Within two minutes he was alone with Lobo, and the drinkers in the bar next door to them had resumed subdued conversation. The air vibrated with tension, half the clientele disappointed by the peaceful outcome of the interchange, the other half relieved and a little shaken, alert to signs of new conflict.

Randy was among those cautiously relieved. It had cost him a lot to get into the Institute of Performing Arts — in effort, in self-discipline, even in money — and he didn't want to jeopardize everything he'd worked for.

Lobo slumped in his chair. Randy knew if he tried to get Lobo out of the place without making any attempt to dissipate the bad feeling, there'd be trouble of the nastiest kind.

'So,' he said, 'where's the best place to pick up a bit of good luck these days?' he asked. 'In case I wanna top up me grant?' Not that he intended to do anything about it, but he had to get Lobo off the subject of students and the best way was to get him to talk about himself.

Lobo slid him a sideways look. 'Supplementary benefits, 'eh, la'?' He took a swallow of beer and shrugged. 'Still doin' the usual. Me and Lee-Anne. There's some boss houses round Mossley Hill, man.' He launched into a description of homes without security systems, gardens with high hedges and nice, quiet streets empty of people between half eight in the morning and six at night, when he stopped, looking suddenly shocked and sickened.

'You all right, mate?' Randy asked. Lobo had lost colour, and for one horrifying moment Randy thought he might be about to burst into tears.

'Gonna puke,' Lobo mumbled, stumbling for the door. Randy followed him a few seconds later, carrying Lobo's cue. Lobo would be really pissed off if he'd lost his cue. Randy lifted his head in salute to the barman, a gesture that said, *See, all it takes is a bit of tact.*

Outside, Lobo was bent almost double, leaning for support on the cornerstone of the building, heaving and splattering his new Nikes with acid-tainted lager. He pressed his face against the pink-speckled granite of the wall.

'Ah, fuck,' he said, when at last he started to feel better.

Randy courteously looked off in the direction of Myrtle Street and waited for the spasm to pass. When Lobo had straightened up and wiped his mouth on his sleeve, he asked, 'Think you can make it back to your car?'

'It was just a bad pint, right?' Lobo said, offended by the implication he couldn't hold his drink.

'Right. And when you get a bad pint, you get the urge to purge.' Randy handed Lobo his cue as solemnly as if it was a ceremonial staff.

They crossed at the lights, Randy slowing his pace, ready to catch his friend if he fell, thinking about the news item on the radio about that woman being murdered in Mossley Hill, already wondering if Lobo and Lee-Anne were the 'youths' seen knocking on doors in the area the previous Friday.

'Hey!' One second Lobo was there and the next he wasn't, streaking over to a silver-grey Peugeot cabriolet, with its roof rolled down. He stood in front of the car, slightly crouched, with that dangerous smile — half-grimace, half-snarl — on his lips.

Randy groaned. Peter was driving. He had a bemused, almost querulous look on his face.

Lobo gripped his cue like a baseball bat and took a swing, cracking a headlamp.

'What the hell are you doing?' Peter yelled. He jumped out of the car. Lobo threatened him with the cue, and he dodged back, then Lobo took another swing, samurai style, straight down the centre of the bonnet.

'Not my car, you bloody lunatic!' Peter yelled. The lights changed, but nobody sounded their horn.

Lobo was screaming. He wasn't saying anything, just screaming while tears coursed down his face, sweeping savagely back and forth with the cue. Peter went for Lobo, his head down, which probably saved him, because the cue caught him on the shoulder, where he would otherwise have taken a crack on the head. He went down and Lobo lifted the now battered cue to finish the job. Randy yelled, lunging at Lobo. He turned, eyes wild, and struck Randy a blow across the bridge of his nose. Randy felt a crunch, but no pain — not yet, that would come later — and fell to the ground, blacking out before he felt the impact.

CHAPTER 23

Shona ran from her car to Max's house. Prayer had no power over him. He must have known she had sprinkled the holy water in his car. It had only made him angry, and now he had her file! What did he want with it? She felt a cold wave of faintness, knowing beyond any doubt that he would use it against her. To find her weaknesses. Perhaps there was evidence of what he had done to her. In the file. He had taken it to destroy it.

She ran to the back of the house. This time the door was locked. She used her elbow against the glass. It would not smash. She took off her shoe and hammered the kitchen window until it shattered, then reached in and turned the latch. A splinter caught her wrist, but she barely noticed. Inside the kitchen, the smell of spices, coffee, strong cheese made her feel dizzy and sick. She resisted, fought the urge to turn and run, the need to vomit, and blundered into the hall.

Her heart hammered in her chest. He might come back any minute, leathery wings creaking, stirring the air next to her cheek, she would turn, and he would be there, teeth bared, ready to strike. Suddenly aware of the blood dripping from her arm, she gasped. The smell! The smell of blood would bring him back. Panting with terror, she clamped one hand over her wrist and hurried to his sitting room. Bookcases with leaded lights stood in the alcoves of the chimney breast. On one wall, an etching of women in the throes of demonic possession.

Shona looked away, but she had seen it. She couldn't unsee the horrible vision of madness and evil: bodies writhing in awful torment, women tearing their clothes, their eyes bulging, as goblins and devils looked on, leering, reaching to touch their bare flesh.

She sobbed, pulling open a cupboard door beneath the first bookcase, looking for her file. It contained CDs. The next was stacked with video tapes. She pulled them out onto the floor, heard them clatter against the floorboards.

The glass-fronted shelves were filled with books. She would have passed them over, moved to another room, continuing the search, but one of them had slipped and lay flat on the shelf. Red and black. The colours of pain and hatred, wickedness and suffering. A vile, reptilian creature, half-human, half-gargoyle stared out from the cover. The title stood out against the rest: *The Myth of Satanic Abuse*.

A pocket of rage burst within her. She fumbled the text from the cupboard and tore off the cover. There were others. Scores of them: some with lurid covers, some with plain leather binding, bound editions of periodicals, encyclopaedias. She felt hemmed in by the sheer weight of them. Perversion, abuse, cruelty, all of them reduced to nothing but faulty memory and hysterical invention. She dragged them out, first in ones and twos, then, as her fury grew, they tumbled like rocks from a hillside, gathering in mounds on the floor.

She trod on them and twisted them, tore and shredded them, her face sweating, distorted, her hands, miraculously strong, healed by the destructive power vested in her.

She moved onward, upward, seeking out the room that was his sanctuary.

* * *

Max noticed the blood first. It had splashed unevenly onto the parquet flooring of the hall and was smeared on the walls and stair rail. The front sitting room door was open, and a sliver of light slashed the dimness of the hallway. He edged up to the door and pressed a hand near the hinge until it swung open with a sigh. The room was in disarray: tables overturned, records and CDs strewn about, pictures askew on the walls and, in a pile in the centre of the room, he saw his books, his precious texts, collected over many years. They had been twisted and torn, pages ripped and ripped again, bindings broken in such a rage that tassels of string hung from the remnants of spines.

This hurt more than the intrusion, this senseless destruction — desecration — of careful, serious scientific study. He felt ravaged. He stood gaping at the ruin of his books, gasping for breath and then, furious, he turned and strode through the house, screaming like a soul in torment, careless of the danger, *wanting* to meet the violator of his world.

Each room was the same. His books, some of which were long out of print and irreplaceable, were ruined. These texts provided historical precedence: past folly illuminating present insanity. In these historical works were the precursors of present psychological ailments: demonic possession supplanted by multiple personality disorder, the horrors of incubus and succubus by alien abduction and experimentation, the current wave of paranoia over satanic abuse, particularly prevalent in the States, mirroring a similar hysterical reaction in the sixteenth and seventeenth centuries. He picked up the torn fragments of a text on demoniacs from the floor by his bed. Its spine had been torn away, and curled, lolling like a dog's tongue, the glue and binding exposed, yellowed and brittle with age. Pages had been dragged from it and screwed up or ripped. Pieces lay strewn about the place.

Max sat on the edge of his bed and put his head in his hands. Who had done this? *Who?* He looked up, his heart suddenly thudding. His office. His files, records, research notes, computer, database — all of it. He ran up the final flight of stairs to the attic room that extended from the front to the back of the house.

He closed his eyes and groaned. The filing cabinet drawers stood open. Papers and hospital records littered the floor. A bottle of ink had been spilled, soaking the lecture notes he had been preparing the previous night and dripping onto the rug beneath.

Frantic, he searched through the records, but they were so disordered and damaged, it was impossible to see what had been taken. He misdialled the first two attempts he made, because his hands were shaking so badly, but on the third try, he got through. 'I need to report a burglary,' he said.

* * *

In the shadows of the street Shona listened. When she heard his yells reverberate through the rooms, the pain of his loss made her tremble with fear. After the frenzy of destruction, she had felt sated, vindicated in a strange way. But now, the thin, shrill scream of adrenaline through her system returned, and in the silence that followed her terror grew.

* * *

Jenny sat up late, working on her lecture notes, trying to make sense of what was happening to her. Sleep was impossible, too trivial to consider under the circumstances, its very necessity seemed an imposition. Since none of it made sense to her, she turned to the boy — Alain. This naming was difficult to get used to.

Max seemed confident that, having made the first steps, Alain would soon confide in her. 'He evidently trusts you,' he had said. 'Otherwise he wouldn't have asked for your help.'

'Or it could be that there was no one else he felt he could turn to and he was desperate.'

Max raised his eyebrows. 'Quite possibly.' He knew better than to bullshit her.

‘What do I do about the grandparents?’

‘Nothing you can do. They have to come. We can’t prevent that. Anyway, most likely Alain feels guilty — he’s tried to be the good little boy, and in his own eyes he’s failed, disastrously. Of *course* his grandparents must come.’

Jenny stood and paced to the French windows. At night, she worked in the dining room because it was beneath one of the spare bedrooms and her nocturnal prowling was less likely to disturb Fraser or the children, if they were fostering at the time.

The work was not going well. Thoughts of her argument with Fraser kept intruding, spoiling her concentration and preventing her from establishing that intense yet essentially detached mood she needed in order to write. Fraser had consistently refused to explain where he had been earlier that day, and of the events of the Tuesday night he would only say darkly, ‘If I could tell you, I would.’ Jenny had made some acid remarks she had regretted immediately, and Fraser had stormed off again.

She sighed, staring over at the small pool of yellow light in which her laptop, notebook and pen sat, almost as if arranged for a photograph. Beyond these, just visible in the gloom was her card index system, which housed her references to articles and texts, with page numbers and brief summaries.

Still life of writer’s block, Jenny thought, allowing her morose mood to make her maudlin and self-pitying. She drew back the curtain, impatient with herself, and looked out over the garden. Its flowers and shrubs could be seen only as lumpy dark masses in the grey light of a waning moon.

After his return from the police station to make his statement, Fraser had kept his distance. Was he afraid that she might ask more difficult questions, or was it guilt, part of the distancing process that preceded separation? She had seen it in him on so many occasions, as the time drew near for a child to leave them. She had always considered the growing reserve towards a child a strangely cold reaction in a man she knew to be warm and loving, but she understood that a degree of detachment was necessary to Fraser to make the pain of loss bearable.

She had felt a glimmer of it herself, as they went through the final stages of Luke's adoption. Writing reports, attending meetings and case conferences in preparation for the adoption became a way of thinking about him as a *foster child*, rather than as the little boy they had loved — even doted on — for eighteen months. Jenny had known the level of Fraser's devastation at their impending bereavement — for that's how it felt — by the degree of aloofness he displayed towards the child in the final weeks. He withdrew, both physically and emotionally, and not just from Luke. A shiver of alarm ran through her. Perhaps she had misinterpreted his quietness, his despondency, in the weeks preceding Luke's placement, thinking it was for Luke when there was another cause entirely.

Fraser was having an affair. The realization hit her with the force of a slap. He must be — otherwise, why the secrecy, the distance, the rumbling gloominess? The telephone calls from Mr Hunter had posed the same question to both of them: *Have you had any children adopted?* Since she hadn't, the call must have been aimed at Fraser. But if that were true, why had Hunter asked to speak to her in the first place? To warn her, perhaps? Or was it an act of impulse, a flash of anger, the desire to hurt someone as he had been hurt? Jenny tried to remember the phone call clearly, the sequence of question and answer, the pauses and the intonation, although she knew it was futile. What she knew now would colour her memory of what had happened then. Did Mr Hunter sound bitter, or did she remember him that way because it happened to coincide with her current theory of infidelity? Her mind went on, constructing a story that wove into her theory, and made sense of the phone calls.

Mr Hunter had recently found out that his wife was having an affair. He had identified Fraser as the lover. Had Fraser and this woman had a child together? Jenny's stomach did a slow, sickening roll. Did Fraser have an affair because she, Jenny, was sterile?

She went through to the kitchen and brewed a jug of coffee, and then left it to go cold while she struggled with the concept of Fraser as an adulterer. She hadn't suspected a thing. She was furious with herself for her own trusting stupidity and stricken by Fraser's cool and callous pretence. How long had it been going on? Long enough presumably for the child to have been born: why else would Mr Hunter ask if they'd had a child *adopted*? If she felt humiliated, an ingenuous fool, how must *he* feel, having brought Fraser's child into his own home — having discovered that his wife had deceived him twice over?

Ever practical, the question of where and when posed itself. Had Fraser carried on an affair with this woman while Luke slept upstairs? Or — the thought made her heart contract with fear — had he left Luke alone and met his lover elsewhere? Either way, Jenny could not prevent a surge of bitter emotion from rising in her, burning the back of her throat.

She felt used, a dupe. How simple she had been, believing all his complaints of extra paperwork, the confusion caused by the new syllabus, his heavy work load, sympathizing with his perpetual tiredness.

'*God*!' Furious with herself, she stood and rushed from the room, unable to bear her own thoughts any longer. As if she could leave these torturing thoughts within the four walls of their home, she grabbed her jacket and keys and quietly let herself out of the house.

The night was clear, noticeably cooler than of late, and a light shower at around midnight had left the garden fresh and the air sharp. The pavements around Sefton Park were pungently fragrant.

Jenny crossed the deserted road, skipping lightly over potholes puddled with tarry water, and debated briefly which was safer: walking around the perimeter of the park, a target to drunks and kerb-crawlers, or taking the more sheltered gravelled path that ran parallel to the road, which presented a greater number of hiding places for a prospective mugger. She opted for the drunks and kerb-crawlers, reasoning that she was likely to be more agile than the former and would hear the latter coming and melt into the shadows.

The thin crescent of moon struggled with the orange glow of the streetlamps. Few stars were visible in the combined pall of mauvish light which hung like a fog over the park.

During her half-hour walk Jenny saw two cars: a private-hire cab and a police car. The police stopped and warned her of the dangers of night-time strolls around the park, and after a short-lived and rather childish rebellion against their good advice, in which she walked a further half-mile, Jenny turned for home, having resolved nothing.

She had almost reached the house when a sudden flare of light caught her eye and Jenny looked towards a car parked perhaps twenty-five yards down the road from the house. It was some dark colour, impossible to discern in the distorting sodium glare of the streetlamps. She hadn't noticed it when she had left the house, but then she had been in a foul mood and had anyway turned left as soon as she'd got through the gate.

The driver — a man? A woman? Impossible to tell at that distance — had lit a match and was shielding it with one hand. The tip of the cigarette glowed red and, as the match flame faltered and died, the figure looked up at Jenny, and although it was too far away for her to see clearly, she felt a shiver run down her spine. It may have been the way the flame played along the lower line of the jaw and threw deforming shadows, but the driver's face had an infernal quality, a look of such malevolent intensity that Jenny hurried into the house, her heart beating fast.

CHAPTER 24

Mike Delaney telephoned at seven thirty a.m., just under an hour into the first deep sleep Jenny had managed all night.

'Did I wake you?' He sounded surprised. He had worked with Jenny long enough to know she could function well even on only four or five hours' sleep.

Jenny surfaced from a cramp-inducing position on the sofa and made a couple of ineffective swats at her hair in an effort to tame it. Her neck was cricked, and her right shoulder felt like it had been wrenched from its socket.

'What do you want, Mike?' she asked grumpily, edging a cushion behind her and grunting as hot needles shot from her shoulder blade to her neck.

'Sorry,' Mike said, then, interpreting her silence as an invitation to get on with it, he took a breath and began:

'The body we found at Mrs Fournier's house,' he said.

'The mother, yes?'

'Not the mother.'

Jenny tugged unsuccessfully at the tangles in her hair. 'Mike, please don't tell me you've found another body.' She answered without thinking, swamped as she was by her own misery, and struggling against tiredness. Mike did not reply immediately, and her heart skipped a beat. '*Have* you found another body?'

'No . . .' Mike began carefully. 'We've just the one victim.'

Jenny stopped tugging at her hair. 'Oh my God . . .' she whispered, guessing what he was about to tell her.

'Apparently they look alike. There's only a year's difference in age. The cleaning woman thought — and the injuries made it difficult . . .'

Jenny visualized the big policeman's helpless shrug.

'Who is it?'

'Her sister, Jeanne-Louise. We think.'

'*Jesus wept!* I thought the police checked these things.'

'We do — which is why we contacted her parents in the first place. And like I say, we haven't had the identity confirmed yet, so . . .'

'Where's the mother?'

'Alive and well, in France. She's over there on a business trip. Asked the sister to look after the boy. She called us.'

Angeline Fournier had got through to him at five a.m., after threatening the duty sergeant who advised her to call back during office hours with an exclusive interview on breakfast TV, reviewing the incompetence of the British police. Rather than disturb DI Crank's sleep, Madame Fournier was put through to Sergeant Delaney.

'Are you the stupid son-of-a-bitch who put the fear of God into my parents, telling them I was dead?' Her English, though heavily accented, was perfect.

'Madam,' he said.

'Shut up and listen. My father has a heart condition and your half-brained message was passed on to him by *telephone* for God's sake!'

'Madam Fournier,' he tried again, pronouncing her title the English way, 'I'm sorry your parents were upset, but we had no other point of contact.'

Mike's wife turned in her sleep and mumbled something incomprehensible. He reached out automatically and stroked her back.

‘Point of contact? What the hell are you on about? If my parents hadn’t thought to telephone me, they would have been on their way to England by now to break the news to my son. Why didn’t you speak to my sister? Jeanne-Louise—’ She stopped and an awful, gaping void of silence opened between them.

‘We had a positive ID,’ Mike explained. ‘From your cleaning woman. Of course, we needed it confirmed by next of kin.’

The silence stretched a little longer, and Mike wondered if she had understood. Then, in a small voice, she said, ‘Please, not Jeanne-Louise. Not my sister—’ She broke off again, and Mike had to wait a few minutes.

‘How?’ she said at last.

‘We don’t know for sure yet if it *is* your sister,’ Mike said gently.

‘Who else?’ she demanded, miserably. ‘Who else if not Jeanne-Louise? I should not have left her.’ She swore softly. ‘My God — Alain?’

‘He’s all right,’ Mike said quickly. ‘Physically, he’s fine. But he’s refusing to talk.’

Angeline Fournier moaned, ‘Mother of God! Did he witness it? Was he there when she was—when it happened?’

‘We don’t know. He was found some miles from home a week ago last Friday night. He won’t talk to anyone.’

‘How . . .’ Angeline repeated, tremulously. ‘How was my sister killed?’

‘We think it was a burglary,’ Mike said, not wanting to go into the other possibilities. ‘We have three suspects in custody now.’

She was adamant. ‘Tell me how. I want to know how.’

* * *

‘What will happen now?’ Jenny asked.

‘The French police are satisfied she is Mrs Fournier,’ Mike said, ‘but we’ll have to check her out over here as well.

She's flying to Manchester with her parents this morning. We'll send someone to meet them. Mrs Fournier will be allowed to see the lad, under supervision.' He heard Jenny catch her breath and added, 'Alain won't be released to her custody until we're sure he's safe with her.'

'And the suspects?'

'One has been charged with criminal damage and assault and battery — unconnected with the murder as far as we know. But he had Miss Fournier's credit cards on him and an expensive new pool cue — as well as the receipt from the shop he bought it from — he'd only got it yesterday. In fact, only a few hours before he used it to panel beat the bonnet of a student's car.'

'D'you think he's the killer?'

Mike shrugged. He wished he knew for sure. 'We picked his girlfriend up from their flat. Looks like they've been out and bought up the entire stock of Argos. She's pretty well pissed off with him, so we might get something out of her . . .' He shrugged. 'After Mrs Fournier's call last night, I don't know what to think. The lad hasn't said anything that might help?'

'He did say he doesn't want to see his grandparents.'

'See what I mean? Everything's arse-about in this case.' There was the briefest of pauses as Mike wondered if he had offended Jenny. 'D'you think you'll be able to get what happened out of him?'

'Eventually, but you can't rush these things,' she said. 'He's obsessed with locking himself in. He checks the doors and windows himself before he'll go to bed. He keeps painting bars on the windows of the houses he draws, and I can't be sure if he's painting what it was like at home or what he *wants* it to be like, so that he feels safe.' She recalled the stranger in the car, the satanic cast the match flame gave to the driver's face, and she asked, 'Mike, do you have anyone watching the house?'

'*Your* house? No. Why?'

'Insomniac paranoia, probably.'

'Your funny phone caller?'

'All I saw was someone lighting a cigarette in a car. I'm just jumpy with lack of sleep.'

'Paranoia or not, if you see him — or her?'

'I'm sorry, I couldn't tell.'

'Never mind. The same car — or another — anything suspicious, get the registration and phone me, okay?'

'Okay,' Jenny said, blushing slightly that he had assumed — correctly — that she hadn't thought to take the car's licence plate number.

'I'll keep you up to date with our records search,' Mike said.

'Thanks.' Jenny wanted the call to end. She wasn't sure she should have mentioned the car parked outside the house, and she was embarrassed by her nervy reaction to it.

'*Have* you had any more calls?'

'Me? No.'

'What about Fraser?'

'What about him?' Jenny wasn't sure if Mike knew about the incident in the railway station car park.

'Has he had any calls?'

'I wish I knew, Mike,' Jenny said with more honesty than she would have liked.

'I'll maybe have a chat with him, later. And Jen,' Mike added, 'Don't worry about the TWOC — others can worry about that.'

Jenny smiled as she replaced the receiver. She had known Mike for eight years — longer — since he had been involved in liaising with Social Services even before they had started fostering. He was friendly with the social workers and the paediatricians, the foster carers and the ed. psychs. Mike moved easily between the different groups, comfortable at each level, approachable and warm. He always knew how much information to give and how much to withhold. He was the kind of man who could be trusted, who invited confidences, but who never pushed his advantage. As her smile faded and the worries of the night once more intruded on her thoughts, she wondered how much Mike Delaney was withholding from her now, of what he knew about Fraser and the incident at the car park, of the man they had arrested, and of the death of Jeanne-Louise Fournier.

CHAPTER 25

Mummy coming home? Alain's heart hammered in his chest. What will she say? He had promised and—

A thin, high-pitched sound, like the squeal of a kettle on a hob — or a woman's terrified scream—

'She asked if you were all right,' Jenny said.

And Jeanne-Louise, Alain thought. *Did she ask about her?*

Hands up. A flash of inescapable steel. Hacking. With contact, a few beads, red, in a fine arc. *Like the spray from my water pistol,* he thinks. *Splat! You're dead! She's dead.*

And now, he wishes he were dead. Or if not dead, for that is too terrible a word for a small boy, then invisible, non-existent.

'I explained that you were upset.' Jenny's hand went to her temple, fingering the scratches on her face, then on and upwards through her hair. 'Perhaps, now Mummy's coming home, you'll talk to her . . .'

Alain hears the swish and chop of the blade. He sees a shuddering fall of petals as the axe swings at the tree, splitting, tearing. As the blade is pulled from the wedge he hears the sinewy squeak of metal on wood; sap bleeds onto the head of the axe. But that was before. Not — not what happened to Aunt Lou. Confused, he tries to reason it out in his mind, so that he can think what to say, what excuse to give. But there is no explanation. No excuse. What excuse could there be? He made a promise. He broke it.

He looks up at Jenny and the soft, saintly glow of light through her hair almost draws him into telling her.

I should have done what I said. I promised.

'No!' Alain jumped from the sofa and ran to the door. *'Ce n'est pas de ma faute!'*

* * *

Lobo picked at the scabs that were forming on his knuckles where he'd hit the arresting officer. His lips were drawn back into a rictus — part pain, part fury at being locked up.

The duty sergeant dropped the flap of his cell door and Lobo stared at him. Jack Nicholson. He had a picture of Jacko in his head, how he looked in *The Shining*, that bit where he's grinning like a skull, swinging the axe.

'*Daddy's home!*' he yelled, then laughed. His voice was hoarse because he'd hurt his throat screaming at the bizzies, and later he'd burned the raw lining of his gullet by throwing up most of the lager he'd got down his neck. He hated that. It was criminal waste of good beer. This struck him as funny — the criminal bit, given where he was, and what he was sure to be accused of sooner or later — and he laughed even louder, but stopped when it felt like the skin inside his throat was being ripped to shreds.

Is that stupid bitch keeping her beak shut? Lobo's thought processes, still a little groggy from the after-effects of the alcohol, slowed a little further.

Bitch and *beak* didn't, like, go together, did they? Why do they say shut your beak? It would've made more sense if he went, 'Is that stupid *bird* keeping her beak shut?' But, I mean, no one calls girls *birds* anymore. Tart, fluff, bint, bimbo, old lady, bitch — and worse — but not *bird*. It almost made him blush to think of it, calling Lee-Anne something antwacky like *bird*.

Lobo, as a rule, was not the thoughtful type, but he'd been going over his shitty situation all night. He was hacked off with Lee-Anne, and in a vague, unresolved way, he blamed her for his arrest. Her, and Randy and his new-found, poncey friends. He was also developing a deep and abiding hatred for the dickhead who kept coming round every five minutes to check if he'd choked on his own puke.

How was he supposed to get a bit of rest with a beady-eyed pig sticking his snout through the observation flap every time he got his head down and started to drift off? Just getting a few zeds in and *clump clump*, as he comes down the corridor, *click creak*, as he flips the catch and opens the hatch, peers in with his little piggy eyes and then *creak click*, *clump clump* — the whole friggin' thing in reverse.

* * *

Lee-Anne was fuming. *I'll kick his bleedin' head in when I see him*, she thought. She had been locked in that filthy, cockroach-infested basement for two hours before someone had rescued her. Lobo's idea of a joke! And after that, the bizzies had come, just like she told the stupid *get* they would.

Mostly, Lee-Anne could handle Lobo, his temper and his moods and his need to vary the monotony of their penny-pinching poverty, to add contours to the featureless flatness of their days with his thrill-seeking.

She sighed, and looked around her cell: cream walls, bottle-glass windows. Nothing to look at. Yeah, Lobo was easy to read, perhaps not so easy to control, but controllable, nevertheless. Except when Randy was around. Lobo always went that bit further with Randy to egg him on — showing off to the *Man*. It didn't occur to her that the notion to go cruising Mossley Hill had been all hers, nor that Lobo hadn't even seen Randy for nearly a year. All she could think was that they'd got the flat how she'd always wanted it — cosy and smelling of new linen and warm plastic — instead of old sweat and dust. These were smells she hadn't been able to get rid of no matter how much she cleaned, because it was ground into the carpets and had seeped into the nap of the velveteen on the settee. Now, when she opened the flat door, she got a whiff of carpet fibres and recent decoration. But the police would take it away, and it was all down to Lobo meeting Randy and having a few more jars than he could handle.

She should be at home, in bed, with the fresh smell of starch and filler and fibre in her nostrils, the slightly scratchy feel of the new bedcovers on her skin, and Lobo standing there in his new pyjama bottoms with that foolish, lopsided grin on his face that made her want to ruffle his hair, because all he usually wore to bed was a pair of ratty old boxer shorts and a hopeful look.

Thinking about him with that soppy look on his gob was more or less guaranteed to raise a smile, even give her a warm kind of tickle inside, but today, locked in a cell with just a steel sink and toilet in one corner, and having to lie on a bed that any old drunk or druggy could've lain, spat, spewed or shat on, Lee-Anne would like to have scratched Lobo's goggly eyes out and feed them to him with HP sauce.

* * *

'Mr Khan.' Mike Delaney said it as a form of greeting, and as confirmation of identity. He introduced himself and invited Dileep 'Randy' Khan to sit.

Mr Khan stood at the table, his fingers lightly pressing the back of the chair. He seemed to consider a moment, and when he sat down it was with stately dignity. He lifted the chair out — a fleeting spasm ridged his forehead — then he placed the chair just far enough away from the table so that he could be seated. He leaned with both hands on the table-top, and using the table for support, he folded himself into the chair and stared solemnly at Mike.

'Are you ready to give a statement?'

Khan's hands rested on the table. He had a strip of white tape across the bridge of his nose and pads of something up both nostrils. His eyes, deep set even without the added shadow of bruising, looked positively sinister.

'Am I being charged?' he answered, and Mike had the immediate impression that Khan was familiar with police interview rooms.

Mike tried to penetrate the depths of shadow, but Khan, frowning magisterially, was difficult to fathom. 'You were involved in a nasty assault, Mr Khan,' he said, avoiding a direct answer.

'I was only *involved* because I tried to help a friend,' Randy said. His voice was nasal and breathy. He was breathing through his mouth in shallow, catching snatches, Mike guessed to save his bruised ribs. 'You can ask Lobo.'

'Lobo?' Delaney said.

Khan looked him over. 'Lobo's well known 'round here,' he said.

Mike stared into the witness's battered face. He had felt Khan's scrutiny and didn't want to give away more than was unavoidable. Khan was right. 'Lobo', aka Derek Spencer, was well known — not so much around the city centre and docks — but police in the Lodge Lane and Princes Park area were well up on his past exploits and present affluence. Lobo had been flashing the cash over last week. Mike had told the constable who'd given him the intel exactly where he thought the money had come from, and after a short silence the constable said, 'Not his usual style. Lobo either robs houses *or* he gets into drunken rucks, but up to now he's never mixed the two.'

'He might be well known in your circles, but he's not exactly public enemy number one in our book,' Mike said, at last.

He detected relief in Khan's demeanour and decided to tip him off-balance again.

'But I keep coming back to the fact that Lobo is dressed up in new gear, and when he was arrested he had what was left of a very expensive pool cue in his mitts.'

Tense again, Khan gave an uncomfortable shrug. 'Said he'd dropped lucky.'

'Did he say how?'

Khan sucked his teeth. 'Not to me.'

'We've had a statement from a Peter Merembe. He says you were trying to protect him from Derek Spencer — Lobo — when you were struck by the pool cue.'

'There you go,' Khan folded his arms and instantly winced in pain.

Mike opened a bottle of water and poured some into a paper cup, placing it in front of Khan.

'Mr Merembe says he was racially abused by Lobo in the pub — in front of you and friends — before the attack in the street. Are you okay with that?'

Khan pushed the water cup aside and stared fixedly at the tabletop.

Delaney rubbed his chin. *Implacable* was the word that came to mind. The heavy overhang of forehead and eyebrows, the natural gravitas this lad possessed at the age of what — nineteen? Twenty? Like a great, immovable rock. How he managed to be so persuasively dignified even with dressings up his nose and a broad white strip of tape across his face, Mike didn't know. Maybe it was all that acting training.

'Are you refusing to make a statement?' Mike asked.

'Do you really need one?'

'Not to convict him of assault.' They had taken statements from two witnesses the previous night, before they'd had a chance to get cold feet. What Mike wanted from Dileep Khan was some background on Lobo — what he'd been doing during the last week, and more particularly the previous Friday night.

'Does this guy scare you, Mr Khan? Are you *afraid* to make a statement? If so—'

He seemed offended. 'Lobo's a *mate*,' he said.

'So, this is you not wanting to grass up a mate?'

'Can I go now?'

'He cracks you in the face with a pool cue—'

'An accident.'

‘And kicks the shit out of you while you’re down.’ Mike saw a definite flash of surprise. ‘Yeah, the bastard put the boot in — that’s what probably did for your ribs.’ Another flicker of response — anger this time. But just when he thought he’d turned the man against his erstwhile pal, Khan placed both hands flat on the table and began to ease himself up from the chair.

‘If you’re not charging me, I’m off.’

‘D’you watch the news, Mr Khan?’ Mike asked, talking quickly now, not wanting to lose him, knowing instinctively that Khan would respond better to the respectful formality that he had maintained throughout the interview than to threat. ‘The little lad we found in Garston last week. The one that was on *Granada News*. We’ve linked him to the woman who was murdered in Mossley Hill.’

Khan grunted and put a hand to his side, obviously in considerable pain. He was standing now — his pallor giving his skin a sallow, almost jaundiced tone.

‘Jeanne-Louise Fournier,’ Mike said. ‘She was the boy’s aunty. We found her credit cards on your *mate*, Lobo.’

Randy collapsed back into the chair with a shout of pain. The constable who was standing at the doorway took a step forward, but Mike frowned, waving him away.

For a few minutes Khan’s raggedly painful breathing was the only sound in the room.

‘Can you help us?’ Mike asked simply.

‘If it helps you to keep him a bit longer,’ Khan said, taking small sips of air gratefully, like water from a glass, ‘I’ll give you a statement about the assault. But—’

He broke off with a grunt of pain, and Mike gave a sympathetic wince.

‘Take your time,’ he said, nudging the paper cup towards his witness.

Khan took a sip of water, his hand trembling. ‘I can’t help you with the rest, because I don’t know anything about it, and I’m not goin’ down for anything Lobo’s gone and done.’

CHAPTER 26

Saturday afternoon. Alain had shut himself in his room and hung the 'Do Not Disturb' sign on the door handle to ward off any attempt at communication. Fraser, likewise, a larger version of the truculent small boy, had retreated to their bedroom to work on what he termed 'schemes'. Jenny had to bite her tongue to stop herself asking if it was schemes of work or some other design he had in mind.

She shuttled between the dining room and the kitchen, unhappily opening and closing cupboards, sorting washing, tidying, returning to the dining room to review her work and type a few words before restlessness got the better of her and she found herself watering plants or sorting through the magazine rack to decide which papers were ready for recycling.

She could hear Fraser moving about upstairs, as restless as she was. They were supposed to be taking Alain to the hospital to meet his mother that afternoon. The interview had been set up for two o'clock and not only was Alain shutting her out — literally as well as metaphorically — but he was still refusing to see his mother. What was she meant to do? She couldn't drag the boy to the hospital screaming and kicking, and Max was against bringing Madame Fournier to their house, in case there was some reason why Alain should be afraid of her: their house, a haven to Alain since the terrible events of the previous weekend, would no longer feel safe to him.

She stood to straighten a ruck in the curtains, lingering to look out over the garden. The sky was a rich dark blue, but a swelling of cloud piled white on cream, towered over the line of the western rooftops. Later, they would have rain. A jet rumbled overhead, the sound of its engine like a roller skate on a wooden floor. Solid, purposeful.

* * *

Fraser screwed up another sheet of paper and threw it at the wall. How could he concentrate on school work? How could he even be trying to think about it? He reached into his trouser pocket and took out the piece of fax paper. Smoothing out the creases, he wondered why had he gone to so much trouble getting the damned address if he wasn't going to use it? He stared at the name at the top of the sheet. He had to find out. He *had* to know.

* * *

Jenny sat again and tried to concentrate on her work. *When a parent is accused of abuse*, she wrote, *dignity, honesty, respect are gone in a moment: the esteem which has taken a whole lifetime to build is lost. Irretrievably gone. What makes it worse for the those accused is that vehement denial is viewed by therapists as an admission of guilt, and confusingly for the supposed victim, the existence of profound disbelief, whether on the part of the accused or her family, is seen as confirmation, as tangible evidence that their memories are 'real'.*

Jenny could not, in her present state of distraction, imagine how it must feel to experience the level of betrayal, the intensity of paranoia, the emotion — hatred — that recovered memory patients must feel, and the horror of parents wrongly accused.

What she felt now herself, suspecting a betrayal of sorts, was disappointment. And a tingling apprehension, a calm which she knew to be dangerous, for although rare, it always preceded one of two things: extreme emotion or drastic action. Jenny feared there would be no going back on the resulting release of pent-up — what? Anger? Sadness? She turned and stared at the grey luminosity of the laptop monitor and saw the text swirl and swim out of focus.

She wiped her eyes and forced herself to be rational. She probed her feelings, exploring the tender spots, and found only that lingering sense of disappointment, of wasted time. Should she speak to Fraser again — demand an explanation?

Standing in the hallway, she heard Fraser moving about their bedroom. The restless pacing had stopped, and his movements had taken on a more purposeful quality. She pictured him picking up his wallet from the bedside cabinet, patting pockets, combing his fingers through his hair, right hand then left. Then he thumped downstairs: one, two, three, four, five — two at a time, leaping the last three, and rattling the crockery in the kitchen.

He already had his house keys in his hand. He stuffed them into his jacket pocket and, after a barely detectable hesitation, and avoiding her gaze, reached for the car keys on the hall dresser.

'What are you doing?'

Fraser wouldn't look at her, but stood, his head lowered, and his hand closed over the car keys, protecting them, possessing them, establishing ownership, and yet there remained a defensiveness in his stance, in his inability to meet her eye.

'Fraser, you're not thinking of taking the car again?'

He twitched, a slight movement of the shoulder, perhaps a shrug. 'I've somewhere to get fast,' he said, almost apologetically.

'Ring for a taxi.'

'Too far.'

'Fraser you *can't* drive.'

'I can drive. I'm just not licensed to.'

'A fine distinction. And while we're on the subject, have you forgotten that you're not insured, either?'

He shifted his weight, left foot, right, but his grip on the keys never slackened.

'What's this about, Fraser — Mr Hunter?'

He looked straight at her then, and she knew that she was right. 'What's her name?' Jenny asked.

'Whose?'

'Don't insult me.'

He frowned, looking away again, looking down. 'This isn't about her, Jen.'

'Am I allowed to know her name?'

'It doesn't matter. She doesn't matter.'

'Of *course* she bloody matters!' Fraser glanced at his watch and she thought, *Is he so obsessed with her that he can't even talk to me, tell me what's going on?* 'She's poisoned our marriage,' Jenny went on. 'She *matters*, Fraser.'

Fraser flinched slightly. 'I know I've no right to ask you to trust me,' he said, 'but I mean it. This has nothing to do with her.'

'Why didn't you just let me bleed to death ten years ago?'

'Jenny!' He looked stricken.

'It would have been better than this slow leaching.'

He reached for her, but she flinched away.

'Jenny, I have to go.' He glanced at his watch again and Jenny saw a flame of anxiety flare briefly in his eyes.

'It's long been over between us,' he said.

He must have seen the shock and pain in her face, because he stumbled on, 'No — not . . . I meant between me and her. Not—' Blood crept into his face. 'How could you think—?'

One look was enough to silence him.

He bowed his head.

'Who is this "Mr Hunter"?' Jenny demanded. 'Is he her husband? What's he threatening you with? Is she pregnant — is that it?'

Fraser flushed more deeply. 'Jenny, no.'

'Well then, you need to explain to me.'

He sighed, wiped a hand over his face. 'I'm not having an affair. At least, not now.'

She'd known it in her heart but hearing him admit it drained any remaining hope from her. She turned and began the long slow climb up the stairs.

Fraser followed her part way. 'It was years ago, Jen! I haven't seen her in over eight years. It meant nothing.'

She turned back to him. 'Don't tell me it was nothing, Fraser. You had an affair. You had a *baby*. What was that?' she asked. 'An assertion of your masculinity? If it was *nothing*, why did it happen?'

Fraser's head dropped. 'I don't know. But it proved one thing to me — that I love you, and that's all that matters.'

'It matters that you had an affair,' Jenny said, clasping her hands in front of her to keep them from shaking. 'Where? Here? While I was on night shift?'

'For God's sake, Jen!'

'I'm sorry if I offend your delicate sense of decency,' she said, then checked, suddenly realizing. 'Eight years — about the same time we decided that we'd start fostering?'

'*You* decided,' Fraser muttered.

'What?'

'It's what *you* wanted.'

'We discussed it,' Jenny said, feeling the ground beneath her shift and liquesce. The certainties that had kept her from giving up and giving in were slipping away from her. So strong was the impression that she grabbed the stair rail, afraid to look down.

'There was no alternative. You gave me no alternative. You were so . . .'

'So what?' Fraser shrugged. 'Say it — I was so screwed up. Are you trying to tell me you felt sorry for me, so you've put up with something you never wanted for *eight years*?'

'You were always so sure this is what you wanted.'

'And what did you want?' Jenny asked. 'It was always so difficult to get you to talk. Emotions are taboo, aren't they? Dirty language.'

'Don't start that.'

'I didn't start anything,' Jenny retorted. 'You did. The phone calls were all for you, weren't they? Am I expected to believe that the poor bastard who made them is freaking out over an eight-year-old affair?'

Fraser gave her a look which said, *You don't seem to be handling it all that well.*

'*Don't,*' Jenny warned. 'Don't try that with me. This isn't about some ancient affair. It's about lies and broken trust. And it's fresh, Fraser. What's happening is happening now. I need you here and you're going to see her instead, and you want me to accept that you're finished with her — that *it's long been over*.' She quoted his words back at him, spitefully.

'Won't you believe I'm not having an affair?'

'No, I won't. I can't.'

Fraser shook his head. 'I have to go.'

'All right.' Jenny stared down at him.

'Jen.' Fraser stepped forward.

'Leave now,' she said, 'and you needn't bother coming back.' She heard the absolute conviction, the unbending decision in her words, and knew that he would, too.

Fraser repeated her name. He reached for her hand, and she tried to snatch it away, but he held her. They struggled briefly, then a loud *crack!* and Fraser let go and crumpled onto the stairs, slipping the few steps to the bottom.

'You leave her alone!' Alain yelled, his voice breaking, rising to a scream.

Fraser put one hand to his head and groaned, while Jenny turned to the boy. He was holding a cricket bat in both hands and his eyes glittered with fear and fury. 'Leave her alone!' he repeated. He began shaking uncontrollably and Jenny put her arms around him. He started to cry, but he never took his eyes from Fraser.

'Get out! Get out!' he screamed.

Fraser hauled himself up, still holding his head, then, bending to pick up the keys he had dropped, he stumbled and almost fell again. He walked unsteadily to the front door, one hand on the wall all the way.

'I mean it, Fraser,' Jenny said, folding her arms in front of her to hold the child safe — and to hold in the pain that threatened to claw its way out. 'If you go to her . . .' But he had already gone.

* * *

Fraser made it as far as the garage before he was sick. He leaned against the door, trembling, then, taking a few deep breaths, he opened up and sat in the car until the dizziness receded.

He backed out carefully, performing the cockpit routine he had practised in his driving lessons, adrenaline high, senses sharply alert. He waited a couple of minutes for a completely empty road, before manoeuvring the car onto the road.

He gripped the steering wheel, checked his mirror, turned on his indicator, looked over his shoulder, grateful that at least it wasn't raining. He edged out from the kerb, feeding the wheel left to right, then straightening up, right to left, letting the clutch out gently, changing up gears as smoothly as his shaking hands and throbbing head would allow. Christ, if he was stopped by the police, they'd throw the book at him.

He couldn't have told Jenny — not yet. 'Aw, fuck,' he said aloud. He had been thinking that he'd wanted to spare her the pain. But she had assumed the worst — that he was still having an affair — or at least that his lover had whistled, and he'd come running, which amounted to the same thing. How would Jenny have taken it if he'd told her the truth about where he was going? He was sure that would have hurt her more.

He drove down to Smithdown Road and turned right, heading towards Penny Lane. As he approached the complicated system of traffic lights and roundabouts at the start of Menlove Avenue his heart began to hammer. How the hell did folk know which lane to go for? His hands were sweating, and he had to will himself to release first one, then the other, to wipe them on his jeans.

A sudden surge of regret swept over him and he groaned. How could he have said those things to Jenny? They *had* discussed fostering over and over in the six months before they had made their final decision. Roz, their social worker, had probed again and again during their assessment their reasons for opting to foster, rather than adopt. Jenny's arguments had been lucid and persuasive: if they adopted, it would be like trying to replace the child they had lost. It would be unfair, imposing all their high expectations onto another child. How could they avoid making sly comparisons: would *my* child have done this, achieved that . . . ? He had been unsure, insecure, but he had been carried along on the wave of Jenny's regained energy and optimism.

He had privately considered the possibility of surrogacy, but couldn't broach the subject with Jenny, not because, as she had assumed, he thought she was screwed up, but because he had at last seen a return to the confident, extrovert Jenny of old. After two years of depression following the miscarriage, she had, it seemed, begun to regain emotional equilibrium.

He had known, even with the first cryptic telephone call, what Mr Hunter had meant. Not the detail — that was sketchy. Not until the message while Jenny had been away. Had Hunter known that she was away from home? Was he watching the house? But even before the telephone call arranging to meet at the roadside café, Fraser had understood in essence who Hunter was and why he had asked the same question of both of them:

Have you had any children adopted?

The lights had changed and the car behind sounded its horn. Flustered, Fraser crunched the car into gear. It bounced a yard or two before stalling. The driver swerved around him and Fraser caught a glimpse of his face, red with anger, mouthing obscenities. Fraser pulled the handbrake on and went through the procedure, smiling sheepishly and lifting his shoulders in apology at a police car which slid past, the occupants eyeing him curiously.

'Sodding hell,' he muttered. Then, taking a breath, he eased the car into gear and shot through the lights as they changed to amber. He trailed behind the police car until it turned off at Speke and then he accelerated out into the middle lane.

* * *

Jenny carried Alain through to the lounge and placed him on the sofa, sitting next to him and hugging him close with one arm, while prising the cricket bat from him hands with the other. He seemed to be in shock. She would have to postpone the meeting with his mother and grandparents. It was too soon to try and get him to talk, although she sensed that he would, of his own volition, if she left him for a little while. She held him to her, his head resting just below her chin, and thought through the last ten minutes. It was as if her entire world, the foundations on which her happiness was built and her security depended were fake, an optical illusion — one movement from the narrow viewpoint and it all came apart, exposed as a trick. Had she been so self-absorbed that she could not see that what she had so passionately needed was not what Fraser had wanted at all?

'Are you all right, Jenny?' His voice, small, anxious, startled her from her reverie. 'I mean, did he hurt you?'

'Fraser would never hurt me,' Jenny said, and felt a simultaneous shooting flame of fear and loss. 'Not deliberately,' she added lamely.

The boy focused on her face. His eyes, so dark, so like Fraser's, stared into hers. 'Is it—?' He faltered and looked away. He sniffed, and Jenny could see by the redness around his eyes that he was fighting back more tears. He glared angrily at the blank screen of the television set.

'Is it . . . ?' Jenny prompted gently, even now more attuned to others' needs than to her own, to their suffering, despite the rising tide of emotion that threatened to swamp her.

Alain shrugged, dashed away a tear with the back of his hand. For a moment he seemed to shrink within himself, then he took a breath. 'Is it okay — I mean, if you don't mean it?'

Jenny felt a tingle of mingled dread and anticipation. 'If you don't mean to hurt someone?' she asked.

Alain nodded, but seemed unable to meet her gaze. The skin over his right eyebrow puckered.

'Alain . . .'

'Just TELL me!' He leapt up from the sofa and stood over her, his fists bunched.

Jenny started violently, and her eye was drawn to the cricket bat, lying on the coffee table behind Alain. She forced herself to relax, leaning back in her chair and looking up at him. His face, red with rage, was twisted into a grotesque mask.

'TELL ME!'

'There is no simple answer, Alain,' Jenny said. 'It depends on lots of things.'

He was breathing hard, and his fists were still clenched, but at least he was listening. 'What things?' he asked.

'What you did. What you were trying to do. And, of course, what actually happened.'

She realized that the same criteria could be applied to her own situation.

What I did, she thought. I persuaded Fraser to accept fostering when he didn't want it. *What I was trying to do.* I was trying to build a family, instead of us just being two people who cared for each other. Should that have been enough? *What actually happened.* I succeeded in making Fraser so unhappy that he had an affair.

Alain seemed to be twitching slightly. He swayed, and his eyes began to roll up into the sockets.

'Alain?' Jenny reached out and took one small fist in her hand. He snapped out of his near-faint and stared at Jenny.

'Jenny . . .' He began to cry afresh. 'Please, Jenny . . . I didn't mean it.'

CHAPTER 27

Fraser parked outside the house, trying to summon the courage to turn in to the driveway and roll up to the front door. Finally, summoning his courage, he swung in to the broad, gravelled drive and stopped outside the house.

Vi Harvey was instantly recognizable, even after eight years. She had the same glossy, glowing look, the same showy confidence, as when he had met her all that time ago.

'Oh, God,' she said. 'What do *you* want?'

'An explanation.'

She looked over his shoulder and Fraser saw a twinkle of malicious humour in her eyes. 'Think you deserve one, do you?'

They regarded each other for a few moments. Perhaps she did look a little older — weathered, rather than worn — too much sun and nicotine, Fraser reflected.

'Aren't you going to tell me I haven't changed a bit?' she asked. That malicious gleam appeared again, and Fraser thought *She's flirting with me — she just can't switch it off.*

'Can I come in?'

She seemed to think about it and then, as if she had lost interest, turned and walked down the hall. 'Shut the door after you,' she said. He followed her into the kitchen where she was preparing a salad.

'He's mine, isn't he?' Fraser said.

Vi widened her eyes. 'Who?'

'Don't piss me about, Vi. Your husband called me — of course he called himself by another name — but it was him all right.'

She frowned, slicing a tomato with elaborate care. 'How did you find us?'

'I didn't know where to look, at first. I tried the phone book, but—'

'We're ex-directory.'

'I got the company name from Yellow Pages,' he said. 'After that — well, you should never underestimate the libraries service — if they can't help, they usually know a man who can. They put me on to the Companies House Register, and Companies House faxed me the managing director's name and address.'

'Obliging of them,' she said. Then, 'He isn't here . . .' She hesitated, seeming suddenly unsure of herself. 'I don't know where he is.'

'It's you I wanted to see.'

'How nice. After all these years.'

'You told me you'd had an abortion.'

For a moment, she was disconcerted. She turned to the sink and rinsed her hands, taking time to recover her composure before answering with her back turned to him. 'Who's to say I didn't?'

'Your husband for one. Otherwise, why contact me?'

'You'll have to ask him that. Are you *sure* it's me you wanted to see?'

'I want to see my son.'

The smile returned, but the malicious edge had sharpened. 'Go home,' Vi said. 'Go back to your wife.' She began to turn away and he caught her just above the elbow.

'Where is he?'

She looked up into his eyes, unafraid, angry. 'You're hurting my arm.' Her grip tightened on the vegetable knife in her free hand.

Fraser let her go. 'I told you I'd provide for the child.'

'What?' she said, flinging the knife into the sink. 'On your teacher's salary? Do you know what a house like this costs, Fraser? Have you *any* idea?'

Fraser blinked. 'You bartered our child for this house?'

'Oh, please. Spare me the Calvinist morality. You make it sound so sordid. The boy was the glue that bound our marriage together. People do it all the time.'

'With another man's child?' He stared at her disgust. 'Where *is* he?' He ran from the kitchen, determined to search the house.

She followed him out, running down the hallway, grabbing the newel of the staircase for support, screaming up at him. 'Don't you watch the news, you *stupid* bastard?'

Fraser stopped and turned. She collapsed against the newel and slowly sank to the bottom step, sobbing. He returned down the stairs, one at a time, unsure if this was just another ploy. At the bottom of the stairs he crouched next to her and suddenly she hit out, punching hard. He raised his hand in a reflex action and her fist grazed his left eyebrow. Her momentum carried her forward, twisting as she fell, and she banged her face on the newel post.

She covered her mouth and sobbed, 'You stupid, self-obsessed *bastard*!'

Fraser stood slowly, bewildered, wanting to help, to console her. He touched her shoulder lightly, but she slapped it away.

'Don't *touch* me!' she screamed. 'Get out of my house! GET *OUT*!'

* * *

Fraser slumped behind the wheel of the car, staring at his hands. They were shaking. He had got as far as backing out of the drive when he felt another bout of nausea overtake him and he had to pull over to the side of the road until it passed.

What the hell had made him come here? He had hurt Jenny so badly that he didn't see how she could ever forgive him, and for what? He still hadn't seen his son — didn't even know if he was safe. What had Vi called him? Self-obsessed. Maybe so, but he couldn't stop now. He couldn't let go. He had to see this through to the end, no matter what the consequences.

CHAPTER 28

'Dr Greenberg?'

'Speaking. Who is this?' Max sounded wary.

'I'm sorry, phoning you at home, and on the weekend as well, but—' She stopped, seemed to gather herself. 'I'm Yvonne. I work on the switchboard at the hospital. I don't know how to say this . . . She'll probably kill me for talking to you . . .'

'Whatever you tell me will remain strictly confidential,' he reassured her.

'I wasn't going to bother. She's not exactly my responsibility. But I couldn't settle to anything. I kept worrying about her.'

She hesitated. Max waited.

'It's Shona,' she said. 'Shona Rhys. Didn't you look after her when she had a — well, when she got sick?'

'I'm afraid I can't—'

'No, I know that, but Shona told me you helped her before — last time — and I thought maybe you could . . .'

'Why are you worried about her?'

'She's been all over the place this week. Turning up late for her shifts, going off without a word of explanation. Crying over nothing. Withdrawn. And she's got these bruises on her hands. I—' She lowered her voice. 'I think she's started hurting herself again.'

Max recalled Shona's wild appearance at the entrance of the hospital on Friday morning. Yes, he should have been more direct, should have insisted she make an appointment to see him.

'Dr Greenberg?'

'I'll talk to her,' he said. 'I'll do my best.'

* * *

It was getting worse. Now she didn't have to close her eyes to see his face, the eyes wide, insane and evil, laughing at her. The destruction of his books had only made him angry and now he was persecuting her so that she dared not sleep, because when she slept, he would hover over her bed, waiting for her to awake and inhale the sickness and putrefaction of his breath. His laughter followed her, cutting across phone calls, insinuating itself into the rhythm of the car's engine, the whirr of her refrigerator, gurgling through the water pipes, hissing through the flames of the gas fire. He whispered to her from the static on the radio, and with the rush, rush, rush of blood in her ears, he urged her on, telling her there was no other way:

Suicide-suicide-suicide.

She telephoned Pam on her emergency number, but he wouldn't let her say what she wanted to say. She had heard Pam trying to reach her over his angry screams:

'How are we healed, Shona? Say it with me.'

'By openness and shared experience, we achieve awareness,' she intoned. 'By the expression of legitimate rage . . .' Here, Pam's voice was drowned out by his furious demands for her to kill herself. '. . . confrontation of our persecutor brings release and the realization of our potential.'

Shona knew it by heart. It was pinned to her noticeboard in the kitchen, but he wouldn't let her say it.

'Confront your demons, Shona,' Pam said. Then he disconnected them.

Shona reached for her address book, and as she put it on the table, it fell open at the page where she had written his number.

Fate. She would be calm.

Max Greenberg picked up the phone on the second ring. He listened for two or three minutes before speaking.

'Yes,' he said. 'It's time we talked.'

CHAPTER 29

Mike Delaney nodded towards the family group beyond the mirror. 'Do they know it's two-way?'

'They're not stupid, Mike.'

He and Max Greenberg sat side by side, their knees almost touching the screen between the tiny office and the interview room.

'I'm not sure this is a good idea,' Mike said in a whisper, unconvinced that the soundproofing really worked.

Max took a deep breath, then exhaled through his nose. 'Jenny said the same thing about Alain. She's not sure he's ready for it.'

'They were very upset.'

'Mm.'

They watched the little group for a couple of minutes. Angeline, Alain's mother, appeared to be trying to calm her mother. Her father sat, frowning, distracted, perhaps in shock.

'All three of them insisted on identifying the body,' Mike said.

Max winced.

'Sorry, Max, but that's what it is.'

'I know, that's not what's bothering me. They're Catholics, aren't they?'

'So?'

He shrugged. 'It beats me why believers in a religion that makes such a big thing of faith — in believing what can't possibly be proven — would insist such close scrutiny of a body before accepting death.'

Mike bridled, despite his long-standing lapse into a troubled agnosticism. 'Haven't they a right to see Jeanne-Louise one last time?' he demanded, falling into the interrogative speech patterns of his mother and father, still devout in their beliefs. 'After all, is it likely they'd have an open coffin with her injuries?'

Max's eyebrows twitched. 'I hadn't expected such fellow feeling,' he said. 'But I'm not disputing their right to view the body,' he explained. 'I'm just noting that it hasn't exactly put them in a sanguine frame of mind to meet Alain, has it?'

'Sanguine,' Mike said, prickly at being subjected to a lecture. 'Is that what they call a Freudian slip?'

Max eyed him coolly. 'I'll go and tell Jenny we're ready.'

Mike began to stand, but Max pressed gently on his shoulders. 'Best you stay here. The boy is a little . . . volatile at present.'

'Frightened?'

'Most likely, but it's being expressed as aggression. He cracked Fraser over the head with a cricket bat this morning.'

'Is he okay?'

He saw a fleeting twinkle of mischief. 'Fraser or the boy?'

'Both.'

Max became serious, reflective. 'Alain is calm. For the moment. Whether he's okay is quite another matter, but he *is* here.'

'Is he communicating?'

'He'll talk to Jenny. Only to her,' Max said, fixing him with a look that said, *He's not ready to speak to you.* 'And then only under extreme conditions.'

Mike did a little mental backtracking. He recalled the day and Diane Seward, the photographer, had gone to take Alain's picture. There was a strained, unwelcoming atmosphere in the house which was quite unlike Jenny and Fraser. He moved on to the morning that he had telephoned Jenny to tell her that the body they had found was not Alain's mother but her sister. Jenny had mentioned a car parked outside their house — a car she had noticed when she had left the house to wander Sefton Drive in the early hours.

'These phone calls Jenny and Fraser have been getting . . .' he began.

'I don't know what they're about, Mike,' Max said, his tone making quite clear that he would consider it a discourtesy if Mike were to inquire further.

Mike responded with a slight lowering of the eyelids, a mental more than physical acquiescence. 'How's Fraser after the crack on the head?'

'I don't know. He buggered off with—' Max stopped, and Mike's ears pricked.

'Off with . . .' *What? Or who?*

He waited, interested to see how Max would resolve his obvious misstep. He was holding back. Who was he protecting — Jenny or Fraser?

'Without a word,' Max concluded abruptly.

Mike had been a policeman for too many years and had heard too many lies to let that go. He studied Max for some moments, then nodded again, once, slowly, thoughtfully.

'Jenny thinks she's being watched,' he said, again waiting for Max's reaction. He gave none, except for a slight lifting of his head. 'And that's on top of these weird phone calls.'

'Can't you put a trace on the line?'

'We could,' Mike said, 'but it'd be a bit pointless if Fraser knows who's making the calls.'

He was asking Max to help him out, and although he couldn't read it in Max's face, the psychiatrist's hesitation said that he was having an inner debate.

'Are you any nearer tracing Alain's father?' Max asked, after too long a silence.

Mike grimaced. 'It's proving more complicated than we expected. I've got a few questions for Mrs Fournier before she leaves, so ask her to hang about when she's finished here, will you?'

'Of course . . .' Another awkward pause. 'The men you were interviewing yesterday—'

'What about them?'

Max smiled. 'You've stolen my line.'

'We let one go. We're still interviewing the other.'

'And?'

Mike gave a slow smile. 'And nothing. We're still talking, that's all.'

It wasn't quite all: they had charged Lobo with the attack on Randy Khan to add to the charges of assault and battery on Peter Merembe and criminal damage to Merembe's car. It hadn't been difficult to persuade his superintendent to grant an extension on Lee-Anne's detention. She hadn't said anything arrestable yet, but she would, he was sure of it.

'I see,' Max said, turning to leave.

'I don't think you do, Dr Greenberg,' Mike said quietly.

He saw surprise — perhaps even affront — in the psychiatrist's expression as he turned back.

'I think you know what's going on with Jenny and Fraser,' Mike said. 'Now, I'm sure you have good reasons for withholding that information — respect of privacy, honouring a position of trust, whatever. But ask yourself this: if you say nothing, and that puts Jenny in danger, will you ever forgive yourself?'

For five seconds he thought Max was ready to tell him all. Then his face closed, and he left the room, closing the door firmly behind him.

* * *

Jenny guided Alain gently towards the interview room. Having told her that the family was ready, Max had retreated to watch the exchange from the observation room. The boy had enough to deal with, he had explained — an additional stranger in the room would only put more pressure on him.

Jenny had only managed to get Alain this far by providing him with a series of achievable goals. First, leaving the house. Next, getting into the taxi, promising him that she wouldn't force him to see his mother, that he could leave whenever he wanted to.

The walk from the taxi to the hospital had proved the most difficult. At first, he had refused to get out of the taxi, then they sat outside for ten minutes on a bench in the sunshine, listening to the distant sound of traffic and the insistent chirrup of sparrows in the bushes nearby. But he *had* made it inside, taking a deep breath and bracing himself as if he were about to take a high dive into deep water.

Now, outside the interview room, Jenny could feel Alain trembling. His hand was deathly cold in hers. He was doing this for her, because she had asked him to, and she felt a little ashamed of herself. Didn't she say she wouldn't force him? And wasn't this coercion a subtle way of doing just that? She told herself that he had to meet his mother, that the authorities needed to know what had happened to him, but looking down at the child now, seeing the curls on his forehead quiver with anxiety, she felt she was being cruel.

'Mummy is inside,' she explained. 'And your grandparents.' Alain made a low, guttural sound like a moan, and Jenny added, 'I'll stay with you, Alain. I'll be with you the whole time.'

He squared his shoulders as if preparing to go before a firing squad. He even nodded to let her know he was ready. She opened the door and stepped inside.

Angeline Fournier was stunningly pretty. She wore her hair in a loose knot, held in place with a mother of pearl comb, tendrils of rich, dark brown curls caressing her cheeks. She held herself erect, her chin slightly lifted, her eyes, big and dark like Alain's, were bright, despite her long journey. Alain's grandmother was small, dainty, grey haired, her make-up subtle, her style understated and elegant. By comparison, her husband looked like a rustic: big, round faced and rather rumpled in appearance.

Mrs Fournier made a movement, as if to stand up, but Jenny gave her a warning glance and she settled back into her chair. Alain huddled closer to Jenny.

'Maman?' He seemed uncertain of her.

Jenny did as Mike had instructed her. 'Alain,' she said, 'can you tell me who these people are?'

For a few moments he said nothing, gazing at the trio with a solemn, sad expression. 'Maman,' he said, with a sigh, 'Grandmère et Grandpère.'

'Come to Mummy,' Mrs Fournier said.

Alain turned a bewildered face up to Jenny. She slackened her grip to allow him to go to his mother, if he chose. He held her hand tightly and shrank back, almost hiding behind her. Mrs Fournier's face was closed, unreadable.

Alain's grandmother opened her arms to him, then, with a little sob, she let them fall. Alain looked away, fixing his eyes resolutely on the floor. 'I want to go now,' he said. It was barely audible, no more than a whisper, but Jenny heard it. She had promised him, if he asked to leave, they would go — no argument, no delay.

She turned, still holding Alain's hand, and heard a gasp behind her. 'No!' Mrs Fournier screamed. 'You can't take him!'

Alain broke free of Jenny and ran blindly out of the clinic, into the corridor, back the way they had come, running, running, until he could no longer hear her screams. He burst out into the sunshine, past parked cars, dodging a man who tried to stop him, stopping only when he got to the main gates and was unsure which way to turn. Jenny caught up with him, and Alain struggled and then clung to her, sobbing miserably. 'I want to go home!' he begged.

'All right,' Jenny soothed, hugging him tightly, stroking his head. 'All right. We'll go home. We'll go now.'

* * *

Max had arranged for Mike Delaney to interview Alain's mother in his office at the Child Development Centre. It was a long, narrow room, with filing cabinets cluttered at one end. The expanse of wall on one side of the room held a giant pinboard, dominated by a year planner. Nearly every weekday was already blocked in, with clinics, talks, seminars and conferences. Max's desk, with its phone and PC, was jammed up against the window, which overlooked slate rooftops and the steam vents of the hospital laundry. Max had cheerily informed him that on a fine day, when the wind wasn't blowing eastward, the window could be opened to allow a little ventilation.

Mike took advantage of that facility now, grateful for a respite, no matter how small, from the roiling heat of the afternoon. He took off his jacket and rolled up his sleeves, wondering where the hell Angeline Fournier had been all this time. Simultaneously there was a loud, confident rap at the door, and then she was in, shouting.

'What have you people done to my son?'

'Done to him?'

'He wouldn't even come to me. His own mother!'

'Talk to the doctors about that,' Mike said. 'It's not my field.' He stared over her shoulder, to a framed cartoon sketch which hung next to the wall chart. A caricature of Max: large head, small body, the great expanse of his forehead puckered slightly. He was seated at a cabaret table with his back to the stage, making notes on the audience, while behind him, a curvy stripper peeled off her stockings. The caption read: *An observer of human nature.*

'I'm told he's under an interim care order,' Mrs Fournier said, coldly. 'My understanding is that you have a responsibility.'

Mike sighed. 'Look, as I understand it, he's in shock. He's not behaving normally.'

'I want him home with me.'

'Not yet.'

'You don't understand — how could you? He needs me.'

'Like you said, we have a duty of care to the lad. We'll keep him in care until we're sure he's safe to go home.'

She looked ready to kill him. 'Are you saying that you don't trust me with him? How dare you! He's *my son*! I've a right—'

'Yeah? Well he's got rights too. And he's requested returning to the foster parents he was placed with when he was found.' Mike was getting sick of people screaming at him. He was tired and he had a headache.

Mrs Fournier crumpled. Sobbing, she fished in her handbag for a tissue. Mike began to suspect that Mr Radleigh's explanation for Alain's persistent absenteeism from school was right: that it was a symptom of his mother's neurosis rather than the boy's anxiety. 'I love my son,' she said, when she had regained some control. 'I only want what's best for him.'

'Look,' he said, relenting a little. 'We're *all* trying to do what's best for Alan.'

'Al*ain*.'

'What?'

'My son's name is Al*ain*. It's a French name.'

Mike rubbed his eye with one finger and told himself that the woman was distraught after the death of her sister. He should be patient.

'I need to ask you about your ex-husband,' he said, trying to keep his voice even.

'What do you want to know?' Her eyes became hooded, wary.

'Tell me why you left him.'

She caught her breath, shook her head.

'Mrs Fournier?' He saw a fleeting look of pain.

'I can't . . .' She swallowed, seemed to collect herself, raised her head and said with some dignity, 'My reasons were — are — private.'

Mike shook his head. 'I can't have that, given the circumstances.'

She flushed angrily but said nothing.

'What's your married name?'

'I am no longer married, Sergeant.'

'Your ex-husband's name, then.'

'No . . . I'm sorry, but no.'

'Mrs Fournier, this is a murder inquiry!'

She flinched, clamping her lips together, avoiding his eye, and Mike said more calmly, 'Tell me why you left him.'

'Because he's a vicious, sadistic bastard who made our lives hell.' She glared at him, breathing hard, daring him to disbelieve her.

'D'you have any proof of this?'

'Have the doctors examine Alain's hands. That will give you proof enough.'

'They have — examined him, that is.'

Her eyes widened a little, then she tossed her head. 'Well then.'

'Do you have an address where we can contact your ex-husband?'

'Why would you want to contact him?'

'When did you last speak to him?'

She looked away, and a petulant furrow appeared between her carefully plucked eyebrows. 'He's not interested in Alain,' she said. 'He hasn't been in touch for over two years. I doubt if he'd even recognize his own son in the street.'

'The natural father has rights of access—'

'Rights!' she exclaimed. 'What about responsibilities? I took Alain away from him before he did my son permanent harm.'

'Try to see it from my point of view,' Mike said. 'You're asking me to believe that your son's injuries were inflicted by his father, but—'

'But it's my word against his, is that it?'

'We haven't even got a *name*, let alone made contact with him. How could it be your word against his?'

She gave an irritated shrug and turned away from him.

'Either you give us the name of your ex-husband or I will charge you with obstruction.' He waited, but she refused to look at him. 'Do you understand what I mean by obstruction, Mrs Fournier?'

He heard a gasp of exasperation. 'I have a degree in English,' she said, turning slowly to face him. Her expression held a mixture of disdain and amusement. 'I have read your English classics: the Brontes, Austen, Thackeray, Dickens. My final thesis was an analysis of the tragedies of Shakespeare.' She sat up straight and met him eye to eye with a look that all but demanded to know what *his* bedtime reading was.

Mike smiled. 'Me, all I got was a grade C in O-level English. *Cider with Rosie*, I think the set text was.' He held her gaze. 'Give me a name, Mrs Fournier. If you're telling the truth, you've got nothing to worry about.'

She snorted.

'Okay, we'll do it the hard way. If your husband assaulted your son, there's bound to be a record of it somewhere. Time frame about two years ago. Maybe he's even in prison.'

He caught a fleeting look of dismay, then she said, 'I — I didn't report it.'

Mike fought a rising tide of anger. If there was one thing he hated, it was being taken for a mug. 'Every finger of both hands were broken, and *you didn't report it*?'

'Of course, I got him treated. I said he'd trapped his fingers playing.'

Mike winced. He saw a sharp, electric-blue image of his eldest, Mary, trapping her fingers in a car door on her ninth birthday. She had been playing in the garage. It was November, he remembered it quite vividly, the strip light was switched on because of the gathering darkness, giving everything that unreal, bluish tinge.

'I can't make up my mind. Are you arrogant or just uncaring, Mrs Fournier?'

'What do you mean?'

'Do you really expect me to believe this crap?'

'I'm telling the truth!'

'That your little boy was brutally attacked, and his fingers broken, and you lied about it. What did you tell the medics? A car boot — a door? Maybe a window? And you coolly "get him treated" and then let the culprit off scot-free?'

Her lip quivered a little as she answered. 'We got out — away from his father — after that. I reverted to my maiden name, we moved north. I made sure he couldn't find us.'

Mike nodded and she seemed to relax fractionally.

He leaned forward, as if about to impart a confidence. 'Who's to say you didn't do it?'

She stared at him, open mouthed. '*What?*' She was angry, offended at being challenged so directly.

'Put yourself in my place. A little boy is found wandering the streets in his pyjamas. Middle of the night. He's so deeply shocked by what's happened to him he can't speak. No one seems to even notice he's gone. We wait four, nearly five days. Not a squeak. We put out a TV appeal. Still nothing, until his headmaster contacts the hotline.' He raised his voice. 'Not his mum or dad, his *headmaster*.'

She began crying, sobbing self-pityingly. 'He was with his aunt,' she wailed. 'I tried to telephone . . .'

'We got you on the answering machine. Once. We had it translated from the French. "Arrived safely. I'll be in touch." Now, if I was away from home, I'd at least leave a contact number.'

'I'm entitled to some time on my own,' she said. She sounded truculent, hurt by the suggestion. He stared at her for a little longer and she blushed.

'Business, was it?'

She wiped her nose before answering, dabbing carefully, to minimize the damage to her make-up. 'Business, yes.'

'So you'll be able to give us a list of people, places, meetings.'

'It wasn't that kind of business.'

'What other kind is there?'

'Don't be disgusting!'

Mike stared hard at her, and she relented. 'I'm an artist,' she said, with stiff dignity. 'I was in search of inspiration. I go places, make sketches, watercolours — and I visit the local potteries. It was informal. Unscheduled.'

'A holiday,' Mike said.

Her blush deepened. Temper or guilt?

'Business,' she replied, flatly.

* * *

'She said they'd moved north after the alleged attack on her son.' Mike sipped from a cup of tea and typed one-fingered at his computer.

'What — from London?'

Mike glanced sideways at DC Sallis. 'She isn't exactly giving us her autobiography, Ron. But her kind of business does best where there's plenty of dosh.'

'We've got someone checking the marriage records in the National Index.'

'Let's hope *he's* not French an' all, or we'll have to set up a search through Interpol.'

'What about her parents?'

'They're refusing to say anything.' Mike sighed. 'I don't know. The kid's mum is accusing his dad of brutalizing them both, but she's making damn sure we don't get his side of the story. She says she didn't report the attack, but she went a funny colour when I said we'd check the files for him. Let's give it a whirl, see what we come up with.'

CHAPTER 30

Lee-Anne seemed torn between admiration and exasperation. 'Lobo's a bleedin' headcase,' she began, minding her language, at least until she was more sure of who she was dealing with.

Mike Delaney leaned in a little. 'Is he?'

Lee-Anne settled back in her chair with a smirk. Apparently, she wasn't so easily drawn out.

'Mr Merembe's car is in pretty bad shape, and we had to send Mr Khan back to the hospital this morning.'

'Wha'?' Lee-Anne snapped to, the smirk wiped off her face and a perhaps a hint of anxiety in the gathering of her brows.

'I think you might know Mr Khan under his nickname Randy,' Mike explained, enjoying the foggy confusion on her face. Her intense concentration finally resolved itself in a look of animal aggression.

'I know Randy. What's up with him?'

'He goes out for a few jars with his old school mate, Derek Spencer — your Lobo — and he ends up with cracked ribs and a broken nose.' Mike winced.

'And you're trying to say Lobo done it? Do me a favour. They were in the same gang at school. They're mates.'

'Not anymore,' Mike said, hoping that she was sharp enough to hear the implied threat, the hint that Khan might have said something incriminating.

She kept her head down but shot him a look of mingled venom and fear from under her eyebrows. 'Fuckin' Paki!' She looked down again, breathing hard. 'Whatever he said, he's lying.'

'You said yourself, Lobo's a headcase.'

'Yeah, but not like that. More, like — off the wall. He wouldn't do that to a mate . . .' She screwed up her face, as if struggling for a way of making him see what it was she was driving at.

'One time,' she said, 'there was this feller Lobo really hated. Maths teacher. Thought he was hard. Dickinson, his name was — Dickhead, for short. "Derek," he says. Lobo hates being called Derek — does his head in. "Derek, nobody thinks you're funny disrupting the lesson like this. Nobody thinks you're clever." Which was soft, because *everyone* thought Lobo was funny and it was pretty friggin' clever an' all, getting us out of maths homework. Two minutes to the bell and Lobo kicks off, what else was he trying to do?'

She chuckled, remembering.

'So Dickhead goes over to Lobo and he like, leans over him and puts his two big hairy hands either side of him and he thinks because he's bigger than Lobo he can scare him. But Lobo's not scared of nothing. He just gives dickhead the mad eye. *He* starts talking to Lobo in a sort of growly whisper and we're all watching, even the creeps up the front of the class have turned around.

'"In fact," Dickhead says, "If brains were dynamite, you wouldn't have enough to blow your hat off!"

'There's a sort of nervous titter goes round the class, like a Mexican wave. Lobo lifts one finger, and he's got that smile on him, like his gob's too big for his face. He lifts his finger and he shows it to us and then he shows it to Dickhead. There's blood under the nail. Everyone stops laughing.

'"See that?" Lobo says, quiet like, but we can all hear him. "That's a bit of razor blade, that is. So, when someone goes for you—" He makes a quick, slashing flick, like Freddie Krueger in *Nightmare on Elm Street*. Dickhead jumps back.

'"They go—" Lobo puts his hand to his face. "What the fuck, man? It's blood! You cut me, man!" And just to show the damage that teeny broke off piece of razor blade can do, Lobo draws a line down the middle of his forearm and watches the blood squeeze out.

'"You bloody mad bastard," the teacher says, and for a minute there, we all think he's going to faint. Lobo laughs and laughs, wild, like a maniac or something.' Lee-Anne faltered, her eyes searching Mike's face for understanding.

At last, she dragged her fingers down her face. 'Ugh! It's coming out all wrong.'

Mike kept his stance relaxed and widened his eyes. 'Is that how it ended?'

She shook her head. 'Nah. For some reason we all start chanting *"Loco Lobo! Loco Lobo!"* and the lads are kicking the desks and stamping on the floor, so it sounds like a train, or the Kop on a Saturday. And Lobo laughs and laughs and shakes his head till you think it's gonna come off and he's cracking up 'cos he thinks the teacher's funny, 'cos he made him swear and 'cos we're not gonna do no homework today. And he thinks *we're* funny, an' all — chanting and bouncing the dust out the cracks in the floor with our stamping. And the blood's funny and . . .' She paused, searching for the words to express how funny it all was. 'And he just bleeds.'

She stopped entirely for a good thirty seconds, then seemingly frustrated by her inability to articulate what she wanted to say, she spoke again. '*Everyone* looked up to Lobo, not just me — all the lads in his gang — and his lot was the hardest in the school. Everyone wanted to be in Lobo's gang.' She exhaled in a great rush. 'I'm trying to say Lobo's a *headcase*, but he isn't a *nutter*.'

Mike let that thought reverberate for a few seconds before he said, 'You think he's putting it on.'

She gave a half-nod.

'Lee-Anne,' he said, as kindly as he could, 'you can't "put on" that kind of fury — because that's what it is. When Lobo smiles and laughs and shakes his head "like it'll come off" — you *know* someone's going to get hurt, don't you?'

She pouted. 'No . . . He's a good *laugh*.' But they both heard the edge of desperation creeping into her voice.

'A good laugh.' Mike considered this point, cupping his chin in one hand. 'Is that what you were doing when you broke into Angeline Fournier's house — having a good laugh?'

Her eyes narrowed. 'I don't know what you're on about.'

He leaned in, closing the distance across the table, robbing her of the safety of distance. She raised herself from her accustomed slouch, a look of alarm on her face.

'You were seen, Lee-Anne.'

She looked away and the furrow deepened between her eyes.

'We've got several witnesses willing to identify you,' Mike went on.

Two bright spots of colour appeared on the sharp blades of her cheekbones. Mike recognized it as temper. 'You were seen around the Fournier house. Lobo was caught with Ms Fournier's credit and debit cards on him, and your flat looks like it's had a make-over by *Changing Rooms*.' She glanced up at him, an eager look of flattered gratification on her face, and Mike, disgusted that she could forget so easily that her gain was at the expense of someone else's life, made the mistake of showing his dislike.

Her expression hardened. 'Yeah?' she said. 'Prove it.'

Mike leaned back, knowing that he had lost this round. 'I will,' he said. 'Just watch me.'

* * *

Mike interviewed Lobo immediately after, while his adrenaline was still high. This was more formal, of necessity. Since Lobo had been charged, his solicitor had been appointed and

Lobo, conscientious about the proper execution of the law and well versed in the provisions of the Police and Criminal Evidence Act, had insisted on him being present. Jack Hughes was in the wrong job: he believed in the inalienable right of every British citizen to protection under British Law, but he worked on first impressions, and if he didn't like the thug he was asked to represent, he just couldn't hide it. His real name was John, but one of the custody sergeants had given him the name, in one of his rare lighter moments, and it seemed so appropriate that now everyone called him Jack — though not to his face.

'Fuckin' snob Paki dropped me in it, has he?' Lobo gripped the table's edges, bending his elbows and leaning forward.

Mike studied him with genuine curiosity. Gargoyles and goblins came irrepressibly to mind. 'You might want to remind your client to curb his racist comments,' he said, looking at Jack.

Mr Hughes had a whispered exchange with his client.

Mike exchanged a look with DC Douglas. 'Witnesses will testify that you took a pool cue to Mr Merembe's car and, when he tried to intervene, you used it on Mr Khan.'

'He asked for it.'

Mike chose not to draw attention to the implied admission and was amused to note that Mr Hughes seemed to be of the same mind.

'How did he ask for it?' Mike asked, in a tone of genuine interest.

Lobo began rubbing his palms backwards and forwards, smearing the edges of the table with grime and sweat. 'He started on that poncey course, didn't he?'

'It was my understanding that you had lost touch,' Mike said. 'And that you didn't know what Mr Khan was doing until you met him yesterday, outside the Liverpool Institute of Performing Arts.'

Lobo snorted, ignoring the logic of Mike's statement. 'LIPA,' he said, working himself into a rage. 'Liverpool Institute of Poncey Arseholes, more like!'

'So, he asked for it,' Mike said, careful to make the intonation a statement, rather than a question.

Lobo stopped the compulsive chafing of his palms against the table. He placed both hands on the table and looked straight at Delaney. 'I should've kicked his fucking *head* in.'

Mike could smell his breath. It reeked of alcohol and vomit and the bitter acid of jealousy.

Jack coughed, politely, clearly embarrassed by his client.

Mike straightened up, exhaling hard to clear the stench from his nostrils. 'Cue's wrecked,' he observed mournfully.

Lobo darted him a quick, cunning look.

'And unfortunately, it isn't going to be so easy getting a replacement, now you've lost your gold card.'

Lobo slipped back, his hands sliding off the table in a fluid, nerveless movement into his lap. He's lost colour, Mike thought. Seems like I'm pushing the right buttons.

Lobo balled his fists and began cracking each knuckle in turn.

DC Douglas handed Mike an evidence bag containing Jeanne-Louise Fournier's cards, sliding Lobo a sideways glance as he did so, smiling a little to himself. Lobo must have sensed the look. He caught Douglas's eye, his anger blazing out briefly, but he seemed to think better of acting on it and stared down at his hands and resumed cracking the joints with increasing ferocity.

'Recognize these, do you, Derek?' Mike asked.

Lobo began chewing the inside of his mouth. His eyes, refusing to obey him, flickered up, up, to the bag and the cards inside. Mike saw his forced effort to look away.

Douglas was watching Lobo implacably, as they'd agreed he would — that lazy smile on his face — and opposite Mike, Jack Hughes had also turned to look at his client. He seemed perplexed, waiting for an answer. Surely Lobo had told him about the cards?

'Mr Spencer?' Mike said.

'I never seen them before.'

'They were in your wallet.'

Lobo shrugged, looking down again, avoiding the three pairs of eyes watching, watching.

'You signed for them when the custody sergeant asked you to turn out your pockets.'

'They're a plant.'

Mike laughed softly. 'You used this one' — he tapped a Visa card through the bag with his index finger — 'to buy the cue.'

Lobo turned down the corners of his mouth. 'Not me.'

'You've been identified. Once seen, eh, Lobo? It was a bit lax, using the card like that, when you could've got cash — or asked Lee-Anne to do the buying.'

Lobo pressed too hard and his little finger gave an exceptionally loud *crack*. He grunted, but his expression never changed.

Mike watched him sweat for a few moments. 'But I'm forgetting, you had a row with Lee-Anne yesterday morning. Couldn't very well ask her to go and get you the cue when she wanted you to get shot of the cards.'

The horror on Lobo's face was a rare treat. It was quickly displaced by rage.

'*Bitch!*' he spat.

'The assistant who served you was a bit lax an' all,' Mike said. 'Not noticing that the card belonged to a Miss J. L. Fournier. All he did was check the signatures tallied. Which they did. I bet you were good at copying in school, weren't you Derek?'

Lobo lifted his head and glared at Mike, grinning, but Mike grinned back with equally feral menace. 'Where did you get the cards, Derek?'

'I found them.' Lobo looked away.

Mike raised his eyebrows. 'Found them,' he repeated. 'Found them where?'

'I don't know. In the street.'

A second mistake — a second concession to the truth that could be used against him. Mike saw sweat pop out of the thug's forehead as he realized that control was slipping from him.

'In the street,' Mike repeated. 'Precisely where?'

'I don't know, do I? Hey.' He turned to face his solicitor for the first time since they had entered the room. 'Aren't you supposed to stick up for me?'

'What do you want me to say?'

Perhaps, Mike thought, Jack Hughes had been disabused of his idealistic notions of fairness and innocence until proven guilty too soon and too decidedly by an early experience representing an out-and-out villain. He couldn't see the young lawyer remaining a duty solicitor for long: he was far too sensitive — and far too inclined to take sides against his clients.

Lobo stared open mouthed. 'What do I want?' he began. '*I* don't know, do I? I'm not a lawyer, am I? Tell him he's being argumentative, or somethin'. Badgering the witness—'

'You're not a witness, Mr Spencer, you're a suspect,' the solicitor said. 'And this isn't a court of law.'

'Could've fooled me!' Lobo folded his arms, scowling.

'Answer the question,' Mike said, playing the unreasonable advantage the solicitor was giving him. He was half inclined to feel sorry for Lobo, but not enough to stop him following through. 'Where — exactly — did you "find" the credit cards?'

Lobo sat with his head down, staring up at Mike. His eyebrows were angled to a V in the centre of his forehead, and the maniacal grin covered a jumpy nervousness and a great mass of guilt.

Mike slid the evidence bag across the table. 'Can you read the name on the cards, Derek?

'I can read.' Lobo said belligerently, taking offence at the implied slur on his intellectual abilities.

'Then read the name.'

He tried to stare Mike down, but when he realized he wouldn't win, he shrugged and reached forward with an indolent movement.

'Don't touch it!' Mike said, sharply.

Lobo's eyes narrowed and Mike focused on them, glittering with rage. He wondered that Lobo could cope with it, burning like a bone-dry furnace within him day and night. He half expected to see signs of cracking — tiny fissures in Lobo's face. Had Jeanne-Louise been the escape valve?

'I can't see from there,' Lobo snarled.

Mike tilted the bag. 'J. L. Fournier,' Lobo said, pronouncing it 'Fornear'.

'Jeanne-Louise Fournier,' Mike repeated, thoughtfully. He retrieved the bag, frowning at it as if trying to remember something. He could see the solicitor in the periphery of his vision, staring at Lobo's profile. Behind the professional mask of impartiality, Jack Hughes's animosity was palpable.

'It was you, knocking on doors round Mossley Hill a week ago last Friday, wasn't it?' Mike asked.

Lobo gave him a look of troubled innocence. 'Knocking on doors. What for?'

'We'll get to the reason in a moment. Let's just establish facts,' Mike said. 'Was it you?'

A pause, then, 'No.'

'That's not what Lee-Anne says.'

'Oh yeah?'

The grin was back, and Mike was well on the way to thinking he'd like to stop it with his fist.

'Something funny?' he asked.

'Yeah, you are.'

'Care to share?'

Lobo thought about it. 'Lee-Anne can be a spiteful bitch, but she's not soft. She wouldn't drop herself in the shite.'

'Okay.' Mike quickly gave the concluding details of the interview and switched off the tape. 'We'll set up an ID parade,' he said, addressing the solicitor.

They had a number of witnesses who thought they could identify the young man and woman seen near the Fournier house on the night of the murder. Since Lobo had already been charged with assault he wasn't going anywhere.

Lobo eyed his solicitor in a decidedly threatening manner. 'That all right with you, Mr Spencer?' he said, laying on the sarcasm with a trowel. 'I mean, it is your right to refuse.'

'Er, yes,' the solicitor said. 'I would have to discuss the pros and cons of agreeing to an ID parade.'

'No need, mate. I've made up me mind — I'm not doin' it.'

Mike smiled. 'Two of our witnesses are willing to meet you face to face, Mr Spencer.'

'You wouldn't want that,' the solicitor hurriedly intervened. At least in a line-up there was a chance that one of the others would get picked out. Narrow the field to one and the outcome was more certain.

'How would you know what I want? You've sat there squinting down your big beak at me like I'm somethin' smelly you got on your shoe.'

'You're mistaken, Mr Spencer, I assure you—'

'You callin' me a liar?'

Mike interrupted. Retrieving the tapes from the recorder, he said, 'I'll leave you two to discuss strategy.' He exchanged a glance with Douglas, managing — with an effort — to keep his face straight. 'The constable will wait outside the door. If you need him, just shout.' His final impression of the solicitor was of the whites of his eyes flashing an SOS signal.

CHAPTER 31

Vi held the receiver in place with her left shoulder as she made rapid notes. 'Yes,' she said. 'Yes, I've got it.' She listened. 'I don't know. An hour? An hour and a half?' She hung up and put a trembling hand to her mouth. Her upper lip was moist. She was sweating.

Money for Connor. That's what he had said. Money for a child, as simple as that. Vi quelled a wave of nausea. She would have to agree. He knew that she had no choice. So, there would be a straight swap: her son, purchased for cash, like a piece of baggage.

* * *

Fraser had given up — even got as far as leaning forward to start the engine — when Vi's pale blue Mercedes convertible pulled out of the drive with the top open. Vi in sunglasses and scarf, looking like a fifties film star. So, she had got her call. Was she going to meet her husband? He had to know. He waited for a delivery van to pass before pulling out. She wasn't looking in her mirror anyway. She drove like fury out of Hale towards Widnes, over the Runcorn Bridge, and into Cheshire. Part of the way, she drove along the M56, and

Fraser had a few heart-stopping moments, trying to gauge the speed of following traffic before pulling out to keep her in sight. She joined the M6 and headed south, turned off at Knutsford and drove down country lanes, eventually turning into a narrow track with a sign, which read 'To Avonlea Farmhouse'. He waited for a few minutes, then drove the Volvo onto the grass verge and started walking down the track.

Harvey was smaller than Fraser remembered. He had first met Vi when one of Fraser's A-level geography teachers' seminars had coincided with a business conference at the same hotel. Bill Harvey had been there to promote his new plastic moulding technique. Fraser even remembered the conference title: 'Fantastic Plastic'.

Vi had apparently despised her husband and his business, but she loved his money, or more accurately she loved to spend it. So, she had attended the conference under protest. He had fallen into conversation with Vi at one of the hotel's bars, where she was sulking because she felt Bill was ignoring her. That weekend he had signed a contract with a major toy manufacturer to provide them with moulded plastic packaging for a range of dolls and figures. He didn't have time to pander to his wife and she wasn't used to being sidelined. Fraser had been angry and frustrated that he hadn't been able to bring himself to broach the subject of adoption with Jenny, and because he couldn't accept this as a weakness in his own character, he'd blamed his wife. He understood that now.

Vi and Fraser had used each other. It was a no-strings, no-holds-barred fling. When she had told him she was pregnant, that had changed for him, but not for Vi. He was convinced that she had told him only to gauge his response. Since he wasn't going to leave Jenny, she told him she wanted an abortion. He pleaded with her, but the next time they spoke, she told him with icy control that it was done.

Eight years. He'd had a son for *eight years* and hadn't known. Instead, she had let Bill Harvey believe that Connor was his own. She must have resented carrying a child, ruining her figure for the sake of the only kind of security Vi craved or respected. Until now, evidently, she had considered the pay-off worth the deception and the inconvenience. Vi had her own distinctive set of values, and Harvey had proved a much better bet, financially, than Fraser. Bill had been an ambitious, driven businessman, whose energy was almost overwhelming. Handsome, slim, always smartly dressed and, Fraser remembered, sporting thick, wavy hair. It was hard to equate that image with this balding, middle-aged, slightly corpulent man. He looked respectable — even a little staid — in his linen slacks and pale blue, short-sleeved shirt. The wind riffled the cuffs as he raised his arm and waved to someone in the distance.

Fraser followed his line of sight. In the field, beyond the garden of the house, was a boy. Fraser ducked down, his heart racing, and crouched behind the fencing that bordered the track to the house. Harvey shouted something to the boy, but the wind carried his words away and Fraser couldn't make it out. The boy smiled, returning the wave, then he turned and ran, disappearing into a dip in the terrain. Moments later, a kite sailed up from the field and lifted higher and higher.

* * *

Connor ran with his kite. Inside him was a knot of excitement, like a tangled ball of string. He laughed, feeling the wind tug at him, lifting the kite, trying to pluck it from his fingers. He loved this place, and he loved the sun on his back and the wind buffeting him, and he loved his daddy. He turned and waved again, even though his daddy had already disappeared beyond the hill, and laughed delightedly as he tugged at the kite string. It soared like a bird, whirring and buzzing, the line carrying the vibrations from the fabric to his hands.

* * *

'I suppose the first attempt was staged to frighten me,' Vi said. 'Or to throw the police off the scent.' She stood in her husband's sitting room, speaking directly to him and ignoring the tall, fastidious presence of their solicitor, Jeremy Byatt.

'It was a mistake, Vi — an error of judgement on my part. But what did you expect? You tell me I'm not the father of my own child and in the same breath you say you'll take him away from me.'

'Evidently the actions of a loving and concerned parent.'

'I would never have done it if you hadn't threatened to take Connor away.'

She smirked, remembering the satisfyingly confused emotions on Bill's face when she told him, *'All right, you can have your divorce. I shan't contest it, but you know you have no claim to Connor.'* She had kept her brief fling with the handsome young Scot from him all those years, had held the child as a kind of trump card, an ace up her sleeve. Her affairs since then had been more discreet — less passionate, perhaps, but safer. 'I hate to sound petulant, but you started it.'

'I think you'll find that Bill has more than adequate grounds for seeking a divorce,' Byatt said.

'If you say so, Jeremy.'

Bill Harvey looked at his wife, then out, through the open French windows, to the field where his son was playing. He looked embarrassed, even ashamed. 'I'm sorry if I frightened you,' he said.

Vi shrugged. For her own part, once she knew the boy was safe, she hadn't wasted her energy on another moment's anxiety. What was the point, since he hadn't been harmed? He had been fussed over by parents and teaching staff after the botched abduction. Tea and cakes in the headmaster's drawing room had soon restored him to his old self. In fact, Connor had thought it a terrific adventure.

'Your little charade certainly convinced the police,' she said. 'Did you hire an actor? I hope you paid Equity rates.'

Harvey ignored the question. 'You have lied and cheated throughout our marriage, Vivienne. You would no doubt have continued to do so, and I probably would have tolerated it. But I couldn't — could never have tolerated — you stealing from me.'

'It's my money, too!' she yelled. His refusal to be baited always infuriated her.

'It was the firm's money,' Jeremy corrected her. 'And what you did was fraudulent . . .' He stared at her, a look of severity on his narrow lawyer's face. 'You could go to prison. Bill would be awarded custody of Connor by the courts.'

'You have no rights over him!' She was screeching now, almost out of control. 'You aren't even his natural father!'

Jeremy broke in: 'The *Children Act* is more concerned with what's in the best interest of the child than genetics, Vivienne.' He had a rich, plummy voice, the sort of accent Vi had been trying to cultivate since Bill had signed his first big contract. She resented it, and she resented him.

'I'll fight you.'

'If you do, you won't get a penny from me,' Harvey said.

'And you could go to prison,' Jeremy reminded her.

Vi laughed, a little shakily, but she was regaining her composure. She flipped open her handbag and retrieved her cigarettes and lighter. 'You wouldn't want any whiff of scandal attached to your precious firm, now, would you? That would be bad for business. And I think you'll find there is legal provision for ex-wives, darling. Isn't that right, Jeremy — or would it be a conflict of interest to speak up for me? I am, after all, your client too.' She lit up, her hands not as steady as she would have liked.

'What Bill means is that he will fight you for every penny. And he has greater resources than you.'

'You're asking me to sell my son to you. Money in exchange for a child. D'you think he'd want to go with you if he knew you aren't his real father?'

'I hope he would, but I want to tell him in my own time, and in my own way.'

'Under the terms of the agreement, if you tell the boy, you will automatically forfeit the right to your annuity, Vivienne,' Jeremy said.

'I should have known there would be a clause in this obscene document to cover that.' Vi laughed. 'You really are a bastard!'

'I don't know why you're bothering to argue.' Bill Harvey turned to his lawyer. 'She called Connor "it" for the first two years of his life. Her own son!'

'We're not here to apportion blame,' Jeremy said, 'only to establish a framework for the benefit of Connor. One which is satisfactory to both parties.'

But Bill could not leave it at that. 'Why the sudden interest, Vi?'

'Oh, you know,' she replied bitterly. 'One has to go through the motions.' Both men watched while she took a deep, nervy pull on her cigarette.

Bill spoke again, more gently. 'I only want what's best for Connor.'

'Which is me out of his life,' she said with an ugly twist of her mouth.

'You would have visitation rights,' Jeremy said. 'But Connor will reside with his father.'

'And who'd look after him when you're away on business, and working late, and too bloody busy to be with him?'

'I repeat my question: why the sudden interest?'

She suddenly realized what he was doing. Bill Harvey was used to negotiation, he understood the delicate nature of bargaining, was familiar with the rhythms of offer and counter-offer. He was looking for weaknesses that he could exploit and force her to compromise. *Well, I've made compromises all our married life*, she thought savagely. *Now it's your turn.*

She stared at him, refusing to answer his question, waiting for an answer to hers and he sighed.

'You know who'll look after him, Vi. The same person who's always looked after him.'

'Oh, perfect! Mimsy, mumsy little Lynn will smother and spoil him to her heart's content, won't she? Did the little bitch lie to me about being ill? Was she in on this?'

'In on *what*? I came home at lunchtime that day to see you. I thought we'd be able to talk, with her not being about. And when I saw Connor playing outside I . . . it was spur of the moment.'

'And what about your actor friend? Was he spur of the moment as well? Don't act the innocent with me, Bill — I know you too well.'

He lowered his head. 'I told you, I regret that. I panicked when you said you wouldn't let me see Connor. I lashed out — wanted to hurt you for what you'd done. You can understand that, can't you?'

'I understand ownership. And revenge,' she said. 'You think you own Connor because you made an investment. And we all know what a good businessman you are. You always did get a good return on your investments, didn't you, darling? You wanted to punish me for having an affair' — she ignored his snort of derision at the use of the singular — 'and for having someone else's child,' she finished.

'I love my son.'

'He's *not* your son!'

'I've cared for him and loved him as my son. He *is* mine.'

Vi turned to Jeremy. She pursed her lips, suppressing a smile. 'See what I mean? Ownership.'

'I don't care what you think of me, but I won't have you thinking badly of Lynn,' Bill said.

Vi snorted derisively.

'She was genuinely ill,' Harvey said.

'I'll bet she's having a whale of a time — is she here?' She saw an exchanged look between the two men and strode past them, out of the room, the tip of her cigarette glowing fiercely.

'Are you here, you little bitch?' She stood at the foot of the stairs, yelling. 'Gloating upstairs, are you? Come out, come out, wherever you are!'

'She's been . . . detained,' Jeremy said, avoiding an outright lie. 'She'll be here just as soon as we've got all of the . . . legalities sorted out.'

'She's always acted in Connor's best interests, Vi,' her husband said. 'She's devoted to the boy.'

Vi wheeled to face him, unable to control her spite, furious with herself that she was actually jealous of the respect and affection he felt for their nanny. 'Sent her shopping to get her out of the way, did you? Now why does that sound familiar? Not that I blame you. She is rather downmarket, even for you.' She glared at him, daring him to come back at her: *You should know. You said it, darling.*

But that was the sort of thing Vi said. Bill was always the perfect gentleman. Blameless Bill was above such malice. She raised her chin, waiting for his reply. He seemed hurt, saddened even, and his injured disapproval incensed her.

'Well, I'm sure you'll all be very happy,' she said, barging past him, back into the sitting room, dropping ash from her cigarette. She should sign the damn papers — sign them and leave. But she couldn't simply give up. 'What he's proposing can't be legal,' she said, confronting the solicitor.

'If you sign it, it *will* be legally binding, Vivienne.'

Her eyes raked the lawyer's face, but she saw no trace of a lie there. 'I want to show it to a solicitor. Of course,' she added with acid emphasis, 'I'll have to appoint a new one, now the firm of Byatt & Son has turned against me.'

Jeremy nodded gravely. 'That would certainly be advisable . . . *After* you've signed the documents, you shall have your own copy to take away and discuss.'

'God!' she screamed, rounding once more on her husband. 'You're so *fucking* sure of yourself, aren't you?'

'You agreed to my terms,' Bill said, a note of pleading entering his voice.

'This is coercion,' she snarled.

'Vi, we had all this out over the phone.'

She heard again, the pleading tone. Bill Harvey knew people — he knew about need and greed — but this went beyond his business skills, market projections and statistical analyses. Vi knew that his love for Connor was the most important thing in his life — she had used it to her advantage often enough to be sure of that — and he would do anything to keep him. She glanced from one to the other, deciding to test him one more time.

'I want to see my son.'

'But you haven't asked to see him in the ten minutes you've been here,' Byatt observed, throwing Bill a sharp look to silence him. 'You haven't even asked after his health and welfare.'

He returned her furious glare with a cool disparaging stare.

'My advice, if I were acting on your behalf, would be to sign,' Byatt said. 'You won't get a better deal than this in a divorce settlement. Think of all the dreary meetings with lawyers, the court appearances.' He paused and his face brightened infinitesimally, a latent smile. 'All those cancelled *lunch* engagements.'

She would have liked to fly at him, mark his smug papery features with her nails, but instead she took a puff on her cigarette, discovered that it had burned down, and finding no ashtray available, savagely stubbed it out in a flower pot. When she looked up at her husband, all she saw was weariness and anxiety. If she had read the tiniest hint of triumph in his face she would have turned and walked out and to hell with the consequences.

'Well?' she said. 'Where are the deeds of ownership?'

* * *

Fraser stood at the open French windows, transfixed by what he had just heard. Vi had let him think she was keeping silent — misleading the police — to protect their son, but all the time she had been negotiating a deal with Harvey. He retraced his steps, moving away from and out of sight of the house, needing time to think. He climbed over the corral-style fence and into the field. He hardly knew what his intention was. A desire to see the boy, to speak to him, perhaps.

The ground dropped away for a short distance and he found himself in a shallow, bowl-shaped depression. Cumulus clouds bubbled up on the horizon, some of them dark and threatening, and the wind had freshened to a north-westerly.

There was no sign of the boy or his kite. Then, in a tree, some thirty yards distant, he saw something. A sheet of bright orange, jerking and bobbing in its branches. Connor stood at its base, frustrated and hot, grunting and tugging at the string.

Fraser strolled over. 'Having trouble?' he asked.

Connor looked around. 'Dratted thing's stuck,' he said.

'Let me try.' Fraser jumped and grabbed at one of the lower branches and dragged it down. 'Now, pull!'

The kite slipped a foot or so and then snagged again. 'Nearly there.' He took off his jacket and studied the tree. It was an old oak, with stout, almost horizontal lower branches and plenty of footholds in the trunk.

He started to climb, under the anxious eye of the boy. The kite wasn't far up, but at the end of a branch. Fraser tested it with his weight, then edged forward on his belly. The kite string had become entangled in a cluster of twigs and he wrapped one foot around the branch before releasing his grip to disentangle it. 'Try it now!' he yelled.

Connor gave the string a mighty tug and the kite fell, showering Fraser with bits of twigs and leaves, caterpillars and insects.

'Sorry!' the boy called, somewhat dismayed.

Fraser laughed, backing cautiously to the trunk, before ruffling his hair to dislodge the worst of the mess. He climbed to the foot of the tree and stood, dusting himself down.

'That was great!' the boy said.

'Well, you know,' he said modestly. 'SAS training.'

Connor looked up at him, round eyed, unsure if he was being teased. 'Really?' he said.

Fraser pulled a face. 'Ranger Scouts.' He felt a thrill of joy when Connor laughed.

'Your shirt's a bit of a mess,' the boy said. 'And your trousers.'

'They'll wash,' Fraser said.

'Have you been to see Daddy? He's taken a week off, so we could come here.'

'Sort of,' Fraser said.

'I'm Connor.' The boy offered his hand with solemn formality.

'Fraser,' he said, taking Connor's hand in his own, then, repeating carefully, 'Fraser Campbell.'

Connor began winding up the kite string. 'Are you a friend of Daddy's?'

The muscles of Fraser's throat tightened, a circle of unbearable constriction. He swallowed, meaning to tell him, but he couldn't speak. Didn't he have a right to know? Shouldn't a boy know his own father? Fraser stared down at the child. Physically, Connor was very like him: the same black, wavy hair, the same dark eyes. He remembered the photograph he had hidden from Jenny. The same open, trusting expression on his face.

The boy looked up, puzzled by his delay in answering, and Fraser thought, *Doesn't he have the right* not *to know? Wasn't his dad — Harvey — entitled to tell him when he was ready, to choose his moment?*

'I was a friend of your mother's,' Fraser said. 'A long time ago.'

'Oh.'

Fraser couldn't blame for boy for not caring. Poor kid, having Vi for a mother! Connor was too young to comprehend the reciprocal nature of love — to know that adults sometimes expect love without giving it.

'You're Scotch, aren't you?' Connor asked, having finished winding the kite string.

'Scottish,' Fraser corrected, with a smile. 'Scotch is what you call whisky.'

'Right,' Connor narrowed his eyes, letting Fraser know that this time he knew he was being teased. 'Are you coming to the house?'

Fraser shook his head. 'I have to get home.'

He watched the boy race off to the rim of the basin. He turned and waved before disappearing over the other side. Fraser walked back to the fence and climbed over. 'Connor Harvey,' he said, trying the name aloud. 'Connor Campbell.'

Behind him, the throaty roar of a sports car warned him to step onto the grass verge, and then Vi sped past, throwing up gravel and dust in her wake. Fifty yards up the road, she stopped, then reversed back to where he was standing, spitting grit from between his teeth.

'You followed me!' The idea seemed to delight and exasperate her. 'Well, did you get what you wanted?'

'Did you?' he asked.

'I got rather more than I'd expected, as a matter of fact.' She was evidently pleased with the negotiations, despite her performance at the house. 'Of course, I didn't let *him* know that. I put the squeeze on. One never knows what one might get unless one tries.' She jerked her head towards the gate he'd just climbed over.

'Did you see him? The fruit of your loins? He's out there somewhere. Playing endlessly with that bloody kite of his. Did you glimpse him from afar?' She eyed his dirty clothes. 'My *God*! Did you climb a tree for him? How heroic. Was it a touching reunion?'

The full significance of her words must have hit home, and she said, aghast, 'You didn't tell him who you are?'

Fraser smiled. 'Worried about your contractual obligations, Vi?'

'*Did* you, Fraser?' All her ironic poise had abandoned her, and she seemed desperate to know the answer.

'It wouldn't be polite, rescuing his kite, and then not introduce myself, now would it?'

She sped off, red with rage, and Fraser grinned to himself as he walked the rest of the way to his car.

* * *

It was raining. It had started as a few random drops. Motorway speed sent them streaking up the windscreen, defying gravity, forming inverted exclamation marks. Pewter-grey clouds gathered low on the horizon, sending down dark veils of precipitation. Stratus, Fraser thought, registering the cloud type from habit. The naming lent an air of familiarity, an illusion of normality in a bizarre situation.

He checked the speedometer. Eighty miles per hour. He had never before driven over sixty. He eased back on the accelerator. It was difficult to judge speed — the distances — to check the mirror without drifting away from true.

Signal — Check again—

A Porsche blasted past him at over a hundred. Fraser muttered an oath and peered more closely through the windscreen, which was so badly smeared it was difficult to see. The bruise on the back of his head was beginning to throb again and he felt sick. What was he going to tell Jenny? Would she give him the chance to explain?

He fumbled with the levers either side of the steering column, trying to find the wipers, flicked one, and jumped, almost swerving the car when the VW on his left blared its horn. He had turned on the indicator. He managed to turn it off again and tried the other lever. It worked.

He slammed on the brakes to avoid tail-ending a van just in front. It was driving without lights and crawling in the middle lane. 'Shit, shit, shit,' he muttered. He hadn't yet found the switch for his headlamps, but he would be needing them if the rain got any worse. He took a moment or two to catch his breath before trying the manoeuvre again and succeeded in easing the car into the outer lane.

The rain began to fall more heavily, and he switched the wipers to fast, pleased that he was beginning to master the controls. Rainfall, he thought, precipitation — a headlong fall. He'd had a couple of those already today, and he suspected there was more to come.

The car was flooded with angry light and a hundred hot needles pricked his spine. *Bloody hell!* A Mercedes behind him, hood down, lights flashing. He glanced left, intending to move in, but there were cars blocking his way. He twitched and the car veered left for a second as the Mercedes' horn blared. He glanced left again, his heart beating fast, and his head pounding in time.

Rain blatted the windscreen. Precipitation, he thought, trying to steady his nerves to pass and pull in without incident. He was breathing fast. Precipitate: a hasty action. 'Wouldn't be wanting one of those, now, would we?' he said, grinning to himself out of sheer terror. He inched forward, hoping to pull into inside lane, out of the way of the Mercedes.

He checked his mirror. Christ! It was Vi!

* * *

Vi pounded on the horn. 'Bastard! You bloody bastard! He'll think I put you up to it. He'll tear up the bloody contracts!'

She had not known what her intention was as she waited for him in the lay-by. When he had driven past her, she felt a sullen hot rage wash over her, and she wanted him to know she was furious. So, she had followed him onto the motorway, becoming more and more enraged by his cautious driving, thinking that it was no mistake the words prudent and prude were so similar. Then he had pulled into the outside lane, *diffidently*, and she roared out from three cars behind to show him how it was done. To show him he couldn't *do* this to her. To *show* him . . .

She flashed her headlamps and stabbed at the horn.

Fraser's car twitched, then swerved and he scraped the central reservation. Splinters of sharp red light burst in a hot shower from the side of his car and she heard the tortured scream of metal on metal. Vi braked hard as he swerved the other way. All around, she saw cars braking and swerving, trying to avoid collision. Fraser's car careered off to the left, spinning as it did so, turning a full 180 degrees until it faced the oncoming traffic, skidding across two — three — lanes.

* * *

'The husband's name is Ligat,' Sallis said. 'Carl Ligat.'

Mike looked up from his paperwork. 'Somerset House or the PNC search?'

'Both.'

'So, he has got form.' Mike had been convinced that Mrs Fournier had been lying, and he was disappointed that he had misjudged the situation.

Sallis's eyes gleamed. 'Not him — *her*.'

'*What?*'

Sallis handed him a print-out. 'There was nothing on Ligat, so I ran Mrs Fournier's name through the computer, just to be sure. Drunk driving, common assault. This one' — he pointed to an assault charge, dated 25 December 1996 — 'was particularly nasty. She attacked Ligat with a knife. Cuts to his arms and hands.'

Mike remembered the defence cuts on Jeanne-Louise's arms. 'The CPS didn't follow through?'

'The neighbours called the police when they heard the row. Middle of Christmas dinner. But he refused to press charges, said it had been an accident. He reached across her while she was chopping veg.'

'Too much sherry,' Mike said. 'It can do that to you. Have we got an address on him?'

'He sold up six months ago, but he gave his mother's address for mail and such.'

Sallis had transferred from Admiral Street Station, just after the new year. At first, Mike had been suspicious of him — he dressed too sharply and he had too many smart answers — but over the past few months he had come to respect Ron Sallis: he was painstaking, he didn't seem to mind the boring legwork that constituted ninety percent of detection and he had an eye for detail.

'You'll go far,' he said. Then, calling over his shoulder as he made his way to DI Crank's office, 'You haven't got anything planned for this evening have you, Ron?'

'Let me guess — a drive down to Surrey?'

'I'll have to clear it with the boss, of course. Why not take Douglas with you? Keep you company.'

CHAPTER 32

Max considered how he would approach the meeting: if what Yvonne said was true — and he had no reason to disbelieve her — Shona was in desperate need of help. The problem was, she probably would not recognize the fact, and even worse, might see his intervention as sinister.

He planned to talk to her, to convince her that he understood her fear, her confusion. Jenny had confirmed that Shona was seeing a therapist, a proponent of recovered memory. He had to get her away from those people. He would suggest that, if she was not comfortable seeing him for therapy, he could arrange for her to speak to a colleague. A friend had already agreed to take her on as a patient. It happened from time to time that changes of personality were needed.

He surveyed his sitting room. His pictures had been sent for reframing, and a specialist firm had managed to clean most of the drops of blood off the furniture and floors. He had boxed up the books that were repairable and shipped them off to an expert in Chester. The rest he had burned, late the night before, not wanting to subject them to the ignominy of a refuse collector's crusher. It was a sombre ceremony, and the effort of burning the tattered remains of his books had left him exhausted but unable to sleep. Now, his favourite room had a bland, empty feel. He sighed — at least there was nothing here to alarm her.

* * *

Grandmère and Grandpère had sat so stiff and still, like they did when they were posing for a picture. He had wanted to go to Grandmère, when she put her arms out to him, but he was so ashamed. What would he say to her? They always said Tante Lou was their precious girl, and she had been so kind to him, but they didn't have their belle Louise anymore, and how would he explain to them? How could he make them understand? Their pain screamed to him, demanding to know why. He could not tell them because he did not understand it himself. He was too young to comprehend the terrors of childhood, the power of adults over children, the magical power of words. All he knew was that he had done a bad thing, and he deserved to be punished, but he was afraid to accept their punishment because he had already been punished more than he could bear.

And Maman. She had spoken to him in English. He closed his eyes and saw her hold out her hand and say, 'Come to Mummy.' She would not speak in French, their language of preference. Her eyes were blank, empty, her foot tap-tapping, as it sometimes did when she was angry with him. He was afraid to go to her.

Alain lifted his hands and let them drop. *Of course they're angry with me. It's all my fault. If it wasn't for me, Jeanne-Louise wouldn't be—*

Lightning flashed, sharp as a knife, bringing red rain. Red rain. A drop fell on his skin — hot, burning.

A shout escaped him, and he jumped to his feet, struggling to banish the image. He had placed the owl and, next to it, a black-and-white squashy Pound Puppy, to keep watch at the window. He resolved to go to the window himself, when he felt a little braver, and look down into the garden.

A noise on the landing. He turned to the door. A semicircle of animals, watchful, unblinking, guard it. He listened, ready to attack, poised on the balls of his feet. The toilet flushed, a pause, and then a knock — soft, almost timid.

He held his breath and waited, dizzy with the sound of blood rushing in his ears, then he heard her sigh and walk slowly down the stairs. He went to the wardrobe. *If I screw my eyes tightly till they're nearly shut, I won't have to look at the—*

'Dirty little pig! *Cochon*! D'you like rolling in shit? Living like a stinking animal in a sty? Let's make it more lifelike, shall we? Make you feel right at home! You disgusting little . . .'

Alain clamped both hands over his ears. 'Help me,' he whispered. He began muttering a prayer. 'Je vous salue, Marie, pleine de grace.'

'PIG!'

'Le Seigneur est avec vous. Vous êtes bénie, entre toutes les femmes . . .'

The voice faded, as if someone had turned down the volume, and he reached into the cupboard, intoning the prayer to the Virgin as if it had the power of exorcism. He turned away — *mustn't look!* — and probed the darkness with his tingling fingertips, recoiling, hissing at the softly yielding contact of pink, piggy flesh. 'Priez pour nous, pauvres pécheurs . . .' A second foray rapped his knuckles against something reassuringly hard. He drew out a baseball bat and tested its weight, holding it in his two small hands, trying a couple of tentative swings. It was easier than the cricket bat, and heavier. He raised it over his head and brought it down with a thud across the width of his pillowcase.

* * *

Jenny paused, frowning up at the ceiling, then glanced at her watch. She was due at work at a quarter past eight, it was already after six, and Fraser still wasn't home. How could she expect him to be? She had given an ultimatum, and

Fraser knew she didn't make such statements lightly. But she wanted him there. She wanted him desperately. She needed an explanation, and she needed to vent some of the hurt he had caused her on him, to tell him how much pain she felt, perhaps even to make him feel some of it.

Fraser was having an affair. He had admitted to it, even though he claimed it was over, done with. If it was over, she reasoned, why the urgency? Why was he so willing to rush off to his mistress (ex-mistress?), a woman he said he had broken up with eight years ago?

Eight years ago, they had taken their first foster child, having made the decision that adoption was not for them. At least that's what she had thought. Except now it seemed that Fraser *had* wanted to adopt. Why hadn't she? It was difficult to remember the muddle of emotions, the emotional turmoil she had gone through after the miscarriage. She hadn't wanted to take another woman's child as her own — was that it? But hadn't she given each of their foster children as much love and energy and commitment as she would her own child? They had discussed it over and over during their assessment. They could help so many children by fostering. With her paediatric training and his teaching skills they were used to dealing with children, they understood their needs, their development.

Because of their work patterns, Roz had advised them to foster school-aged children. It had worked remarkably well. Sometimes it had been hard to give up a child, and sometimes it had been a huge relief, but they were happy that they had helped a child in crisis, had made a difference.

Then Luke came along. He was younger than their usual placements, but he already had a full-time place at a local authority nursery, which made his care manageable, and as usual the social workers were desperate for a placement. Decisions about Luke's future had dragged on and on, once the courts became involved, and they had grown more and more attached to him.

She stared out of the window. If she had allowed herself to think about it at the time, she would have realized that adoption was the right — the best — way forward for Luke. How could they have let him go like that? In truth, she knew why: she had avoided thinking about adoption for so long because it meant admitting to her childlessness, and she didn't know how to broach the subject, even in her own mind. Fraser should have helped her — talked to her. From the very first, when she had mentioned fostering, he should have made his feelings known. She would have resisted, but they could have compromised, and eventually, he would have won her over. Instead, Fraser had had an affair with this woman.

If she had borne him a child, it would be about Alain's age now. Jenny felt the hairs on her arms rise, and a sudden chill ran down her spine. The way Fraser had looked at Alain all those times, the boy's strange reaction to Fraser, even the fact that Mrs Fournier had refused to name Alain's father, could it be that Alain was Fraser's son? Alain was so like him. She had found the photograph from their bedroom. Fraser had hidden it in the wardrobe, in an empty suitcase, and the similarity between the two of them was striking. But Mrs Fournier was claiming that Alain's injuries — the damage to his hands — had been caused by his father. She knew Fraser could not have done that, and not only because he had never so much as raised a finger to any of the children they had fostered. Alain could not have been left in the care of his father for a week while Mrs Fournier was away, but she and Fraser had never been apart for more than a few days at a time. Mrs Fournier was lying, which meant it could have been she who had hurt Alain — after all, he had seemed afraid of her at the hospital. But Fraser had also lied.

Conflicting emotions, conflicting loyalties, fought for control of her, and she knew that if he walked through the door right now, she would want him to take her in his arms and tell her that they would work things out — that everything would be all right. She would fight him if he tried it, but she would still want him to try.

After a few more minutes of worry, looking at her watch every thirty seconds or so, she telephoned Max.

'Right,' Max said. 'Best phone and tell them you won't be in this weekend. Doctor's orders. Alain should be with someone he trusts just now.'

'Thanks,' Jenny said. She rang off, then tapped in the hospital number and waited. It was answered on the third ring.

'Hi, it's Jenny . . .'

* * *

'Jenny! How's the little lad? I heard about the meeting,' Shona went on without waiting for an answer.

'Nothing gets by you, does it, Shona?' Jenny was not in the mood to humour her.

'You know what I think's up with him?'

'Shona—'

'Well,' she laughed, 'never mind what I think. Don't let me tell you your job.'

'I won't,' Jenny said, heavily.

'It's just — I feel like we've got a bond. Me and Alain . . .'

'I need to speak to the ward manager on C4,' Jenny said, more insistently.

'You want to have him admitted? Is it his hands?' Her voice took on a breathless, expectant quality.

His hands? For a moment, Jenny was alarmed by the question. But she was tired, and she had worries enough of her own, without taking on Shona's as an extra burden. 'I need to arrange cover,' she said. 'I don't want to leave him tonight.'

'Oh! If you need a babysitter, I'll sit with him.'

Mistake, Jenny. *You shouldn't engage* . . . 'Thanks for the offer,' she said, firmly. 'But that's not possible.'

'Only, I'm due to knock off soon — it'd be no bother.'

'Thanks, Shona, but there are rules . . .'

There was a silence which Jenny longed to break. Although Shona was interfering and insensitive, she meant well, and she would be hurt by the refusal, but if Jenny spoke first, she felt sure that Shona would not let go until she had access to Alain. That, Jenny knew both instinctively and rationally, would be disastrous for the boy.

'I'll try to connect you,' Shona said, and Jenny winced, hearing the tears in the operator's voice — but she bit back an apology.

Shona put her through to the ward and she spoke to the ward manager. It was Jarmon Willis. Jenny relaxed a little, knowing she had a sympathetic ear. She explained the situation. 'We'll manage,' Jarmon said. 'Just you take care of the boy.'

'Thanks, Jarmon. I'm really worried about him. It's a relief getting through to you. I thought Officious O'Flynn was on duty tonight.'

Jarmon laughed, and she felt the balm of his good nature wash over her like a wave of summer warmth.

'She got the 'flu,' he said. 'She was really put out the nasty little bugs hadn't filled in a permission slip for the privilege of infecting the sacred temple of her upper respiratory tract.'

'I wondered why you were on C4,' Jenny chuckled. 'Will Officious ever get over the shame of actually taking a day off?'

Jarmon laughed again. In the background, Jenny heard someone speak to him. 'Be right there,' he said. 'Listen, Jen, I'd love to sit and catch up on gossip, but I gotta go.'

'Sorry, Jarmon.'

'I said, *don't worry*.'

'Sure.' She hung up.

Was Alain at the window now, keeping vigil? Against what? He had not spoken to his mother or to his grandparents. Jenny felt her palms begin to sweat, remembering Angeline Fournier's stilted greeting and the stricken look on Alain's face.

Mrs Fournier had spoken in careful English to her son, instructed by the police and the hospital authorities that only

English must be spoken. She seemed formal, stiff. And her parents seated next to each other, backs straight, lips pale and eyeing their grandson. Were they anxious for Alain? It was hard to say.

Why wouldn't he look at them? Was he afraid of his mother? She could see why he might be. But when he ran from the hospital, he'd seemed upset but not frightened. What had he meant when he asked if it was okay if you didn't mean to do something bad? She remembered the crack he'd given Fraser across his head and the way he'd stood over her with his fists bunched, screaming 'TELL ME!' Alain's sudden outbursts were violent and frightening. Violence begets violence, she knew. And Alain had been violently assaulted at some time in his young life. She thought of Jeanne-Louise, slashed and stabbed with such terrible violence and felt a terrible chill. *Surely*, she thought. *Surely to God, not the boy?*

* * *

Shona looked down at her hands — at the carefully applied rings of plaster, at the padding and bandaging on her wrist.

There had been a bond between her and the boy since he was first admitted. She felt she knew him, knew what he was afraid of. Her fingers throbbed with pain just thinking about him.

Why was Jenny being so mean? She was only trying to help. She could've looked after the kiddie — would've kept him safe. But in the next instant her seesawing emotions told her that it was for the best. Pam would say that in offering to babysit she was trying to escape the frightening prospect of meeting *him*, talking to *him*, *confronting her demons*. She would feel better when the job was done. And it was true that the whispering of his voice had receded since she had made the call to Max, arranging to meet. She felt more in control.

Shona heard the rumble of a metal drawer sliding home on its castors, felt the slam and shrieked in pain. She knew what had happened to little Alain — he didn't need to tell her — she *knew*. She began to cry silent tears — for the boy and for herself. For the misery Max had caused her. For in the hours since her telephone call arranging to meet Max Greenberg, she had muddled the times and sequence of events, and was certain that she had taken an overdose *after* she had been referred to Max. Now she knew that it was Max who had driven her to the point at which life became unbearable.

* * *

Mrs Ligat invited detectives Sallis and Douglas into her sitting room and invited them to sit, lowering herself onto a wooden-armed cottage armchair and folding her hands calmly in her lap, before fixing Sallis with a sharp, intelligent eye. Sallis found her composure impressive.

'We're trying to locate your son, Mrs Ligat,' he said.

'In connection with?' she asked.

'I'm afraid we can't discuss that at present.'

'If it is in connection with the disappearance of my grandson, I think I have every right to know.' She had, it seemed, decided that Sallis was the man to talk to, and she waited for his response, fixing her gaze on his face, ignoring Douglas's presence. The gold clock on the mantelshelf chimed the quarter hour, and Sallis was struck by the peace, the stillness of the house. It was furnished with antiques like the clock — beautiful things that glowed as she did — denoting care and, Sallis thought a little cynically, money.

'Disappearance?' Sallis repeated, deciding that he would get as much as he could out of her before explaining the purpose of their visit, but Mrs Ligat wasn't the type to fill in the gaps with nervous burbling, she merely nodded, a graceful inclination of the head. Her hair, pure white, shone with health.

'When did he disappear, Mrs Ligat?'

'The tenth of April.'

'That's very precise.'

'When one's grandson disappears, one remembers the date.'

'You didn't report that he'd gone missing.'

'No.'

She wasn't making this easy. 'Why didn't you?'

'Because Carl asked me not to.'

Sallis was a patient man, methodical, but Mrs Ligat's replies were bordering on the obtuse. 'You wouldn't like to explain that, would you?' he asked, half expecting a simple 'yes' or 'no', and then for her to wait for the next question. She surprised him.

'My son lived — lives — for his family, despite his wife's excesses. She is fickle, shallow and violent, but when she disappeared, he was distraught. You see, he didn't want to lose either of them. He was afraid that if Angeline knew that the police were looking for her, she might do something drastic. She is a very unstable woman, constable.'

'All the more reason to tell the police, surely?'

She straightened her back and looked Sallis in the eye. 'Carl knows what he's doing. He has his own way of going about things. He usually gets what he wants.'

'What triggered it? I mean, her running off like that.'

'She had been away the week before she left. Called it a business trip, but she'd been having an affair — someone she met on her trips to France. When she left, Carl thought she'd gone off with the fellow — I can't remember his name — but when Carl went to see him, it seemed he hadn't seen her since her return to England. He's been looking for them ever since.'

Douglas said, 'He sold his house.'

The look she gave Douglas said that the implied question was impertinent. She did not answer but turned again to Sallis. 'Why are you here?' she said. 'Has something happened to Alain?'

Sallis deliberated, decided it was time to come clean. 'We're not sure. He was found in the middle of the night, wandering the streets of Liverpool in his nightclothes. He won't talk to anyone about what happened.'

She nodded as if this was exactly as she had expected. 'If you take my advice, you'll keep his mother away from him,' she said.

'Where is Mr Ligat?' Sallis noticed that she didn't offer to come and see her grandson herself.

'My son is away at the moment.'

'Have you spoken to him?'

'He rings every day, without fail.' Her satisfaction was evident. 'He brings me flowers every week.'

'So, where can we find him?' Douglas refused to be ignored this time. 'An address or a telephone number will do.'

'Carl travels about a lot. He's a financial consultant. He has a part-time secretary to help him with the administrative tasks. You might try her.' When she stood, there was no hint of arthritic stiffness. She picked up her address book from its place next to the telephone and jotted the number down for them. 'You may use my telephone, if you like.'

* * *

The doorbell rang as Jenny reached the foot of the stairs.

'Mike?'

The big man seemed flustered. 'Can I come in, Jen?'

She stood back and he walked through to the hall.

'Is everything all right?' Jenny asked. He looked pale, uncertain of himself in a way she had never seen in him before. 'Mike?'

'Look . . .' He glanced past her to the stairway, then, touching her elbow lightly, he said, 'In here . . .'

Jenny understood. Something he didn't want Alain to hear. 'Sure.' She led the way into the sitting room. The news presenter was giving an emergency number — a multiple pile-up on the M62. In the background, in an oblong frame, the drama continued: flashing blue lights and wreckage and acid yellow reflective jackets.

Jenny picked up the remote control. Mike was staring at her. She switched the television off and the silence in the room became a roar. She looked at the remote control in her hand and then up into his face, still uncomprehending.

'There's been an accident,' Mike said.

The remote control slipped from her fingers and bounced on the rug, falling apart with the impact. Mike saw her sway and grabbed her by both elbows, easing her into a chair.

'He's at the Royal,' he said.

Jenny tried to get up, but Mike held her firmly. 'Give yourself a minute.'

'I've got to go to him, Mike!'

'I'll take you. Just wait until you feel a bit steadier.'

'How bad is it? Is he—?'

'He's unconscious,' he said, speaking slowly. Jenny's mind raced through the possible degrees of injury, the events that had led to Fraser taking such a rash decision, the guilt and the if-onlys and the what-ifs, unable to take in much of what Mike was saying.

'. . . skull fracture,' she heard him say.

Fracture. The word seemed to echo, and she shook her head in a large, exaggerated sweep, left to right, to clear it, as well as to negate the awful truth. If Mike had let go of her, she would have covered her ears. She struggled half-heartedly.

'He's in Intensive Care.'

She looked up again, tugging ineffectually against his gently restraining hands.

'Jen.'

'How bad is it, Mike?' she repeated.

He hesitated and she waited until she had eye contact.

'They don't know,' he admitted.

'No!' She twisted, almost pulling free of him, but he held her to him and finally she yielded, resting her head against his chest and sobbing uncontrollably, giving vent to the fear and sadness, the frustrations, the sense of betrayal and loss — and yes — the bitterness of the past week.

CHAPTER 33

The bell rang. So, she had come. Given her hectic emotional state, Max had half expected her to cancel or simply to not turn up. He quelled a flutter of excitement, perhaps even of nervousness. He often felt this quiver of anxiety before a session. It denoted a new phase, occasionally the proximity of a breakthrough.

He smoothed his hair in the hall mirror. It was in need of a trim. *Leave it any longer and it'll look like you're trying to hide your bald patch*, he told himself. Max was not a vain man, and only rarely in social situations did he wonder what sort of impression he made on others. In the consulting room the persona of psychiatric counsellor generally served him well. He adopted and adapted the usual tricks to convince his patients of their uniquely interesting stories, was careful of his body language and worded his responses with circumspection.

During this session he would assess Shona's state of mind and persuade her, if necessary, to accept medication or even a voluntary hospital admission until she felt more able to cope.

She had scrubbed her face clean of make-up. Without it her features seemed curiously bland, like a painting with no shadows or depth, waiting for the few deft strokes that would bring it to life, give it character and perspective, the illusion of reality.

'I hope you don't mind coming here,' he said. 'I didn't think it would be appropriate to see you at the hospital.' It was difficult enough for her coming to see him, he was sure, without running the risk of being seen by friends or colleagues. She stared at him in silence. 'I thought,' he said, turning to gesture to the half-open door, 'we might talk more informally in the sitting room.'

She stared back at him from the threshold, a fearful yet determined look passing over her formless features, as if she were bracing herself for something daunting. Then she stepped inside the house, clutching her big, grubby holdall across her front like a shield.

He led the way, turning to face her as he reached the centre of the room, rotating his palms upwards and outwards in the universal gesture — *See, I'm harmless.* He had practised this, in his mind, as he had practised what he would say. He would go to the window, as far from the door as he could get, and he would sit in the window seat. Then he would ask her where she would like to sit, so that she didn't feel threatened or coerced, physically or mentally. He would make himself small, reducing the chances of her misinterpreting his presence as intimidating. When he had reassured her, he would coax her to speak.

As he turned towards her, smiling, he was already bending his knees, lowering himself onto the broad wooden bench-seat.

He didn't even see it coming — only felt the pain, like a flash of light — then searing, livid heat in his shoulder. His momentum carried him forwards and he crashed to the floor, rucking the corner of the rug and dropping two circular gobs of blood that splashed and then coalesced on the newly waxed floorboards.

Shona took a step back, splaying her hands, flicking them away from her body, as if to rid herself of something clinging and disgusting. She screamed.

* * *

'The news said a multiple pile-up,' Jenny said.

Mike glanced into his rear-view mirror. She was sitting on the back seat, her arm around Alain, who was holding the big white polar bear close to his chest.

'Mike?'

He sighed. 'Twenty injured. Mostly minor.'

'What the hell was he *doing*?' Jenny asked, tears muffling her voice.

'We aren't sure, Jen.' Mike felt the need to apologize, to find some way of conveying his sympathy for her, but an apology would be absurd, and what he did know of the background was unsubstantiated, as yet, so he said nothing. Vi Harvey had been injured in the pile-up. The motorway police had received reports of her sports car following Fraser's Volvo at speed in the outside lane. Fortunately, a number of drivers had dropped back, seeing a potential disaster looming, otherwise there might have been more casualties. There was no point in troubling Jenny with speculation. Until they could speak to Vi or Fraser, they couldn't be sure of anything.

He drove around to the car park at the back of the hospital. He didn't want to risk being wheel-clamped for parking outside the ambulance bay at the other side of the building, and he didn't like Jenny going in alone. He flashed his warrant card at the barrier and parked close to the concrete steps down to the rear entrance.

Inside the building, the lifts seemed to take an age to arrive and he could see that Jenny was barely managing to keep control. He reached out and took her free hand and she squeezed it with a gasp of anguish and gratitude.

They were met at the doors of the Intensive Care Unit by a young SHO who looked close to exhaustion. He offered Jenny his hand, and as she let go of Mike's he saw her sway a little and steadied her with a touch to her elbow. The SHO launched in with a description of Fraser's injuries.

'We don't think the head trauma is serious,' he continued, then shook his head as if incredulous of his own words. 'Of course it's *serious*,' he went on, 'But we don't think it's erm . . .'

He's trying to think of an alternative to 'fatal', Mike thought.

'It's not—His condition is *serious*, but it's not . . . not *grave*,' he said at last. 'Preliminary scans are . . .' — he wavered — 'promising. We'll send him for another scan when we're sure he's stable. The pelvic fracture may account for the . . .' He seemed to lose the thread again for a moment and stood staring down at Alain, with a slight frown drawing a line between his eyebrows, then he shook his head again and continued. 'He's in shock, you see. That's as much part of the problem as anything. Do you . . . Would you like to . . .' He turned, gesturing towards the glass-fronted cubicle.

Mike nodded. Jenny looked up at him, uncharacteristically unsure of herself, then down at the boy. He seemed almost to have shrunk, and he buried his face in the white fur of the polar bear. Mike crouched down beside him.

'Alain,' he said, making an effort to get the pronunciation right, 'Jenny wants to go and see Fraser. How's about you and me go and get something to eat at the restaurant?' He held out his hand and Alain shrank back as if he had raised his fist. Mike glanced up quickly at the SHO. 'Or maybe we could sit in the waiting room?'

The SHO stared for a moment as if trying to decipher a foreign language, then he realized that Mike was waiting for a response from him and made an extra effort. 'Oh, yes! Of course.' He pushed open the wooden door leading to the private waiting room. Alain did not move.

Mike understood. 'We can move one of the chairs and prop it against the door to keep it open,' he said.

Alain lowered the polar bear to watch him perform this operation, then he walked silently past Mike and the puzzled SHO, into the waiting room.

* * *

The room smelled of cigarettes and stale coffee. Alain did not mind this, because Maman sometimes smoked cigarettes when she was worried about something. It reassured and unsettled him simultaneously, for he had learned to be sensitive to his mother's moods. Her worries became his.

There were four chairs in the room and a shiny coffee table with a gold rim around the edge and black, splayed legs. It had coffee rings and spills and a couple of polystyrene cups, half empty, a skin of greyish scum filming the surface.

Alain wanted to sit on the chair holding the door open, but then he would have had to sit with his back to the big dangerous emptiness beyond, so instead, he chose the chair next to it — the green one with the patches where it had worn thin and foam bulged out, yellow and grubby.

He sat on the edge of the chair and hugged the polar bear — he hadn't given it a name — with his left hand and picked at the foam with his right and worried about what the doctor said.

When he had come towards them, with his white coat billowing behind him like the sail of a boat, Alain had wanted to run away.

'Head trauma,' the doctor had said. Maman didn't like him to watch *Casualty*, but sometimes, on the rare occasions when she got a babysitter, he would hear the music from his bedroom and creep down to watch it from behind the sofa. 'Head trauma' was something they said on *Casualty*.

Trauma was a word he knew from before, when he had been in hospital that time. They would talk over and across him, as if he was deaf or an imbecile. Alain knew what trauma meant.

The doctor had had red spots on his jeans. Alain had a niggling anxiety that doctors weren't supposed to wear jeans and thought he might get into trouble. Also, the red spots brought flashes of—

'*Run*, Alain!'

—something he had been trying to shut out.

The doctor had stared and stared, as though he knew what Alain had done, that he had hit Fraser, and now Fraser had a head trauma.

Alain made an involuntary noise at the back of his throat, drawing the attention of the policeman. He had blue eyes, empty and clear, like a swimming pool, but also hard, like the powder-blue stones in Maman's earrings. He *knows, too*, Alain thinks. *He knows that I hit Fraser with a cricket bat and now Fraser is going to die.*

Alain jumped from the chair and dodged past the policeman, running into the dark room where Jenny is.

'Fraser, please don't die!' he begged. 'I didn't mean it!'

* * *

Seconds? Minutes? Hours? Longer? Max groaned — he felt it in his throat but could not hear it above Shona's screams. Seconds, then, or minutes at most, for surely she could not have continued screaming for longer. The calm logic of his thoughts struck him as incongruous: he should be terrified, and yet he was not. He was able to think rationally, to reason that if Shona had continued screaming for more than a matter of seconds, the neighbours would have come to see what was the matter, or at least they would have telephoned for the police. This, he told himself, is the rationality of the dying — the drowning man, too exhausted to fight death.

This realization galvanized him, and he tried to push himself up from the undignified forward slump in which he had awakened, feeling a mixture of indignation and surprise that he was unable to move. The pain had receded now, and he felt nothing so much as cold: a chill that penetrated to his core and made him shiver violently. A second attempt to rise to his knees failed and, giving in to the inevitable, he rolled instead onto his back.

Shona gagged and choked, but mercifully it stopped her screams. Max struggled with a wave of nausea. *God, what did she hit me with?* He lifted one shaking hand to his shoulder. It was wet, and, from the corner of his eye, he could see the dark outline of the hilt of a knife. Shona leaned over him. He brought a hand up to protect himself. A shaft of sharp, cruel pain shot through him, and then he felt nothing.

* * *

A candle flame, unsteady in the humid heat, first called her back. The water was at body temperature, warm as the womb. A thick froth of bubble bath covered the water's surface, and on the rim of the bath, the bottle stood open, next to the candle. Geranium and rose petal — pink, the colour and scent of restfulness.

She spoke the word aloud: 'Wretchedness,' then frowned. What had made her say that? She hadn't meant to say it. It wasn't even the sort of word she would use, as a rule. She lay still for a moment, testing her feelings, and found that she was, indeed, wretched. The combined magic of bubble bath and candle scent wasn't working. She sniffed experimentally and discovered that she could not smell the healing balm of geraniums and roses. A solitary drop of mucus fell from the tip of her nose and the massed foam fizzed and crackled as a thousand tiny bubbles burst. Her face was wet. She was crying, her head ached, and she could not think what had upset her. She lifted her hands to her face and wiped it, listening with pleasure to the musical tinkle and splosh of water droplets. Through the open bathroom door she could see light flickering — blue light, flitting from wall to ceiling — and she guessed that the TV was on. The light played tantalizingly, running along the wall of the narrow hallway, now dimming, now flashing with sudden brilliance through the glass panel that separated the hall from the living room. In the kitchen, the washing machine droned steadily.

Shona jerked convulsively, making the water crash with angry violence against the sides of the bath. *The blood!* She leapt out of the bath and dragged the towel from the rail, drying herself hastily, waiting until the last moment to pull the plug, for she never could watch the awful downward swirl of water without fearing that she would be dragged into its hungry maw.

She tiptoed to the kitchen as if she were afraid that she might surprise some dangerous animal skulking there. Her clothing turned and dropped, turned and dropped in the drum of the machine, tingeing the water pink. The colour of wretchedness.

'Oh, God!' she moaned. She had to get dressed. As she passed the open door of the living room, she glanced in and let out a breathless scream.

A body! On the settee! Blue jeans, a baggy shirt, one arm flung outwards, the other across its midriff. The image changed shape and seemed to flatten and lose its density and mass, finally resolving itself into her own clothing, clean, ironed, fresh from the airing cupboard, laid out ready to wear.

A creeping terror came over her and for a moment she was unable to move. She could not remember any of this: driving home, turning on the TV, running a bath, washing her clothes, laying out a fresh set — it was all a complete blank. Her eyes were drawn to the television set, to seek out the pictures which so often soothed her, but her vision was blurred because she had left her glasses in the bathroom and all she could see were confused colours in soft focus.

She went to the settee and shoved the clothing to one side without looking at it, afraid that it would metamorphose again into the terrible outline she had first seen. Her hair dripped down her back and, shivering, she tried to blot some of the water out of it with a dry corner of the towel, then began dressing.

The volume was still turned down, but the remote was on top of the TV set, and it seemed an impossible distance to go and retrieve it. If she screwed up her eyes, she could just make out the face of a newsreader. One of the local ones, *Granada* or *North West Tonight* — she couldn't remember which.

Had they found him?

What if he's dead?

They would come for her. She couldn't go to prison. Oh, God! She was seized with a new kind of terror and began searching the shelves of her bookcase. 'Please, God, where is it?' In her panic, she threw books, ornaments, pens onto the floor. It wasn't there. She'd left it on the shelf. Someone had—

She began riffling the drawers of the sideboard, and finally her hand closed on a fist-sized cylindrical object. She ran to the kitchen and threw it in the bin, then, horrified, tore the lid off it and rooted through the rubbish to retrieve it. 'Stupid! Stupid! That's the first place they'll look.' She returned to the sitting room and placed the voice changer in her big canvas shoulder bag, intending to dispose of it somewhere safe.

She shrugged into her shirt and pulled on her jeans. There was a jumbled mass of coloured blocks on screen, then a picture of a child. Of *Alain*? She moved closer to the TV, but already the image was gone and a new story was being related.

Alain. She had promised Jenny. Hadn't she? Promised Jenny she would babysit. She was sure she had. Because Jenny had to go to work, and Shona understood Alain. She could help him. Jenny recognized that. She knew. Shona never broke her promises. She always . . . That's why she had to come home. To get ready. To go to Alain. To show him that you can stop the people who hurt you, make it — make them — stop. They were just people. They could be hurt, too.

My God! Max!

She mustn't be found here. How could she explain? And what if Dr Greenberg *was* dead?

* * *

'Jen?'

Jenny closed her eyes briefly.

Mike hesitated, abashed. His interruption had been ill-timed. He glanced at Alain, who was sitting next to Jenny.

The polar bear was in his lap and he hugged it, sobbing miserably. Jenny had her arms around both the boy and the bear. The devastating sobs continued, but Mike sensed an alertness, as if Alain was bracing himself for bad news.

'I've got to go,' Mike said quietly. Lee-Anne had demanded to speak to him. She wasn't interested in talking to anyone else and he couldn't afford to miss the opportunity to persuade her to cooperate.

Jenny nodded. She was dry eyed, but her face was pale, and the strain showed in the fine lines around her mouth and eyes. 'We'll be leaving soon ourselves,' she said.

Mike checked his watch. 'I'll run you home. The wait'll do her good.'

Jenny managed a smile. 'You go ahead,' she said. 'We're not ready yet.' One hand went to the boy's head, and she stroked his hair. It was damp, plastered to his scalp, and Mike wondered at the energy children expend in their tears, the passion with which they abandon themselves to their unhappiness.

He shrugged an apology. 'I'll call round later,' he suggested.

'Perhaps best if you leave it till tomorrow,' Jenny replied, with a brief nod at Alain. 'I'll phone Max when I get home. I'm sure he'll babysit so I can come and sit with Fraser for a while.'

CHAPTER 34

Lee-Anne had the kind of face that a good disposition and a ready smile could have transformed to prettiness, but the down-turned mouth, too apt to curl into a snarl of aggression or a sneer of contempt, reflected a general attitude which betrayed a customary ill temper, bordering on maliciousness.

Mike had seen hundreds of them in his years on the force: girls whose lives turn sour before they reach eighteen, girls whom fear and worry — and, too often, alcohol and drug abuse — would ravage before thirty. At just under twenty years of age, Lee-Anne had already lost the bloom of youth. She stared up at Mike, truculent, unable to convey so dignified a sentiment as disdain, resorting instead to hostility.

Mike returned her stare, wondering why she had dragged him back to headquarters, if all she intended to do was scowl at him and give monosyllabic responses to his questions. For this he had been forced to leave Jenny at the hospital, when she really needed someone with her. He hadn't seen his family for three days, beyond a numb half hour in front of the television before crawling off to bed, and Lee-Anne was keeping him late again, wasting his time and wearing his patience.

'All right,' he said wearily. 'Let's start with the new stuff in your flat.'

'Me sister give me them.' She lowered her head so that her chin almost rested on her chest.

'What about that jacket?' Lee-Anne had slipped off a little Versace number and tossed it carelessly over the back of the chair with the label showing.

She fixed him with a flat, colourless stare. 'Got it from the Oxfam shop, didn't I?'

Mike leaned forward. 'We've got the receipts, Lee-Anne, remember?'

They could have charged her with fraudulent use of the credit cards, but Mike had persuaded his senior officer that they could get both of them for stealing the cards from the Fournier house on the day of the murder.

Lee-Anne tutted and slumped even lower in the chair.

She had planned to tell Delaney everything when she asked the custody officer to call him. Lobo had kicked off on average once every half hour for the past few hours and it was getting on her tits. She was beginning to think he'd lost it all together: first putting the boot into Randy Khan, now screaming and ranting at the police, even at her. He was blaming her for the fact that he went off on a final shopping spree — blaming her for the fact he lost his rag and cracked the black feller with the cue. *Blaming her!*

That made her mad. She'd waited until the duty officer had come on his rounds and told him she wanted to see Mike Delaney, to tell him just what Lobo had done. Now, sitting in an interview room with a tape running and no solicitor to advise her, it seemed a stupid idea. The tape could be used in evidence, which meant Lobo would know exactly who to thank for grassing him up. She should've asked for a solicitor, but she'd thought if she refused legal advice they could have an informal chat, clear the air. It hadn't turned out that way, and now Lobo would be out to get her. Delaney was trying to make her say they'd done that woman, and she didn't know how to get out of it.

'Fourteen hundred on a new bed, bedding and curtains in Lewis's. Eight hundred and odd on carpets — feel free to correct me, I'm working from memory here,' Mike said. 'Five hundred on kitchen goods, including a washing machine from Comet, three-fifty on a couch from Uno.'

'Sofa.' Lee-Anne spat the word, making it sound like a threat.

'Sorry,' Mike said, smiling. 'Sofa.'

'What're you laughin' at? Have you seen where I live? Oh, of course — you've poked your big fat nose into everything, lookin' for *evidence* haven't you?'

She was sitting up straight now, her hands flat on the table, ready to spring over and grab him by the throat. The WPC who was chaperoning stirred, but Mike signalled for her to be still. Lee-Anne bunched a fist.

'Yeah, I s'pose it is funny, paying out fifty quid a week for a flat with no heating, and light switches that spark when you touch them — I near piss meself laughin' every time the bastard comes round for the rent. The leccy man won't go into the basement to check the meters no more 'cos he near broke his neck falling through the steps down. Rotten they were. I bet he laughed all the way to the hospital. The windows threaten to fall in if there's a breath of wind — probably all that's holding the bloody things together is the plastic and sealing tape I use to try and keep out the draughts.'

She was breathing hard, and little black spots came and went in front of her eyes.

'I've got silverfish in me bathroom and woodlice in me kitchen. What's so funny about tryin' to make it nice — looking *decent*?' Her voice rose to a scream.

'Nothing wrong with that, Lee-Anne,' Mike said, quietly. 'Except you used a dead woman's credit card to bring about all your home improvements.'

Lee-Anne slammed the table with her fist. 'What'm I supposed to do? D'you even *know* what you get on the dole these days? *Fuck all* is what!' she shouted. 'Fifty quid a week he gets for twelve flats in that bleeding death trap. Two years I've lived there. You know how much maintenance the landlord's done?'

Mike raised his eyebrows, like he was interested.

'He put a timer switch on the hall light, so's we wouldn't waste the leccy leaving it on. Six hundred quid a week he gets, all told, and you think *I'm* the criminal!'

'You were desperate, you needed the money and . . .'

'And . . .' she mocked him, her face twisting with hatred and bitter, bitter disappointment. 'And we took what we needed.'

'Took it,' Mike said softly.

Lee-Anne felt her eyes bug as she screeched, 'Well, she wasn't gonna have no use for it no more, was she?'

'Wasn't she?'

'Are you *thick*, or wha'?' *Stupid big lump.* Mike looked at her. 'She was *dead*, wasn't she?' Lee-Anne flung herself back in her chair, exasperated.

'We know that, Lee-Anne. We also know that you stole her credit cards. What we don't know is who killed her.'

'Well, don't look at me! She was dead when we got there. *We* never done it.'

'Didn't you?' he asked. 'Do it, I mean.'

'She was *dead*! We got in round the back. The door was unlocked. She was already dead when we got in.'

'Was she?'

'There was blood everywhere!' She blinked, realizing she was supposed to stick to the story that they'd found the cards, and she'd just admitted to being inside the Fournier house with blood all over the place. 'No. No! It's not what you're thinking, it wasn't us. We never touched her.'

'What I'm asking is, are you sure she was dead? Did you check, either of you?'

'You didn't need to.' She couldn't look him in the eye. She was thinking about that dream, the obscene gurgling gash in the woman's neck, the words . . . *Help me* . . .

'What time was it when you arrived?'

'I don't know! Eleven? Half past?'

'Did you see anyone else?'

'Like who?'

'You know about the boy . . .'

'Ah, look . . .' For the first time in the entire interview Lee-Anne seemed chastened. 'If I'd've seen the little lad, I would've—'

'What, Lee-Anne? What would you have done? Called the police?'

'Fuck off!' she snarled, sick of being judged. 'I never touched her, and neither did Lobo. All you can do us for is credit card fraud.'

'I think we can do a little better than that, Lee-Anne,' he said. He charged her with the theft of the credit cards, and with failing to report the murder of Jeanne-Louise Fournier, then he concluded the interview, repeating the caution and informing of her right to a solicitor.

As he reached the door, with the sealed interview tapes in his hand, she called to him and he turned.

'What?'

'D'you think they'll let us keep all the stuff we bought?'

CHAPTER 35

Sallis called Mike on his mobile as he was heading for home. 'We've got an address for Ligat.'

'About time,' Mike said.

'It is the weekend, Sarge. We had to get his secretary's home address and call round. He's got a little flat in Sefton Park.'

'What? Here, in Liverpool?'

'Apparently.'

'How come he didn't come forward when we splashed his son's picture all over the news, then?'

'His mum said his business takes him from South Devon to North York. The TV reports on the lad were only broadcast in the North West region.'

'And if Mr Ligat happened to be selling an AVC to a kipper-smoker in Whitby on the day of the broadcasts . . .'

'Precisely,' Sallis said.

'Have you spoken to him yet?'

'No . . .' Sallis said. 'But I could go round now if you want?' He didn't sound too thrilled at the prospect, and Mike couldn't blame him.

'All right,' Mike sighed. 'Give me the address — I'll have a word with him.'

'You finished with Lee-Anne?'

'She coughed to the break-in, and to stealing the cards. Claims Jeanne-Louise was dead when they got there.'

'Aren't you gonna have another go at her tonight?'

'I'll need a few hours' sleep before I can stand to look at that snarling face again,' Mike said. 'Anyway, we'll have to give her a chance to talk to a brief — if she did have something to do with Jeanne-Louise's murder, we need everything watertight.'

'Well, if you're sure — only, it's my nephew's birthday, and I promised I'd pop in before his bedtime . . .'

Mike smiled. Sallis was full of surprises — he hadn't seen him as a dutiful uncle.

'Go and eat some cake,' he said. 'I've got a call to make in the area before I head home. Ligat's is on my way.'

Mike jotted down the address as Sallis dictated it. He would call in on his way to Jenny's. Despite what she'd said about leaving it till the morning, he wanted to be sure that she was all right before knocking off for the night. He glanced at his watch — with a bit of luck he'd manage dinner with his family tonight.

* * *

For a long time, Alain couldn't stop crying. But Jenny was kind and patient. She murmured little cooing sounds, over and over, like the wood pigeon he heard during the early hours outside the Irregular's dorm at school, and after a while he felt sleepy. She wrapped him in a blanket she must have borrowed from the hospital and carried him into a waiting taxi.

On the journey home she continued her murmured reassurances, and Alain lay comforted in her arms, though he was aware of every jolt of the taxi, and the rattle of its diesel engine and the squeal of its brakes seemed unbearably loud. Because, as they had left the building, his heightened senses had noticed something that had set his nerves a-tingle.

A smell, perhaps, or a sound — *Yes*, he thought, *it was a sound*. He had been in a pleasant state between waking and sleeping, when distant noises become woven into snatches of dreams. Then suddenly he was alert, vigilant — for what, he could not quite recall, but he remembered the feeling of old, and it meant danger.

* * *

Neither Jenny nor Alain would notice the car following them from Prescot Street, lagging two cars behind, speeding up when traffic lights threatened to separate them in Upper Parliament Street, falling back again on the long, straight stretch of Smithdown Road, with its built-up, soot-blackened terraces of shuttered shops and warmly lit restaurants, its four lanes of traffic and its thin band of sky, narrow as a lath.

There was no need to follow this time. The Campbells' address was circled in red on the map on the passenger seat. This was purely for the thrill. Whatever happened next was meant to be. It was ordained. The car was directly behind them as they turned into Ullet Road. From here, they entered the broad avenue of Aigburth Drive, astonishing in the suddenness of its green and open vistas, with Sefton Park on one side and Victorian mansions on the other. The following car pulled in a hundred yards down the road and waited.

Shona watched their arrival. She had been up to the house and knocked, but there was no answer. She waited and waited and saw no sign of movement in the house, and after a while she developed the terrible notion that Jenny had left Alain inside and gone to work, leaving him alone. But perhaps Fraser was looking after the boy. She shook her head — no, that wasn't right, Jenny had asked for the night off. She was sure she had, because she had listened in on Jenny's call to Jarmon Willis. Why would she ask for the night off if Fraser was at home? Remembering this only confused her further, since she now recalled that Jenny had refused her help, remembered Jenny's frosty tone when she said, 'There are rules.' She was not required for babysitting at all.

'I was crying,' she said aloud, trying to make sense of the events of the evening. Failing entirely.

She noted the weak state of the boy as Jenny lifted him out of the taxi, the hospital blanket, and thought, blanking out what she had done only an hour earlier, that she would like to kill anyone who knowingly hurt a child. What had possessed Jenny to take him out, away from the safety of her home?

* * *

It was after eight p.m., the clouds that had gathered and bunched in ominous banks throughout the day seemed to bear down, sinking under their own weight, ready for a storm.

Jenny cooked Alain a cheese omelette and was relieved to see him wolf it down with bread and a mug of tea. She explained cautiously that she needed to return to the hospital and, although he seemed uneasy at the prospect of spending the evening with Max, he took the news quietly.

Alain showered as the first flashes of lightning lit the distance in sheets of lilac and mauve. Rumbles of thunder followed, leisurely at first, but gaining volume and chasing the lightning flashes with increasing rapidity. As Jenny towelled his hair dry, a ferocious crash overhead made him shout, and he turned his face to her shoulder.

'There's nothing to be afraid of in a little thunder and lightning, sweetheart,' she said, ruffling his hair. 'Listen.' An echo of the thunder crash rumbled in the distance. 'It's the angels ten-pin bowling. Can you hear the ball roll along the lane?' The rumble ended in a muted *crump*. 'How many pins d'you think he got down with that one?'

Alain learned away from her, his brow furrowed in concentration. 'One,' he said. 'Two at most.'

'The biggest ones are a strike,' she said, helping him into his pyjamas. 'D'you know how many there are in a strike?'

''Course,' said Alain, with an insouciance she had never seen before, and which almost made her hug herself with glee at this show of confidence, a degree of normality she had almost given up hope of ever seeing. 'A strike is ten.'

They got through the worst of the storm by arguing how many pins had tumbled with each thunder crash, and then Jenny tucked him up in bed and kissed his forehead. It was cooler now, and although he seemed terribly tired, he was calm. She dimmed the switch on his bedside lamp and patted the covers one last time.

'Jenny . . .'

'Hmm?'

'I'm sorry about Fraser.'

She put a finger to his lips. 'You can't keep shouldering the world's cares, Alain. It can only make you unhappy.'

He gave an unhappy nod.

'Jenny . . .' He fidgeted, tucking the polar bear and the lion inside the covers and Jenny helped him.

'Hmm?'

'D'you think . . . ?' Two bands of livid colour appeared across the ridges of his cheekbones. Jenny took his hand and after a couple of deep breaths, he said, 'D'you think Grandmère hates me, because of Aunt Jeanne-Louise?'

Jenny was dismayed to see his dark eyes fill with tears. His little frame had been so racked with weeping already that she feared he would make himself ill. Even so, she felt it was imperative that she gave Alain an honest answer.

She thought about the stiff formality of the family group in the hospital interview room — his mother's reserve when she spoke to him, his grandmother's attempt to smile at him, her beckoning to him to come to her, abandoned with a sob.

'No,' she said, 'I don't think she hates you.' He hadn't asked the question of his mother, and Jenny thought how he had shied away from her, refusing contact. What was Alain's hurt? Guilt, certainly, but that was not all. And guilt for what? What had he done or failed to do that had made him feel so responsible for his aunt's death?

‘I think your grandmother is very sad about Aunt Jeanne-Louise, and I’m *certain* that she loves you, and would like to comfort you.’

Alain nodded, sniffing slightly, but apparently accepting what she had said, and Jenny went downstairs to telephone Max. The telephone rang five or six times and Jenny replaced the receiver, thinking who, of her nursing friends, would be best to ask this favour of. She needed someone who would be willing to come to her: Alain should stay put. He had been upset enough for one day. Then, if she got someone who was free, and willing, she would have to clear it with Social Services. She sighed and started thumbing through her address book.

* * *

The boy watched, solemn and pale, from the dining room windows. He was locked inside the house, while his father worked with frenzied energy in the garden. The cherry trees were just beginning to unfold their petals — their russety bark gleaming and silky in the morning sun. He felt a pain just beneath his heart. Every year, he and his mother would bring the branches, laden with white and pink blooms, inside to decorate the house. He winced, juddering as each bite of the axe shivered through the trunk and sent a snowfall of petals fluttering to the ground. His father’s lips were moving. He was muttering and sweating as he worked on the trees. Suddenly, unable to bear it any longer, the boy ran through the hall and up the stairs to his bedroom. He pulled and dragged at the sticking drawer of the tallboy until it gave, then he reached to the back, beneath his jerseys. For a moment he thought it had gone and he whimpered in fear — if his father knew he had taken it — but then his fingers brushed something hard and plastic, and he sobbed with relief and grasped the screwdriver firmly.

He trod the red-and-blue pattern of the carpet towards the front sitting room, missing the tips of the swirls that looked like snakes' heads, humming to himself for courage. He trailed his fingers along the top of the wooden dado, accumulating grey dust that his mother would never have allowed to build up. But Mummy wasn't home, and something was wrong with Daddy. He carried on walking, the screwdriver in his pocket becoming heavier with each step. At the door to the sitting room he had to stop, his heart was beating so fiercely in his throat he thought it would choke him. The sofa had been pushed back against the window, and he climbed onto it to reach the lock. His father had fixed a screw dead centre of the frame, securing the upper and lower sashes of the window.

He fitted the blade of the screwdriver into the head of the screw, but his hands shook so badly that it jumped out again. He took a deep breath, then tried again, pushing hard and turning. At first the screw would not budge, but then it gave a little and he worked at it, a quarter of a turn at a time until his hands cramped, and he had to stop to wipe the sweat from his eyes. He had no clear idea what he would do once he was free, he only knew that he had to get away from his father, away from the terrible sound of the axe. At last the screw yielded to fingertip pressure and he eased it out. The latch slid back easily, but the sash lifted only an inch, no matter how hard he pulled. He would have to move the sofa and get to it from below. He jumped down, then, satisfied that he was still alone, and put his shoulder to the faded silk of the sofa. Its wheels squealed in complaint, rumpling the rug in the centre of the room, but gradually it inched away from the window, leaving dark tracks on the wooden floor. He pushed harder until the gap was wide enough for him to squeeze through. Then, sliding his fingers under the opening between the window and the frame he pulled and tugged until the window gave another inch.

'How did you—?'

His heart contracted at the sound of his father's voice and he had a strong sensation of falling. Falling very far and very fast.

'Of all the *deceitful—*' His father had seen the stolen screwdriver, lying discarded on the sofa.

The boy tugged wildly at the window sash, desperate to escape. His father reached his side in two, long strides. 'You bloody little thief!' He slammed the window shut and for one unreal moment, the boy felt nothing. Then he began screaming and could not stop. Screaming in pain and terror. His father pulled the sofa away with one hand and grabbed the boy by the belt of his trousers with the other. His screams increased in pitch and intensity as his trapped fingers were jerked and pain jolted through every bone, every joint in his hands. Then his father thrust the window open and snatched him away, carrying him to the door of the basement.

'No, Daddy. Please, Daddy. I'll be good, I promise, I promise, *Daddy Daddy Dad! Please!*' He screamed over and over. Even after the door had been bolted and he was in the darkness he swore to be good to be quiet to be—

'Jenny!'

Alain was standing at the top of the stairs, holding the baseball bat in one hand. He looked ghastly. Jenny ran towards him, fearing that he would fall. The doorbell rang.

'Don't answer it!'

Jenny half turned to the front door, then back to Alain. Exhaustion and worry had befuddled her.

'He's come back.' Alain's voice quavered with terror and disbelief. He had been drifting off to sleep when the thing that had so disturbed him on their way out of the hospital had reasserted itself. It was a cough — light, no more than a clearing of the throat — and yet he had heard it at some subconscious level, separating it from the telephone trills, the footfalls and the voices in the main foyer, and the sirens and traffic buzz beyond. He had known it at once and yet had buried it deep, not wanting to believe that he was so close to the terrible events of the previous week — so close to death.

Suddenly wide awake, he had gone to the window to set up his animal sentinels to watch through the night and had seen him arrive.

His fear cut through the layers of misery and tiredness, and Jenny felt a sudden chill run down her spine. 'Who is it, Alain?'

Alain's voice was no more than a breath. '*Daddy*.'

The blade gleams as a spotlight flares from it.

'*Run, Alain!*'

'*Daddy, NO!*' Aunt Lou steps between them. He sees the point slash once, twice, and Aunt Lou falls. Again Daddy strikes, and again. Her arms are no protection, and he hears the awful slice and chop of the blade. He must run from it or he will go mad.

* * *

Mike Delaney parked outside a rundown terrace in a Toxteth street. It was a far cry from a flat in Sefton Park, but it must have sounded so much better than a bedsit in Toxteth when he gave the address to his secretary.

Since the eighties riots, everyone had heard of Toxteth, and it didn't conjure up an image of leafy suburbs in quite the same way Sefton Park would. The landlord let him in to the house. The hall carpet was a filthy, threadbare runner that might once have been red, and the air reeked of damp, curry spices and cabbage.

The landlord let them in to Ligat's flat. He was a small, thin man, not much over thirty, with dark hair and a goatee beard.

'Haven't seen him for a couple of days,' he said, pushing open the door to let them through first.

Mike recoiled at the smell, then, bracing himself, stepped into the room. Fungus had blistered the plaster and spread like an enormous cloud over the ceiling, belching green spores at its edges. Mike stared about him at the peeling wallpaper and bubbling plaster, the fur of mould on the walls and ceiling, the accumulated filth of blackened, tacky grime on the carpet.

'It's people like you give landlords a bad name,' he said.

The landlord smiled. 'He's never complained.' He lifted his chin, challenging Mike. 'Look how he lives.'

The sink in the corner was crammed with plates, mugs and pans. Those that wouldn't fit were piled on the floor. The old, two-ring cooker was tarry with layered deposits of fat and spills. There was a huge dip, the shape and colour of a massive cocoon, in the middle of the unmade bed. The same smell of damp pervaded the room, with an added undertone of dirty linen and cigarettes, but overlaying all of this was something that made Mike's stomach do slow rolls. Rotting meat? Or maybe some dead animal trapped behind the skirting boards — the place must be infested with vermin.

Mike had once heard someone on a radio programme ask, 'What's wrong with squalor?' The man who'd said it could never have been close to it. *What's wrong with squalor?* he thought, looking again around the crumbling walls. *It degrades and dehumanizes. It creates people so alienated from society that they forget that this isn't the norm.*

'Where is he?' Mike demanded, clenching his teeth against rising nausea.

'How should I know?'

Mike suppressed a desire to grab the landlord by the throat and asked, 'When did you last see him?'

'When I collected the rent. Thursday night.'

'And you're sure this is the man.' He showed the landlord the photograph of Ligat that Ron Sallis had borrowed from his mother and faxed through to Merseyside HQ from Surrey.

'That's him, all right. He's a bit thinner. A bit madder-looking maybe, but it's him.'

Mike tucked the photograph back in his pocket and tried to purge his nostrils of the ripe stench of rotting meat. His eye snagged on a black plastic bag in a corner of the room. Clothing was spilling out of it, and moving closer, Mike realized that it was the source of the smell.

He took a biro from his inside pocket and hooked a shirt by its collar from the pile. It was stiff with brown, dried-in blood.

* * *

The door knocker rattled suddenly, and Alain jumped. Behind her Jenny heard the caller turn away and walk down the front steps.

'He killed her, Jenny,' he whispered. '*He killed Tante Lou.*'

Jenny snatched up the telephone receiver and began dialling. The line went dead. Alain ran down the stairs to her. 'We have to get out,' he said. Simultaneously, they heard glass shattering behind them, in the kitchen. 'He's coming!' His voice was a breathless squeak.

Jenny pushed him towards the front door. 'Go next door. Ask Mrs Lucas to call the police,' she told him.

Alain grabbed her arm with both his hands, clunking her elbow with the bat, and clung to her. 'Not without you.'

Jenny understood: he had left Jeanne-Louise, and now she was dead. He would not leave Jenny.

Jenny could hear Ligat clearing the glass from one of the panels of the back door. He would be inside the house within seconds. 'Okay,' she said. 'We'll go together.' She opened the front door and a sea-spray of freezing droplets blew in at them. She tugged the baseball bat out of Alain's hands and bundled him into his coat, then slipped on her own waterproof jacket. 'Shoes,' she said. While Alain forced his feet into his trainers, she snatched the front door keys from the hall stand.

Jenny used the latch key to close the door quietly behind her, then double-locked it: if Alain's father had to retrace his steps to get out of the house, it would give them extra time. Too late, Alain realized he had left his weapon inside the house.

They ran to the adjoining house, but there was no reply. The next house was divided into flats, but if they ran to the house on the corner—

A cascade of glass exploded from the front door. Alain shrank to Jenny's side and she heard his father's voice for the first time.

'Come back here, you little bastard, or I'll tear your fucking *heart* out!'

Jenny grabbed Alain's hand and ran to the edge of the road. It was twilight, and the heavy storm clouds increased the gloom. It was raining heavily. If they knocked on a few more doors they might find someone at home, but Ligat might catch them first. It was half a mile to the nearest public phone box, if it hadn't been vandalized.

'We need to get to where there are more people, Alain,' she said. 'But we need to hide.'

The road was flooded. Water swept down it, carrying twigs and odd bits of litter. It cascaded over their ankles. She led Alain to the low wall at the edge of the gravel path around the perimeter of the park, and from there through the holly hedge into the park itself. She intended to keep low, next to the hedge, and make a run for it once they got to Lark Lane.

Ligat headed straight for the park, working by some kind of predator instinct. They got no more than fifty yards away when he spotted them and yelled. The hedge was dense at this point, and there was no escape back onto the roadway, so Jenny had no choice but to sprint for the cover of a small copse, a little further inside the park.

* * *

Mike was driving fast, siren blaring, lights strobing in the lightning flashes. He had radioed for double-crewed units, directing them to Jenny and Fraser Pearson's house. His radio crackled and he answered his call sign. It was the sergeant in charge of the control room.

'There's a substation blown out in Kensington,' he said. 'A number of casualties. No units available.'

Mike braked, flashing his headlights, siren screaming, as he crossed Tunnel Road and Lodge Lane from Parliament Street into Smithdown Road, against the signals. A van skidded to a stop directly in front of him and, cursing, Mike drove around him.

'I'm on my way,' he said. 'Keep trying her number — we've got to warn her.'

* * *

Shona was trying to sort out in her mind what had happened during the phone call. Had Jenny really refused her help? She wasn't at work, so she wouldn't need a babysitter, but Shona couldn't shake the idea that Jenny *needed* her. No — that wasn't quite what she felt — it was *Alain* who needed her. It had something to do with his hands, and the bruises on her hands. Something to do with Max . . .

She reached forward and switched on the radio, turning the volume up loud. She wouldn't, *wouldn't* think about Max. It wasn't her fault . . .

She started singing along with the band, rocking backwards and forwards, staring out at the rain and crying.

Two figures ran across the road. Shona snapped to, instantly alert, and peered through the windscreen. She flicked the windscreen wiper lever, but nothing happened. Flustered, she turned the ignition on and tried again, but the two had already disappeared through a gap in the hedge. 'No,' she said, her voice inaudible over the throb of the music on the stereo. 'It can't have been.'

A minute or two later she saw a man run out of Jenny's driveway. Hadn't he arrived just after Jenny? But he had gone to a house further down the road. She had watched him go into a driveway two doors down. What was he doing at Jenny's house? He looked up and down the road and then ran across to the park. In a flash of lightning she saw that he was carrying something metallic, with an evil-looking hook at one end.

'God help us,' she muttered. 'that was Jenny and Alain . . .' She reached for the door handle, then, changing her mind, turned the ignition key the final quarter. The engine caught and she revved, accelerated towards the man, but he dodged through the hedge, apparently unaware of her.

Shona swung the car round in a U-turn, throwing up a bow-wave through the floodwaters on the road. There was an entrance into the park a little further down the road, and she made for it.

The tall pillars of the old gateposts were all that remained of the park gates, and she drove through, into the parking bay. *Which way?* To her left, two broad paths, high and low, leading to the park café, to her right, a narrower track. She eased the car right and turned on the headlamps, catching the man in her main beam. He put one hand up to shield his eyes. She didn't stop to think but accelerated straight at him. He froze momentarily, then ran to his right, down the grassy slope. Shona slid to a halt, the wheels skidding. The man ran down the pathway, in the direction Jenny and Alain had taken, towards the boating lake.

Shona turned the car and followed him. Lightning flashes froze the fleeing figures of Jenny and the boy and their pursuer in a grotesque tableau. With every dazzling flare, he seemed to be gaining on them.

The car slewed and bumped over the uneven grass and Shona hit the horn in staccato bursts, driving relentlessly at the man. She was almost on him when he turned and hurled something. The windscreen shattered and Shona threw up one arm to shield her face. The car slithered into a turn, the rear end clipping the man and knocking him to the ground, the front sliding into an oak tree, crushing the side panel and driver's door and trapping Shona against the steering column. The car horn blared.

* * *

'Down there,' Jenny said. 'Towards the stepping stones.' The pond which fed into the boating lake had overflowed and they had to wade across the pathway before reaching the stepping stones. In the distance, a car horn suddenly gave a few short blasts, then sent up a continuous blare of noise.

'Go left,' Jenny said, raising her voice over the noise of the rain and the thunderstorm and the rushing water cascading over the flat rocks. 'Hold on to the rail,' she cautioned. 'It's uneven here.' Alain reached for the rail, but the pull of the water made him lose his footing and he fell with a cry of pain. Jenny hauled him to his feet and they carried on. She shepherded Alain up the stone steps to the statue at the top of the hill, carrying him half the way. From the top they would be able to see where Ligat was.

'Keep low,' she warned. 'Do you see anything?'

Alain dropped to a crouch beside her. His teeth were chattering, and she put her arm around him. Behind them, the cast iron skeleton of the palm house gleamed white in the flashes of light, flecked with rust, open to the torrents of rain that fell unremittingly.

'There!' Alain said, pointing. 'Over there!'

Ligat was making his way towards them, limping, using the crowbar as a walking stick. Jenny debated what to do. If they stayed put, hiding themselves in the shrubs on the hillside, he might find them, but if they went on, he might catch them in the open.

'He's injured,' she said, arguing against her own timidity. 'Let's go.' She grabbed Alain's hand. He stood, then crumpled with a shout.

'My ankle!'

Jenny sat beside him under the statue. His foot was swollen. 'I'll carry you,' she said.

'Jenny, he'll *catch* us.'

'No,' Jenny said, taking his face in both her hands and looking into his eyes. 'I won't let him.' She cast about in the undergrowth of the shrubbery on the slope of the hill and found a rock. 'Hold that for me. And *use* it if you have to, okay?'

Alain took the smooth, egg-shaped rock in his hand and nodded, dumbly.

'Now jump up,' Jenny said. 'You're going for a piggy-back ride.'

She started at a run, but soon slowed to a trot, breathing raggedly. 'Jenny, he's coming,' Alain said, his voice rising in panic.

'Hear that?' Jenny said. Sirens howled through the night. 'Someone must have phoned the police. They're looking for us! See the lights?'

From where they stood, they could see blue flashing lights and crazily bouncing headlights as unseen vehicles, obscured by trees, bumped across the fields.

'They're down by the lake!' Alain shouted. 'But Jenny, *he's* down there! How are we going to get past him?'

Jenny ran one hand over her face to wipe off some of the rainwater. 'All we have to do is hide until they find him,' Jenny said. She darted for the cover of a planting of mahonia and birch and dog roses and gently eased Alain to the ground. For ten minutes they waited in the dark, waiting for someone to come up the hill to find them, focusing on the flashing lights of an ambulance and a fire engine, watching them cut away the driver's door and unhurriedly carry a lifeless woman out of the car.

'Jenny!' Alain gripped her arm. 'They're going away!' The lights seemed to be retreating. The fire engine and the ambulance were moving off, across the field. They drove slowly, their strobe lights had been switched off, and Jenny realized that they hadn't come to find them at all. Nobody knew they were there, nobody was looking for them. Only Ligat.

Jenny leapt to her feet and waved frantically. 'No!' she screamed. 'Come back!'

A sudden flurry of movement to her right warned her and she ducked just as Ligat burst into the shrubbery, flailing the crowbar. The chisel-sharp hook thudded into the trunk of a birch tree, just missing her neck. Jenny picked Alain up under one arm and made a run for it, down the hillock, slithering on her backside for most of the way, scratching her hands and face on the thorns of the dog roses and mahonias that snatched at her as she slid.

Once on level ground, she ran for the stepping stones, desperately trying to attract the attention of the ambulance, which was making slow progress in the mud and standing water left by the storm, but Ligat was there ahead of her. He turned to face her, raising the crowbar, but as he did so, he lost his balance and stumbled backwards, trapping his foot between two of the stones. Jenny ran past him, feeling Alain's arms slip from her neck, clearing the stream in two long strides and running up the hill, faltering when she recognized Shona's car. It stood silent now, its roof peeled back and the passenger door thrown carelessly to one side on the grass.

She switched Alain to her left hip and ran on, but Ligat was gaining on them. He made a sideways swipe with the crowbar and Jenny fell. Instinctively she rolled away from Alain and saw the vicious claw of the crowbar coming at her.

Then something hit Ligat squarely between the eyes and he stood for a second or two, while his grip on the crowbar slackened, and then he dropped it and clutched his head in both hands.

'You fucking little bastard!' he screamed.

Jenny lunged for the metal bar, but Ligat caught her by the hair and pulled her to him.

'What do you *want* from us?' she screamed. 'Why can't you leave him alone?'

He took her by the throat and squeezed. 'I want my son,' he said. '*My son!*'

Jenny tried to break his hold, but he was too strong. She fished around in the mud, feeling her strength drain from her, seeing the sky, even the flashes of light, darken and fade. Then she found the smooth rock that Alain had thrown at his father and brought it in a short jab to the side of his temple. He grunted, but his grip did not slacken. The rock tumbled from her grasp and Jenny felt a terrible pressure in her head. Just before she blacked out, she thought she could hear the sound of a car horn.

CHAPTER 36

Jenny woke fighting.

Something was covering her face and she struggled with it, slapping away the hands that held it in place.

'Jenny! Jenny, it's all right. You're safe now. You have to keep still.' The voice was authoritative, and it was a woman's.

Jenny made an effort to calm down and take stock of the situation. She was inside a vehicle. *Ambulance?* The thing covering her face was an oxygen mask. Her throat hurt dreadfully. Her eyes widened. 'Alain?' She could not make herself heard and so tried to sit up. Again, the restraining hands held her. She fought again, crying now. 'Alain!'

The name came out as a croak, and the paramedic spoke again, speaking loudly, trying to make her understand.

'He's here, Jenny. He's all right.'

Jenny sobbed, trying to push the paramedic out of her way.

'Look.' The woman beckoned to someone behind her and Jenny strained to see.

Alain. She fell back on the stretcher, sobbing, trying not to because her throat hurt so badly. Alain stood by her, frowning, biting his lip. He was soaked through, and a blanket had been draped around his shoulders. He offered her his hand as if afraid she would reject it. Jenny took it, laughing and crying. The paramedic offered her a handkerchief and allowed her to remove the mask long enough to wipe her nose, and then Jenny subsided, her breathing becoming laboured.

'I thought you were dead,' Alain said.

Jenny gave him a rueful look. 'So did I.'

'This young man saved your life,' the paramedic said. 'He sounded the car horn — we turned back to see what the trouble was.' She paused to wipe Jenny's forehead. 'We got there just in time.'

'Where is—?' She could get no further.

The paramedic shot a look at Alain, then, deciding it was safe to tell her, she said, 'He's under arrest. He's been taken to hospital because of his injuries.'

'He'll be kept under police guard the whole time,' a second voice chimed in.

'Mike?'

Mike leaned forward so that Jenny could see him. 'And in a different hospital,' he added. 'You've nothing to worry about.' He put one hand on Alain's shoulder, meaning the reassurance for him as much as for Jenny.

'How did you—?'

'Get here?' he said, finishing for her. 'I was on my way to your house when I saw all the fireworks in the park.' He exchanged a look with the paramedic. 'When we arrived,' Mike said, 'young Alain was beating seven bells out of Ligat.'

Alain quailed at the mention of his father, but then Jenny watched as he straightened himself up. He seemed to be steeling himself, and she squeezed his hand, gently in encouragement.

'I let him in, Jenny. When Tante Lou was looking after me. Mummy was away and . . .' He shrugged, disconsolate. 'I thought he'd come on a visit. I *had* to open the door or he'd be angry with me . . .' A look of pain crossed his face and he cupped his hands gently before him as if remembering the fearful injuries his father had inflicted on him before. 'I shouldn't have, but I was afraid to say no . . .' He started to cry.

Jenny placed her hand over his. 'You aren't to blame, Alain. Daddy did a terrible, terrible thing. You did what any little boy would have done. You did as your daddy told you.'

For a moment, Alain simply looked at her with a harrowed, haunted expression that made him look much older that his eight years, then he threw himself on his knees beside her and sobbed.

EPILOGUE

Mike closed the interview room door. Angeline Fournier sat in the chair on the other side of the desk, perfectly still.

'Madame Fournier.'

'Before you say anything, I want to apologize,' the woman said. 'I thought I was protecting Alain. I didn't know.' Her forehead wrinkled in pain. 'I thought I was keeping him safe from his father.'

Mike nodded. 'What about the assaults on your husband?'

'Self-defence.' She shrugged. 'Why should you believe me? I lied before. But it is true. Every time—' She frowned, then corrected herself. 'Each time, I was protecting Alain, or myself.'

'And the drunk-driving charge?'

She stared at her hands. 'It gets to the point when you would do anything to make it stop. Sometimes, if I drank enough, it would go away, for a while — the pain, the fear, the . . . awfulness of it. Everything would go away. Jeanne-Louise understood that. She never judged me for it. My parents . . .' She shrugged again. 'They don't understand . . .'

Mike waited, letting her take it at her own pace.

'He was so unpredictable. He could be so charming to his clients, with his mother, even with the two of us — with me and Alain — that when it first started, I would almost convince myself that I had imagined it.' She fell silent, and for some time, she sat, frowning at a cigarette burn on the tabletop.

The WPC coughed and Mrs Fournier stirred and sighed. 'Eventually, it was like Carl was two different people — the public person who was charming, witty, humorous, light-hearted. But behind closed doors he was a petulant, depressed, violent, paranoid tyrant.'

She looked up at Mike for the first time. 'He didn't give us a moment's peace. We never knew what was going to set him off. He would ask you a question and you knew it was a trick. No matter how you answered, it would be wrong. "How do I look tonight?" And if I said fine, he would scream: "You fucking little liar! I know how I look. If I can't trust my wife, who can I trust?" If I said, "You look a little tired," he would say I was constantly running him down, that I'd never loved him, and then he'd hit me and hit me, and hit me and—' She balled her hand into a fist and struck the table, hard.

Mike leaned forward and placed his hand over hers. 'I was terrified that Carl would come looking for us if you got in touch with him.'

'He was already on your trail,' Mike told her. 'He traced you via your business transactions.' She nodded, resignedly, as if it was what she had come to expect from her husband.

'We think he waited outside the children's hospital every day for a week, until he saw Jenny take Alain home after one of his therapy sessions. He followed them home.'

She retrieved her hand, placed it in her lap. 'I was on holiday in France' — she made a slight movement, an apologetic little shrug — 'with a lover, when the final attack on Alain took place.' She reddened a little and gave him a fleeting, embarrassed look. 'Lou was mostly able to look after him when I went away — she was a freelance journalist — but that time . . . It was short notice. She couldn't . . .' She shook her head, staring intently, seeing something in the coffee-stained tabletop, reliving the event. 'I should never have gone. But I wasn't — I couldn't think straight. I only knew that I had to get away from Carl. I took a chance. He — Carl . . .' She fell silent, still finding it difficult to make sense of what had happened. 'Carl got it into his head that the cherry trees in the garden were undermining the house. Alain watched him cut them down. All of them. Like a madman. Alain was so afraid. He stole a screwdriver . . . Carl had screwed all the windows shut. He tried to escape. Carl caught him. He—' She closed her eyes for a moment. 'Alain had managed to get a window open. Carl slammed it shut on his hands.'

Mike expected her to cry, but she kept rigid control, although her skin was paper-white, and her hands, tightly clasped in her lap, trembled with emotion.

'He kept Alain at home, delirious and in terrible pain, for three days until I returned. Then he went off to work, as though nothing had happened. "Alain has a touch of flu," he said. He left my little boy in his own filth, half dead with shock and fever — he didn't even know me. Just kept repeating over and over. "I'm sorry. I'll be good." Begging, "Please, please, please."' This time she did break down. Mike slid a box of tissues over to her and waited. At length, she went on. 'We ran from him, left home and just ran. I was certain then that he was capable of anything.'

* * *

Jenny sat in an armchair, next to Fraser's bed. He had been moved from the intensive care unit to a high-dependency ward, and was no longer on the respirator, but he was still attached to a heart monitor, and although he had woken twice in the night, he had not yet spoken. She felt a movement behind her and turned.

'How is he?'

Jenny turned at the familiar voice.

'Max!' she winced and put a hand to her throat.

The nurse who had wheeled him down parked Max's wheelchair next to Jenny's.

'You shouldn't be up,' she whispered.

'Just try telling him,' the nurse grumbled. 'Five minutes max. . . . Max.'

Max narrowed his eyes at her, and she sauntered out, with a smile.

Jenny touched his arm lightly. His left shoulder was bandaged, and his arm strapped up.

'It isn't as bad as they first thought,' Max said. 'The blade glanced off my collar bone. Proved my mother right, after all these years.'

'How's that?'

'She always said I was a little bleeder.'

Jenny smiled, but it was a half-hearted attempt, and after a moment's silence she said, 'Shona . . .'

'I know, they told me.' He was silent for a few moments. 'She called for an ambulance before she left me.' He shook his head. 'I should have acted faster. I should have seen—'

'She saved our lives, Max. If it wasn't for Shona . . .' Her hand strayed protectively to her throat.

'Where's young Alain?' Max asked.

Jenny roused herself from a morbid reliving of the event. 'He went home. His home.'

Max nodded. 'About time, too.'

He sat next to Jenny for a few minutes, saying nothing. They both watched the monitor tracing the rhythms of Fraser's heartbeat.

'He'll be all right.' Max said, placing his free hand on Jenny's.

Jenny looked at Fraser. There was an immobility in his face that seemed in some way profound, untouchable. 'I barely recognize him.' She felt a tear brim over her lower lid and slide down her cheek and realized that she meant more than just the physical change in him.

Max watched her closely in silence for some moments and then said, 'What will you do?'

Jenny sighed. 'I hate what he did — the fact of his betrayal — but I can't bring myself to hate *him*. You must think me terribly weak.'

'Fraser has stood by you and shared your happiness and sadness for fifteen years,' he said. 'You've accepted your childlessness and made something positive from it. You've given a home, love and stability to dozens of children — perhaps the warmest and closest family experience of their lives — and never regretted it, never stinted, never resented the demands those children made on you.' He smiled. 'Of *course* you're not weak — you're the strongest woman I know.'

Jenny nodded. It was reassuring to have the affirmation. She was surprised that Ligat's physical assault on her had so emphatically undermined her confidence, her centre of inner calm seemed to have evaporated in the heat of the attack and she felt vulnerable and alone.

Max sighed. 'It's a shame about Luke.'

Jenny felt the blood drain from her face, and she gripped his hand tightly. 'What's wrong with Luke?' she whispered, afraid to look into his face.

'Nothing *wrong*, exactly,' he said. 'But his adoptive parents have asked for him to be taken back into care — they simply can't cope with him any longer.'

Jenny searched his face, suspecting one of Max's manipulations.

'Surely not,' she said.

Max tilted his head. 'He simply won't settle. I've never seen him so monstrous. You wouldn't believe it was the same little boy who charmed everyone while he was with you.'

Jenny tried not to feel a degree of satisfaction in this.

'We'll have to find him another foster placement, but what he really needs is to be with someone he trusts.' He slid her a sly look, her eyes snapped to his again.

Now she was in no doubt — this entire visit was a set-up.

Fraser stirred and moaned. At the same moment, the nurse returned. Max patted Jenny's hand before he was wheeled out.

Jenny wet Fraser's lips with the sponge and he licked them greedily. She took fresh cotton-wool swabs and wiped his eyelids with gentle care.

He was still for a time, then slowly, experimentally, he opened his eyes. For a long time, he didn't speak and Jenny was afraid that his injuries had been more severe than the hospital had realized. Then, after swallowing, he managed to croak, 'I'm sorry.'

'So am I.' She wanted to say, 'It's all right.' But it *wasn't* all right, and she *was* sorry. Sorry that they could never go back to where they had been — to *what* they had been — before her lost innocence. She mourned her loss, understanding fully what Alain had lost and knowing that innocence, like trust, once lost is irretrievable.

Fraser slipped off again into unconsciousness and Jenny leaned back in her chair and rested for a few minutes, slipping lightly in and out of sleep as she would when they had a new child in the house, as she did every night for three months when Luke had first come to them. The next time she opened her eyes Fraser was watching her.

'Forgive me,' he said. It sounded like a question.

'I'm trying.' It was easier, somehow, to make the effort after what she had been through last night. In the context of what had happened to her — to both of them — it didn't seem an unreasonable request.

She saw Fraser's look of gratitude and it grieved her.

'What will you do?' he asked, and Jenny glanced sharply at him, wondering if he had heard her answer to the same question that Max had posed earlier.

'Take it a step at a time.' She shrugged. 'It's all I can do.'

He nodded and she felt again a stab of regret at the humility of his acceptance. She wanted him to shout, to throw some of the blame back at her, but he took it meekly. Too meekly.

'What happened to you?' He pointed to her neck.

'Nothing,' she said. 'An accident. I'll tell you when you're more up to it.' To change the subject, she said something she hadn't intended to, simply because it was uppermost in her mind.

'Luke's miserable with his adoptive parents.'

She didn't have to try and gauge his response: the systolic trace on his heart monitor increased and his face flushed slightly.

'We've spoilt him for anyone else, you know.'

Fraser frowned, nodding. He turned his head away, and a tear slipped from beneath his closed eyelids.

'Maybe I should have a word with Max,' she suggested. 'About fostering him. Yes.'

'Max wouldn't countenance that: it would only unsettle him more, coming back to us, only to be uprooted again in a couple of months.'

'Oh,' he said. 'Of course, you're right.'

'I was thinking — maybe we should make it a permanent placement.' She tried to sound casual, but her voice was uneven, as she said it.

'Adoption?'

'That sort of thing.'

'What the hell is going on?' The ward manager had hurried into the room, expecting to see Jenny, whom she knew to be a nurse, administering CPR: Fraser's heart monitor had triggered an alarm in her office.

'Some good news,' Fraser said.

'Well you'd better calm down or I'll have to sedate you,' she said, then, turning to Jenny, 'You should have more sense.'

'I know,' Jenny said. 'I really should.' She glanced at Fraser and he smiled.

* * *

Perhaps it would be all right again, Fraser thought — not now — the present was too achingly raw, too painful to dwell upon, but at some time in the future. The present held practical concerns: his recovery, and the acceptance that his son would be happier living with a man who was not his natural father. Was it so different from his relationship with Luke? Perhaps not, but it would be difficult to let Connor go. The future, with its fuzzy edges, the misty promise of a mirage, held hope, and hope, it seemed, was more resilient than trust.

THE END

ALSO BY MARGARET MURPHY

CLARA PASCAL SERIES
Book 1: DARKNESS FALLS
Book 2: WEAVING SHADOWS

DETECTIVE JEFF RICKMAN SERIES
Book 1: SEE HER BURN
Book 2: SEE HER DIE
Book 3: DON'T SCREAM

DETECTIVE CASSIE ROWAN SERIES
Book 1: BEFORE HE KILLS AGAIN

STANDALONE NOVELS
DEAR MUM
HER HUSBAND'S KILLER
THE LOST BOY

FREE KINDLE BOOKS

Thank you for reading this book. If you enjoyed it please leave feedback on Amazon or Goodreads, and if there is anything we missed or you have a question about, then please get in touch. The author and publishing team appreciate your feedback and time reading this book.

We're very grateful to eagle-eyed readers who take the time to contact us. Please send any errors you find to corrections@joffebooks.com. We'll get them fixed ASAP.

Printed in Great Britain
by Amazon

54822832R00196